THE FAMILY T

①   ZELAPHCHAD ↔ ACHLA

THE DAUGHTERS OF ZELAPHCHAD
(in order of Birth)
MACHLA   TIRZA   HOGLA   MILKA   NOAH
(in order of Torah Listing one and two)
MACHLA   NOAH   HOGLA   MILKA   TIRZA

②   AZRIEL ↔ YISCAH

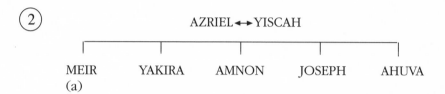

MEIR   YAKIRA   AMNON   JOSEPH   AHUVA
(a)

③   SHAFAT ↔ ADINA

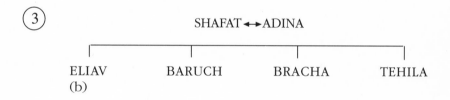

ELIAV   BARUCH   BRACHA   TEHILA
(b)

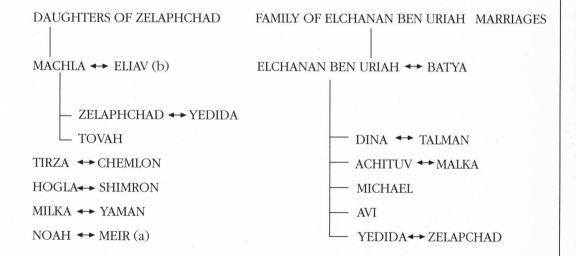

DAUGHTERS OF ZELAPHCHAD   FAMILY OF ELCHANAN BEN URIAH   MARRIAGES

MACHLA ↔ ELIAV (b)   ELCHANAN BEN URIAH ↔ BATYA

    — ZELAPHCHAD ↔ YEDIDA
    — TOVAH   — DINA ↔ TALMAN
TIRZA ↔ CHEMLON   — ACHITUV ↔ MALKA
HOGLA ↔ SHIMRON   — MICHAEL
MILKA ↔ YAMAN   — AVI
NOAH ↔ MEIR (a)   — YEDIDA ↔ ZELAPCHAD

THE
DAUGHTERS
VICTORIOUS

Rabbi Shlomo (Stanley) Wexler

gefen
publishing house

JERUSALEM ◆ NEW YORK

Typesetting: Marzel A.S. – Jerusalem
Cover Design: Studio Paz, Jerusalem

1 3 5 7 9 8 6 4 2

Gefen Publishing House   Gefen Books
POB 36004, Jerusalem 91360, Israel   12 New Street Hewlett, NY 11557, USA
972-2-538-0247 • orders@gefenpublishing.com   516-295-2805 • gefenbooks@compuserve.com

www.israelbooks.com

Printed in Israel   *Send for our free catalogue*

Book Web Page: www.thedaughtersv.co.il

ISBN 965-229-255-9

Library of Congress Cataloging-in-Publication Data:

Wexler, Shlomo

The Daughters Victorious: Fictional recreation of the Biblical story of the daughters of
Zelaphchad / by Shlomo Wexler

1. Daughters of Zelophehad (Biblical figures)—Fiction. 2. Bible. O.T. Numbers—History of
Biblical events—Fiction. 3. Bible. O.T. Chronicles—History of Biblical events—Fiction.
4. Inheritance and succession—Fiction. 5. Women in the Bible—Fiction. I. Title

PS3573.E976 D3 2000 • 813'.6—dc21 • CIP Number: 00-034047

Contents

DEDICATION

To my devoted wife, Chaya Sarah (Irene) Wexler, who for half a century has lovingly assisted me in all my creative endeavors.

She is a true disciple of the daughters of Zelaphchad — described by Chazal as possessing wisdom, righteousness and exegetic skills.

Let me also thank my dear sister, Shirley,
and my wonderful children and grandchildren,
for their support and encouragement:

Rabbi Dr. Shaya and Dina Wexler and
children, Tehila, Esther, Shmuel and Yehuda

Eliezer and Adele Wexler and
children, Shmuel Ari, Daniel and Benjamin

Dr. Chaim and Batya Wexler and
children, Chana and Nava

הסכמה

The story of the litigation of the daughters of Zelaphchad to gain recognition as the legal heirs of their deceased father's shares in the West Bank of Eretz Yisroel, and its far-reaching influence on the extensive Torah laws of inheritance, is set out in great detail in the latter portions of the book of Bamidbar and in the book of Yehoshua. The complex issues raised and the masterful presentation by the victorious five daughters compelled Moshe Rabeinu to seek Divine guidance in resolving the case. Chazal in the Talmud and Midrashim understood that the Torah wisdom, legal acumen and deep religious piety of the sisters, were the decisive factors that won for them esteem and grace in the eyes of God and Man.

It is thus to the credit of my distinguished colleague, friend and chavrusa, Rabbi Shlomo Wexler, that early in his studies he grasped that the qualities of mind and spirit, as displayed by the daughters of Zelaphchad, could only be acquired by a deep, thorough and intense Torah education. This led him to years of research on the subject of Torah education for both men and women in the early years of Jewish history as seen by an active rabbi and teacher. The result is this well-written, informative, inspirational and entertaining book. The Rabbi's literary talents, subtle wit, and sociological insights are manifest throughout the work.

The fictional format chosen by the author enables a very vivid presentation of the sojourn of the children of Israel in the desert in general, and the dramatic experiences of the daughters of Zelaphchad in particular. It was during this period that the Hebrew people were transformed from the status of lowly slaves to a nation of men and women imbued with Torah knowledge and determination to possess and settle their ancestral land. The struggle of the daughters of Zelaphchad to acquire a Torah education, as well as the right to be recognized as the spiritual successors of their parents, will forever be a source of inspiration to generations of Jewish women. The "Daughters Victorious" will bring an awareness to the public that it owes a debt of gratitude to many unsung figures of the past who made heroic sacrifices to advance causes that we deem vital to Jewish survival today.

I enjoyed reading this book immensely. I therefore give it my full endorsement and recommend it to the general public.

Rabbi Dr. Chaim Heifetz

Rabbi Dr. Chaim S. Heifetz

Formerly the Legal Advisor to the Ministry of Religious Affairs of the State of Israel 1964-1994, until mandatory retirement.

I have read with great interest Rabbi Shlomo Wexler's The Daughters Victorious. While it is essentially fiction, it is based upon historic facts. The author has successfully woven the Biblical and Rabbinic texts that detail the saga of the daughters of Zelaphchad into the novel. It makes for fascinating and inspiring reading. Biblical figures come to life and one feels the heartbeat of the generation that left Egypt and continues on to the Land of Israel. The daughters of Zelaphchad emerge as exalted figures. The reader rejoices in their victory.

I can highly recommend this novel to those who read analogous literature. This time it will be enhanced by the Biblical and Rabbinical overtones.

Rabbi Dr. Aaron Rakeffet

Professor of Rabbinic Literature at Yeshiva University's Caroline and Joseph S. Gruss Institute in Jerusalem Author of The Rav: The World of Rabbi Joseph B. Soloveitchik

The Talmud in the tractate Baba Bathra states: "It was taught: The Daughters of Zelaphchad were wise women, were conversant with the law, and were virtuous."

Our author, in his recreation of the Daughters of Zelaphchad, has developed in a most beautiful manner, these three characteristics.

The fictional format used by the author, enables him to present the very strong impact the daughters have made on Jewish Law and Jewish Life. So strong is this impact that the names of each of the daughters is mentioned thrice in the book of Numbers and once in the book of Joshua.

The author has been blessed with an excellent gift for writing. He beautifully develops themes of the daughter's love for their forefathers, their struggle for an inheritance in this beloved land, their intense efforts to receive a Torah education for themselves, and to expand religious education for women.

It is with great enjoyment that I read "The Daughters Victorious." I strongly recommend its reading to everyone who seeks a deeper appreciation of these exceptional Biblical women.

Reuven Aberman

Rabbi Dr. Reuven Aberman
BA., MA., PhD.
Smicha Yoreh-Yoreh, Yadin-Yadin
Currently: Midreshet Moriah
Lecturer in Jewish Law
Formerly: Michlala-
Jerusalem College for Women
Director of Foreign Student Program
Yeshiva Kerem B'Yavneh
Rosh Yeshiva (RAM)
Yeshiva University
Dean and Rosh Yeshiva

הסכמה

בע"ה

לכל מאן דבעי,

בנות צלפחד תבעו את משפטן בשני פסוקים בתורה. כמובן, חכמי התלמוד הרחיבו לבאר גם את דמותן של אותן בנות חכמות ואף את הרקע הכללי לטענותיהם.

ידידנו היקר, הרב שלמה וקסלר יצ"ו הוקסם אף הוא מאותן הדמויות. לאור ההתפתחות הברוכה בלימוד התורה ע"י נשים בדורנו, החליט הרב המחנך הותיק לדרוש ולחקור בחכמתן של אותן הבנות. נהניתי מאד מהשילוב המוצלח של תורה שבכתב עם מפרשיה, מגידיה בתורה שבעל פה ואף מהדמיון הפורה של המחבר. הקורא יוכל לקבל תמונה כללית ולהרגיש ולהרגיש את האוירה של אותו דור. והלומד המעמיק יוכל לעיין אף במקורות שצוינו ולעמוד על דברי חז"ל ולהבחין בין השלבים השונים של פרשנות חז"ל ולראות איך שאפשר לשער ולהוסיף רקע דמיוני לתיאורים. הדברים נאמרו ונכתבו בטוב טעם ודעת ואפשר ללמוד הרבה מספר זה.

בכבוד רב,

ובברכת התורה

הרב בנימין תבורי

הסכמה

The Daughters Victorious — an extraordinary historical novel rooted in the truth of Torah tradition and the immediate concerns of today — is Rabbi Shlomo Wexler's superb gift to the literary world.

The daughters of Zelaphchad have always been the symbol of womanly courage and dauntless faith. They were the pioneer molders of true feminine spirit in Torah Judaism, long before the daughters of Rashi and the founders of Bais Yaakov. It would not do to belittle the traditional role of the woman — as illustrated by Sarah — who tended to the "ohel," the home, whilst hand in hand with Abraham built Klal Yisrael. Nonetheless, these courageous daughters raised the flag of fairness and were justified by G-d Himself.

Rabbi Wexler has provided a marvelous service to the correct interpretation of traditional Judaism by assembling — with proper annotation of sources — the story of these brave women who were leaders and teachers before their time. The author has put to rest the theories of those who castigate our forebears and besmirch Yahadut, for consigning women to the roles of domestic servants and producers of children.

Chazak U'Varuch, Rabbi Wexler! Your enthralling tale deserves a long period on the best seller charts. You have succeeded in opening the eyes of our generation. Koh Lechai!

Hersh M. Galinsky

Rabbi Hersh M. Galinsky
Dean and Director General Educational Centers in Israel of The Rabbinical Council of America

INTRODUCTION

It was in the summer of 1941, some fifty-eight years ago, that I first became interested in the story of the daughters of Zelaphchad. Shortly after my Bar Mitzvah, I had undertaken to read several portions of the Torah for a vacationing Sexton in a nearby synagogue. As luck would have it, my first public reading consisted of the portions of Matot-Maseh. The last section of the fourth book of the Torah, in the sidra of Maseh, tells how the elders of the family of Gilead, from the tribe of Menashe, petitioned Moses to prohibit the daughters of Zelaphchad from marrying men from other tribes. This request was granted by the Almighty.

Since I had to review this section many times in preparation for my first Torah reading, my curiosity about the events was aroused. I was moved to check on the first part of the story in the portion of Pinchas, in which the daughters of Zelaphchad first appealed for the right to inherit land in Canaan. I may have heard something about this subject in my elementary Yeshiva, but I had not studied it in depth.

On and off, over the years, I reflected on the story and read all the material that I could find about it. My first written draft of an interpretation of the events was actually composed more than forty years ago. Serious writing of the current book was undertaken a full decade ago.

What troubled me with the story was the fact that many religious people were not aware of the full details of the lives of the daughters of Zelaphchad and their extraordinary accomplishments. The Torah is remarkably brief in relating these events. Unlike the experiences of Eliezer — the servant of Abraham — spread across an entire portion and related in painstaking detail (Genesis

XXIV:1-61), the exploits of the daughters of Zelaphchad are recorded in a few terse verses of the Torah. This is done despite the fact that their deeds resulted in the enactment of new laws in the Torah text and in Jewish legal procedures. That such laws could emerge as a result of the efforts of a small group of women some 3,300 years ago, was nothing short of miraculous.

The Talmud is more generous in its description of the daughters of Zelaphchad, but the main sections dealing with the subject are off the beaten track. They appear beyond the 115th folio in the Tractate of Baba Bathra. In effect, this means that the details are rarely studied by men and virtually never by women. While the stories of other great Jewish women may also not be studied from Talmudic sources, the Torah itself is more generous in its description. Men and women do study the Written Law. Even if they do not study the Oral Law, the tales of other Jewish heroines are at least popularized and glorified. All Jewish children quickly learn about Sarah, Rivkah, Rachel, Leah, Miriam and Devorah.

Information about the daughters of Zelaphchad that is not familiar among fairly knowledgeable people includes the following:

How many people realize that the daughters of Zelaphchad all deferred their marriages till well beyond the age of forty in pursuit of their cause and were later rewarded with children born in a miraculous manner?

Although the daughters in this family were acknowledged in the Talmud to be brilliant Torah scholars, how many know how they acquired their religious education?

How many are aware that many Talmudic Rabbis felt that Zelaphchad was not the wood-gathering Sabbath-violator mentioned in the Torah, and resented that other Rabbis considered him guilty of this sin?

How widely known is it that the restriction on property-inheriting women marrying outside their tribe was abolished after one generation and that the children of Israel made a holiday to celebrate the occasion?

Other remarkable facts emerged from my research. The daughters of Zelaphchad were listed by name on three successive occasions in the Torah — the only men or women of their generation to be so honored. What is even more remarkable is that the listings do not always occur in the same order.

Only two occasions are recorded in the Torah in which laws were enacted as a result of requests made in the desert. One is the question of the second Passover and the other is the inheritance case of the daughters of Zelaphchad.

The issues that arise from the story in this book are far more significant today than in Biblical times. Equality for women before the law; quality Torah education for women; love for the Land of Israel and the right to be heard on important matters, are all included in the women's agenda today. Women who are concerned about these issues today will be pleased to learn — on reading this book — that these issues were current 3,300 years ago and the daughters of Zelaphchad made a monumental contribution to such causes. They should be inspired from this knowledge to seek to improve their religious background, to possess the Land of Israel and to express their feelings on matters of significance to them.

There were many factors that prompted me to write this book in dramatic form. The primary reason was a lack of background material in the Torah and traditional sources. This material had to be reconstructed in the form that would make the struggle of the daughters of Zelaphchad comprehensible to the modern reader. Although there are some Rabbinic scholars who are not sympathetic to historical fiction, I feel that an exception is warranted in this case. Although the book is in fictional form, all aspects of the events are based on traditional Torah, Talmudic and Midrashic sources and are heavily documented. For greater enjoyment of this book, the reader is advised to read the General Notes before embracing the novel. The Detailed Notes may be read as the reader goes along, or after the novel is completed. Footnotes are recorded in the text within each chapter. The notes relating to the numbers are found in the Detailed Notes section, immediately after the General Notes. There is also a bibliography and a glossary.

An internet web page is being established to accommodate comments and corrections that readers wish to present to the author. The site will be registered at the time the book is published and will be addressed as www.thedaughtersv.co.il. The author will attempt to answer all inquiries and make necessary corrections in future editions.

For readability, certain concessions were made. Times and dates are given in the modern idiom. When classical measurements are used, they are translated to modern terminology in the glossary by meters and feet. The names of classical Biblical figures are translated into English or Latin equivalents. Words such as "Moshe," "Paroh" and "Bereishit" appear as Moses, Pharaoh and Genesis. Younger readers who are not familiar with these versions may find the original Hebrew form in the glossary.

Where Biblical verses are translated into English, I made use of the translation of the Jewish Publication Society. The translation of Rabbi Aryeh Kaplan, of blessed memory, was also of value.

For many years I labored on this research in solitary pleasure. As a decision to publish became firm, it was necessary for me to seek the help of others and many people were gracious in the support of my efforts. First and foremost, I wish to thank Rabbi Dr. Chaim S. Heifetz for his encouragement. Rabbi Heifetz was a classmate of mine at Yeshiva University and we studied together with Rabbi Soloveitchik, of blessed memory. After receiving Smicha, Rabbi Heifetz made aliyah to Israel and embarked on a new career. He became legal advisor to the Ministry of Religious Affairs of the State of Israel and served in that capacity for more than thirty years. He also was an instructor in Tanach and Jewish Law at various schools of higher education. Rabbi Heifetz read the original draft and made many valuable suggestions and corrections.

Numerous other friends and members of the family, particularly daughters-in-law and granddaughters, read the book in pre-publication form and made comments. Based on these suggestions, substantial changes were made. Students at the Neve Yerushalayim Seminary helped with the manuscript on their own time.

Professionals who worked on the book included editor, Roberta Chester. Mrs. Chester, an Instructor in English at Hebrew University, served as the manuscript editor. She made invaluable suggestions for the enrichment of the text and its readability. Mrs. Ada (Sefton) Apfelbaum served as editorial assistant and provided service of very high quality. Following her marriage, Mrs. Apfelbaum was replaced by Mrs. Miriam Landon, who maintained the high quality of assistance. Others who helped with the editing included my devoted wife, Chaya Wexler. Rabbi Joseph Epstein provided good counsel in matters relating to publication. Rabbi Dr. Aaron Rakeffet, author of the book, *The Rav: The World of Rabbi Joseph B. Soloveitchik*, provided similar advice. Assistance was also received from Mrs. Linda Derovan, formerly the Director of Yeshiva University's Educational activities in Israel.

Five Rabbis read the book and provided written endorsements. In alphabetical order, they include: Rabbi Dr. Reuben Aberman, Rabbi Moshe Galinsky, Rabbi Dr. Chaim S. Heifetz, Rabbi Dr. Aaron Rakeffet and Rabbi Binyomin Tabori.

My sincere thanks to Gefen Publishing House for their efforts on behalf of this publication. Ilan and Dror Greenfield, and other members of their staff, provided the highest quality of service in a patient and courteous manner.

Although many people assisted with this book, the ultimate responsibility for it rests solely with the author. To err is human and, undoubtedly, errors may have crept into this work. The author would appreciate corrections and comments from readers.

PROLOGUE

The Daughters Victorious is a novel of the type classified as historic fiction. This means that the book is based on events that actually occurred but for which the description in historic sources is brief and limited. In the case of this book, the primary source is the Torah itself. The brief summary in the Torah is expanded in various books of the Talmud and the Midrashim. Elaborations notwithstanding, the story that emerges from these sources does not capture the imagination or generate appreciation for the greatness of the daughters of Zelaphchad.

In using the fictional format, the author intended to integrate all the basic material and present the story in dramatic and readable form. To do so, it was necessary to introduce persons who may not have existed and events that may not have occurred. The challenge is to be certain that the fictional elements in the book in no way contradict any of the traditional teachings concerning the daughters of Zelaphchad. The author feels that he has succeeded in this regard. Nevertheless, to be sure that no misunderstandings arise, he has put into the General and Detailed Notes a clarification of which material in the book is fact and which is fiction. He also wishes to add the following warning:

> The Daughters Victorious should not serve either as a text of Jewish history or as a guide to Jewish laws and customs. The proper place to seek such material is in the existing Codes of Law and the traditional history books. The author's interpretations of certain actions and events are his own, and may not reflect all of the authoritative opinions of accepted scholars and commentators.

The reader is invited to consult the Detailed Notes on each chapter which provide the sources for the elements in the story. By studying the sources, the reader may determine the extent to which the author succeeded in capturing the spirit of the historical period and the character of the protagonists.

Part 1

THE EARLY YEARS

CHAPTER
ONE

"FROM THE DEPTHS WE CALLED UNTO THEE O LORD"

"Get back to work now, Zelaphchad," the Egyptian taskmaster yelled to his Hebrew foreman at the top of his lungs, "or I will have my guards beat you mercilessly. Your job is to lay bricks, not to play nursemaid to weak Hebrew slaves." Once again, the combination of fierce heat and superhuman toil had taken its toll on one of Zelaphchad's crew of slaves. The man had collapsed and was mumbling incoherently. Although Zelaphchad had run to his assistance in an attempt to revive him, there was little cause for hope. Slaves frequently died from exhaustion in Egypt, and Zelaphchad's men were no different than the others.[1]

Zelaphchad ignored the taskmaster for a few more minutes before returning to work. His crew would have to work harder to make up for the missing man and the extra toil would deprive them of the time to grieve. For Zelaphchad, however, the emotional pain burned within him and the callousness of the taskmaster did nothing but add fuel to the fire. He cursed the man under his breath and prayed for the day when retribution would be forthcoming and his Hebrew brothers would be free.

Like his father and grandfather before him, Zelaphchad, the son of Chefer, was born into slavery in the Land of Egypt. It was of little comfort to him that he lived in the most advanced society the world had ever known. Towering pyramids, truly awesome constructions, formed a distant backdrop for his arduous efforts. They were beautiful geometric structures encasing the bodies of departed Pharaohs, but their majesty did nothing to alleviate the pain of the blistering sands and backbreaking toil.

He was a Hebrew — a member of the nation of Israel that had suffered in bondage for two full centuries. It was an unusually cruel and severe oppression, motivated not only by economic considerations, but also by racial hatred and political goals. Though the Egyptians profited handsomely from store cities constructed by Hebrew slave labor, they derived far more satisfaction from the knowledge that their programs were crushing the spirit of what was once a proud and autonomous people.

Zelaphchad was only sixteen years of age when he joined the ranks of the slaves. A tall, muscular man, with inordinate strength and stamina, he was designated almost immediately by the Egyptians to fill a supervisory rank. At the age of nineteen, he was made foreman of a crew of laborers, reporting directly to a taskmaster. Despite opportunities to do so, Zelaphchad never took advantage of his rank. He toiled alongside his men and did not seek to avoid actual labor. Nor did he dress differently because of his position. As a working slave, he labored with his body bare from the waist up. The lower part of his body was covered with a short cloth garment held in place by a belt.[2]

Many of those he supervised were members of his own tribe. Among them were his three younger brothers — Azriel, Shaphat and Ram — who joined the ranks of the slaves when they came of age. All of the brothers and their parents lived in a family house in the province of Goshen by the shores of the Nile River. Zelaphchad dealt firmly with those who were in his charge, enjoying the confidence of his Egyptian overlords and meeting their imposed quotas with high quality work.[3]

Despite his success, Zelaphchad was never reconciled to his fate as a slave. Sitting with his father and brothers in the family home, he frequently brought up the subject of resistance to the Egyptians. "We slaves," he argued, "far outnumber the Egyptian taskmasters and guards. If we rebelled against our oppressors, we could easily overpower them and break away."

Chefer understood his son's frustration for he, himself, had toiled as a slave for over thirty years. The work had taken a huge toll of his physical resources and lines of weariness were deeply etched in his face. Although no longer able to do heavy labor, he spent time with the working slaves, sharing his experiences and rendering minor assistance. "Son, you are dreaming about something that is impossible for many reasons. Long before you were born, there was a Hebrew by the name of Moses who was raised as a prince in Pharaoh's home.[4] When he left the palace, he was shocked at the suffering of his brothers. Moses was the only Hebrew who offered resistance to our enslavement. Once, on seeing a Hebrew being beaten by an Egyptian, he struck down the oppressor and buried his body in the sand.[5] When Pharaoh learned of his deed, he sent soldiers to kill him, his own adopted grandson. Moses managed to flee into exile, but he has not been heard of since. If he were still alive, he would be more than seventy-five years old and hardly in a position to lead rebellions.

"Any act of insurrection would be put down by the Egyptians with force. Some slaves might attempt to flee but, given the harsh environment of the desert, nothing will remain of their efforts other than withered bones in the sand. Only with the total defeat of the Egyptian nation, will we achieve our freedom."

Zelaphchad never could accept such a passive philosophy. He felt that the Almighty could, if appealed to, shorten the exile and redeem His people. Despite his father's words, he also could not bring himself to exclude the possibility of resistance. These were his secret hopes and they strengthened his determination to survive. When he attempted to convey such ideas to others, however, they had no sympathy for his unpopular cause. Not wishing to enter into polemics, Zelaphchad generally maintained his peace. He also felt that he might endanger his parents and brothers, if he were to become known to the Egyptians as a revolutionary.

What Zelaphchad knew about the history of his people came from his father, who was steeped in the traditions of the Hebrews. There were some schools for the younger Hebrew children, relics of a massive school system built by Judah, son of the patriarch, Jacob.[6] Given the exigencies of slavery, however, most Hebrew children, including Zelaphchad, did not attend them. It was Chefer who told his son the story of Joseph, the patriarch of his own tribe of Menashe. It inspired Zelaphchad to hear that Joseph achieved success in Egypt despite starting as a slave imprisoned in a dungeon.[7]

Joseph was one of the twelve sons of Jacob and a great-grandson of Abraham, the founder of the Hebrew faith. He had arrived in Egypt as a slave after being sold into bondage by his jealous brothers. It did not take him long to work his way out of slavery and attain the rank of second in command to Pharaoh, in charge of a food program that saved Egypt from a disastrous famine. As a child, Zelaphchad pictured Joseph riding in his chariot with a host of armed soldiers running before him crying aloud, "The Prince is coming! Bend the knee!"[8] He could see Pharaoh's signet ring on Joseph's finger flashing in the sun as he waved to the multitudes.

The Egyptian famine spread over the entire region. It affected Canaan and forced Jacob and his sons to migrate to Egypt. After their reconciliation with Joseph, the brothers settled in the Egyptian province of Goshen. There, they were given land by Pharaoh and permitted to pursue their occupation of sheep raising.[9]

The children of Israel prospered in Egypt during Joseph's reign, and developed into thirteen large tribes. Eleven of the tribes were named after the eleven sons of Jacob other than Joseph. The remaining two tribes were named after Menashe and Ephraim, the first two sons of Joseph born in the Land of Egypt. Although there were actually thirteen tribes, Zelaphchad kept hearing people describe his nation as the twelve tribes of Israel. He understood that they excluded the tribe of Levi, because that tribe was involved only in religious work and was exempt from slavery.[10]

Concerned by the rapid expansion of the Israelites and their entry into Egyptian society, Pharaoh undertook to suppress them by enslavement. He hoped thereby to gain cheap labor and diminish the Hebrew birth rate. His plan failed because the more the Israelites were persecuted, the more they multiplied. The women of Israel refused to allow their husbands to abandon the deeply-rooted tradition of family building. They kept bearing children even when it meant that their sons would face a lifetime of forced labor.[11]

When the slavery did not achieve his intended goal, Pharaoh issued a gruesome decree commanding his officers to drown all newly-born Hebrew boys in the Nile. Heroic measures were taken by the Hebrew midwives to conceal the male babies and thwart the Egyptian terror. Despite brave resistance, the decree took a heavy toll of Jewish life and threatened for a while to curtail Hebrew fruitfulness. A number of men delayed starting families while others, who were already married, refrained from having relations with their wives. Such a separation occurred in the family of Amram, chief judge of Israel. It was his daughter, Miriam, who convinced him that he was making a grievous error.[12]

She argued that at least half of the children born would survive because they would be female. Even when boys were born, some could be hidden from the Egyptians and saved. Miriam felt it was wrong for the Hebrews to abet their own national suicide. She demanded that Amram resume normal family life and instruct all other Hebrew families to do likewise. Amram acceded to her logic and, in time, his wife, Yocheved, gave birth to Moses. Through a miraculous set of circumstances, the child survived the death decree. His mother placed him in a basket in the Nile, where he was found by Pharaoh's daughter and adopted by her. Moses grew up in Pharaoh's palace as a prince and did not leave until he was a grown man. While he was aware that he was a Hebrew, being isolated in the royal environment prevented him from fully understanding the desperate situation of his people.[13]

In time, the genocidal decree was withdrawn. Zelaphchad was fortunate that the evil law was not in effect when he and his brothers were born. The Pharaoh who issued the decree was ultimately succeeded by his son but the slavery remained unabated. Under severe conditions, the forced labor continued to build the Egyptian infrastructure. The main projects erected by the Hebrew slaves were the great store cities of Pithom and Rameses.[14] It was Joseph who had originally developed the plan of storing grain in special cities. In years of bountiful crops, the government bought surplus grain for storage. In the event of a drought, the government opened the store cities to feed the population. While projects of this nature were of commercial value, others, such as pyramids and monuments, were not. The brutal work took a large toll of the exploited slaves and only the strongest ones survived.[15]

Upon reaching his twenty-first birthday, Zelaphchad had a long talk with his father. "It is wrong," he said, "for your children to delay building families any longer than necessary. It is the sacred duty of our people to do so, for we have been taught by our elders that our strength is in numbers. If we fail to reproduce sufficiently, the bondage will totally destroy our people."

Chefer was beginning to sense the import of his son's words, but wanted him to be more explicit. "What exactly are you driving at?"

"Father, the time has come for your sons to get married. Since my brothers will not do so before me, I would like your assistance and blessing."

Chefer was not really surprised to hear his son's request. "It so happens that your mother thinks as you do. We most certainly will help you find a suitable mate. Do you have a particular young woman in mind?"

Zelaphchad blushed. "Yes I do, father, a very pretty girl. She is the sister of a man who works in my crew. I find her very attractive."

Zelaphchad did not dwell on his relationship with Achla because he felt that his father would not understand the delay in bringing the matter to his attention. Long courtships were generally not approved of in Hebrew families, and Zelaphchad had been friendly with Achla for more than a year. He first noticed her when she came to the construction area to help her brother. She would bring him a basket of food and a flask of water. When darkness fell, she would walk her brother home. Zelaphchad got to know her well, and was impressed by her regal bearing. Although she dressed modestly, he could see that her garments were in a class of their own. They reflected an element of quality and style that was not customary in slave families. He later discovered that Achla was particularly gifted in work with cloth. She fully mastered spinning, weaving, sewing and embroidery. She worked best with the linen that was derived from the abundant flax in the Goshen area.

A happy smile appeared on Chefer's face. "Since all the members of your group are related, perhaps I know the family. I will be glad to speak to her father on your behalf."

Zelaphchad shyly revealed the name of the girl and her family to his father. "Her real name is Achlama, but everyone calls her Achla for short. She is seventeen, and mature for her age."

"I know the family well," Chefer said. "I know, too, that the parents have had a solid religious training, but I am not sure how they educated their daughters." After a brief pause, his voice changed to a more philosophical tone. "Surely you know that beauty is not the most important thing in a marriage. Over the course of time it fades away. What is most essential is that your bride be wise and have a good heart."

Zelaphchad's response had apparently been rehearsed well in advance. "From all that I have seen of Achla, I feel that she has those qualities. She shares my dreams of the Land of Canaan and I am sure that she will pass on this love to my sons. She is familiar with our customs and national history. If you were to meet her, father, I know that you would share my sentiments."

"I am delighted to hear that. Why don't you bring her home so that your mother and I may see her?"

Zelaphchad conveyed the invitation to Achla but she was hesitant. "Are you sure you need parental approval, Zelaphchad? Most men of your age just choose their brides in the marketplace and ask no one for consent. Our people have no special rituals of consent and approval these days." Achla was troubled by the possibility that Chefer, a very distinguished member of the tribe, might look with disfavor on her.[16]

"I am aware of what people do, Achla, but we are not talking now about rights and legalities. As a matter of courtesy to my parents, who have been very good to me, I would like them to feel that they are performing part of the sacred tradition of finding a bride for their son. Tomorrow night, I want to take you home and present you to my family. You have no reason to be apprehensive."

Zelaphchad was not alone in thinking that Achla was attractive, as there were many others who shared his judgment. She was of middle height with broad shoulders and fine form. Standing next to Zelaphchad she looked small only by comparison. Her skin was dark from long exposure to the sun, but was smooth and clear. Her black hair was long and straight and flowed gently to her waist. She was endowed with soft features that made her look very youthful.

For her visit to the Zelaphchad home the following night, she selected a black robe. Except for a white scarf, she avoided any bright colors that would make her look younger and lessen the seriousness of the occasion. The scarf emphasized her dark features, which were considered very attractive in Egypt.

When Achla saw Zelaphchad's home, she was impressed with its size. She realized that the home had been in the family for many generations and had been erected at a time when the Hebrews were very prosperous. The walls were built with bricks similar to the ones used by the slaves in their building work. Except for the central area, the rooms extending from the sides of the main room were small. The ceiling of the central room was supported by four brick pillars.

Achla made a winning impression from the moment she entered the Chefer home. In fact, Zelaphchad's parents spent more time praising their son than asking her questions. Escorting Achla back home, Zelaphchad was filled with joy at his parents' approval. "What name shall we give our first son?" he asked.[17]

"Zelaphchad, you're rushing things a bit. Besides, not all children are boys. I will do my best, but sometimes girls are also born. You may have the honor of naming all of our sons. If, by chance," she said teasingly, "we have daughters, I will name them."

"Bite your tongue," he said. "I suppose I could live with one or two daughters if they happen to arrive. By no means can I make peace with the idea of more than that. You know that our traditions regard the birth of a male child as a special blessing, especially when he is a first-born child."

Achla chose not to dwell on the subject. She understood that Zelaphchad reflected the prevailing prejudices about females both in the Egyptian society and among the Hebrews. Her mother had told her that such attitudes were not a problem. If her husband were a good man, he would love his children, both sons and daughters. Achla's parents knew Zelaphchad well, and had long since given their approval to the match. Her mother did not want anything to cause Achla to have any doubts about the marriage.

"The sex of a child is determined in heaven," Achla said to Zelaphchad. "We have no choice but to accept whatever God gives us. Speaking of marriage, how soon will it be and where will we live?"

"For my part I am ready tonight. But, if you cannot put things together that quickly, I am willing to wait until tomorrow. There is a room in my house that is available. Right now, my brothers and I sleep together in one of the side rooms. My father said that if I get married, he will give us a room of our own."

"Zelaphchad, you know that we Hebrew women observe a few customs before marriage. I will be able to perform them tomorrow. Afterwards, I will gather my things in a sack. You may then take me to your home."

It was a joyous evening in the Zelaphchad home the following night. Achla and Zelaphchad were glowing and happy. Achla's family was represented by her parents, her brother, her sisters, and her cousins. The food was ample, and there was singing and dancing. There were some speeches, but the festivities did not last long, as most of the men, including Zelaphchad, had to report to work the next morning. The Egyptians had no regard for the personal lives of their slaves nor for any family traditions they may have had. Zelaphchad then took Achla to his chamber to start their married life.

The following years passed by quickly. Slavery lends neither excitement nor variety to the human experience. Slaves rose at dawn and worked in the blistering sun until dark. The pervading atmosphere was one of fear and despair. The smell of sweat and sounds of groaning under heavy burdens filled the air. At night, the laborers were so exhausted that they could barely think or speak. Despite their degradation, the slaves defiantly retained their Hebrew names and spoke amongst themselves in the sacred tongue.[18] Otherwise, the prevailing culture was Egyptian, and there was a high degree of assimilation.

The young couple quickly adjusted to married life. Zelaphchad waited in vain for a chance to bestow a name upon a son. Achla, though, named the three daughters that were born in quick succession. Machla, the eldest one, was born within their first year of marriage. She was followed a year and a half later by Tirza and a year and a half after that by Hogla. The Chefer home was getting crowded because, as soon as Zelaphchad got married, his brothers began to follow his lead.

Azriel, next in order of birth, married a year after Zelaphchad. Shafat was wed a half year later. Both were blessed with sons which made Zelaphchad feel somewhat envious. Shafat, who married Adina from the tribe of Ephraim, named his son Eliav. Azriel, who married Yiscah from the tribe of Menashe, named his first-born son, Meir. Although Ram was approaching twenty, he seemed in no hurry to get married. His parents did not believe in pushing him before he himself felt ready.

Azriel was the scholar in the family, having surpassed Chefer in this regard. He was not nearly as militant as Zelaphchad but his faith was much deeper, his intellect far keener. As he learned about the values and traditions of the Hebrew people from the elders of the tribe, he shared the knowledge with his family. His teachings served to reinforce Zelaphchad's religious beliefs.

One night, shortly after Hogla was born, Zelaphchad came home extremely agitated. He gathered his brothers and their wives in the main room and spoke to them as a group. "I heard some wonderful news today. The slaves were whispering that Moses, son of Amram, has returned from exile with a message from the Lord, God of Israel. He and the elders of our people plan to approach

Pharaoh and request, in the name of our God, that we be freed from bondage and allowed to proceed to our homeland, Canaan." His announcement caused a flurry of excitement among the members of the family.[19]

When pressed for details, Zelaphchad could not provide too much information. "I have no idea what Moses was doing for more than half a century of exile. From what he related to the elders, he married Tziporah, the daughter of the Midianite priest, Jethro, and they had two sons. Several weeks ago, while tending Jethro's sheep in the Sinai desert, he had a revelation in which he beheld a bush that was burning, but was not consumed. You know the bushes in the desert. Sometimes they flare up from the heat and burn out in a few minutes. Well, this one kept on burning and Moses, being curious, went over to see what was happening. It was then that he heard God's voice saying to him, 'Moses, remove your shoes, for the place you are standing upon is holy.'"[20]

Azriel was familiar with earlier revelations experienced by the Hebrew patriarchs and he and other slaves had long been praying for heavenly redemption. Still, it was hard to believe that the prayers were actually being answered. "What else did God say?" he asked, anxiety etched on his face.

"I can't repeat the exact words," Zelaphchad said. "There was a complicated discussion about the names of God. I also heard that there was considerable resistance from Moses to the idea of being selected for the mission of leading the Hebrews out of Egypt."

Azriel pondered the report. "I can understand the part about Moses not being eager to go. To begin with, he is still a fugitive wanted for murder. Even if that were no longer a factor, there are other problems. He has to convince the elders that God really sent him, and he has to persuade Pharaoh to listen."

"I wouldn't worry about the elders," Zelaphchad said. "He performed some awesome miracles to convince them that God actually did appear to him. Speaking to Pharaoh will be a harder problem. Even if Moses were a persuasive speaker, Pharaoh would not be inclined to listen. Unfortunately, reports have it that Moses is afflicted with a speech impediment and is not at all an eloquent speaker."[21]

"What miracles are you talking about?"

"When he throws his rod to the ground, it becomes a serpent. He is able to turn pure water to blood and make healthy skin leprous. He can also reverse the miracles so that the serpent becomes a rod again and the leprous skin is restored to its normal appearance."[22]

"Is that all?" Shafat interjected in a cynical tone. "Pharaoh's magicians can certainly equal that and probably do a lot more. Personally, I think that Moses is wasting his time. In the end, it will probably be a lot worse for all of us. Pharaoh will be furious if he is asked to release his slaves."

Zelaphchad became a little heated. "You have the same attitude as the elders. We will never end the slavery if we remain silent. I know that Pharaoh won't be impressed in the beginning, but we have to start. Surely, if the Lord sent Moses to Pharaoh, deliverance must be close at hand."

With that, the gathering came to an end. Zelaphchad and Achla went to their room and continued the discussion. "Shafat is like many of our people who can not sense the impending redemption," he complained bitterly. "They have become so accustomed to slavery that they are afraid of freedom. They can not bring themselves to believe that salvation may be imminent. How can they doubt that our Lord is incapable of doing anything He wishes? Didn't He create the entire world?"

Achla felt the need to temper some of Zelaphchad's enthusiasm. She didn't want him to build up his hopes only to have them cruelly dashed. "You are letting yourself get carried away with this news," she warned him. "It will take much more than one petition to get us out of this country." Nevertheless, Zelaphchad remained agitated. Tired as he was, he found it hard to sleep.

Early the next morning, while he was at work, Zelaphchad paused to watch the procession of Hebrew elders pass by on its way to the meeting with Pharaoh at the banks of the Nile where the king went for daily worship. After the services, Pharaoh would usually receive a few petitioners, mostly Egyptians, with personal or political problems.

The procession was led by Moses and Aaron. Zelaphchad recognized Aaron who had succeeded his father, Amram, as the spiritual leader and chief judge of the Hebrew people. At various times, Aaron had visited all of the Hebrew tribal areas in the performance of his duties. He was known for his flowing white robes, white beard and delicate, friendly face. Moses, by contrast, projected a totally different appearance. He was much taller than Aaron and had the darkened visage of a shepherd. His eyes burned fiercely. There were stories of his compassionate nature but, looking at him, no one would ever imagine it. He had returned to Egypt in haste at God's behest and was still dressed in simple garments. Zelaphchad trembled in fear as he beheld the legendary figure.

In his hand, Moses carried the rod with which he performed the miracles. Aaron was wearing the garments of a judge. After years in public office, he was a polished statesman, well-versed in protocol and affairs of state. A short time earlier he had been prophetically summoned and advised by the Lord that Moses was returning. He was instructed to prepare himself to meet his brother at Mount Horeb and then to serve as spokesman at both the meeting with the elders and the confrontation with Pharaoh.[23]

Walking proudly behind Moses and Aaron were the elders of Israel. Although well beyond working age, they were younger than their two leaders who were in their eighties. Zelaphchad recognized his tribal chief, Gamliel, and bowed to him as he passed. Gamliel saw him and smiled, pleased to see a member of his tribe and rejoicing in the attention that was being focused upon him. Zelaphchad had little use for Gamliel's politics but he respected the man for his knowledge and dedication. Gamliel worked hard on tribal matters, settling disputes and helping people in trouble.

When the procession passed out of view, Zelaphchad resumed his tasks. Returning home after work, he heard what had happened with the elders when they were no longer being observed by the people. One by one they dropped out of the procession and left Moses and Aaron to speak with Pharaoh alone. They justified their cowardice by saying that Moses was being too aggressive in making such strong demands of Pharaoh. The fear that Moses always had about weak support from the leadership of the Hebrews was quite justified.[24]

When the pair arrived at the royal encampment, they did not have long to wait. Aaron was well known in royal circles as the spokesman for the Hebrews. When the Egyptians wanted to convey a message to the Israelites, they relied upon Aaron to transmit it to the tribal leaders. They, in turn, would report it to the masses. Aaron was soft spoken, popular and congenial. He commanded close attention whenever he spoke.

While waiting to be heard, Moses studied the Pharaoh sitting in a richly upholstered chair. Having grown up in the royal palace, Moses knew the king's late father quite well. The present Pharaoh was only a baby when Moses had to flee the country. Like his father, this Pharaoh had a lean frame and sharply chiseled features. He conveyed the same cruel, hard-bitten appearance that characterized all members of the dynasty. The king's teachers had told him about the rebellious prince, Moses, but left him under the impression that the man had died in exile.

"Your Majesty," Aaron said, when the king turned to him, "My brother, Moses, is with me today. We thank Your Highness for granting us this audience." Pharaoh allowed only a few minutes of general conversation before asking Aaron about the purpose of the visit.[25]

"My brother has had a vision in which our Lord, the God of Israel, appeared to him and commanded him to come before you and convey a special message."

"And what does your so-called God have to say for himself?" Pharaoh scoffed, glancing knowingly at his advisors to share his contempt.

Moses fought to control his anger. Aaron put a restraining hand on Moses and continued, "The God of Israel requests that you grant His people the right to worship Him in the desert."

Pharaoh reacted violently. He was thoroughly convinced of his own divinity and had no desire to share it with anyone else. "Who is your God that I should listen to him?" he snarled. "I recognize no such God, and it goes without saying that I have no intention of letting the Hebrews go anywhere!"

"Fear not, we are not seeking the full liberation of our people," Aaron said in a moderate tone. "What we are asking for is a respite, a three-day holiday to travel to the desert and worship our God. If we neglect our religious duties, the Lord may punish our people with a plague or with the sword."

Pharaoh was not moved by Aaron's mollifications. With growing impatience he replied, "Hear me out, Aaron. Your people are now reconciled to their condition. Why should you disrupt them from their tasks and foment unrest? Why don't the two of you go about your work and leave well enough alone? Do not forget that you are dealing with vast numbers of people. Do you think I can entertain the idea of holidays for so many workers?"

With a wave of the hand, Pharaoh signaled that the audience was over. Moses and Aaron left the reception area without delay. They were, of course, disappointed at the abrupt rejection of their demands but they weren't totally dismayed. They had no reason to doubt the Divine prophecy. They realized, though, that it would take much more heavenly intervention before tangible results could be achieved.

Pharaoh, on the other hand, was far more concerned than he had revealed. The look on the face of Moses and his piercing eyes left him unnerved. The man did not seem to be part of the real world. He possessed an unworldly quality, a remoteness that made it difficult to relate to him. Aaron was his usual friendly self but he seemed under the sway of Moses. It would become difficult, under those circumstances, to have Aaron continue his role as a buffer between himself and the Israelites.

As far as the Hebrew God was concerned, Pharaoh had no cause to fear. He was not much of a believer in his own gods and he certainly wasn't going to respect any others. He performed worship as part of the kingly role but mostly for public consumption. What he did believe in was strength of arms coupled with political skill. In that area he was a superb player.

He realized that any insurgency among the slaves had to be quelled immediately before it got out of hand. The Hebrews, like any other slave group, craved their freedom. At the moment, however, the long years of slavery had weakened any resolve on their part to seek it. A cause endorsed by the chief judge of their tribes might encourage them to put aside their passivity and embark on revolution. He was sure that his troops could contain the slaves but an uprising would be costly in terms of manpower and lost production.

Pharaoh then instructed his chief of staff to gather the ruling council at the palace immediately after the noon meal. When the meeting was convened, Pharaoh reported on his discussion with the Hebrew leaders and solicited advice. The advisors did not feel much of a threat in the matter but they deferred to Pharaoh's anxieties. "If it please the king," a junior advisor volunteered, "we could easily remove the men who trouble him."

The senior advisor quickly stepped in. His face reflected a measure of contempt for younger men whose rash actions bespoke much passion and little experience. "That is not the way to proceed at all. Aaron is our surest link to the Israelites and he serves our interests in controlling them. Without the subversive ideas of his brother, he could continue to be a valuable asset to us.

Besides, the last thing we want to do is to provide the Hebrews with a pair of martyrs whose murder would fan the flames of resentment."

"What do you suggest?" asked Pharaoh.

"The wisest way to proceed is to undermine the stature of Moses in the eyes of the Hebrews. We must thoroughly discredit him. It would be wise to enact a decree that will further oppress the Hebrews and cast the blame for it on Moses."

Pharaoh was not convinced. "If the slaves are further afflicted, that in itself might bring about rebellion."

"It is not the slaves that I intend to oppress," the advisor said, attempting to clarify his ideas. "The slaves do not have a mind of their own. If their captains and leaders tell them to follow Moses, they will do so. We must aim this new decree at the Hebrew leadership by inserting a wedge of hatred between them and Moses."

At this juncture someone suggested increasing the brick quota. Depending on local circumstances, a crew of fifty slaves produced and emplaced about 2,000 bricks a day. "You are missing the point," the senior advisor objected. "We are not trying to increase production at this time. We are aiming at creating conditions that would make it impossible for the slaves to meet the existing quota. When the men fail to produce enough bricks we will punish their captains. If we were to increase the present quota, then we would have to use more men of our own to prepare the materials. We certainly do not have them to spare." In light of his statements, the suggestion was rejected.

The advisor who had proposed the higher quota quickly reversed himself. "In that case, I have an approach that will satisfy both requirements. We can release manpower by relieving our own men of the chore of providing straw for the bricks. We will maintain the existing brick quota but it will be impossible for the Hebrews to meet it if they have to scrounge for straw." The suggestion was quickly approved by a council that had long-standing tendencies to deviousness.[26]

The decree was transmitted to all the Egyptian taskmasters who were told to call in the Hebrew captains and foremen and advise them that on the morrow there would be no straw provided. The brick quota would remain the same and, if the crews did not meet it, the captains and foremen would be punished.

Zelaphchad, as the leader of a crew, received the news late in the afternoon. He fully understood the intent of the decree. He held his peace, however, until he could consult with his brothers and relatives after the evening meal.

The family turned to Azriel for help in analyzing the turn of events. The latter had been thinking about the problem while walking home with his brothers and was ready when called upon. "We have three approaches to this situation," he said. "We can refuse to work altogether, we can work as usual and fail to reach the new quota, or we can make heroic attempts to meet the challenge."

Zelaphchad ruled out the first approach immediately. "This decree," he said, "is aimed only at the captains. If all of us cease to work or utterly disregard the quota, then everyone will get beaten. That is definitely an unacceptable course of action."

Ram, who was Zelaphchad's closest confidant, spoke up. "Somehow we must try to meet the new quota. If we do, we can spare our brother the agony of a beating. Even if we can come close, the Egyptians may ease up on the brutality."

Azriel was satisfied with Ram's suggestion. "How do we go about it, Ram?" Ram, although the youngest of the brothers, was the most astute in technical matters and all the brothers relied heavily on his skill.

"The situation is not too promising. Our crew is divided into two units, one making bricks and one laying them. Remember, these are heavy bricks, as long as a man's arm.[27] We have about 1,000 bricks on hand, so the bricklayers have enough to work with until early afternoon. The brick makers form the bricks in the morning and put them out in the sun to dry. They produce about 2,000 bricks each day. Half are used in the afternoon and the rest are reserved for the next day.

"How much production would we lose if we had to gather our own straw?" Zelaphchad asked.

"That is hard to say," Ram responded. "We need lots of straw to put in the mud. It is early fall now. While there is straw around, it takes much effort to gather it and cut it to size. As a guess, I would say that our production might very well be cut in half."

"That doesn't seem so bad," Azriel said. "We could first use up the 1,000 bricks that we have on hand. Let's say that we only produce 1,000 new bricks instead of the usual 2,000. We could meet the quota by using the full 1,000 on hand and not worry about a reserve for the next day."

"We cannot do that," Ram answered, "because it is not feasible. Bricks made in the afternoon are not sufficiently dry to be laid before dark. Working at night is out of the question because we cannot emplace bricks in the dark. But even if we could find a way of doing it and the Egyptians did not object, what would be the purpose? We would only succeed in delaying Zelaphchad's beating for a single day. Bear in mind that royal decrees are never issued for only one day. No, we have to find a better solution."

"What if we were to work faster?" Zelaphchad asked.

"You work the men pretty hard now. We could make a special effort for a few days at the expense of quality. At best, though, you are talking of forming and laying several hundred additional bricks, hardly enough to meet the quota."

"What then are our alternatives?"

Ram thought for a second and said, "We might try something new. In Egypt, straw is used to give strength to the mud as it is pressed in the molds. The Babylonians don't use straw at all. They use clay and then fire the bricks in an oven. Maybe we could try it."[28]

"There is enough clay around," Zelaphchad said. "What are you going to use for fuel?"

"We have some tar, some brushwood and, even if we burn straw, it doesn't have to be cut to size."

"Will we be able to fire enough bricks?"

"There is a slight chance. I would feel more hopeful if we had some experience in the method."

"We have nothing to lose," Zelaphchad decided. "It's worth a try for sure."

At this point, Achla, who was following the discussion with mounting fear for Zelaphchad's safety, made a suggestion. "Perhaps the women can help in gathering the straw?" Some of those at the table were surprised that she spoke up because the women usually sat very quietly at such meetings.

Her father-in-law, Chefer, who also had been listening, intervened. "I know that you want to help, Achla, but I cannot allow it. Thus far, the Egyptians have not enslaved our women. If we show them that they can do that, it will destroy our homes and families."

In the privacy of their bedroom, Achla told Zelaphchad that she didn't mean to make an improper suggestion. She only wanted to save him from a beating. She had already heard from some other women that they were planning to help gather straw.

"Don't worry about me," he said. "I am strong enough to withstand the pain." He was, however, quite afraid.

"Why are they doing this to us?" she asked.

"I am not sure," he answered. "It may have something to do with the visit of Moses and Aaron with Pharaoh."

Ram was at work before dawn the next morning building a crude oven. Zelaphchad sent part of the brick-making crew out to gather straw while the rest stacked bricks for the oven. He didn't want to risk all his efforts on an experiment so, as soon as Ram had enough clay bricks to get started, he had the men resume the standard brick-making. He also shifted some of his slower bricklayers to the brick-making work.

The firing of the bricks was not a total failure. Ram, however, had trouble maintaining sufficient heat in the oven and the process did not meet expectations. Many of the bricks crumbled in his hand. Zelaphchad pressed his men as hard as he dared but, in the end, it was obvious that the quota could not be met.

The taskmaster, who was no lover of Hebrews, arrived at the scene before dark. While he may not have been a vicious person in his basic nature, his zeal in carrying out the royal edicts caused him to lose his self-control. That his actions might hurt innocent people was of no concern to him. This was especially true if the victims were Hebrews. He shouted at Zelaphchad in front of his men, "Don't you know what the daily brick quota is?" Zelaphchad maintained a sullen silence.

"Have your men done their regular amount of work, today?"

Zelaphchad didn't feel the need to dignify the cynical performance with an answer. It wasn't the taskmaster who had created the situation so nothing could be gained by defending himself before him.

The taskmaster summoned three guards who bound Zelaphchad to a post and took turns applying the lash to his bare back. The pain was excruciating. Zelaphchad bore it as long as he could until he finally collapsed on the ground taking the post with him. At that point, the guards desisted and went with the taskmaster to the next crew.[29]

Zelaphchad's brothers cut him loose from the post and washed the bleeding welts. They gave him some water and assisted him to his feet. Wearily he trudged home, leaning on Ram and Azriel. Achla was glad to see him alive and helped him to bed. There she rubbed his back with ointment to ease some of the pain.

The family was finishing dinner when a messenger arrived. He advised Zelaphchad that the tribal leaders had decided to gather a representation of captains to appear before Pharaoh and appeal for leniency. When Zelaphchad was asked to participate he readily accepted. He didn't have much hope that Pharaoh would be receptive to any pleas, but the visit would give him an opportunity to learn first-hand what had caused Pharaoh to issue the oppressive order.

The captains gathered outside the royal encampment at about ten in the morning. They were quickly ushered in to see the king. The encampment was not nearly as lavish as the royal palace in the city of Memphis which the Hebrews called "Noph." The walls were made of cloth curtains suspended on wooden beams. Several smaller chambers were curtained off for the king's convenience. The open area was used to conduct meetings or receive visitors.

Pharaoh was determined to deliver his tirade against Moses as soon as possible. He felt that the bruised and battered captains would make a receptive audience. Protocol demanded that the king speak first, so the captains waited in deference for the meeting to get underway.

"I have before me a petition," Pharaoh announced, "to revoke or annul the royal decree issued two days earlier with regard to the daily production of bricks. Who speaks for the petitioners in this matter? Let him step forward and state his case."[30]

The tribal leader of Asher moved to the speaker's stand. "I am Pagiel, leader of the tribe of Asher. I speak on behalf of the captains and foremen of all your Hebrew servants. Your Majesty, each of the group leaders gathered here was savagely beaten last night for failing to meet the brick quota. They still bear the welts of their punishment on their backs. Under the conditions of the new ordinance, it is absolutely impossible to produce the number of bricks requested by the king."

Pharaoh remained unmoved by the leader's presentation. His face was frozen in a mask of apathy and disinterest. After a short pause, he asked in a loud voice, "Who among you is Zelaphchad, son of Chefer?" Upon hearing his name, Zelaphchad came forward and walked to the speaker's stand. His body ached and his ribs were sore but he mustered all the dignity he could. Although he was nervous in the presence of the Pharaoh, he was not afraid. Rather he was angry and embittered with the cruel treatment meted out by the Egyptians.

"I am Zelaphchad, His Majesty's servant. I await His Majesty's bidding."

"I have been advised by my taskmasters that you and your crew almost reached the quota yesterday, falling short by a mere hundred bricks or so. Do you, too, feel that I have imposed an impossible quota upon the Hebrew slaves?"

"If it please His Majesty, I will speak the truth. My crew made a very determined effort to work under the new conditions. We worked harder than ever before, even introducing some new methods. Still, we fell short and I was publicly beaten. If my men continue to work at yesterday's feverish pace, they will all die. His Majesty must realize that if we are not given the straw, we cannot produce the same amount of bricks as we did in the past."

"You are a brave and devoted captain, Zelaphchad," Pharaoh said. "Your special effort is commendable and will be noted. I will not, however, change the new edict in any way and I shall explain why. The other day, your leader Moses came before me and said that the slaves wanted time off from their work in order to worship their God in the desert. To me, such requests are a sign of indolence. Slaves who are working to the utmost of their ability do not have time to think of vacations. If we allow such nonsense, it will not be long before they start dreaming of not working altogether. Tell me, Zelaphchad, do you share the subversive views of this man, Moses?"

Zelaphchad realized that he could not answer this question in the affirmative even though he did support Moses with all his heart. Nevertheless, he was not willing to betray Moses openly in front of the royal court. He did not know whether the other captains would follow his lead, but he understood his own duty clearly.

"The King knows full well that it is the desire of every slave to be free. We, of course, would not have had the temerity to ask His Majesty for a respite. Moses, however, was sent on his mission by the Lord of Israel. He had no choice but to approach His Majesty."

Pharaoh was visibly angered by the response. He shouted in rage, "Do you also believe in the God of Israel and this stupidity about visions?"

Zelaphchad used every ounce of self-control to suppress his seething rage. "I have been brought up in the traditions of my people which taught me from birth to believe in the God of our fathers. We believe that God appeared to our forefathers, Abraham, Isaac and Jacob. It is apparent to me that He has now appeared to Moses as well."

Pharaoh was irate and turned to his advisors. "I told you that this man Moses is insidious and has wide support." To Zelaphchad he said, "You and your fellow Hebrews would be well advised to disassociate yourselves quickly from this traitor, Moses. You have already felt a taste of the troubles that he will bring you. Indeed, there is more in store if you don't tell Moses to leave matters as they are and cease spouting wild ideas. He will not gain you your freedom. Rather he will cause you to be further oppressed. My new decree will not be revoked until you convince Moses to go back to where he came from and not speak another word on your behalf."

Zelaphchad was badly shaken by these harsh words. Before his very eyes the last hope for freedom was being quenched. He returned to his place among the captains as Pharaoh waved the meeting to a close with an imperious gesture. With bowed heads, the captains backed away from the royal presence and left the chamber.

Once outside, they saw Moses and Aaron waiting to greet them and secure a report on what had transpired. The captains related the essence of what had occurred without casting any aspersions on their leaders. Soon a crowd gathered around them. Two elders of the tribe of Reuben, Dothan and Abiram, began to berate Moses publicly. "See what you have done," they angrily accused him. "Your imprudent intervention has destroyed our reputation with Pharaoh. The good will that we have accumulated over the years has been erased in one moment. May God judge you for the evil you have done to us. You have given the Egyptians a sword with which to slay us."[31]

Heavily burdened with guilt over his actions and fully aware of the harm which had resulted from them, Moses beat a hasty retreat. He could now seek comfort only from God himself. For his next prophetic session, he waited in an isolated field by the river Nile.

> "O LORD," HE PRAYED, "WHEREFORE DIDST THOU ALLOW
> THIS EVIL TO BEFALL THY PEOPLE. WHEREFORE IS IT THAT
> THOU HAST SENT ME ON THIS MISSION? FROM THE DAY
> THAT I COMMENCED TO SPEAK TO PHARAOH ON THY
> BEHALF, THE SITUATION OF THIS PEOPLE HAS BECOME
> WORSE. NOR HAST THOU YET REDEEMED THY PEOPLE."[32]

Moses was not one who uttered long prayers. He came to the point directly and waited quietly for the Divine answer. It was not long in coming. As the spirit of God descended upon him, he heard the heavenly voice. Once again the Lord assured him that the pledges made to Abraham, Isaac and Jacob would be fulfilled. He was commanded to return to the children of Israel and repeat the various promises of Divine redemption given to them.[33]

Moses wanted very much to believe the prophecy that he was experiencing. He reasoned that the first failure may have been a test of faith. Abraham, the first Hebrew, had been tested many times and never ceased to believe. A man must trust in God not only in times of prosperity but also in times of adversity. Thus he raised no further objection. He returned to his brethren, speaking to them once again in the name of the Lord.

The children of Israel, though, did not possess the same degree of faith. Oppressed by the harder work now required, disappointed by the failure of the first mission and burdened by the knowledge of the severe beatings being administered to their captains, the Hebrew slaves and their leaders turned their backs on Moses. The words of Divine prophecy, spoken by Moses, fell on deaf ears.[34]

A bitterly disillusioned Moses was then the recipient of another revelation in which he was instructed to speak directly to Pharaoh and order him to release the Israelites from bondage. This time Moses could not control his protest.

"Behold," he cried, "the children of Israel, who in their hearts crave freedom, no longer listen to me. Why should Pharaoh, who has no interest in freeing the Hebrews, pay any attention?"

The question raised by Moses reflected only the deep feelings of despair in which he was engulfed. When he did regain control of his thoughts, he fully realized that he would have to return to Pharaoh and once again speak to him in the name of the God of Israel.

Zelaphchad went from the captain's meeting with Pharaoh directly to the work area where he was pleasantly surprised. Everything was in order and Ram was directing the operations. Ram had had a little more success with the brick hearth and the straw gathering had been better organized. The men were hopeful that they would meet the quota and spare Zelaphchad another beating. Zelaphchad was grateful to them and joined in the work. Once again they came close to the required amount and, with a little extra effort in the fading light, they installed the final row of bricks. Zelaphchad was vastly relieved although he realized he would not be as successful every day. A shortage of fuel or straw, an unexpected interruption or any of a number of other problems, could cause a loss of production and leave him standing at the whipping post again. Zelaphchad decided to take one day at a time, however, and joined his brothers in the long walk home.

That night, Achla listened attentively as Zelaphchad spoke to the family and related the details of the meeting with Pharaoh. Not wishing to appear haughty, she kept her peace until she was alone with her husband. "I am proud that you were the spokesman of the captains in the presence of Pharaoh. I am even more proud that you had the courage not to betray our prophet, Moses."

Zelaphchad held her closely to him. "No one can be certain that Moses will succeed, but far be it from me to withhold my support. I can only pray that my next child, our first son, will be born in the Promised Land of Canaan or on the way there. Achla wisely refrained from warning him that the next child might not be a boy. She felt the warmth and comfort of his presence and chose not to dampen his ardor by bringing up the possibility of daughter number four.

CHAPTER

TWO

*"ON THAT DAY THE LORD
REDEEMED ISRAEL"*

Zelaphchad rose at daybreak and woke his brothers. Together they trooped out to the work area and rounded up their fellow slaves. Zelaphchad was anxious to get started early because the morning hours were the most productive. All night he had thought of new arrangements to reduce the strain on his men.

One of Ram's suggestions was to work in cooperation with other slave groups. If Zelaphchad's men were able to exceed the brick quota, they could possibly trade the surplus with groups that were more proficient at gathering straw. Zelaphchad thought it was a good idea but unduly optimistic. He had not heard of any crews that had extra straw. Until he could locate such a group, he would simply have to carry on with the work as usual.

Zelaphchad organized the crews and began. Sweat poured down his brow as he tried to do many things at once. Under the pressure of the work, he put aside thoughts of his meeting with Pharaoh to secure freedom for the children of Israel. About an hour into the morning tasks, a stranger came by and asked for him by name. "Are you Zelaphchad?" he asked, when he saw him directing the crew.

Zelaphchad could not recall ever seeing the man before. He seemed to be more of a scholarly type than a working man. His hands were not callused and he wore an outer garment. Instinctively, Zelaphchad felt that the visitor could be trusted. "Yes, I am," he said. "What can I do for you?"[1]

"I have a message for you, but I must deliver it privately." Zelaphchad signaled Ram to take over and walked with the messenger some distance away from his men.

"I come with word from Moses," the man said. "He knows that it would be dangerous for you to be seen talking to him, so he sent me to tell you what he wishes you to hear."

"Who are you and what is your name?" Zelaphchad asked, sensing the special importance of the message.

"I think it would be safer if I didn't reveal my name to you at this time. Suffice it to say that I am close to Moses and serve him. He wishes to tell you that he is deeply grateful for your loyalty to him when you spoke to Pharaoh yesterday morning. He wants you to know that the Lord will reward you for your faith and courage."

Zelaphchad was pleased with the words. "What is Moses going to do now? I heard that he spoke to the elders again but they refused to listen to him."

The messenger shrugged, illustrating his obvious dismay. "Our leader, Moses, can no longer rely upon them. He will single-handedly perform the Divine mission, save for his brother, Aaron. In fact, this morning they intend to speak to Pharaoh once again."

At that very moment, Moses and Aaron were on their way to another meeting with the king. They had no difficulty in securing an audience because Pharaoh was eager to see them. "I am pleased that you have come today," Pharaoh said to Moses, gleefully. "I have heard that the leaders of your people hold you personally responsible for the trouble you caused them. They do not wish to hear your wild ideas and they no longer want you to speak on their behalf. The captains have also rejected you and want no further part of your leadership. I, too, am not impressed with you, as you have not shown me any sign or miracle that you speak in the name of a God. If I were you, Moses, I would cease all political activity before you cause your fellow Hebrews additional trouble."[2]

In response, Aaron advised Pharaoh that Moses was not free to cease his efforts to achieve freedom for the Israelites. In an unusually firm tone, he proclaimed, "Moses is the servant of God and his master has commanded him to appear before you. If you need miracles to convince you, I shall perform some signs given by our God as proof that Moses speaks in His name." At that point,

Aaron dropped the staff from his hand and what was a straight rod when it fell, became a slithering snake. Pharaoh was startled for a brief moment but quickly regained his composure.

"If that is the extent of your miracles," he said, "then I have nothing to fear from you. Even the most poorly trained magician in my service can perform a similar feat. In fact, I will prove it to you now."

He thereupon called in his magicians who quickly duplicated the sign of Aaron. "See, I told you that what you did is in no way unusual here." While he was speaking, Aaron's snake began swallowing up the snakes produced by the magicians. Pharaoh, however, was not at all impressed.

"So you have a slightly more aggressive snake. Your miracle, though, does not exceed in essence that which our own magicians commonly do. Moses, it is time for you to abandon your sedition. It will only compromise the well-being of your own people."

After Moses left the meeting, God appeared to him again. "It is obvious," the Lord said, "that Pharaoh is stubborn and will not listen. Set no more meetings with him. Tomorrow morning, take the miracle rod and confront him as he walks to the river for prayer."

Moses rose early and waited with Aaron at a point along the route of the royal procession. From his position, he could see the gently flowing waters of the Nile. The floods had passed and the river was no longer swollen with raging torrents. Within a short period of time he saw the heavily armed soldiers who always marched before the king. They were followed by a phalanx of horsemen who rode behind the guards. The impressive entourage served not only to protect the King but also to emphasize the majesty of the royal establishment.

Pharaoh was annoyed when Aaron and Moses stepped up from their waiting place and stood before him in the center of the road. "What do you want now?" he shouted, "Can't you see that I am on my way to prayer?"

Moses responded immediately. "The Lord, God of the Hebrews, sent me to instruct you to release His people so that they may worship Him in the desert. Thus far you have not heeded His command. Thus says the Lord: 'I will smite the waters of the Nile with my rod. All water in the Land of Egypt will turn to blood. In the seas and in the pools of Egypt, the water will no longer be fit to drink.'" So saying, Moses handed the rod to Aaron and signaled him to wave it over the river. Before Pharaoh's horror-stricken gaze, the waters of the river began to darken. While the Nile was never a crystal clear body of water, it was always considerably transparent in the fall. Now it was completely opaque. The morning sun reflected the deep crimson color of blood from the surface of the shimmering waters.[3]

Transformation of the Nile waters to blood was the first of a series of harsh plagues that the Lord brought upon the Egyptians. It was followed by many others, equally severe, throughout the winter and early spring.[4] It was after the plague of frogs that Pharaoh first mentioned releasing the Hebrew people.[5] It was not a serious gesture for, as soon as the frogs were gone, he quickly forgot his promise. A similar suggestion was made after the fourth plague.[6] Under the stress of the wild beasts that were invading Egypt at the behest of the Lord, Pharaoh made an offer that would allow the Hebrews to have a religious holiday within the confines of the country. Moses rejected the offer on the grounds that sacrifices of sheep were part of the Hebrew holiday rituals. Such rites could not be performed in the presence of Egyptians who worshipped the sheep. Pharaoh then agreed to allow the Hebrew people to venture out into the desert for their religious services. This was more acceptable to Moses but did not result in anything concrete. As soon as Moses caused the wild beasts to disappear from Egypt, Pharaoh reneged once again on his commitment.

The same thing happened after the seventh plague. A promise made by Pharaoh to release the Hebrews was not kept. It was only during the eighth plague that serious negotiations commenced. Pharaoh's advisors were no longer supporting him in his stubborn resistance to the demands of Moses. Earlier, the magicians had withdrawn their support of the King because they were personally afflicted by the plagues and could not continue to stand in his presence. The common people began to withdraw from Pharaoh during the seventh plague. When they heard that the country would be afflicted by violent hail storms, many of them moved their cattle to shelter despite Pharaoh's order not to do so. Now it was the turn of Pharaoh's main advisors. "Send these people out," they said to him, "before the whole country is totally destroyed." These defections weakened Pharaoh's resolve.[7]

"Moses," he began, wishing to clarify a dark foreboding in his heart, "if I were to release the Hebrews, who is it that would be going?"

Moses quickly answered, "Everyone. Our young people, our old folks, our wives, our children and our cattle, will all join the men on this holiday."

"What are you saying?" Pharaoh cried. "Was it not a religious holiday that you requested? I know that only men actually participate in such worship. I am willing to allow the Hebrew men to leave the country for several days for a holiday. The women, children and cattle must remain in Egypt." Moses would accept no such limitation and Pharaoh began to awaken to the awful truth. The bargaining terms had changed drastically and were no longer limited to a request for a short vacation. It was apparent to Pharaoh that Moses would settle for nothing less than the complete exodus of the Hebrew people from the Land of Egypt. Pharaoh had absolutely no intention of making a concession of that magnitude.

"Accept my final offer," Pharaoh said, "and let the males go for a respite. I will never allow more than that."

Moses left Pharaoh without saying anything further. He understood that additional plagues would be necessary before Pharaoh would surrender. After the ninth plague of darkness, Pharaoh offered a further concession. "You can take all of your men and women, all of your old and young folks and go for your festival. All that I request is that you leave your cattle within the country."[8]

For a fleeting moment, Moses realized the impact of Pharaoh's words. Accepting Pharaoh's offer would achieve the long sought goal of freedom for his people. He knew that many slaves ran away from their masters with nothing more than the shirts on their backs. By leaving at once, the period of slavery would be shortened. Nevertheless, Moses dismissed this option for several reasons.

First and foremost, was the Divine promise made in the covenant with Abraham, wherein the Almighty pledged to the father of the Jewish people, that his descendants would leave their bondage in Egypt with great wealth.

In addition to the Divine promise, there was a consideration that related to the psychological state of the Hebrews. The rigors of the desert without material possessions would be too much for them to bear. They weren't spiritually strong and slavery had diminished their confidence. Moses was afraid that in the face of hardship, they would opt to return to bondage in Egypt. As such, they would not be the first slaves to return voluntarily to their masters after failing to adjust to life as free men. Above all, he was absolutely certain that the Almighty would perform additional miracles to help him achieve a complete victory over Pharaoh.

"Your terms are unacceptable to me," he advised Pharaoh. "When we go forth from this land, not a single hoof will remain. What is more, your own people will bestow upon us gifts of silver, gold, garments and utensils, in order to hasten our departure." The discussion soon became very heated and both Moses and Pharaoh lost their tempers.

"I've had enough of you," said Pharaoh. "I have no desire to talk to you anymore or even see your face. If you show up here again, you will die."

"That is entirely agreeable with me," countered Moses. "The next time you wish to see me you will have to come looking for me." So saying, he stormed out of the meeting.

Zelaphchad and his family followed the course of the plagues with great interest. They were among the first to realize that the hand of God was punishing the Egyptians. The rest of the people and their leaders soon came to understand the situation as well. Moses was no longer being shunned. Wherever he walked in the Hebrew areas he was cheered. In fact, Zelaphchad himself had an opportunity to greet him personally. Those who had earlier criticized him now maintained a discreet silence. For all intents and purposes, once the plagues struck in their full fury, Egyptian slavery had come to an end. The Egyptians were too demoralized to impose any discipline upon their slaves. Their homes were a tableau of human suffering and misery. Their cattle were destroyed, their crops ruined. The furthest thought in their minds was the continued oppression of the Hebrews.

Zelaphchad finally sent his crew home and thanked them for their valiant efforts to save him from beatings. "Go home," he said to them, "and begin preparing for the journey to the Promised Land. It is only a matter of time before we shall depart this accursed country."

It was on the second day of the first month that Zelaphchad gathered his family in the main room. "We have two important matters to consider this afternoon. Moses addressed the elders of our people yesterday and advised them of the date of our departure from Egypt. He directed them to command all of our families to conduct a religious ceremony on the eve of the departure. That is one of the matters that we will deal with. The other concern is preparing ourselves for a long and arduous journey."[9]

Azriel, who was always interested in religious duties, asked Zelaphchad to elaborate on the nature of the special rituals.

"As I understand it," Zelaphchad answered, "the final plague will be inflicted upon the Egyptians on the night of the fifteenth of this month. At that time, the first-born son of each Egyptian family will be struck dead. There is no doubt that as soon as the plague strikes, the Egyptians will hasten to send us out of the land, hoping to save as many of their first-born as they can.

"We have been instructed to select a lamb on the tenth day of the month and slaughter it on the afternoon of the fourteenth. We must mark the doorposts of our homes with the blood of the lamb. The Angel of Death will descend, pass over those homes which are marked and strike at those which are not. While waiting for the plague to start, we will eat the roasted lamb with matzos and bitter herbs. At the meal, we must wear our shoes and have walking sticks and backpacks ready. When the signal is given at dawn, we are to leave our homes and proceed to the meeting place in the city of Rameses. I am appointing you, Azriel, to conduct the religious ceremony of the evening." In deference to his religious scholarship, Azriel was asked to perform the services despite the fact that he was not the oldest son. He was deeply honored by the recognition.

It was Ram who presided over the second half of the meeting. He was fully informed on the events to come and had prepared for them. "I understand that we have the right to help ourselves to some Egyptian wealth before we leave. I am not talking of looting. We shall just borrow and not return those items that we may need. It is justified as a form of reparations for the many years that the Egyptians exploited our labor. Incidentally, I know that we may also borrow gold and silver in this manner but those things do not interest me."

Adina, Shafat's wife, felt the need to interrupt the proceedings. "I take it that you are speaking for yourself," she said. "As for me, I feel that a pair of gold earrings and some bracelets would vastly improve my appearance."

"You look fine as it is without jewelry," Ram answered. "You may, however, indulge yourself, if you feel that the Egyptians owe it to you and got rich at your expense. I would like to remind you, though, that you cannot eat earrings in the wilderness and that bracelets will not protect you from the desert storms."

"What do you suggest with regard to what we really need?" asked Zelaphchad.

"Our first concern is carrying the children. The older Hebrews who have teenage children can simply walk with them. In fact, they can take their sheep and cattle. Our family is comprised of young people and we have children who cannot walk by themselves. The most urgent need, then, is for three ox carts, which will carry the children plus some very critical supplies."

"We own a cow, a pair of oxen and quite a few sheep," said Zelaphchad. "We can trade a number of sheep for a third ox but what are we going to do for carts?"

"The carts are not as important as the wheels," Ram said. "At the very least we need six wagon wheels. The other parts of the carts we can build by ourselves. I would suggest that before we go for the gold and silver, we try to find wheels, wood and leather in the Egyptian homes. While there, we should also seek poles and cloth for tents. Twelve days is not too much time to prepare everything."

"My good friend, the taskmaster, spoke to me the other day," Zelaphchad said. "He asked me to intervene with Moses to spare him further agony from the plagues. He told me how much he respected me and admired my work."

"I hope you reminded him of the beatings that his guards inflicted upon you," Achla said.

"That I did," said Zelaphchad. "He then said that he would be willing to make amends if I were to help him. He is a wealthy man and I think we can obtain most of the material we need from his estate. You, Ram, will supervise the construction of the carts. Shafat and I will start gathering the needed supplies."

Achla then came to the defense of Adina who was still pouting about her jewelry. "We could all use a few nice trinkets," she ventured. "I distinctly remember that Moses spoke very emphatically of the gold and silver that is to be our reward. It is not just vanity. If we cannot borrow all the material that we need, we may be able to trade for it with precious metals."[10]

"Go ahead, if it will make you happy. Just be sure not to interfere with our securing what we urgently need," Ram warned her. With that, the family gathering ended and the couples retired to their rooms.

"I have more good news for you, Zelaphchad," Achla said when they were alone. "I am with child and you will be a father once again."

"That makes me very happy," Zelaphchad answered, "and I pray that we will finally have our first son. Of course, it may be a little difficult for you to lead an ox cart in your condition, but I am sure we will manage."

The next twelve days were very busy ones at the family home. Ram built the carts, Azriel prepared the lamb and the matzos. Zelaphchad and Shafat gathered various supplies and the women amassed quantities of jewelry. On the afternoon of the fourteenth day of the month, the family gathered to watch Azriel slaughter the lamb and dip the hyssop into the basin containing the blood. With the hyssop, he smeared the blood on the lintel and the two doorposts. All the adults and children remained at home, abiding by the Divine instruction not to leave any dwellings before daybreak.

The Egyptians had been more than glad to bestow their wealth upon the Hebrews in the hope that it would somehow ease their punishment on the day of judgment. Their belated generosity, however, was of no avail. At midnight, the angel of death struck the Egyptian first-born sons with fierce wrath. The stricken families ran to the palace to beg Pharaoh to release the Hebrews. Angry mobs gathered in front of the royal estate. Pharaoh's troops were barely able to contain them. "Let the Hebrews go," the people shouted. "Let the Hebrews go before we all die."[11]

Pharaoh was astute enough to know that he had been defeated. He hastily sent messengers to call Moses. Moses, however, was in no hurry to be found. He felt that the additional delay would prolong the tenth plague and bring the full punishment the Egyptians so richly deserved. The King himself had to run around in an attempt to locate Moses. When Pharaoh's troops finally found him, Moses taunted them, "The King himself said that he never wanted to see me again. Why should I trouble him?"[12]

The guards answered, "You must come now. The people are about to storm the palace and take matters into their own hands."

When Moses arrived at the palace, Pharaoh was waiting. The loss of his eldest son had been a severe blow for him. He was panic stricken but, for the sake of his nation, he had overcome his personal anguish. "Leave this country now," he cried, "and take your people with you. Take everything you want, Moses, and bless me with your departure."[13]

While Pharaoh announced to the mob that the Hebrews were leaving and the plague was over, Moses left to take command of the Exodus. He sent word that everyone should leave home at the first light and proceed to the rendezvous at Rameses. He requested the people not to take the time to bake bread. "Where necessary," he suggested, "the men may carry the dough on their shoulders."[14]

Tension ran high in the Hebrew homes as they waited for the dawn. Until the sun rose, the sky was lit up with a pillar of fire that illuminated the countryside. It was the Divine light sent by the Almighty to guide the Israelites on their way. Within a short interval, it would be replaced by a heavenly cloud that led the Hebrews during the daylight hours. Long before the cloud appeared, a stream of excited humanity started to pour forth from each household. The freed slaves merged into a massive procession that flowed endlessly in the general direction of the city of Rameses.

Zelaphchad placed his three children in a cart which was standing in front of the house and his brothers did likewise. Each of the married brothers led a cart while Ram and their parents walked alongside. The former slaves were in high spirits and waved to the dejected Egyptians as they passed. The Egyptians were beginning to bury their dead and hardly noticed the departing Hebrews. Some of the Hebrews joined in prayers of thanksgiving.

By late morning, all of the Hebrews had gathered in Rameses for the impending departure. At precisely noon, the official march began from Rameses to the city of Succoth. The afternoon sun was hot enough to dry the soil which had been soaked by the spring flood. Progress was steady but somewhat disorganized. Above the marchers, the Cloud of Glory moved slowly eastward. When it was replaced at dusk by the pillar of light, the direction of travel remained unchanged. Fearing the Egyptians would pursue them, the fleeing masses marched both day and night.

The turmoil slowly subsided in the royal palace, but the trauma of the defeat was more than Pharaoh could bear. Added to the pain of his personal bereavement, was the dismay engendered by the report of his advisors that Egypt had not only lost the Hebrew slaves, but thousands of others as well. Large numbers of non-Hebrew slaves took advantage of the opportunity to join the Israelites in the Exodus from Egypt. They reasoned that the defeat of Pharaoh was an opportunity that would come only once. Nor were slaves the only ones to join the Israelites. There were also free Egyptians who were so moved by the awesome power of the Hebrew God that they decided to cast their lot with the people of Israel.

There were strong doubts among the Hebrew leaders whether the non-Hebrews should be allowed to join the ranks. Some of them suggested that this element lacked the Hebrew heritage and would ultimately corrupt the children of Israel with their idolatrous and immoral practices. For reasons of compassion, Moses allowed them to come along although he understood that they might become troublesome at a later time. He felt that freedom was a universal right to which every human being was entitled. It was not for him to reject any of the wretched masses who had toiled and suffered alongside the children of Israel.[15]

By the third day, Pharaoh had completed an assessment of the losses that he had suffered. The entire slave enterprise had been destroyed and, with it, Egypt's economy. He would now have to depend on his own people to continue his massive construction projects. He quickly concluded that he had neither the manpower nor the resources to finish his projects without slave labor. His own people, depressed by their suffering and disillusioned by the king's policies, would not support his projects.

With characteristic stubbornness, he chose to forget the night of fear and panic when the Egyptian mobs were ready to storm the palace. He gathered his generals in an emergency meeting. The army men were called because his political advisors would no longer support any of his actions. "Men," he said, "we have made a grave error in permitting the Hebrews to depart. Our country cannot stand the loss. We must pursue the departing slaves and force them to return. We can trap them when they reach an impassable body of water. Gather all available troops and chariots and prepare to set out after them. I myself will accompany you and, together, we shall bring them back. If they refuse to return, we will slaughter them and retrieve all the wealth they have stolen from us."[16] Reports reaching Pharaoh that the Hebrews had slowed down and changed their direction of travel, encouraged him to proceed.

Pharaoh was impatient to get started. He personally donned his military uniform and supervised the yoking of the chariot horses. While the Hebrews had a head start of a few days and were marching day and night, he felt it would be only a matter of time before his troops caught up with them. His men could move rapidly, while the Hebrews were burdened with children, household goods, sheep and cattle. The savage nature of the Egyptian army was well known. Pharaoh had spared no efforts to establish it into the most powerful fighting force in the world with 600 massive horse-drawn chariots. The foot soldiers wore armor and were equipped with well-honed swords.

The escaping Hebrews trudged slowly across the sands of Goshen, traveling for hours on end, pausing only briefly when necessary. The march followed a straight easterly course for two days and then veered to the southwest. The new direction of travel surprised many who assumed that a northern route would be taken in order to travel along the well-known highway to Canaan. They were not aware that the change in direction was part of a Divine plan to lure the Egyptians into pursuing the Hebrews and thus expose themselves to additional retribution. By the sixth day, the Hebrews reached the Sea of Reeds and came to a halt. It was then that they heard the clamor of the pursuing Egyptians and were overwhelmed by fear.

As the last rays of daylight began to fade, the Hebrews encamped near the sea. The camp stretched from the sea to the city of Pi Hahirot. The city was originally called Pithom — one of the store cities built by Hebrew labor. To the left and right of the encampment were the cities of Migdol and Baal Zephon, a center of Egyptian idol worship. Zelaphchad didn't even attempt to pitch the tents at the camp because, with the Egyptians approaching, the tension was extreme and the panic palpable. No one knew whether anyone would survive the next few hours.

Not wishing to frighten the women, Zelaphchad gathered his brothers for a quick conference some fifty cubits from the carts. "We are in very serious trouble," Zelaphchad said. "I do not see a way out."

"Why did God lead us to the sea in the first place?" Shafat asked.

"I am sure," answered Azriel, "the Lord knows that we were not ready to fight the inhabitants of Canaan. If our people had to face war they would certainly flee and return to Egypt."

"It would have been easier to fight the Canaanite people," Zelaphchad responded, "than the entire Egyptian army."

"We could surrender and return to Egypt," Shafat offered. "Right now our options are to be killed fighting, or to drown in the sea."

"We are by no means certain that the Egyptians would accept our surrender," said Zelaphchad. "They are embittered over the loss of their first-born sons and the spoils we took from them. They will probably attack us without any negotiations. Once they get a taste of blood, they will not stop until they have slaughtered us all."

As they were talking, the vanguard of the Egyptian troops rode up into the area. Behind them the hills were black with chariots and infantry. The first troops to arrive pulled up no more than 150 cubits from the edge of the Hebrew camp and waited for the commanders to survey the scene and coordinate the attack. The brothers were surrounded by a rising crescendo of wailing and crying. "Can we make a break for it?" Zelaphchad asked Ram. "We are on the north side of the camp. Maybe we can work our way over the hills under the cover of darkness."

"No chance of that," Ram answered. "The Egyptian forces are spreading north and south to completely encircle us."

"What do you suggest?"

"I think we should head for the water. It is probably shallow for about fifty cubits. The chariots cannot follow us into the water. Even the armored foot soldiers will be at a disadvantage. We can offer better resistance that way."

"Ram, you have to stop looking at everything from a technical point of view. Your idea won't work because we cannot fight holding our children and we cannot abandon them. Furthermore, if we go into the sea first, the rest of the Hebrews coming in afterwards will push us into deep water."

As they were talking, an arrow whizzed by and landed near the carts. "Get down behind the cart!" Zelaphchad yelled to Achla. He and his brothers rushed back to the carts to get their families under cover. Other families whose backs faced the Egyptian lines did likewise. The area was soon enveloped in ghostly silence. No one spoke and no one moved. Once the women were safely under the carts and the children inside of them, Zelaphchad whispered to his youngest brother. "Look after my family, Ram, while I run to the center of the camp where our leaders are. I want to find out what is happening. I am fairly certain the Egyptians will not attack before dawn but I'll return as quickly as possible."

So saying, he headed southward toward the camp center. Where word of the arrival of the Egyptian troops had not yet spread, families were sitting quietly or putting their children to sleep. Fairly soon, Zelaphchad came to an open area near the center of the camp where two men stood guard near a richly decorated coffin. Even though he had never seen it before, he recognized it at once. The coffin contained the remains of Joseph, father of the tribes of Ephraim and Menashe. Moses had fulfilled a promise made to Joseph, who asked that his remains be carried to Canaan when the Hebrews left the Land of Egypt. Passing the area, Zelaphchad followed the sound of a large group of men arguing near the center. When he joined the crowd, he saw that a tribal elder was about to speak. The people quieted to hear his words.

"You have led us into a death trap, Moses. We are between the sea and the Egyptian army. It is only a matter of time before we are attacked and slain. Were there not enough graves in Egypt," he cried with a dramatic flourish, "that you took us out of the land to die and to be buried in the desert? This is what we told you in Egypt. 'Leave us alone,' we begged you. 'Leave us alone and let us serve the Egyptians.' Is it not better to be alive and enslaved in Egypt than free and dead in the desert?"[17]

This time Moses was not at a loss for words in the face of the savage tirade. "Do not be afraid, my brothers," he said. "Stand firm and observe the Divine salvation. The Lord will fight for you. As you see the Egyptians today you will never see them again."

Moses then turned away to receive further prophecy from the Lord. Zelaphchad rejoiced in his heart for he was pleased that Moses was in control of the situation. He returned to his family and as he came close to where they were huddling behind the carts, he was suddenly swallowed up by a thick black cloud of smoke. "What's happening?" he heard Achla scream as he groped his way over to the carts.

"Fear not," he said. "It is the Cloud of Glory that leads us by day. It is moving behind us and heading for the Egyptian lines." As the cloud moved on, the air cleared over the family. They could see each other once again in the glare of the pillar of fire which still hovered over the Hebrew camp. Within moments, the

Cloud of Glory stopped its journey and completely blocked the Egyptian army. The Egyptians could no longer see the Hebrews and the barrage of rocks and arrows ceased.

"We now have an opportunity to escape, if we wish," Ram said.

"We are not going to do so," Zelaphchad ruled. "It is very clear that the Lord of Israel is protecting us. The Egyptian army is absolutely no match for Him. I just heard Moses tell the elders to stand firm and wait for the salvation of the Lord. That is exactly what we will do."

No sooner had he finished talking when a severe gust of wind passed over the carts and blew off the covering cloths. "A storm is arising," cried Zelaphchad. "Lash down everything that can blow away and get under the wagons again."

It was a difficult assignment in the face of a howling wind. When Zelaphchad finished securing his cart, he ran to assist the others. Heavy though he was, he was bowled over by the force of the gale. Holding on to a wheel, he picked himself up and helped Azriel secure his cart. "Do you think the carts will tip?" Azriel asked in fright.

"They are heavily laden," Zelaphchad answered, "but they might go." Just then Ram ran over. He was out of breath after violent exertions helping Shafat secure the last cart.

"We must link all three carts together," he said, "or they will turn over and the children will be hurt."

"I never experienced a wind of this force," said Zelaphchad, as the brothers labored to tie one cart to the other.

"This is not an ordinary storm," said Ram. "There are no such winds in this part of the world."

"Then it must be another Divine miracle that we are experiencing," said Azriel. He was one who quickly sensed supernatural events and, as usual, he was right. The brothers later found out the full story of what had happened. During the prophecy that came to Moses after the debate with the elders, the Lord told Moses to command the children of Israel to enter the sea. Most of the tribes did not respond because they were afraid of the raging waters.[18] The tribe of Benjamin, though, was courageous and started to advance to the edge of the water. They were outdone only by Nachshon, leader of the tribe of Judah and brother-in-law of Aaron. He actually plunged into the water to demonstrate obedience to the Divine will. The people on shore watched in horror as he moved deeper and deeper into the raging currents. They were certain he would drown as the waters covered his neck.[19]

At that precise moment, Moses was ordered to wave the Divine rod over the sea and cause it to be split. Moses did as he was instructed and the fierce blast of an eastern wind passed over the water. It persisted for many hours and caused the waters to recede. Azriel, who had guessed the nature of the wind, also fathomed its purpose. "This wind will blow a path in the sea and I am sure that is already happening." The Chefer family watched in awe as the Lord demonstrated his power by carving a huge path of dry land between two opposing walls of solid water.

The pillar of light, which had remained in a stationary position overhead, suddenly started to glide eastward. A cry went up in the camp as people ran to prepare for the advance. Ram unleashed the carts and each of the brothers yoked an ox to his cart. They finished just in time as they were already being pressed by families behind them.

They reached the shore of the sea in less than an hour. The sea bed was completely dry and easily supported the weight of the multitudes, their cattle and their carts. It was a long path between the standing walls of water. It took the Zelaphchad family more than an hour to reach the opposite shore. The sea on either side was swollen with the runoff of the spring rains and was extended to its maximum depth.

On the eastern shore of the sea, Zelaphchad ascended to higher ground. There he got a complete view of the spectacle. He clearly saw the last of the Hebrew tribes rushing to reach the opposite shore. To his great surprise he also beheld hordes of Egyptians entering the path between the walls of water in pursuit of the Hebrews. He was worried that they might overtake the stragglers who had not yet reached safety.

Yet he had no cause for concern. The path which had been bone dry when the Israelites crossed, suddenly turned soft. The heavy Egyptian chariots started to bog down in the mud. The drivers jumped from their seats and began turning the wheels by hand. They prodded the horses to move. The harder the horses pulled, however, the worse the results. The wheels pulled loose from the axles and the heavy chariot coaches crashed into the mud. Once that happened there was no way to lift up the coaches and reattach them. The horses couldn't pull the mired coaches and all movement ground to a halt. The back ranks of the Egyptian army, unaware of what was happening up front, continued to press into the sea bed. Soon the entire force was jammed in the quagmire, unable to extricate itself.

It was exactly then that the Almighty chose to even accounts with the Egyptians who had cruelly enslaved the Hebrews for centuries. The Lord ordered Moses to wave his rod over the sea. The same rod that had caused the sea to open, now caused it to close. The Egyptians who saw the columns of water cascading down upon them realized too late that they were not fighting hapless slaves but the Lord, God of Israel.

Zelaphchad put Machla on his shoulders to watch what was happening. At four years of age, she had no true understanding of the great miracle but he hoped she would preserve the picture in her mind. When she would hear the story in future years, it would be that much more meaningful to her. He was sad that his younger daughters could not even grasp the picture but he was sure that they, too, would someday learn the story.

Inspired, Moses began to sing a great song of triumph.[20] Zelaphchad was too far away to hear the words directly but he could see the stage upon which their leader stood during his recital. As Moses spoke, his words were relayed to the multitudes by strategically placed interpreters. Zelaphchad was thrilled by the closing verses which promised that the Lord would plant his people on the holy mountains of Canaan.[21]

Achla, for her part, was also celebrating. Miriam, the sister of Moses, had organized the daughters of Israel in a joyous dance accompanied by musical instruments. Over and over again Miriam chanted as they danced, "Sing to the Lord for His great victory. Horse and rider He drowned in the sea." Achla rarely had a chance to sing and dance. She did so exuberantly despite her pregnancy.

The Hebrews did not tarry long at the Sea of Reeds but proceeded to march southward in the Desert. Moses was leading his people to Mount Sinai, sometimes called Horeb. It was here that God first revealed Himself to him in the form of a burning bush. It was here, according to the Divine promise, that the children of Israel would worship on their way out of Egypt.

The trip to Mount Sinai had taken only six weeks but it was a very arduous one. The original supplies that the Israelites took for the trip were quickly exhausted. Water was even in shorter supply and the barren desert had nothing to yield. Once again the miraculous hand of the Lord came to the rescue of the Hebrews. Wells developed where none had previously existed, brackish water turned sweet and a heavenly food called manna fell daily on the edges of the camp to feed the hungry Hebrews.

Zelaphchad soon became accustomed to the rigors of the desert. There were many complaints from those who could not make the adjustment. Moses was constantly beset by unhappy Israelites who rapidly forgot their suffering in Egypt. Whenever they faced a hardship in the desert, they reminded Moses of the good times in Egypt and complained that he took them away from a land of plenty. The worst carping came from the non-Hebrews who left with the Israelites. The Promised Land was not the dream of their ancestors. It meant nothing to them and provided no reason to endure any hardships to get there. Their discontent spread to Hebrews who should have known better.

As far as Zelaphchad was concerned, the ungratefulness of his people was beneath contempt. He had felt the lash of his persecutors in Egypt, and would never forget the abuse and suffering. He would remain loyal to Moses and follow his commands no matter what the price. The idea of the Hebrews returning to the Promised Land was the core of his existence. Exile and slavery could not be the status of a people who taught the world that there was one invisible God in heaven. He knew the names of every city in Canaan and which of the ancestors lived where. He didn't know where in Canaan he would settle but, given a choice, it would be the central part of the country where his tribal ancestor, Joseph, tended sheep.

Finally, the experience at Mount Sinai reinforced his convictions. The Torah was a book of law that would elevate the Hebrews above all peoples. It meant that life in Canaan, when the Israelites took over the country, would be on the highest moral level. As Moses put it, the Torah would make the children of Israel a chosen people, a kingdom of priests and a holy nation.[22]

Once again he held Machla on his shoulders to see Mount Sinai as it erupted in smoke and flame. This, too, was a tableau that he wanted her to frame in her mind and keep until she was old enough to understand the full impact of the event. As thunder rumbled and lightning streaked, Zelaphchad himself began to tremble. It is one thing to hear about revelation, another to actually experience it. The spectacular visual display came to an end and the sound of the ram's horn issued forth. This was followed by the voice of God.

> "I AM THE LORD THY GOD WHO BROUGHT THEE FORTH FROM THE LAND OF EGYPT FROM THE HOUSE OF BONDAGE.
>
> "THOU SHALT HAVE NO OTHER GODS BEFORE ME..."

The sound continued until the end of the second commandment and then there was a pause. After an interval of silence, Zelaphchad beheld from afar a solitary figure, slowly ascending Mount Sinai. "That most certainly is Moses," said Zelaphchad to Achla who was standing nearby, white as a sheet, eyes full of tears. "He is ascending the mountain to gain further revelation."

"I am happy the voice stopped for I couldn't have endured another moment. It is hard to believe that I, a simple woman, was privileged to hear the actual voice of God and understand the meaning of what the Lord was saying."

The Lord had intended to deliver the remaining commandments directly to the ears of the children of Israel. After the second commandment, however, the elders pleaded with Moses to speak to God alone and convey the commandments to them afterwards. They claimed that the people were absolutely terrified by the voice of God and many were wailing hysterically. Moses acceded to their request and, to the relief of the frightened masses, the Divine voice was halted.

After receiving the balance of the ten commandments, Moses was told to ascend to the top of Mount Sinai for an extended stay of forty days. There, in supreme solitude, he communed with God and received the Torah. Atop the mountain, Moses transcribed that part of the Torah that covered events from the creation of the universe to the covenant at Sinai. The balance of the Torah was dictated to Moses by the Lord at intervals over the next forty years. Whatever was revealed to Moses for inclusion in the sacred text was thereafter considered the Written Law. All supplementary information and insights given to Moses, served as the basis of what would be called the Oral Law. Furthermore, since the ten commandments were carved into two stone tablets by Divine will, Moses had a prototype script which he used when writing the Torah. That script has became known as the Torah script or the Hebrew script.[23]

Before leaving for the long session on Mount Sinai, Moses appointed his brother, Aaron, and Miriam's son, Chur, to look after the affairs of the children of Israel. The choices were not successful. Chur was exceedingly strong-willed and would brook no compromise on any matter. Aaron, on the other hand, was too moderate. He could not stand up to the stubborn Israelites.

The substitute leaders were able to maintain order until the fortieth day when it was assumed that Moses would return. The assumption was based on an unfortunate misunderstanding. Moses had advised the people that he would be absent for forty days. He took it for granted that they realized he would be away a full forty days and not return until the forty-first. The people, though, expected him to return on the fortieth day itself. When the day arrived and Moses did not, large masses of Israelites gathered and spoke to Chur. They claimed that Moses was gone, perhaps dead, and would not return. This would leave them without access to a God. Accustomed to idol worship in Egypt, they requested Chur to fashion a golden calf, an idol to replace Moses. Chur flatly refused and the mob turned ugly. The raging hordes beat Chur to death and then proceeded to make the request of Aaron. Sensing the mood of the mob, Aaron sought the path of appeasement.

His plan was to delay the project until Moses would return. He promised the mob that they could have their idol the next morning if they would gather a sufficient quantity of gold from their women and children for the purpose. He was hoping that the women of Israel would refuse to part with their jewelry for such a sinful cause. It made no difference how the women felt, however, because the men were so inflamed with lust for idolatry that some donated their own personal gold adornments, while others tore the jewelry off their hapless wives and daughters. The contributions were presented to Aaron who cast the gold in a furnace. The golden calf emerged shortly thereafter.[24]

Zelaphchad was repelled by the idolatry. "These people heard the word of

God only six weeks ago forbidding them to make idols," he told his family. "They will surely bring down the wrath of God upon us all."

"It should make you happy that none of the women in our family contributed to the golden calf," said Adina, shaking her arm to display her bracelets.

"That it does," said Zelaphchad. "Now I want all of you to promise me that you will not go near that entire area tomorrow. There is no telling what the Lord will do in his wrath."

At first light, the eager idolaters arose to worship their new god. They encircled the golden calf and chanted over and over again, "This is your God, Israel. This is the God that brought you forth from the Land of Egypt." After that, they begin to sing and dance frenetically and indulge in acts of gross immorality. Moses, still on the mountain, was advised by the Lord that his people had gone astray. After a passionate prayer, he hurried down with the two tablets in his hand and beheld how far the situation had deteriorated. Thereupon, he lost control of himself and angrily smashed the heaven-made tablets on the rocks by the foot of the mountain.

Moses then strode into the camp to get a full report on the events. After hearing what had transpired, he berated Aaron for his share in the affair. Then he walked to the center of the camp and cried aloud, "He that is loyal to the Lord, gather around me." The tribe of Levi responded to the call. Moses commanded them to pass through the camp and destroy by force those who were still worshipping the golden calf. The Levites complied and killed a large number of idolaters. Order was restored and Moses personally ground up the golden calf, dispersing the remnants in a nearby stream.

The Lord fully intended to destroy all of the Hebrews for this grievous sin, but Moses intervened and secured their pardon in a series of eloquent prayers. Now he had to return to the Lord on Sinai for a new set of tablets to replace the original ones. He carved a set of bare tablets and the Almighty Himself inscribed them. This time he was able to leave the Israelites to fend for themselves in his absence. They had learned the hard way of the bitter end which awaits those who bow to the works of their own hand.

With the revelation over and the sin of the golden calf put aside, the Hebrews resumed the task of organizing life in the desert. As excited as

Zelaphchad was to enter Canaan, he realized that it would take many months before the Israelites were ready to invade a heavily fortified country. To develop into a first class fighting force, they needed military training, a command structure and considerably more self-confidence. It would take many months for the former slaves to rid themselves of their poor self-image.

What pleased Zelaphchad immensely was the progress made by Moses in developing an administrative structure for the Hebrew people. Much of the framework was designed by Jethro, the father-in-law of Moses. As an experienced national leader, he realized immediately that Moses could not carry the burdens of the Hebrew people all by himself. Moses tried to do so at first but it kept him busy from morning to night. Instead of devoting his full attention to the major problems confronting his people, he was spending precious hours settling petty disputes and answering trivial questions.

Jethro advised Moses to delegate the work by appointing officers within the tribes to be in charge of groups varying in size — a thousand, a hundred, fifty or ten. Anyone with a problem or dispute would first have to get a ruling from the officer of ten. If the matter could not be resolved at that level it would be moved to the next higher level. Only matters that could not be handled on the tribal levels would come to the attention of Moses. With the implementation of the new system, Moses was relieved of many time-consuming matters.

The new government plan affected Zelaphchad directly. Moses remembered him as a loyal follower in Egypt. He also remembered how effective he was in managing a crew of fifty slaves. He sent for Zelaphchad and personally asked him to assume supervision of a group of 100 families. Although Zelaphchad argued that it was easier to look after 1,000 slaves than 100 free Hebrews, in the end he accepted the assignment.

Reporting directly to Zelaphchad were two captains of fifty. Each of them, in turn, supervised five men in charge of groups of ten. Zelaphchad himself was one of ten captains reporting to a group commander of 1,000. The system worked downward as well as upward. When Moses wanted to reach all of the Israelites, he issued the command to the officers of 1,000. They passed the information to lower ranking captains. Parts of this system were later used to spread Torah teachings in addition to the day-to-day commands. Zelaphchad quickly distinguished himself in his work. He had a flair for leadership and his captains had great trust in him.

As a free man, he now had more time to devote to his wife and daughters. On the eve of the fall holidays, Achla went into labor. The midwife was called and assisted Achla in a relatively easy birth. After the midwife completed her work she quietly left the tent without saying anything to Zelaphchad who was waiting outside with his other children. She apparently didn't have the courage to tell him that his dream of having at least one son did not yet come to pass. Achla had given birth to her fourth daughter whom she named Milka.

*"TRANSGRESS YE NOT THE WORD
OF THE LORD"*

Fall arrives rapidly in the Sinai desert. Days are shorter and the midday sun is a little more tolerable than during the summer. Desert life for Zelaphchad settled into a daily routine of gathering food for the family and maintaining the tents and carts. Every morning, Israelite families went to the borders of the camp to collect the manna. Seed-like and crystalline, it was easily scooped up in pitchers. The daily allowance of manna was one omer for each member of a family.[1]

On Fridays, the collectors were allowed to gather double rations of manna. One share was used on that day and the remainder was processed for use on the Sabbath. Gathering extra manna on days other than Friday was a waste of time because manna was highly perishable and rapidly became wormy and inedible. Only Friday's extra manna did not spoil. This feature made it possible to maintain the Sabbath as a day of rest, undisturbed by food-gathering activities. Although manna was highly perishable, it was still a very versatile food. It could be cooked or baked or prepared in many other ways. The Zelaphchad family processed the manna into flour using a mortar and pestle. They preferred to bake the manna into cakes for in that way they could carry smaller amounts of processed manna wherever they went.

The manna was similar in taste to honey cake. Despite the pleasant taste, however, there were some Hebrews who tired of the same diet day in and day out. Craving variety, they began to glorify Egyptian foods in their complaints to Moses. In glowing terms, they recalled the leeks, the melons, the cucumbers and other delicacies surrounding the Egyptian fleshpots. Needless to say, the heavenly diet plan was not changed for those ungrateful people. In addition to other acts of ingratitude, the complaints served to further distance the Almighty from the children of Israel.[2]

Zelaphchad worked out a satisfactory daily schedule. After gathering the manna for his family, he met with the captains of fifty who reported to him on the status of the families they supervised. If there were any matters which had to be settled on a personal basis, he would take care of them immediately. If not, he usually went to the center of the camp to socialize with friends. The change from very arduous labor to the relative idleness of the desert was not easy for an active man like Zelaphchad, but it provided him with a restful period after his brutal experiences in slavery.

In the eighth month of the first year after the Exodus, a national project was undertaken that broke the daily monotony. At the request of the Lord, Moses announced that a Tabernacle was to be built in the desert that would serve as the religious sanctuary of the children of Israel. This would be the first worship center for the Hebrews as a nation, and they were excited at the prospect.

The Mishkan, as the Tabernacle was called, had certain architectural requirements. While the building had to serve worship functions, it also had to be portable. Mobility did not mean that it could be transported as a unit, but rather that it could be dismantled and reassembled each time the children of Israel moved from one encampment to the next.

Building and maintaining the Tabernacle required the full-time services of many men. Moses assigned the tribe of Levi to devote itself to the religious needs of the children of Israel. Their elevation to Divine service was a reward for their strong show of faith in the aftermath of the golden calf incident. In addition to carrying the Mishkan and assembling it at each location, they were also responsible for the worship services. These services, consisting of animal sacrifices, were conducted by Aaron and his immediate family who were designated as "Cohanim." The rest of the members of the tribe were called Levites. Once Levi was designated as the holy tribe, Zelaphchad was relieved of additional responsibility. Prior to the elevation of the Levites, the first-born sons of each family conducted family worship.[3]

The daily walks to the center of the camp became far more interesting when construction of the Mishkan commenced. Zelaphchad could watch the chief architect, Bezalel, fashion its vessels. There were many volunteers assisting Bezalel, but Zelaphchad was not among them. He had no particular skill as an artisan. He did, however, think of Ram, who had a knack for various crafts. He spoke to his brother and suggested that he volunteer his services. Ram, who was also finding time heavy on his hands, undertook to work with the goldsmiths. Most of the Tabernacle furnishings were plated with gold including the ark, the table and the altar.[4]

A large amount of precious metals was needed in the construction of the Mishkan. To acquire them, an appeal was made to the people for donations of gold, silver and copper. The only gold available to Zelaphchad consisted of the earrings and bracelets that Achla had garnered from the Egyptians. Zelaphchad knew that they were the only items of jewelry she had ever possessed, so he was reluctant to ask her for them. Achla herself found it hard to make the sacrifice, but she knew that it had to be done. Tearfully, she dropped the precious adornments into the collection box. She was comforted in the knowledge that her donation was for a most worthy purpose, fully sanctioned by the Lord.

In addition to giving up their jewelry, the women of Israel worked hard to weave the cloth needed in the Mishkan. They used blue wool, scarlet cloth and white linen. Achla, who was highly skilled in weaving and embroidery, did more than her share. She enjoyed sewing and managed to do much of the work by herself. Of greater importance was the time she spent guiding and supervising the work of others, who were eager to help but lacked the required skills. Achla patiently trained the novices and improved the efforts of those of average experience. All of the curtains, draperies and covers used in the Tabernacle were made by female volunteers.[5]

The most exciting part of the construction was the casting of the Menorah. Moses himself was on hand for this phase, conveying directions that he had received in a vision from the Lord. The candelabrum had to be cast in a single piece of solid gold. The work was extremely intricate, as each of the seven branches was carved with cups and flowers. Large crowds gathered for the casting and watched as it was successfully executed.

Each night, upon returning from watching the work of the Mishkan, Zelaphchad informed his wife and family of the progress that had been made.

"They are working at an extremely rapid pace," he said. "There is every reason to feel that the Mishkan will be dedicated by the start of our second year in the desert."

Zelaphchad was using a new frame of reference in dating current events. The children of Israel no longer marked the years in terms of Egyptian kings. The Lord gave them a new calendar when they became a free people. In the desert, year one was the year in which the Exodus took place. Month one, which coincided with the onset of spring, was the month in which it had occurred. Thus the Exodus was considered to have begun on the fifteenth day of first month of the first year. The length of each month was based on the lunar cycle.[6]

"I would like to visit the construction," Achla said to Zelaphchad upon hearing his dramatic reports.

"I don't see why not," he answered, "if you can find someone to take care of the children."

"We can take Machla with us and I will ask Adina to look after the others. That means, of course, that I will have to watch her children some other time." They had no qualms about taking Machla. Not only was she well behaved, but she was already displaying indications of superior intelligence.

The next afternoon, Zelaphchad took the family to see the Tabernacle being built. "That is the holy ark," he said, pointing to a box-like structure plated with gold. "On top of the ark are a pair of golden cherubs."[7]

A wide-eyed Machla studied the dramatic sculptures. "Those are angels," she said. "I know about them." The parents evinced a measure of surprise. Neither could recall telling their daughter about such beings. "Where did you hear about angels?" Achla asked.

"Grandfather called me 'his little angel' so I asked him what angels were. He told me all about them."

Machla loved the attention she was getting from her parents. With three younger sisters at home, she didn't receive sufficient notice. Chefer, who no longer was active, was able to grasp the child's potential. He spent a lot of time teaching her the history of the Hebrew people.

"What else did grandfather tell you?"

"Lots of things. He told me how God created the world and gave Moses the Torah."

"You're very smart, Machla. I'm truly proud of you," Zelaphchad said. He lifted her on his shoulders. "Look, there is the Menorah. Isn't it beautiful! Somewhere in all that gold are your mother's earrings."

The Mishkan was assembled and dedicated on the first day of the first month of the second year after the Exodus. The timing was intentional for it allowed the children of Israel to observe the rituals of the Passover holiday in a Tabernacle of their own. Each day, from the first of the month, leaders of the various tribes made special presentations to the Mishkan. Zelaphchad and his family attended the dedication services on the eighth day of the first month, the day chosen for his tribe of Menashe to make its offering. He watched as Gamliel delivered various gifts on behalf of the tribe.[8] Gamliel and the other tribal leaders actually donated the offerings from their own personal resources. To avoid any feelings of ill will, each tribe was required to bring identical gifts of silver, spices and animals.

Returning to his tent, Zelaphchad began preparations for the Passover holiday in earnest. This Passover differed from the one which was held in Egypt on the night of the Exodus. The first seder was a hurried affair which had to be finished quickly. The seder in the desert was leisurely. The family gathered outside the tents to rejoice in the meal and eat the lamb that had been slaughtered earlier at the Mishkan. Machla was old enough to understand some of the discussion that took place at the seder meal. She was a very inquisitive child and asked questions about life in Egypt before the Exodus. Her father told her the story of the Exodus and was amazed at her retention of even the slightest detail. Zelaphchad conducted the seder because he was the first-born. Azriel, however, added the scholarly touches. It was to her uncle that Machla addressed the question as to why the Paschal lamb had to be selected ahead of time and watched for four full days. He told her that this was to show that the children of Israel were no longer afraid of the Egyptians who worshipped sheep.

After Passover, a chain of events began that had a profound effect on Hebrew history, and on Zelaphchad as well. For over a year, the children of Israel had dwelt in the desert experiencing a process of rehabilitation and training following many years of slavery. At the end of the year, the children of Israel were ready for the initial steps that would lead to the conquest of Canaan.

The first action taken by Moses consisted of elevating the tribal leaders to the rank of tribal presidents. Gamliel, the son of Padahatzur, was made president of Menashe, a choice which pleased Zelaphchad. Gamliel's views on the Promised Land had become more positive once slavery had ended and the Hebrew people were en route to Canaan. The next step was to organize the desert marchers into a tight formation. The time had come for the children of Israel to cease resembling a group of hapless refugees and become a disciplined people.

The departure from Egypt had been a disorganized affair. People marched haphazardly without concern for tribal identity. To correct the situation, Moses — at God's behest — arranged the marching Hebrews into distinctive groups. He divided the twelve tribes into four units of three tribes each. Each unit was an entity unto itself. When the children of Israel marched, the lead unit consisted of the tribes of Judah, Issachar and Zebulun. Following them came the second unit of Reuben, Simon and Gad. After two units advanced, the Levites, who were in the center of the tribes, moved forward with the dismantled Tabernacle. The third group of tribes, consisting of Ephraim, Menashe and Benjamin, followed the Levites. The final grouping comprised of Dan, Asher and Naphtali.

The start of each march was signaled by the sound of trumpets and by the movement of the Cloud of Glory. At the time of the dedication of the Tabernacle, the cloud hovered over the Mishkan. As long as the Mishkan was assembled and functioning, the cloud stayed in place. When the time came to advance, the cloud moved ahead of the tribes and served to guide them on their way.

It was on the twentieth day of the second month of the second year, that the children of Israel commenced their march to the Promised Land. Zelaphchad's joy knew no limits. He imagined that within the space of a month or two his nation would invade Canaan and restore the homeland to the tribes of Israel.

The leaders of the Hebrew people, however, were not yet confident of their ability to capture the Land of Canaan. They desired human assurance in addition to Divine promises. They therefore requested that an investigative mission, composed of distinguished men, be sent to the Land of Canaan to determine whether the country could be conquered. Although Moses had some misgivings about such a venture, the Almighty allowed it to happen.[9] The twelve men who were appointed by Moses to undertake the mission were all important figures in their tribes.

Two outstanding choices for the action were Joshua and Caleb. Joshua, representing the tribe of Ephraim, was a full-time disciple of Moses. He had led the Hebrew people in the war against Amalek when that desert tribe attacked the Hebrews who were leaving Egypt. After the war, Joshua continued to serve Moses. Caleb, a very distinguished man from Judah, was related to Moses by marriage.

The other ten spies were men of lesser quality. Zelaphchad was particularly disturbed about the appointment of Gadi ben Susi of Menashe. True, he was an elder of the tribe, but he was a man of little faith or courage. Zelaphchad debated whether to challenge the appointment openly. In the end, he felt that it was not for him to do so. He confided his fears to Achla. "This project is not a true spying mission, as we already know enough about the Promised Land. I am sure that Moses expects these men to encourage the children of Israel by convincing them that it is possible to defeat the Canaanites. If that is true, I am concerned that he has chosen the wrong person from Menashe for the task. Gadi is a man who is afraid of his own shadow. He will never convince anyone that we can stand up to the nations in Canaan. Perhaps Moses should have sent women who love the Land of Israel rather than men who despise it."[10]

Moses may also have been doubtful of some of the spies who were chosen. He hoped that Joshua and Caleb could control the others and convince them to join in a positive report. The mission was planned to last for forty days. It would start in the Negev, the southern part of Canaan, and proceed as far north as possible. Moses instructed the spies to take note of the nature of the cities and the type of people who inhabited them. He also asked them to judge the agricultural potential of the land and bring back samples of the fruits.

The men performed their mission largely as they were told. They traversed the land from one end to the other. In the city of Hebron, they selected clusters of grapes to bring back with them for display to the children of Israel. The fruits were so heavy that most of the spies were involved in carrying them.

The day the spies were supposed to return — the ninth day of the fifth month — was an exciting one. Zelaphchad awoke early, gathered the manna for his family and took care of his tribal affairs. In mid-afternoon, he walked to the area of the Tabernacle where a platform had been erected for the spies to address the nation. The people milled around the platform until the end of the daily afternoon sacrifice as they waited patiently for the presentation.

Shamua, the first spy to be appointed, acted as spokesman. He represented the tribe of Reuben, the eldest son of Jacob. "We came to the land that our revered leader sent us to investigate and it truly is a land of milk and honey. Here before you are the very fruits of the land." He pointed to a mote that was suspended from raised blocks at the end of the platform. A huge cluster of grapes was tied to the mote, weighing it down. "This is typical of the fruit which grows in the Land of Canaan." The people stared at the grapes and gasped aloud. Nowhere in Egypt could such fruit be found.

Other spies continued to report in a more subdued tone. "There is a problem, though, with the Land of Canaan. The people there are mighty and their cities are extremely well fortified. Some men that we saw there were the children of giants. The Negev is occupied by the Amalekites. The Hittites, Jebusites and Amorites live in the hills while the Canaanites occupy the seashore, central Canaan and the Jordan Valley."

A hush fell over the anxious audience. The elation they felt at the sight of the fruits from the Land of Canaan quickly dissipated. Concern started to mount as the words of the spies sunk in. Aware of the reputation of these warrior nations, the people began to understand that conquering the Land of Canaan was a formidable task. At this point, Caleb interrupted his fellow spies who were making the report. He had been on the mission with them and knew how much they feared the Canaanites. He felt that if the spies were to continue with their negative views, wide-spread panic would result. He therefore took the floor and quieted the people. In a voice that projected faith and confidence he proclaimed, "There is no problem with the Land of Canaan. We can go up and take the land, and we must do so."

What started out as an orderly presentation of a report on a mission, quickly became a heated debate between Joshua and Caleb on the one hand, and the remaining spies on the other. The speeches became emotional, rather than rational. "We cannot do it," the majority screamed. "Those nations in Canaan are stronger than us. The land that we visited consumes its inhabitants. The men that we saw there were great and mighty. Compared to them, we felt like grasshoppers, and we are sure that we seemed that way."

They continued to disparage the Promised Land with such vehemence that the children of Israel began to weep, "Oh, that we had died in the Land of Egypt or in this desert. Why is the Almighty bringing us to a land in which we will fall before the sword of our enemies and our wives and children will become captives? Come, brethren, let us turn around and go back to Egypt."

When Moses and Aaron heard these words they became terrified of a Divine retribution. They fell on their faces in prayer to avert the punishment that was inevitable for those who spoke evil of Canaan. They also prayed for those who preferred to believe the spies instead of trusting the Divine promise. When they heard the Land of Canaan being maligned, Caleb and Joshua rent their garments. They made one last attempt to reason with the enraged mob of Israelites.

"The Land of Canaan that we toured is a good land. If the Lord wants us, and we find favor in His eyes, He will bring us there and give us the Land. Brothers, do not rebel against God, do not fear the natives of Canaan. God is with us, do not be afraid."

Their words were lost amidst a rising tide of voices. The people who did hear them were enraged with what they were saying. When Caleb and Joshua saw the children of Israel gathering stones to throw at them, they quickly retreated.

The Lord was filled with rage against the children of Israel. He told Moses that he was going to destroy the entire nation with a plague and build a new and mightier nation from the family of Moses. As he had done many times before, Moses launched into renewed prayer to save the lives of his people. But, unlike previous occasions, he was not entirely successful. The Lord, who readily forgave other sins, was unwilling to forgive those who spoke against the Land of Canaan. Although He would spare them immediate death, He would exact retribution over the course of time.

The heavenly verdict was swift and harsh. Moses was instructed to announce to the children of Israel, "The generation of people who went forth from Egypt and who have shown their lack of faith in the Divine word, will not live to enter the Land of Canaan. Every man among them who was between the ages of twenty and sixty at the time of the departure from Egypt, will die in this desert. The only exceptions will be Caleb and Joshua who have shown a different spirit. For the next forty years, one year for each day of the tragic mission, the children of Israel will wander in this wilderness and fall by the wayside. Their children, for whom they were concerned, will live to enter Canaan and inherit the Land."

Zelaphchad was stunned. He could not believe his ears. He and all of his brothers, who were over twenty when they left the Land of Egypt, would never enter the Promised Land. Instead, they would wander in the wasteland until they died and were buried in the sands. Oh, what an injustice this is, he thought to himself. We who love the Land of Israel and are willing to fight to the death for it, are being punished for the sins of those who are cowardly and lack faith.

Zelaphchad left the gathering in a daze. He didn't even see the hand of God strike down the ten spies with fierce anger. Nor did he hear the announcement that, on the morrow, the children of Israel would reverse their direction of travel and return to the desert from which they emerged. All he could think about was the sentence of virtual death that had been imposed upon him. Life without reaching Canaan had no meaning for him. He might just as well be among the dead.

Zelaphchad wandered around the camp for a long time. Everywhere, he heard muted discussions of the situation and cries of fear and anguish. He wondered how his own family was reacting to the heavenly pronouncement. Concerned as his family members were for themselves, he knew that they would be very worried about the effect of the decree on him as he was more obsessed with the desire to reach Canaan than any of the others. He could not tarry any longer among the tribal tents.

Although Zelaphchad was returning home after nightfall, the waxing moon, the bright desert stars and the heavenly pillar of light lit his way. When Zelaphchad did not find anyone in front of his own tent, he walked over to his father's tent where his family usually gathered when they had matters to discuss. There he found everyone conversing in hushed tones. His wife and children, his brothers and their families and his parents, were sitting as if in mourning. The heavy gloom came as no surprise to Zelaphchad. On his walk through the camp he had noticed a pall everywhere. Voices were subdued, while the banter that usually filled the air was noticeably absent.

When Azriel saw Zelaphchad, he greeted him quietly. "We heard the terrible news. Now we are sitting here trying to understand the full impact of these tragic developments."

Zelaphchad started to release some of the resentment that had built up within him. "There is injustice in the decree," he cried, "God is punishing the righteous for the cowardice of others."

Azriel tried to calm Zelaphchad and console him. "Compose yourself, Zelaphchad," he said. "Let us reason and see what can be done."

When Zelaphchad sat down in his designated place, Achla gave him some water to drink. "How long has the family been sitting here?" he asked.

"Not more than ten minutes," she answered. "Your captain of the fifty brought us the details. He said that the officer of 1,000 wanted to hear from you later this evening."

The call to duty did not please the very depressed Zelaphchad. "I am not sure that I am ready to continue my work," he said. "I am not inclined to see him, for it is all in vain. What has been said at the family meeting thus far?"

Achla answered him, "When you came in, Azriel was explaining why the Lord enacted this harsh decree against us." To Azriel she said, "Continue with your explanation. I am sure that Zelaphchad wants to hear what you have concluded."

Azriel resumed his analysis of the events. "Before you arrived, Zelaphchad, I was telling the family that I do not believe that the decree of the Almighty was due entirely to this incident with the spies. We must remember that our people are common folk with little training in politics. When ten distinguished leaders tell them that capturing the Land of Canaan is impossible, it is natural for them to be upset and panic. Of course, they should never have suggested returning to the Land of Egypt because that idea is hateful to the Lord. What apparently happened is an accumulation of events, each of which tested the patience of the Almighty. In His words to Moses tonight, the Lord stated that our people have tested Him ten times since they went forth from bondage. They expressed their desire to return to the land of slavery at the Sea of Reeds. They protested about the lack of water and the lack of food. They worshipped an idol within weeks of receiving the ten commandments. They also complained about the manna which keeps us alive in this desert.

"On many occasions, the Lord threatened to wipe out the entire people and Moses saved them with his timely intervention. This most recent rebellion against God was the act that finally tipped the scales against our people.

"Look, we must understand that we are dealing with a catastrophic situation. The Lord took us out of Egypt to bring us to the Land of Canaan. Our nation is in no condition now to wage war against the Canaanites. Only with God's help can we defeat those nations. Even if such a miracle were to come to pass, we would still have the problem of maintaining our existence in Canaan. I believe our people here do not have the moral strength to maintain a nation in a way that would be acceptable to the Almighty. For people who lack faith, it would only be a matter time before they reverted back to the idolatry and immorality that they knew in Egypt. Sadly, it is clear to me that this generation of Israelites is not ready to meet the challenge of nationhood. Only the Lord's mercy keeps us from being totally destroyed."

Zelaphchad listened closely to Azriel's explanation but found it wanting. "I do not disagree with what you are saying," Zelaphchad answered. "I know that our people are not ready to enter Canaan. I would be prepared to wait ten years or twenty years, if necessary, for that day to come to pass. What is unjust is that no distinction has been made between those who have been faithful to the Lord and those who have betrayed Him, between those who believe in settling the Land of Canaan and those who wish to return to Egypt. Even if the righteous people are in a minority, there should still be enough of them to save the lives of the rest of the Hebrews.

"We all learned that Abraham, our ancestor, prayed for the people of Sodom. At the end of his prayer he was told that if God could find even ten righteous people in Sodom he would not destroy the city. Wouldn't you assume that among the hundreds and thousands of Hebrews who left Egypt, scores of righteous individuals can be found? Why are we not being given as much consideration as the wicked Sodomites?"

Azriel countered almost at once. "The analogy is not a good one, Zelaphchad. The issue in Sodom was the total destruction of the city and all its inhabitants. A small number of righteous people is enough to save a city from that level of destruction. Now we are not being threatened with immediate extinction. Most of us will live out our normal span of years. On average, we will probably live longer than under slavery conditions in Egypt.

"What we are being denied is a chance to be the generation of Hebrews entering the Land of Canaan. Remember that the Almighty did not promise any individual here that he would enter the land. The promise was made to an entire nation. The Lord said that he would bring the children of Israel into the Land of Canaan at some time. It was never clear which generation would be the one chosen to enter. This is an area where a few righteous individuals cannot outweigh a majority of faithless ones. The righteous may be able to save the lives of the sinners, but they cannot capture a country and establish a government for them."

Zelaphchad was not convinced. "In this case, the righteous are being denied a promise that was made to our generation by Moses. Our own family is made up of young men who left Egypt shortly after their twentieth birthday. Certainly, some of us who have not committed sins should be allowed to enter the Promised Land with the generation that is first growing up. Why must we die too? Why can't an exception be made for us righteous people?"

At this point, Ram, who had been sitting in desolate silence, interjected. "That's not quite true, Zelaphchad. Two exceptions have already been made. Joshua and Caleb, who were both over twenty when they left the Land of Egypt, have been exempted from the decree. They will be allowed to enter the Land of Canaan. Are you comparing yourself to them?"

Zelaphchad paused before delivering his answer. "I cannot compare myself to those men. Joshua is now being groomed as the successor to Moses and will be the future leader of the children of Israel. Caleb is a towering figure who commands the respect of an entire nation. I am convinced that the courage of those two men, in seeking to counteract the report of the spies, saved the people of Israel from even worse punishment.

"Nevertheless, there is no reason for me to be ashamed of my own record. I fully supported Moses from the first day he appeared before the elders of Israel with his message of freedom. I was loyal to him in the presence of Pharaoh at a risk to my own life. I accepted with pleasure the position of trust that he gave me, and I performed to the best of my ability. What is more, when the followers of Korach sought to enlist me in their planned rebellion against Moses, I refused to listen to them. What else could have been expected from me?"

To this Azriel responded, "In Sodom, that would have been sufficient. But once the Torah was given to us, the conditions of judgment changed. We must now bear collective responsibility for all of our brethren." The impact of Azriel's words struck Zelaphchad immediately. He stared into the distance as if he suddenly caught a glimmer of what such a philosophy could portend for Hebrew life. Azriel drove the point home. "It is no longer enough that we can save our own souls, we must be able to convince all other Hebrews to act in a righteous manner. It will ever be so, Zelaphchad, because when we stood at Sinai we were a nation reborn. We became a united people with one body and one heart.

"In the days of the flood, it was also different. Although Noah wasn't able to save his generation, he himself did not perish. In the days of the Torah, we must cause righteousness to prevail everywhere. If we cannot do so, we ourselves will be responsible for the failure and will have to pay the price."

Zelaphchad had no answer and merely sat in deep depression. If what Azriel said was true, he was being judged by a standard that he could never hope to meet. He was now beginning to understand what the Almighty intended when He spoke of a holy people and a nation of priests. What it meant was that one or several irresponsible Hebrews could cause the entire nation to be condemned. Tragically, that was happening now.

At this juncture, Shafat made his first contribution to the discussion. "I know that you feel sorry for yourself, Zelaphchad, but we are all in the same situation. I feel it was a merciful act on the part of the Almighty that he did not condemn me to an immediate death. I, for my part, will go on living. I have my family to live for and I have my children to bring up and educate with love for God and Torah. Even in the desert, life is better than it was in the Land of Egypt. There were many generations before us who lived in total slavery and never even aspired to go to Canaan. Nor is this situation entirely without hope. If we abide by the will of the Lord, it may well be that in time we will again find favor in His eyes. He may then revoke the harsh decree that He has pronounced against us. It is not outside the realm of possibility that I will be privileged to join my children in the Land of Canaan."

Zelaphchad answered, "I wish that I could share your outlook. Your sons will inherit your share in Canaan and that gives you a greater basis for hope. I, however, do not yet have any sons to prepare for life in the Holy Land. If my daughters reach Canaan, they will not live on my land since women are not allowed to inherit property under our laws. I can only see that my fate at this moment is to die in the desert with no memory of my name after I am gone."

At this point, a stranger approached the family meeting area and asked for Zelaphchad. When Zelaphchad identified himself, the messenger asked him to leave the family gathering for a minute. When they were alone he said, "I have word for you from Arad, leader of 1,000 in the tribe of Ephraim. Your name was given to him by your leader of 1,000, as a man of great courage and a lover of the Land of Canaan. Arad is organizing a group that will venture forth tomorrow to attack the Canaanites directly."[11]

Suddenly Zelaphchad awoke from his stupor. At last, he thought, someone else is also not willing to accept the situation passively. "Where is Arad now?"

"He is in the camp of Ephraim," the man answered.

The tribe of Ephraim bordered on that of Menashe and, by making a few inquiries, Zelaphchad reached the tent of Arad within fifteen minutes. "I am Zelaphchad," he said. "You sent for me?"

Arad looked him over. "Zelaphchad, we are looking for brave volunteers. We need men who are physically strong, and are consumed with passion for the Holy Land. You certainly look strong and I was told that you share my love for the Land of Canaan. We have all heard the severe decree that was pronounced against us that we will die in the desert and never see the Promised Land. This must not be allowed to happen. I am organizing a group that will attack the Canaanite stronghold on Mount Paran tomorrow morning."

From the point where the spies had embarked on their mission, it was about a half-day march to the foothills of Mount Paran. The mountain was the southernmost border of the Land of Canaan. To prevent an invasion of the Land from either the south or the east, the Canaanites, jointly with the Amalekites, had fortified the mountain. They kept a considerable number of soldiers there because they understood that if an enemy force passed Mount Paran, the entire southern part of the land would be exposed.

Although Arad did not look particularly strong to Zelaphchad, he had an air of determination that inspired confidence. "I have nothing to lose," Zelaphchad said to him, "as I am doomed to die in this desert anyway. I would rather die fighting for what I believe in than wait idly for the angel of death. I will join you and, possibly, my brother Ram will do so as well. What is your plan?"

"I do not want to mislead you, Zelaphchad. There are fierce warriors in the mountains who may very well outnumber us. They have superior arms and years of experience in warfare. I am working on one assumption. If God sees that we are serious about the Land of Canaan, and are willing to die for it, He may repent his decree. In His mercy, he will give us victory over the Canaanites. Even if we lose the battle, He may still reward our sacrifice by being merciful to the rest of the children of Israel. If you share my faith, you may join me. It would also be good if you could recruit others to join in this effort."

"I am with you in this regard," answered Zelaphchad, "and I will make this plan known to my captains. I won't recruit anyone individually because I do not want to be directly responsible for causing his death, but I will not dissuade those who wish to volunteer."

"Very good," Arad answered. "Be here tomorrow morning. We will plan the action at eight. At ten in the morning we will advance against the enemy."

Zelaphchad walked home, feeling that a heavy burden had been removed from his heart. He never could have made peace with the idea of waiting passively for his life to end without some effort to reach the Land of Canaan. True, the plan was rash and foolhardy, but at least it was better than doing nothing.

By the time he returned to his tent in Menashe, the family had dispersed. Achla was putting the children to bed and Ram was sitting outside the tent that he shared with his parents. He took him into his confidence and Ram reacted as expected. "I am going with you, Zelaphchad. There is no way that I will absent myself from a battle for our homeland."

When Zelaphchad returned to his tent, Achla had finished putting the children to sleep. He called her outside and walked with her some distance from the tent. It was there that he disclosed his intentions for the next day. Achla began to cry as soon as she heard his plan.

"You cannot do that Zelaphchad. You are a married man, with a wife who loves you and with four daughters and another child on the way. If you get hurt or killed, I will not be able to raise the children myself. This action is not called for. You have always obeyed the word of God. A man like you should not dare venture into battle on his own without the Lord's blessing."

While Zelaphchad understood Achla's concerns, he was not going to be dissuaded. "I believe in a merciful God. He will not let His children be killed when they venture on the path that is in keeping with His promise and His will. When He sees us fighting for Canaan, He will vanquish our enemies before us."

"You are making an assumption," she cried. "It is wrong to risk your life on it. For my sake, Zelaphchad, and for your children, please don't leave me."

Her pleading was to no avail. Zelaphchad did not respond. His silence indicated that his mind was made up and that he would not entertain further debate. Instead, he removed a little sack from his pocket. "I was planning to present these to you upon the birth of our son, but I will give them to you now."

Achla's hands were shaking as she undid the sack. Through her tears she saw a pair of golden earrings similar to the ones that she had reluctantly donated for the construction of the Holy Tabernacle. Zelaphchad knew that she missed her earrings very much and he had managed to gather up enough goods to trade for an equivalent set.

"They're beautiful," she said to him, "but they will not console me if anything should happen to you." Hand in hand they walked back to the tent. "I want you to promise me, Zelaphchad, that you will be very careful and resist putting yourself in the front ranks."

Zelaphchad awoke early the next morning to gather the manna for his family. He kissed Achla and the children and went off with Ram to the camp in Ephraim. On the way, he stopped at the tent of one of the captains of fifty and advised him of what was underway. He told him to speak to the other captain and to the officers of the tens. When he arrived at the tent of Arad, a meeting was getting underway to discuss the battle plans.

"There is only one route to the Canaanite fortifications atop the mountain," Arad said. "All we can do is charge up the hill and confront them straight on. I will lead our men up the hill."

Listening intently, Ram interrupted at this point. "While you see only one way up the mountain, there are smaller side paths cutting into the main road. I am afraid that we will walk into a trap. The Canaanites will let us advance close to the top without resistance. Then, troops who have been waiting in hiding on lower levels will seal the main path behind us and leave us with no way out."

Arad soon realized that he was talking to a very knowledgeable man with considerable experience. "What do you suggest we do?" he asked. "There is no need to change your plan," said Ram. "Lead the main force up the hill as planned but leave a smaller force with me and Zelaphchad to cover you from the rear. If we see that there are troops waiting in ambush who want to entrap the main force, we will sound two blasts on the horn. If you hear the sound of the horn, retreat immediately down the path. We will hold off the troops trying to cut off the path until you can pull back the main force."

This suggestion made sense and Arad agreed to it. He then assigned a number of men to Zelaphchad's group and advised him that the force would leave in an hour. He would use the time to gather more equipment and brief any additional men who were coming to join the attackers.

While waiting for Arad, Zelaphchad had a visitor. Moses himself had left the Tent of Meeting to persuade the group not to venture an attack without Divine approval. Moses was looking for Arad but, when he did not see him, he addressed Zelaphchad instead.

"Zelaphchad, I want you to convey this message to Arad and all his helpers. 'You are transgressing against the Almighty in this venture. The action will not succeed. Do not ascend the mountain because God is not in your midst and you will be routed by the enemy. The Amalekites and the Amorite Canaanites are in the mountains and they will destroy you with the sword. You will earn your fate because you are not listening to the Lord. What is more, I cannot allow the ark of the Lord to go into battle with you. Without the ark there is no chance of victory.'"

Zelaphchad answered Moses that he would convey the message to Arad. At that point Moses turned to Zelaphchad. "I am not sure that Arad will listen. What I will say now is addressed to you, personally. You have been a faithful servant to the Lord from birth. In Egypt, you supported me in front of Pharaoh and you have taught the word of God to the families of whom you were put in charge. At this time, you are still without sin. I request you to withdraw from this group and accept the decree of God, even though it will deprive you of setting foot in the Promised Land."

Zelaphchad turned to Moses with tears in his eyes. "I am a condemned man. I will die either in this desert or in this battle. I remember when Nachshon plunged into the waters of the Sea of Reeds and, on his behalf, the Almighty split the waters. I feel in my heart that the Almighty will not let his children go into battle for the Land of Canaan and fail to come to their assistance. This battle is my form of repentance for the sins of the children of Israel. If it is the will of the Lord that I die, then the only sin on my record is that I loved Canaan so much that I gave my life for it. If I cannot have what I desire on earth, I know that this will at least insure my admission to the eternal life."

Moses was greatly moved by this display of faith but knew that Zelaphchad's hopes were futile. Again he warned, "It is in the nature of things that God tests man frequently. It is not proper for men to test God, yet that is precisely what you are doing. You are putting yourself at risk and challenging God to rescue you. It may have worked for Nachshon when he plunged into the sea, but that does not mean it will work for you." So saying, Moses departed from the tent leaving Zelaphchad wondering if today would be the last time he would ever see his beloved leader.

The determined Hebrews chose to ignore all warnings and, a short time later, Arad's men marched off. Zelaphchad's group followed thereafter. Both groups walked steadily and, within several hours, Ram and Zelaphchad could see Mount Paran in the distance. The realization that he was actually in the Land of Canaan had a remarkable effect on Zelaphchad.

"We are in the Holy Land," he shouted to Ram. "We have reached it."

Ram did not respond but the excitement clearly showed in his eyes. The long hill leading up to the Canaanite stronghold was steep. The Hebrew troops ascended the mountain and met no resistance at all. Zelaphchad was almost half a parsang behind the main force keeping a close watch on both sides of the path. When the lead force was near the peak of the mountain, Zelaphchad heard movement on the right. He looked quickly and saw a large number of Amalekites advancing towards the main path. He realized that he was badly outnumbered by a heavily armed force. He seized the horn at once and sounded two loud blasts on it.

When Arad heard the sounds of the horn, he understood that the advance force was in serious trouble. He immediately ordered his group to retreat down the path. Suddenly, vast numbers of Canaanites emerged from hiding on both sides of the path and pursued the Hebrews as they fled. Zelaphchad moved his men off the main path to a narrower location on the side path. His task was to hold off the Amalekites for the time it would take for Arad to retreat down the hill. Within moments, he and his men were engaged in bitter hand-to-hand fighting with the enemy. He was amazed at the strength and skill of these warriors, and he realized that only with God's help had Joshua been able to defeat the Amalekites. Zelaphchad's efforts were successful in delaying the enemy but he paid a very heavy price. Ram was killed by Amalekites in the early phase of the battle.[12] He himself was heavily wounded and could no longer stand on his feet. All of his men would have been slaughtered but for the fact that when the Hebrew troops passed the ambush point in their frenzied retreat, the Canaanites signaled the Amalekites to join them in the pursuit of the fleeing men. The Amalekites disengaged from Zelaphchad's men, who were badly battered and could no longer block the main path. They joined the Canaanites and pursued the Hebrews for many parsang until the city of Hormah. The toll they exacted from the Hebrews was enormous. Only the swiftest escaped. The rest were mercilessly slaughtered.

Zelaphchad's men realized that they had to leave the battle scene before the Canaanites returned and completed the destruction of their entire group. The dead, including Ram, were abandoned on the mountain side. Several men assisted Zelaphchad, who was weak from the loss of blood. He had great difficulty walking, even when leaning on two of the men surrounding him.

The stragglers made their way back to the Hebrew camp where Zelaphchad was brought to his tent. The men who helped him told the family that Ram had been killed and that they did their best to get Zelaphchad back home. The brothers were in shock because they weren't even aware that the two had left the tents to venture into battle. Achla knew, however, and became hysterical. It was clear that Zelaphchad's wounds were mortal, and that he would never recover.

Azriel and Shafat did their best to help Zelaphchad, but there wasn't much that could be done. When Achla gained control of herself, she helped staunch the bleeding and bind the wounds. "He is bleeding inside," Azriel said, "and he is in shock. If he does not die from the loss of blood, he will die from infection and fever." The brothers placed Zelaphchad on the mat in his tent and took the children away so that Achla could devote her full time to him. Achla called to Adina, "I cannot leave Zelaphchad alone in his condition. I know that Moses will not pray for him because Zelaphchad sinned against God. Go to the bier of Joseph and offer prayers for his life. Maybe the father of our tribe — who himself loved the Land of Canaan — will intercede with the Heavenly Father on his behalf." Adina did as she was told.

Zelaphchad was weak but still conscious. He told Achla, "I have no regrets for my actions. I fought to the best of my ability and I will die knowing that I was in Canaan, if only for a few moments. I am sure that God will be merciful in his judgment."

"You are a brave man, Zelaphchad," Achla said, fighting to hold back her tears, "I am praying for you to recover."

"I thank you for your prayers and for the love you have given me over the years. I know that I leave you with a terrible burden but you are strong and will raise our children well. Achla, my beloved, if God gives us a son, call him Zelaphchad. Then, someday, when our nation captures Canaan, people will point to a section of land and say that it belongs to Zelaphchad, the son of Zelaphchad, the son of Chefer." Those were the last words he uttered. He lapsed into unconsciousness and, after a few hours in a coma, his soul terminated its earthly existence.

The funeral was held the next morning for Zelaphchad and his brother, Ram, whose body was never recovered. The service was conducted by Gamliel, the tribal president. In his eulogy, he recounted the heroic services of Zelaphchad, his faith in God and his dreams of the Land of Canaan. The most telling words that he uttered were these: "Zelaphchad was driven to his final deeds by the lack of faith of his fellow Hebrews. They failed to believe in the Divine promise that we would be brought to Canaan. Their lack of trust in God condemned us all to die in the wilderness. Let us elevate the memory of Zelaphchad and Ram by dedicating ourselves to faith in the Lord and His pledge to return us to the Land of our Fathers. Let us work to implant this belief in the hearts of our children so that someday they may inherit the Promised Land."

Azriel followed with a sad personal message. "Ram, was our eyes. He helped us see many things and understand them. You, Zelaphchad, were our heart. You made us do things that we could not have done by ourselves. Achla, we stand with you in your hour of travail. We will support you and help you raise your children. You shall always be part of our family."

Chefer was overwhelmed by the loss of his oldest and youngest sons and entered a period of mourning from which he never emerged. On the third day of mourning, Aaron, the High Priest, came to comfort Chefer, who was well known to him. "Moses could not come for obvious reasons but he shares your grief. I, of course, know your feelings well and can only pray that God will give you strength in your hour of trial." Aaron had also lost two sons on one day. At the time of the dedication of the Tabernacle, his sons, Nadab and Avihu, introduced a strange fire in the Tabernacle, one that they had not been commanded by the Lord to bring. They were immediately consumed by Divine fire and left no children after them. Despite his severe personal loss, Aaron continued to function as the High Priest, performing his duties with courage and conviction.[13]

After consoling Chefer, he blessed Achla and said, "May God grant you courage and fortitude to raise your children in the spirit of the Torah and the traditions of Israel."

CHAPTER

FOUR

"THUS SHALL YOU SAY TO THE HOUSE OF JACOB"

Many people mourn the passing of a righteous man. Mourning, though, is not the same as bereavement. In the latter instance, the loss is felt personally and far more acutely. Even "bereavement" can not fully describe the impact of Zelaphchad's death on his widow. Achla had been married to Zelaphchad for six and a half years and had borne him four daughters. For the next six months, she would be carrying still another child in her womb without the aid and comfort of a husband. Before her twenty-fourth birthday, she would be a widow with five children. Her desolation was overwhelming.

The first three weeks of her sorrow were spent in a trance which left her totally oblivious to the world around her. She ate and slept irregularly, her feelings were a mixture of grief and guilt. The emotional strain had a drastic impact on her otherwise splendid appearance. Her eyes were red and swollen, her complexion was sallow and her dress was unkempt. Except for the immediate family, other members of the tribe would be hard-pressed to recognize her.

She was most troubled by the fact that she hadn't made more of an effort to prevent Zelaphchad from joining the ill-fated venture that cost him his life. If she were thinking rationally, she would have realized that nothing could have stopped him. But reason and good sense had deserted her and she could not think coherently.

Immersed in her pain, Achla neglected her duties as a mother. Shafat and Azriel had to gather food for her family. Her sisters-in-law, Adina and Yiscah, were taking care of the children, even though they had their own children to care for and each of them was expecting an additional child. The help they received from Achla's mother, who came whenever she could, was far from sufficient. The woman was well-meaning but incapable of handling four young children under the age of six. It was not long before the burden became oppressive to the sisters-in-law and they consulted with Azriel.

Azriel was torn between his concern for his brother's widow and worry about the pregnant wives. As was his custom, he sought a compromise. "Let us continue what we are doing for Achla until the thirty day period of mourning is over," he said. "If there is no improvement in her condition by then, we will have to ask Barak, our captain of 1,000, for assistance." Since Zelaphchad was a captain of 100 when he died, the family could approach Barak directly without presenting the matter to lower ranking officers.

The formal mourning period passed and Achla could still not pull herself together. At Azriel's request, Barak came to see her the following morning. Achla rose to her feet out of respect, but there was no smile on her lips and none of the usual sparkle in her eyes.

"How are you, Achla?" he asked.

"How can I be? The Lord has punished me severely. My whole life has been destroyed," she sobbed.

"Nothing I can say will ease the pain," he replied softly. "You must understand, however, that even those afflicted with grief are not free of their obligations."

"I don't know what you mean."

"What I am saying is simple. There is a tradition amongst the children of Israel that a mourning period for any person must not exceed thirty days. Even if Moses our teacher would pass on, God forbid, the people of Israel would not mourn him for more than a month."[1]

"Are you asking me to forget Zelaphchad, my husband, the father of my children?"

"No, not at all. I very much want you to think of him and what he would ask you to do if he were sitting in my place. He would not want to let relatives take care of his children. He certainly would want you to resume your normal life. In fact, he often told me how competent you were and how well you looked after the children."

Achla shrugged hopelessly. "I cannot do it yet. I look at my children and feel that I have betrayed them, that I let their father go to his death without making enough of an effort to prevent him."

"There was nothing that you could have done. What I am asking you is not to betray Zelaphchad any further by deserting his children. It is your duty to gain control over your emotions and begin life anew. Not all at once, but gradually. Rather than speak in general terms, I will tell you specifically how to get started. This afternoon, I want you to take Machla for a walk and talk to her. The child feels that you have abandoned her and that now she is a total orphan."

The words cut through the fog that was shrouding Achla as if awakening her from a long trance. "I wasn't aware of it because I was so engrossed in my misfortune. I will make an effort today and do more in time. You must be patient with me, though, for it will take me a very long time to recover."

Achla mulled over the conversation with Barak for the next few hours and finally resolved to take the first steps. After Adina finished feeding the children in the afternoon, Achla came to see her. She had discarded her dark mourning garb and changed to clothes of a lighter color. Adina was not surprised to see her because Barak had indicated that he had achieved a measure of success in his attempt to rouse her from her lethargy. Achla's two middle girls were happy to see their mother and cried, "Mommy, Mommy." She picked them up and kissed them. Machla, though, maintained a stony silence and didn't respond to her presence. Achla was hurt by her coolness but said nothing.

"Adina, I would appreciate it if you could put the younger girls to sleep. I want to take Machla for a nice, long walk."

Machla did not object. She missed the long walks with her father who took her to interesting places and told her exciting stories. "Where are we going, Mommy?"

"Maybe we will go see the sheep in the tribe of Reuben. They are lots of fun to watch."[2]

Machla smiled for the first time in weeks and joined hands with her mother. At first, Achla had been worried that she would have to explain to the child what death meant and why Zelaphchad was absent. Then she recalled that Machla was the only one of her daughters who was allowed to be present at the funeral. When the girl saw her father being lowered into the ground she probably understood that he was gone forever. That also reminded her that Zelaphchad once took Machla to the bier of Joseph. There, he would have had to tell her about life and death. She regretted that she did not know the level of understanding that her daughter had reached in her talks with her father. Zelaphchad always insisted that Machla was very smart, but Achla regarded her as just a little girl. That is why she was stunned by Machla's first question after they left the tent area. "Why did you let daddy go and get himself killed?" she asked, with a tone of accusation in her voice. Achla paused for a long time before answering. She realized that her future relationship with her daughter depended on her reply. She also gathered that Machla must have overheard conversations like this in the tents of the sisters-in-law.

She gained time by asking Machla, "Does anyone think that I could have stopped him?"

Although only five years old, Machla was smart enough not to name those who had expressed opinions on the matter. That would be tattling, and she had been told it was wrong. She also did not want to admit that she was eavesdropping. She looked up at her mother with eyes on the verge of tears, "I don't think it's important who said it, mother," she finally answered.

"I have thought about it many times in the last month," Achla said. "I don't know what more I could have done. I told him that he was the father of four children who loved him very much. Even that was not enough to prevent him from going. I could have asked grandfather to stop him but I know that he would not have done any better. He probably would not have even tried."

"Why is that, mother?"

"Grandfather Chefer brought up his children to believe in the Promised Land. As soon as your father was old enough to understand, he was told that every Hebrew child must pray to return to the land of his ancestors. That was the land that God promised our forefathers, Abraham, Isaac and Jacob. This was the land that our tribal father, Joseph, loved and that is why he requested his brothers to bury his remains in the Promised Land after they returned to it. The Land of Canaan was in your father's mind and in his heart and in his blood.

Before he married me, he wanted to make sure that I understood how much the dream of Canaan was part of his life.

"From the day that Moses appeared on the scene and repeated God's promises about the homeland, your father could think of nothing else. He was counting the days until the prophecy would come to pass. When the evil spies said bad things about the Land and the Lord said that no one in your father's generation would enter Canaan, your father became very angry. He couldn't think straight and that is why he went to fight that awful battle.

"He was a brave man, Machla. Those who weren't killed in the battle owe their lives to him and your uncle, Ram. Even though he did the wrong thing by joining the attack, I want you to remember him as a hero and as a loyal Hebrew. The only sin that he ever committed resulted from his great love for Canaan. Before he died, he made me promise him that I should keep his beliefs and try to have his name kept alive in Canaan. Do you know that Moses himself said your father was a man of great faith and courage?"

Achla's words had a profound effect on her daughter. She now understood that her father didn't die in some unworthy adventure but for a noble cause. She felt a need to learn more about the Land that had been promised to the Hebrew people and she wanted to realize her father's dreams. In the ensuing years, she would often raise the subject with her mother.

With the passage of time, Achla regained her composure. She managed to resume most of her normal activities even though she was hindered by the approaching birth of her child. Zelaphchad had always been helpful to her in the late stages of pregnancy. Now she was totally alone. She hated to ask for help but had no choice. She never discovered who in the family held her responsible for not restraining Zelaphchad, but she came to realize that her young daughter was right when she said that it didn't matter. Knowing the guilty party would have only caused a rift in the tightly knit family and would not have helped anyone.

As the birth approached, she turned to God in prayer that she have a son and be able to fulfil her husband's deathbed wish. The wise men have always said that one should not pray for a child of a certain sex after the onset of pregnancy because the Almighty had already made His decision at the moment of conception. While the parents might have to wait nine months before finding out God's will, any prayer in this matter would be considered as supplication after the fact.[3] Nevertheless, Achla prayed for a son. The other members of the family, however, were hoping for a girl. It took her a number of years to discover what prompted their perversity. As time passed, she realized that Zelaphchad's shares in Canaan would fall to his brother's children if she did not have a son. They were moved by greed while she was thinking only of perpetuating the name "Zelaphchad."

The birth was difficult. Zelaphchad was not among those waiting outside the tent and she felt isolated and afraid. When the baby did emerge, she was so physically and emotionally depleted that she didn't even bother to ask about the sex. She felt that the hand of God was out to punish her once more and that she was destined never to know happiness again. Thus was born the last of the daughters of Zelaphchad. Achla named her new daughter Noah, which meant the restless one.

During the next few years, nothing of great significance occurred. The Hebrews kept wandering in the deserts of Paran and Shur, burying the members of the generation that had left the Land of Egypt and had incurred the wrath of the Lord with its faithlessness. Memories of life in Egypt began to fade. The survivors still complained about their lot, albeit less than before. They became involved with their daily affairs and went about bringing up the new generation of children. Korach, an overly ambitious member of the Levitical family, led his long planned rebellion against Moses and paid for it with his life. As Korach and his supporters confronted Moses and accused him of various improprieties, the ground underneath their feet suddenly opened and swallowed them alive. Moses was not challenged thereafter and continued with his dedicated work of developing the Hebrew nation and instilling in it the spirit of Torah.[4]

In addition to the commanders of the thousands, Moses was given a court of seventy elders who were blessed with the prophetic spirit. They heard the words of the Torah directly from him and conveyed the teachings to the commanders.[5] This simplified matters for Moses because it meant that he communicated with seventy men instead of 600. After hearing the Divine teachings, the commanders transmitted the words of Torah to lesser officers who, in turn, instructed the individual families. The Zelaphchad family now received instruction from Azriel, who became a commander of ten. He was a replacement for Ram, who formerly held that post. Azriel reported to Abiram who was still a commander of fifty. Arnon, the other commander of fifty under Zelaphchad, was then promoted to fill the position of his fallen supervisor. Within Achla's immediate family, the daughters began to grow into women and developed the personalities that would differentiate them. Living without a father, however, meant that the girls received less religious training than they should have.

Azriel and Shafat continued to add children to their families. In addition to his first-born son, Meir, Azriel next fathered a daughter, Yakira, two sons, Amnon and Joseph, and a daughter, Ahuva. Shafat, in addition to Eliav, fathered Baruch, Bracha and Tehila.

Machla was moved into her grandmother's tent. Her presence was essential because the latter was now a widow and needed help in managing her affairs. Chefer's heart was weak after a life of slavery and the shock of losing two sons was more than it could bear. He lingered for a few years after the incident but his movements were limited. Often he had to lean on Machla to get around. She helped prepare the food and clean the tent. She was only eight years old when he died, and was terribly sad. To the limit of his ability, Chefer had been a father to her in the absence of Zelaphchad. Machla cared for her grandmother thereafter and took care of her personal needs. Her relocation helped the family because space was at a premium in the main family tent where Noah now slept with her mother in the back half while Tirza, Hogla and Milka slept in the front part. The extra space that Machla now had gave her a measure of privacy and insulated her from the petty haggling of her sisters.

At thirteen, it was clear to everyone that Machla was going to be a serenely attractive woman when fully mature. She had long black hair, brown eyes and high cheek bones. Her lips were somewhat thin but all other features were perfect. She resembled her father in every respect, much more so than the other daughters. She was also his spiritual heir, incorporating his noble ideals into the fabric of her being.

Early in her thirteenth year, an interesting development took place. Her cousins, Meir and Eliav, were both eleven and approaching manhood. Shafat conferred with Azriel about their religious training and an arrangement was worked out between them. Since Azriel was more learned, he would undertake to instruct both children in Torah and traditions for two hours each morning. Shafat, in turn, would gather the manna for both families. Since Machla and her sisters were already capable of gathering their own food, Shafat was able to manage his share of the understanding with Azriel during his two daily trips.

Neither Achla nor her daughters knew about the arrangement. There was a growing coolness and absence of communication between Achla and her sisters-in-law. She joined the family at Passover but, other than that, she no longer socialized with them. If their paths crossed anywhere, they exchanged only the most formal of greetings. With her brothers-in-law, the situation was not much better. Occasionally, they would help her in cases of obvious need, especially when the children of Israel moved from one location to the next. They dismantled her tent and loaded it in the cart. At the new location, they assisted her in setting it up. Otherwise, they kept their distance. Machla assumed that the cause was due to the absence of her father, who was the cement that bonded the family. Achla, of course, knew better. She realized that the coolness was generated by her sisters-in-law who feared that Achla had designs upon their husbands under the ancient tradition of Levirate marriages.

One morning, Machla had occasion to walk by the tent of Azriel. Coming from the tent were the lilting sounds of classic Hebrew phrases. They were far beyond the simple Hebrew spoken in the daily course of events. Despite their high level, she clearly understood the words she was hearing, "And God spoke to Abraham: 'Get thee forth from the land of thy birth, thy native city and thy father's house to the land which I shall show thee. And I will make of thee a mighty nation and I will bless thee and make thy name famous and thou wilt be a source of blessing to mankind.'"[6]

Machla's father and grandfather had told her stories about Abraham but she had never heard the actual Torah text. She realized that the words she was hearing were those written in the holy book and she was overwhelmed by their beauty. Something moved within her soul, something sublime, a mixture of awe and terror. For a moment she was transfixed, weighing her subsequent actions. She then walked to the back of the tent where she could hear the voices very clearly. She sat down outside the tent cloth, listening intently and not moving for the next two hours. She heard Azriel explain not only the literal meaning of the words, but the significance and message of the text. In a lucid voice, he expressed his understanding of the historic events. "Abraham's concept of God was more advanced than that which prevailed in the world around him. Our patriarch was told to seek a new country because it would have been impossible for him to develop his faith in a single and invisible God within the idolatrous environment of his native land. The Hebrew religion could flourish only in a new location. He migrated to Canaan at God's behest and the Lord promised him the land as an eternal inheritance." As he spoke, Machla could hardly catch her breath.

This Torah lesson was particularly meaningful to Machla. Now she realized why the Land of Canaan played such a central role in the history of her people, and why it had been so important to her late father. She resolved that she would continue learning Torah in this surreptitious manner. Every morning, a few minutes after the Torah lesson started, she would take her position in the back of the tent and quietly listen. In moments between the verses, Machla wondered how her cousins were responding to the teaching. Azriel's son Meir, participated more actively in the lessons. He would frequently interrupt his father with questions that indicated good understanding of the subject matter. Eliav, on the other hand, was quiet and Machla didn't know how well he understood the teachings. Their classroom responses were in sharp contrast with their usual social behavior. Eliav was far more outgoing than Meir and had many friends. Extremely sociable, he got along well with everyone. Meir, on the other hand, was very introspective and kept to himself.

After several months, Machla's luck ran out when Azriel began to cough in the middle of teaching and walked out to get a drink of water from the cistern behind the tent. Machla tried to scramble away but was too slow. Azriel spotted her and understood that she had been listening. He didn't say anything at the time because he wanted to complete the lesson. He returned to the tent and went on teaching while Machla, returning to her place, was fully aware that it would only be a matter of time before Azriel called her to account.

When Azriel finished teaching, he walked out to speak to Machla. "What are you doing behind my tent and how long has this been going on?"

Machla decided it would be best to tell the truth. "I was listening to you teach the Torah," she answered, "and I have been doing so since you started the story of Abraham."

"Your behavior is highly improper. You should never eavesdrop on people, and I doubt very much that anyone gave you permission to study Torah."

To this Machla responded, "I know that I should have had your consent to listen to the lectures. As far as learning Torah, no child of Israel needs permission to study it. The Torah is the inheritance of all the children of Israel. The Torah makes our nation holy."

Azriel was not intimidated by Machla, whose intelligence he had encountered on previous occasions. "A book may be owned by many people, but that does not mean that all the owners may study from it. There is a tradition amongst our people that only men learn Torah from the source. For women to keep the laws, they must be instructed by their fathers and husbands in a simple manner in keeping with their ability to understand."

Machla immediately saw an opening in these words and pounced on it. With tears in her eyes she said, "I have no father and my mother does not know enough to teach me. How will I be able to keep the laws until I get married?"

Tugging at Azriel's heart strings won the point for her. He could not shift the burden of Machla's education anywhere else. "Granting that you should be taught," he said, "there is still the question of your ability to learn the Torah from the original text. Perhaps, with your mother's help, we can arrange some tutoring for you on your level."

"It will not work," Machla protested, "because a man will not want to teach me and I know of no women in the tribe who are on my level."

"What do you mean, no women on your level? Do you know more Torah than the married women in our family?"

"I do not wish to say anything that would make me sound haughty, but I know of no women who can quote a single verse in the Torah, let alone understand its significance. I already know from Abraham to the end of the story of Joseph, the parts that you have taught your students. What is more, I know them by heart."

"What do you mean by heart?"

Machla took the next few minutes to recite verbatim many of the Hebrew verses that she had heard from Azriel. She did not miss a single word in any verse she cited. Azriel stared at her, his mouth agape in amazement. "Do you understand the meaning of all that you have memorized?" he asked.

"You are free to ask me any questions that you wish," she said. Azriel felt the need to verify her assertions. At first he asked her simple things and Machla found no difficulty in responding. He then went on to areas that he had refrained from teaching his own son because they were too complex. Here, too, Machla was not in the least stymied. Where she had not heard the answer, she projected the most logical approach that she could think of. More often than not, her answers were correct. On occasion, her words coincided with theories expressed by the commanders who were instructing their subordinates in the latest Torah lessons.

It did not take long for Azriel to grasp the reality of the situation. Not only was this young girl far ahead of his own son in knowledge of the Torah, but it was only a matter of time before she would exceed his own knowledge. She had an unbelievable memory, a fierce desire to learn and a brilliance that made the most difficult concepts simple. As a man of integrity, Azriel had no alternative but to make the proper moral decision.

"Machla, I cannot deny you the right to listen to the study of Torah. I must, however, impose certain conditions if I am to let you continue sitting near my tent."

"I am willing to do anything to learn," Machla said. "What are your requirements?"

"You must promise me, Machla, that you will never embarrass my son or Eliav with your superior knowledge. That is the first condition. You must also agree not to tell anyone who taught you Torah. Finally, you must give me your word that you will not use your knowledge to escape your responsibility to observe the commandments. In your studies you may learn that some laws carry more weight than others. When we instruct our women, we never make such distinctions. We tell them that all laws are equally important and that they all have to be observed."

Machla felt relief and elation. "I promise you, uncle Azriel, that I will meet all of those terms."

Thereafter, Machla did not feel guilty as she sat outside the tent. After a while she gained more confidence and was able to ask Azriel to clarify some of his ideas or to give her an understanding in depth of some of the points of law. She mastered all of the Torah that was available to the Hebrew people up to that time. While Moses had heard many additional laws at Sinai, he did not reveal them all at once to the elders. He chose to release sections at intervals in amounts that could be easily absorbed by the elders and the commanders whom they instructed. What had been released already was all of the history of the Hebrew people up to Mount Sinai, many of the laws governing relationships between men and their neighbors and the laws of sacrifices and worship. Machla never missed a day during the time she studied in this manner. Azriel taught the boys from Sunday through Friday. On the Sabbath, Shafat, who did not have to collect manna that day, examined his son to see how he was progressing in his studies. He was apparently very satisfied with the quality of Azriel's teaching.

When Machla was fourteen, major changes began to take place in her life. With growing maturity, she was able to relate to her mother not merely as a child but almost as an equal. One afternoon, following her studies, she passed her mother's tent and heard an ear-splitting scream. She recognized the voice as that of her youngest sister, Noah, who was eight years old. While she was accustomed to hearing Noah yell on many occasions, it had never reached such a volume. She quickly ran into the tent and there she saw her mother in a violent rage. Achla had Noah over her knees and was spanking her.

Nothing like this had ever happened before in the Zelaphchad household. Zelaphchad never had to lift a hand to any of his children and, as far as Machla could remember, her mother had never hit a child either. Machla immediately intervened without debating parental rights. She pulled Noah loose from her mother's grasp and whispered to her to run away as far and as fast as she could. Achla did not resist releasing Noah but burst into hysterical sobs and cried bitterly for a number of minutes. Machla stood by patiently and waited for her mother's anger to subside. Her mother was still enraged, however, when she told Machla what had happened.

"I was telling Noah to clean up her part of the tent because she had messed it up. Do you know what she said to me? She said, 'You are picking on me because you are a frustrated old woman and you need a man.' Can you imagine such nerve from an eight-year-old child!"

Machla understood that Noah was merely repeating someone else's words without understanding their import. She had obviously heard them from an adult, or from some child who had overheard the remarks and sensed that they were intended to be spiteful. Machla then suggested to her mother, "Let us go for a walk and you can tell me all about it. Maybe I can be of some help."

They set out on the path in front of the tents and headed toward the eastern border. The sun had moved past its zenith and the heat was tolerable. With the sun at their backs, the desert glare was not as harsh. While they were walking, Machla's mother told her the full story of what had happened and what was the probable source of the snide remark. "The reason that Noah's words hurt so much is that they are true. It is eight and half years now that Zelaphchad left me and I miss him terribly. A couple of years ago, when I passed the age of thirty, I couldn't bear my loneliness any more. I thought of getting married again, but no one ever proposed to me. There are very few single men of my age and they are reluctant to marry a woman with five daughters and not a single son. As far as being a second wife, husbands in our tribe do not frequently take additional mates. There is not enough wealth around for them to have that luxury. Even if they were so inclined, they would look for a young, single woman. I can't imagine anyone in Menashe taking a second wife with five daughters."

"What did you do about it mother?"

"I went to see Barak, our commander of 1,000. He knew Zelaphchad very well and he was extremely helpful to me when I was in mourning. I told him my problem and he asked what he could do to help. It was then that I mentioned to him that I heard that in the Torah there was a tradition among the ancestors of Israel of Levirate marriage."[7]

"I know about those laws, mother," Machla said. "It occurred in the days of Judah. Judah's eldest son, Er, married Tamar, and died without having children. Judah then asked his next son, Onan, to marry Tamar and produce a child who would bear the name of his dead son, Er." She did not mention that Onan had disobeyed his father and refused to perform the Levirate marriage properly.[8]

Although Achla knew that Machla had been listening in while her cousins were receiving Torah instruction, she was surprised that her daughter was so thoroughly versed in Hebrew history.

"I told Barak that under these Hebrew traditions, Azriel or Shafat should take me as a Levirate wife and try to produce a son with me who would bear the name Zelaphchad. Barak listened to me with compassion but wasn't ready to help me. He told me that while there may be new laws revealed to Moses on the subject, such commandments of the Torah had not yet been released. When they would become available, they would spell out the terms of the Levirate laws. For the moment, there were only the traditions of the Hebrews to go by. As far as these traditions were concerned, it was certain that Levirate laws applied only when a widow had no children at all. Just as the birth of a male child disqualified a woman from Levirate marriage, so did the birth of a daughter. Since Achla had children, the brothers-in-law could claim exemption from Levirate responsibility.

"I said that I could not understand that. If the purpose of the law was to produce a child who could bear the dead father's name, it had to be a boy. Barak told me that I may very well be right in theory but, when it comes to traditions, practice is far more important. Azriel and Shafat would probably claim that they are not required to perform a Levirate marriage with a woman who has had female children.

"I then told him that he could not be sure that Azriel and Shafat would take that attitude and that he should speak to them. He agreed to do so. He warned me though, that if they were convinced that they were not legally obligated to enter such a marriage, they could not undertake the marriage on a voluntary basis either. Under the laws of the Torah already available this was absolutely clear. It was strictly forbidden for a man to marry his brother's widow, even after the brother's death, except where a situation of obligatory Levirate marriage was in effect."

Achla continued with the remainder of the story. "Barak spoke to both men and asked them if they would consent to a Levirate marriage. Azriel knew the laws very well and said absolutely not. As far as he was concerned, as long as I had daughters there was no basis for a Levirate marriage and it would therefore be forbidden under Torah law for either brother to marry me."

Achla did not want to tell Machla that she suspected the motives of the brothers-in-law. She knew that they were using their interpretation of the law simply to avoid marrying her. It was not because she didn't find favor in their eyes. It was due to their fear that if a son were born to Achla in a Levirate marriage, the child would be the legal heir of Zelaphchad. As matters now stood, the brothers were entitled to inherit Zelaphchad's property in Canaan and there was a substantial amount of land involved. As a first born son, Zelaphchad was entitled to a double share in Chefer's property. As one who left the Land of Egypt past the age of twenty, he was entitled to a share in his own right as well. He would also get a third of Ram's property by inheritance. While Azriel and Shafat would not live to enter Canaan, their five male children would enjoy major estates in the Promised Land.

Achla refrained from relating this to Machla because it would have required her to reveal to Machla that women do not inherit property under Hebrew law. Where there are no sons in a family, the father's property goes to his brothers. Knowing how much Machla grew up in her father's image and shared his passion for Canaan, she was afraid to mention to her that she was not going to have a share of the Promised Land.

"I understand now," Machla said, "why your sisters-in-law have been so cool to you. They must have felt that you were trying to share their husbands with them and they were afraid that you would take them away."

Achla answered, "I know that they didn't want to share their husbands but I am not sure that they were afraid of any competition. The Lord has dealt harshly with me and left me with burdens that have marred my beauty and youthfulness. It is true, though, that once they heard of my intentions they regarded me as a rival and cut themselves off from me. They have also influenced their husbands to put some distance between themselves and me." Machla studied her mother's face intently and noticed the changes that she had not been aware of in the course of their daily existence.

"I guess that was the source of Noah's nasty remark," Machla said. "You must be having a very hard time with this, but I have a few suggestions."

"What can I do?" Achla asked with little cheer in her voice. She was beginning to realize how mature Machla was and she had no misgivings about soliciting her advice.

Machla answered at length. "You are not going to meet anyone who might wish to marry you if you stay at home and take care of your children. You have to get out into the public areas of the tribe and become more visible. Even if you have to travel to other tribes, it will be worth it, because there you may find more men who can afford an additional wife."

"And who is going to take care of my children?"

"I will," Machla said. "I am now old enough to supervise them by myself. What is more, there is another matter that concerns me. All of my sisters are growing up without religious education. They know nothing of Torah and tradition. I have managed to gain some of this knowledge on my own, but they haven't. The loss of our father has been very costly to them."

"You know that I have tried my best, Machla, but I do not have the knowledge that is necessary and I have no ability to teach."

"I am not blaming you mother but, when I am taking care of my sisters, I will also start teaching them the Torah that I have studied."

"That is very thoughtful of you, dear. I know that you can get the older girls to listen to you but how will you get Noah to sit for instruction? She is terribly spoiled, wild and different from all the rest. She never even knew what it meant to have a father and I cannot control her at all."

"Noah is the smartest of my sisters. If we could only get her to listen for a few weeks, she will continue with it of her own accord. It will give her a chance to show off and gain more attention."

"And what do you think I should do with my time? I can't just walk around idly. If I tried that in some other tribe where they do not know me, they would think I was engaged in immoral activity."

"You must find some voluntary work," Machla said. "I know that you cannot work as a teacher. Perhaps you can become a midwife."

"I would not consider that. It would be too painful for me to watch other women giving birth while I am denied that blessing."

"I have a better idea, mother. You are very skilled in embroidery and work with cloth. In fact, some of your work is in the Holy Tabernacle. There is no reason why you cannot teach these special skills to a class of young women. They would be very grateful to you for the instruction. I suggest that you speak to Barak and have him set aside a location for you in the Tribal Center where you could teach the class. Word would spread throughout the tribe of what you are doing and it would be good for your self-esteem." Achla couldn't suppress a smile as she mused on the role reversal of her situation.

The walk with Machla did much to cheer her mother. Achla was determined to take advantage of her daughter's offer to look after the children, at least in the afternoons. She would speak to Barak as soon as possible and ask him to make the arrangements.

Meanwhile, Machla had some business to attend to. She knew where Noah liked to hide and went out to look for her. She found her behind the tents of another tribal family. "Come here, Noah, I want to talk to you." Her voice was ominous but Noah thought that she could evade any unpleasantries. Noah had a long record of charming people with her smiles and eye gestures. Her curly hair added to her irresistible qualities.

"It was very nice of you, Machla," she said, "to save me from a worse beating. I appreciate it." Her eyes looked sincere but Machla could never be sure with her.

"You are not out of danger yet," Machla said. "I want you to tell me whether what you said to mother was your own idea or you heard it somewhere."

"Come on, Machla," she answered. "I don't even know what the words mean. I just wanted to stop mother from picking on me so much."

"From whom did you hear them?" Machla demanded.

"Oh, I can't tell you that. That would be tattling and I will get someone into real trouble," she responded in a sing-song voice.

"Listen Noah, I am not your mother. With me you can't weasel out of things and get away with bad behavior. I will give you three seconds to tell me where you heard that nasty remark or I will break you in two."

Noah knew with whom she was dealing. What she did was almost instinctive. "Look Machla," she said, "there is someone coming down the path."

When Machla turned around to look, Noah took off in the opposite direction and, for the second time that day, ran for her life. Of course, her flight was futile. Machla was twice her size and ran twice as fast. Within fifty cubits, Machla overtook her and grabbed her by the arm. "Are you going to tell me right now or do I have to use force?" To emphasize the point, Machla twisted the arm a little harder and Noah quickly realized that she had no further choice in the matter.[9]

"All right, you may let go of my arm. I heard it from Bracha, who overheard her mother talking with aunt Yiscah."

Machla then said, "I will take care of Bracha when I finish with you. You are to go right to mother and tell her you are very sorry for saying such terrible things. You will also be required to attend the afternoon Torah class that I am organizing for you and your sisters.

"How long will I have to go to the class?"

"You will have to attend at least until you learn the fifth of the ten commandments which were given to us on Mount Sinai."

"What does that commandment say?"

"That commandment says that you must honor your father and mother. You have no father, but you must honor your mother. In fact, the elders have taught us that just as one has to honor his parents, so, too, does he have to honor his teachers. Since I will be your teacher now, you had better listen to me."[10]

Noah was smart enough to sense the power behind the orders and she went quietly home to apologize to her mother. Later that day, Machla caught up with her cousin, Bracha, and had a talk with her. She related what Noah had said and added, "Bracha, you have been eavesdropping on your mother and aunt and telling Noah the nasty things that they say."

Bracha, a tall, thin girl, was not as afraid of Machla as Noah was. "What does it matter to you what I do and what I tell my friends? You cannot twist my arm the way you did to Noah."

"You have caused my mother great pain and that is why it matters to me." Machla gave her a withering expression and added sternly. "I do not think that you would want me to tell your mother about your behavior but I fully intend to do so."

"You can't do so because that would be tattling."

Machla had heard that excuse one too many times and replied at once, "That may be what you think. I for one consider it a case where correction is required under the laws of the Torah. I will not hesitate for a minute about informing your parents if you fail to make amends."

"What can I do?" Bracha said submissively.

"You march right over to aunt Achla's tent and tell her that you are sorry for what you told Noah and that you will never do such things again."

Reluctantly, Bracha trudged over and did as she was told. Achla thanked her for the apology. She was amazed how quickly Machla had brought two of the most stubborn children in the family under control. She knew then for sure that she could leave her daughters in Machla's care.

Machla began teaching her sisters the Torah that she had learned over the previous year. She started with the story of creation and then taught them about Abraham, Isaac and Jacob. After finishing the historical parts of the Torah, she taught her sisters the laws of the Sabbath and the laws of ethics and kindness. The girls enjoyed the learning and took to it well. After a few weeks of token grumbling, Noah also became interested and paid attention. There was no question of her ability to understand the material. Even though she was only eight, she easily kept up with her sisters.

Machla was an excellent teacher. She had not only learned Torah from Azriel but also copied his teaching methods which reflected great skill and devotion. She added a few improvements of her own and made a rule that Torah texts had to be memorized by constant repetition. Each of the sisters took turns reciting passages and explaining their importance. At night, Machla could hear the sounds of Torah verses emerging from the main tent.

As long as Azriel was teaching the boys, Machla was able to keep ahead of her sisters. But when the boys reached the age of thirteen, Azriel's class came to an end. Meir, who was an excellent student, was sent to learn in a class of superior students that was being taught at the Tribal Center by Barak and others. The purpose of such a group was to prepare men for positions as tribal leaders. Shafat felt that his son, Eliav, had secured a sufficient foundation and he directed him towards more gainful work. Eliav joined the shepherds and learned how to take care of a flock.

Machla was thus left without a source of Torah information. New laws were being released to the commanders every week and Machla had no access to them. She used more of her resourcefulness to overcome the problem. A few discreet inquiries convinced her that the one to solve her needs was Barak.

Barak was blessed with seven children and, as far as Machla knew, he had no household help. Here was an opportunity to put her domestic talents to good use. One morning she went to see Barak and a cursory inspection of his tents confirmed her suspicion that the household was not in good order and that the family urgently needed help. Thereupon, she made an offer to her commander. "I see that you are blessed with many children. Doesn't your wife find it hard at times to cope with so much work?"

"She does indeed. She is somewhat frail and I cannot help her as much as I should because I am very busy with my communal responsibilities."

"Wouldn't you think she should have some help with the children and the extra tents?" As commander of 1,000, Barak had a tent in which he received his subcommanders as well as other individuals who needed personal attention. He also had an additional tent for his older children.

"Of course she should. I have no spare resources of my own, however, and I receive no compensation for my work as a group commander."

"What would you say if I were to come each morning and help your wife on a purely voluntary basis?"

Barak was quite skeptical. "I have heard that you are already taking care of four sisters while your mother does educational work. Incidentally, while we are at it, I want to say that your mother is like a new person. I hear wonderful reports about her teaching and she is far more cheerful than she has been since she became a widow. I also understand that you are instructing your sisters in Torah. You certainly have no time for extra burdens." He looked at Machla with a doubtful expression. "Why would you want to work for me?"

"I feel that you were very helpful to us in our time of need."

"Machla," he said sternly, "I have no time for nonsense and I know you too well to be fooled by it. If you are willing to work for four hours a day without charge, you must need a mighty big favor, something you are afraid to ask for."

Machla became a little less composed and tears filled her eyes. "If I were a man," she said, "I would not have had to mislead you to get what I need. I would not have had to beg and plead. I could have demanded it and you would have had to oblige."

His interest was aroused by her words. "What do you really want, my daughter?"

Machla poured out her heart to him. "I have been teaching my sisters Torah based on what I overheard when my uncle was instructing Meir and Eliav. Now that the boys have completed their early education, I have no further source of Torah knowledge. No one in the tribe will teach Torah to a woman. I even had to promise my uncle that I would not tell people that he taught me. In fact, he didn't really teach me. I hid outside in back of his tent and listened. Now my sisters have learned so quickly that I will soon have nothing left to teach them. I am aware that new laws are being taught every week but I know nothing of these commandments. Not having a brother or father, I do not have any idea of what they are."

Barak's heart was moved by her words and tears. "You are not expecting me to teach you?"

"No, not directly. I know, however, that you lecture to your commanders of

100 three times a week. My father was a commander and he told my mother that your presentations were so perfect that they must have been rehearsed. I know that I practice my lessons before I attempt to teach them. I was thinking that if I work in your tents, I would hear you prepare for teaching the new laws that you hear from the elders."

"I do in fact prepare my presentations carefully and I recite all of the actual texts. Some of the material I just review in my mind. I do all of that in my receiving tent on the mornings of those days that I lecture, the first, third and fifth days of the week. Most of the time I have ten subcommanders present. Sometimes I add the twenty commanders of fifty. If I include them, each of the ten commanders of 100 avoids having to repeat the entire lesson for only two students. Now, what would you have me do for you?"

"I will work for your family every morning. On lecture days I will work in the public tent. I can clean the tent and listen at the same time."

"That sounds fine to me. I do not stop rehearsing when my wife or daughter prepares the receiving tent and the refreshments. I would not have to stop in your presence. You will, of course, not interrupt me."

"Indeed not. You are very kind Commander Barak. You will be happy with me and my work."

Machla reported for work at Barak's area the next morning. She cleaned, washed and took care of the children. The children became attached to her and Barak's wife greatly appreciated her help. It was not easy for Machla because many times when she was concentrating on the words of Torah, she would feel a little hand tugging at her skirt, demanding attention. Machla persevered, however, and increased her knowledge. Barak did not tell his wife the real reason for Machla's presence because he was afraid that word would get out. He simply told her that he had invited Machla to help her because she was overworked and he couldn't give her any more assistance himself.

On lecture days, Machla cleaned the public tent so thoroughly that it literally shone. Nevertheless, she didn't miss much of the lecture rehearsals and proceeded to memorize each new verse of the Torah. Things were proceeding well until, one morning, Barak was preparing to lecture on the population of the tribes of Israel based on the census first taken by Moses. Barak was giving the figures for the tribe of Levi and he apparently transposed the figures of the families of Gershon and Merari. Machla, who had taken every precaution against interrupting, inadvertently let a sound escape her lips before she could suppress it.[11]

Barak heard it and paused. "What is it Machla?"

Machla could not avoid the question. "May I respectfully say that the family of Gershon numbered 7,500 while the family of Merari totaled 6,200."

"Are you sure, young lady?" he asked somewhat annoyed.

Machla didn't answer directly. She merely recited the entire selection of the Torah starting with, "And God commanded Moses in the Sinai Desert saying: 'Count the sons of Levi according to the families of their fathers, all males older than one month shall they be counted.'" She continued without missing a word until the numbers of each Levitical family were given.[12]

Barak realized his error and acknowledged the correct figure. He was astounded at her total recall. "I thought you were not supposed to interrupt," he said without any anger.

Machla was prepared for such a contingency. "One may not hear an error in the teachings of the Torah and remain silent. If those who listen to you are not aware of the truth, they will transmit the error to countless others. If they do know, it would cause you great embarrassment. I really had no choice."

"You are right, Machla. Since you know the numbers so well, can you tell me why, of all the tribes, Levi was so small?" This was a question that he planned to ask the commanders to test their powers of analysis. He himself had ideas but he had not worked out the exact answer.

Machla didn't hesitate for a moment. "The two most frequent explanations given are that the rapid multiplication of the Hebrews was a God-given blessing to those tribes which were enslaved, to offset their oppression. Since the tribe of Levi was not enslaved, they were not blessed with great fertility. The second reason is that when Pharaoh ordered all male children to be thrown into the Nile, the tribe of Levi was more observant of the original suggestion of Amram to discontinue family relationships during the period of the evil edict."

Barak was impressed with the rapidity and accuracy of her answers. The scope of Machla's scholarship was becoming clear to him. "Tell me, Machla," he asked, "are there any words of the Torah that you can not recite by heart?"

"I am not aware of any."

"Are there any explanations of Torah verses that you can not expound on request?"

"I can recite all of the teachings I have ever learned. Whenever I hear any interpretations of a Torah theme, I commit them to memory and repeat them to myself over and over again."

"I wish I could say that for my students, Machla, or even for myself. I give you permission to correct me when you hear I am in error."

"It will not be often. You are a true scholar and very dedicated to your studies. I have learned a great deal since I came here."

It was not long before Machla began incorporating her new knowledge into her daily lessons with her sisters. They, too, began to gain deep Torah wisdom. Each sister studied in the group until she was sixteen, when it was deemed that she had completed her training. By the time Machla reached her twentieth birthday, only Milka and Noah were formally left in the group although Machla kept the others informed when significant new laws of the Torah were revealed.

Informally, though, there was an extra member of the class. From the time Machla was eighteen, Eliav hovered in the background when she was teaching. He never missed a day and never said a word. It was clear that he was absorbing all the teaching that was offered. Machla regarded him in a friendly way and noticed that he was developing into a handsome and gregarious man. "Eliav," she asked him one day, "why do you sit in on my class? You are a man and you could join Meir's group and study with the advanced students at the Tribal Center."

Eliav looked into Machla's eyes. "Machla," he said, "I cannot say for certain that you are the greatest Torah scholar in the tribe, although I have reason to believe that it is so. What I am sure of is that you are the best Torah teacher anywhere. The Torah comes alive when you teach it. You make it so clear that even I understand it."

"You don't feel strange learning Torah unofficially and from a woman?" she asked.

"For a girl who employed every devious device known to master the Torah, that is a very odd question. Torah is acquired only by those who are humble and who are willing to make great sacrifices to learn it."

It was the first time in Machla's life that anyone had ever bested her in a discussion and put her in place. "You are right, Eliav," she conceded. "I am sorry. Feel free to attend my class anytime."

When Machla related the incident to her mother, the latter took her aside and revealed the truth to her. "You are the smartest girl in Menashe when it comes to Torah but, when it comes to real life, you are an idiot. Even Noah knows that Eliav attends the class not so much for the love of Torah as for the love of you. He is totally smitten. He worships the ground you walk on and thinks of you day and night." Overwhelmed by this information, Machla was suddenly aware that she still had a lot to learn about life.

CHAPTER

FIVE

"YE SHALL INHERIT THE LAND AND DWELL THEREIN"

Achla's words had a profound impact on Machla. In essence, they signaled the end of one period in her life and the start of another. She had been so busy learning and teaching Torah, that she had never given any serious thought to love or marriage. Growing up in a fatherless home, she lacked understanding of the role of a husband. Nevertheless, she had enough experience with other families to realize that a man could be very supportive and a source of deep intimacy and companionship. She also thought of children and felt that it would be wonderful if she could bring her own into the world.

Such feelings, however, were neither immediate nor urgent. She was in a shell, closed to everything except her present objectives. Eliav's feelings for her pierced the wall that she had erected between herself and the outside world. It was now time for some serious adjustments.

Walking alone in the twilight, she started taking stock of herself. From what others had said, she was a good-looking woman. As far as she could judge from the mirror, they were making a fair appraisal. With the exception of Noah, she was as attractive as any of her sisters. Noah, of course, was in a class by herself. Aside from being beautiful, she had a dazzling personality. When she entered a group, all eyes focused upon her. She had a broad circle of friends and was constantly involved in some social activity. Machla often wished she could have the softer features with which Noah was graced, but she realized that her desire was nothing more than an idle daydream. She would have to live with her sharp, chiseled features even though they gave her a hard appearance. In one way, they were beneficial. Machla's fame was beginning to spread in Menashe as more people heard about the Torah scholar who was a woman. Perhaps her appearance didn't arouse desire in the hearts of men, but it certainly increased the respect that she commanded.

Machla was very much aware of Noah's attractiveness and desirability. When their grandmother passed on, Noah moved in with her. The two girls shared the tent, with Machla sleeping in the back half. This was the only sensible arrangement because Machla went to sleep early and didn't want to be disturbed by Noah who tended to come in late. In Achla's tent, Tirza was now sleeping with her mother while Hogla and Milka slept up front. All of them were delighted to have Noah elsewhere because her housekeeping was poor and her lifestyle too active. She was always doing something, going somewhere or congregating with groups of friends.

Machla continued to reflect. Giving in to some self-criticism, she had to admit to excessive ambition plus a fierce desire to succeed. This made her wonder how Eliav could love her. He was gregarious, outgoing and had many friends. His intellectual level was more difficult to determine. At one time she had dismissed his scholarly abilities out of hand. When he had joined her class and obviously understood everything, she had revised her evaluation of his comprehension and motivation. But she had some doubts about the latter quality. One should learn for the love of Torah, she thought to herself, not for the love of a woman.

Almost in spite of herself, Machla enjoyed her conversations with him and the time spent together passed pleasantly. They talked about many things and were quite compatible. She was, however, not in love with him. Possibly, her feelings for him were tempered by familiarity. After living in adjacent tents all their lives, it was hard to view him objectively. She was also uncertain as to whether differences in their intellectual levels would bar a meaningful relationship. At any rate, Eliav was only eighteen and not yet ready for marriage. It would be at least two to three years before a proposal would be forthcoming. She was flattered by the thought that someone loved her, but she realized that it would be wrong to encourage Eliav when she had no strong emotional feelings for him. She was equally sure that she didn't want to hurt him in any way.

With her thinking proceeding along these lines, she began to wonder about what she wanted for herself as a woman. Did she want to get married at all and, if so, with what sort of a man would she like to share her life. These questions were too complex for her to deal with casually. Typical of her intellectual approach, she decided to set aside a more appropriate time for the subject and think the matter through systematically. Although she was of age, there was no immediate hurry. In the meantime, she would talk to people close to her and get their feelings on the subject.

After dinner, she took Noah aside and invited her for a walk. Noah had other plans for the evening. The serious look on Machla's face, however, convinced her that it would be best for her to go along.

Quickly Noah reviewed her latest sins which included messiness, irreverence and late hours. She wondered for which transgression she was going to be admonished. "You are not going to twist my arm?" she asked, in genuine fright.

"Not unless it is called for," Machla answered, "but, if it will make you feel less anxious, I want to talk about myself for a change, not you."

"That's a lot better," Noah said, as they started down the path. "Now that I know you will not get violent, you may tell me what is on your mind."

Machla hesitated for a few moments. "Don't rush me, it's a delicate situation."

"Alright, take your time. I think I know what is coming."

"Noah, how long is it that Eliav has been attending our class?"

"Since he was sixteen, I guess."

"Do you know why he has been coming to the class?"

"Of course I know. He has seen the error of his ways in becoming a shepherd instead of a scholar. He has fully repented and now his heart yearns for Torah."

Machla knew that Noah was having fun at her expense. "I think it's time for a display of brute force," she threatened.

Noah had prepared a defensive strategy. "You touch me and I'll tell Eliav you're madly in love with him."

"So you knew what was going on all the time?"

"Of course I did. One month after he started coming to class, I told mother that we have a problem."

"With Eliav?"

"No, with you. You are totally oblivious to anything that isn't written in the Torah. We also have doubts about your emotional makeup. You always teach us about the good inclination and the evil inclination and how a person is supposed to have the good overcome the evil. In your case, though, we have never been able to discover the evil inclination. What ever happened to it?"

"If you are talking about physical desires, you have no cause to be concerned. If you are talking about sensing and understanding the feelings of others, I am worried. I should not have been the last one to know about Eliav. If you knew, why didn't you tell me? Why didn't it bother you that I was unaware?"

"For one, we were afraid that if you understood the real reason for his presence you would have become nervous and flustered. It would have affected your teaching. Secondly, and more important, Eliav is a decent sort of fellow and we didn't want to hurt him. You might have chased him away and he would have been terribly upset."

"How did you know why he was there? I'm sure he didn't tell you."

"That is the crux of your problem. A man doesn't have to spell it out. You see it in his eyes. You can tell just by looking at him."

Machla was not eager to accept the fact that Noah was a better observer of human emotions. "Are you sure you are not imagining things or projecting your own feelings?"

"No, Machla. The other day I asked him, 'Eliav, how come you don't look at me the way you look at Machla?' Do you know what he said?" The question was rhetorical and Machla didn't answer.

"He said, 'You're not bad looking, Noah, but when Machla speaks it's like pearls. When you say something, it sounds as if the devil has taken possession of your tongue.'"

Machla burst out laughing. "At least, there is no problem with his perception."

"No," she said, "only with his good taste and judgment."

"That's enough, Noah. I asked you to assist me, not to make me feel worse."

"If you are willing to listen, I'll help you. You are just about finished at

Barak's. Let us use the time to go out, preferably in tribes where you are not too well known. Forget for awhile that you are the holy lady, blessed be she, the greatest female Torah scholar that ever lived. Listen to people instead of lecturing them. Every person is a book. You remember how you explained, 'This is the book of the generations of man.' You can learn something from everyone and you can learn more about yourself when you converse with others."[1]

Several days later, Noah took Machla for a walk to the center of camp. All along the way, people greeted Noah and stopped to talk. She would introduce Machla as an older sister and encourage her to participate. If the subject turned to religious matters, she would give Machla a sharp kick or nudge to keep her mouth shut. The walks did a little for Machla's social graces, but much for her spirits.

It was about a year later that she saw Barak again and heard from him about a whole series of Torah provisions dealing with the land and economy of Canaan. "Can you give me a summary sometime?" she asked. For some reason, she felt uneasy about the new laws, a premonition of something of far-reaching consequences.

"I am free tomorrow afternoon," he said. "Come over to the public tent and I will explain them to you."

Late the next afternoon, she was introduced to the new set of Torah commandments. These laws had already been given to Moses on Mount Sinai but were first being taught now. They dealt with the Sabbatical and Jubilee years in Canaan, which regulated the economy of the land so that no single group or family could accumulate unduly large land holdings.[2]

"These laws are important to me," Machla said. "As a landowner in Canaan, I will be in a position to observe them."

A look of pain passed over Barak's face that he couldn't hide. "Barak, is everything all right? Are you feeling unwell?"

Barak realized that it was time to tell Machla the truth before she became totally obsessed with owning land in Canaan. He remembered all too well how this passion cost Zelaphchad his life and left Achla in widowhood. "Machla, I want you to understand something. These laws are not as important for their observance as for their moral and ethical values. They teach equity and social justice. It is not necessary to be a landowner in Canaan to benefit from them."

Machla was sharp enough to catch the drift of the commander's remarks. She was overcome by a sick feeling in the pit of her stomach. "Do I understand you correctly? Are you saying that I may not be a landholder in Canaan?"

"Don't misunderstand me, Machla. We have to work with certain assumptions. I take it that you will marry a man in the family or in the tribe. All men in our tribe are entitled to part of the Land of Canaan through inheritance from their fathers. You will live on land that belongs to your husband and you can share with him the observance of the laws."

"What will happen if I do not get married? I mean," she quickly corrected herself, "what will happen if no one asks me to become his wife?"

"That is hardly likely to happen with an outstanding woman such as yourself. I have already received requests from a number of families who are interested in arranging a marriage between you and their sons. I also know that your cousin Eliav has a romantic interest in you."

"Commander, please don't do that to me. Tell me the truth and answer my question," Machla said in a state of great agitation.

Barak sensed that evasion would only make matters worse. "Machla, I am very much afraid that unless you get married to a landowner in Canaan, you will never even feel as if you own the soil of the Promised Land, let alone actually possess it."

"If so, what will happen to my father's property and the land that he inherited from Chefer and Ram?"

"I cannot enter into a lengthy discussion of inheritance laws at the moment. Briefly, they allow only for sons to inherit a father's property. If a man dies without children, or only with daughters, his brothers inherit the property. Just as Zelaphchad inherited from Ram, so will Azriel and Shafat inherit from Zelaphchad. Since those two will not live to enter Canaan, your father's property will become the inheritance of your five male cousins."[3]

Machla became distraught and began to weep. "I don't understand, I don't understand," she kept repeating. Unable to continue the conversation, she left the tent and headed home. Although she ached to share the burden, she kept her peace when she got there and didn't tell anyone the devastating news. Instead, she lay down in her tent and cried herself to sleep. Noah heard her crying when she came home, but the hour was late so she said nothing. The next day, Machla was still despondent. The sisters sensed that something was wrong and asked her what happened. She shrugged her shoulders and simply said, "I don't want to spoil the Sabbath spirit. We shall talk about it tomorrow night."

The Sabbath meal passed quietly and Machla taught her sisters the section of the Torah dealing with laws of the Land of Canaan. The girls were interested and asked many questions. Machla answered as many as she could and said that she would have to study the subject further to answer the rest. She reminded the family about the urgent meeting Saturday night and indicated that it would be a long one. Since the meeting concerned her uncles, Machla gathered the family after the Sabbath and walked to the Tribal Center. There she was sure that she would not be overheard by her relatives. Outside the main council tent, there were empty benches and the center was otherwise deserted. Her sisters sensed a major problem but Noah wanted to ease the mood. "Quiet, everyone," she said. "I think Machla is about to announce her engagement."

Even Machla couldn't hide her smile. "Noah, be serious for a change. I have heard the most devastating tidings and they are not a laughing matter. I have been advised by Barak of certain Torah laws that will have a direct bearing on our future in the Land of Canaan."

"Are those the laws that we heard today?" Tirza asked.

"No, based on what I have to tell you, those laws are of no significance to us unless it will be our fate to walk in the fields of Canaan picking up the droppings and the leftovers in the fields."

"What are you talking about, Machla?" Tirza asked. "I thought we are getting big parcels of land in Canaan as our inheritance."

"I will outline the problem as briefly as I can," Machla continued. "When I finish, we will discuss the situation to see if anything can be done." Machla noticed that her mother was brushing away tears. This was the moment that Achla had been dreading for years.

"The Torah does not specify any general rules of inheritance," Machla started in a low voice. "In such cases we tend to abide by existing practices. That there is such a thing as inheritance we know from the Torah but, in all cases, it applies to sons inheriting from their fathers. There is no provision anywhere for females to inherit parental property. We shall not be inheriting any of our father's property in the Land of Canaan."

The sisters sat silently trying to understand the significance of Machla's words. "Who will get it?" Noah asked, her usually cheerful face now distorted with anger.

Machla went on, "When a man dies without male offspring, his property is inherited by his brothers. Azriel and Shafat have inherited all the property of our father and our uncle, Ram, of blessed memory."

Cries of disbelief rose up from the sisters. "But are they not also doomed to die in the desert and not enter the Promised Land?" Tirza asked.

"It doesn't matter," Machla answered. "The land will then go to our five male cousins. They will inherit everything."

At this point, Achla spoke up. "There is nothing new in what Machla has told you. Your father explained it to me after Milka was born. He was desperate to have at least one son in order to allow some property in Canaan to be known as the Land of Zelaphchad. That is why your uncles were not anxious for me to have a son after your father died and that is why they would not accept me for a Levirate marriage that could have perpetuated the name of Zelaphchad. I had hoped that this moment would not come, that you would all be married before you discovered the bitter truth."

"Why are women not entitled to inherit in their own right?" asked Hogla.

Her mother had once asked Zelaphchad that question and he had given her the answer that she now passed on to her daughters. "It is apparently the way of the world. Not in Egypt, not in Canaan, not in any country of the world are women treated as equal to men. The rationale behind the inheritance laws in those cultures stems in part from the feeling on the part of men, who legislate the laws, that women may not be competent to manage the property that they acquire. So, instead of allowing women to inherit real property, they bestow the property on the men and suggest to the women that they get married."

"You are saying," Noah asked, "that if we don't get married, we have no property and could die of poverty?"

"It is entirely possible," Achla said. "Of course, younger women might find work and subsist. For an older widow like myself, it is a very serious problem. But why think in terms of not getting married? I can personally tell you that life for a woman without a husband is intolerable. Single women are feared by married women and shunned by everyone else."

"What if we make money and buy property in Canaan?" Tirza asked.

"That is impossibile under the new laws of the Torah," Machla said. "The Torah forbids the permanent sale of any land in Canaan. You can buy the land for a number of years until the Jubilee year. At that time, the land reverts to the original owners. It is part of the Torah's plan to maintain the original division of the Land of Canaan. If we get land in the first division of Canaan, we will have it in perpetuity. If not, we will never have any land that is truly our own."

"What are the chances of the inheritance laws being changed by the Torah?" Hogla inquired.

"It is possible. My understanding is that there are not too many laws that are still unrevealed," Machla stated. "Nevertheless, some of those that have not as yet been taught deal with certain aspects of family law such as marriage and divorce. There is a chance that the subject of inheritance may yet be covered."

"Even if they are covered," Noah said bitterly, "we do not know whether they will be any more favorable to women. Speaking of marriage, that is no guarantee either. Say a husband dies or abandons his wife. In that case, she is left destitute. Widows and deserted women are not well situated."

"The Lord protects widows at least," said Machla. "It is so written in the Torah. The laws relating to the termination of marriages have not yet been revealed. Anyway, at least we now know the nature of the problem that confronts us."[4]

A gloomy silence settled over the six women clustered in the Tribal Center. The daughters realized why Machla had been so upset before the Sabbath. Noah, who was as committed to Canaan as Machla, was the hardest hit. She couldn't bring herself to say anything, an unusual state for her. It was Milka who was the first to seek some constructive solution to the problem. She turned to Machla and asked, "Do you have any ideas as to what we can do?"

"I have thought about the matter for two days and I have come up with a clear statement of certain goals that we must set to overcome our trouble. I also have a few ideas about how we may attempt to achieve such aims but they are not fully formulated. The first and foremost of our objectives must be to get the laws of inheritance changed to allow for full equality for women."

There was an immediate chorus of objection. "If you go that far, you will be defeated before you start," Noah objected. "Our strongest point is that we don't want our father's name omitted from the records of the Land of the children of Israel. In any family where there are both boys and girls, the father's name will be preserved through the sons. Giving girls property in such families would not mean anything in terms of preserving a name. However, many problems would arise if both a husband and a wife came into marriage with property. Where would they live? Which property would be maintained and which would be sold?"

"Are you suggesting," Machla asked, "that we urge the change only in cases in which the family is comprised of all girls and not where the sex of the children is mixed?"

"Right. It is more practical to get a change that effects a few thousand families than seek a change that will result in a major social upheaval."

"What if we ourselves inherit property and then get married? Wouldn't we face the problem that you brought up of both husband and wives owning property?" Machla asked Noah.

"Yes, but only to a slight degree. Remember, our purpose is limited to having the name Zelaphchad on some land. For that, it would be sufficient if only one of the five of us stayed on the property. The rest could marry and live elsewhere. Considering that we would stand to gain a very sizable property, there should be men in large families who would be willing to give up their small inheritance to benefit from our bigger parcel."

"Your logic is not quite fully thought out on that," Machla said, "but you have a point when you suggest that we aim for a limited goal that can more readily be achieved. Very well, then, if no one objects, we will list as our main goal the revision of the inheritance laws so that women in families where there are no sons will be entitled to inherit property."

All of those present voiced their agreement.

"What's the next goal?" Hogla asked.

"If we cannot get the inheritance laws changed, we turn to the tribal council and ask them to compel our uncles to cede some of their land to us under a concept of equity and social welfare. Since we are poor and without land, it would be the duty of the tribe to support us. It is within the power of a tribe to confiscate land for such purposes. Why shouldn't they take it from those who took the land away from us and also denied our mother a chance to produce a son by a Levirate marriage?"

"Azriel and Shafat would fight to the end," Achla said, "before yielding a cubit of their soil. I don't know whether their sons would be more charitable but I have no reason to think so."

"There might be an alternative. If the council is able to award land that is owned by families, it can certainly give away land that is owned by the tribe itself. Perhaps the tribe can allocate public property to families without sons. If we get such land, we can give it Zelaphchad's name."

"Both of these ideas depend on the sympathy and good will of the council," Achla said. "They certainly have not been helpful to me in the past."

"What's next, Machla?" Noah was anxious for a feasible solution.

"Well, we can marry our cousins. In that case we will actually live and work on our father's land. It wouldn't bear the name but at least in our hearts we would know whose land it is."

"I, for one," said Hogla, "would rather go back to Egypt than have Bracha as a sister-in-law."

"Not all of us would have to do it," said Noah. "Machla could marry Eliav and we could delegate her to assume that the Zelaphchad property exists for us."

"Thanks a lot," Machla said. "The last possibility of all is to admit defeat, get married to the best men we can find and abandon all hope for perpetuating our father's name."

"Now you are finally coming to your senses," Achla said. "I lost my husband because he was obsessed with the Land of Canaan. I don't want to see my daughters throw away their lives on a goal that cannot be attained. Get married and forget about it. Remember that what is important is perpetuating your father's memory, not inheriting his property. That you can do in your hearts."

Out of respect, Machla chose not to respond directly to her mother. "You have all heard the objectives. Does anyone have any suggestions?"

By now, Noah was sufficiently composed to give vent to her creative nature.

"I can only see three options here," she said. "We can petition the council for the lesser goals or we can bring a case to the highest court to change the inheritance laws."

"That's only two," Machla said.

"I am not sure that you are ready for the third."

"It can't be worse than most of your other brilliant ideas. Speak up and we will listen."

"Look," she said, "we have no reason to rush in these matters. It will be another twenty-three years until we are entitled to enter Canaan. Even if God shortens the period, it will be another ten to fifteen years. If we went to the court or council now, we would lose by vast majorities. What we have to do for the next ten years is build public support for our cause. There must not be a single Hebrew in the tribe who has not heard of us. In fact, the nation as a whole must know about us. What is most important, is that if the Lord sees that we are dedicating ourselves to the Land of Canaan, He may then soften the hearts of the judges."

Achla was the first to shout her objection. "I heard that argument before and it left me a widow. Your father thought that if he were fighting for the Promised Land, God would save him from the enemy. Some of the survivors told me that Moses warned him that he was testing God and that is forbidden."

Machla was more restrained. "A campaign such as the one you suggest is a very good idea but it will exact a heavy toll. If one or two of us were to undertake it, it would have little effect. As a unit of five attractive women, we are novel and unique. We can draw a lot of attention. The problem is that if even one of us gets married the battle is lost. I personally am willing to wait twenty years before I get married if it will win the struggle. After all, it is not just for us. We are fighting to advance the cause of all Hebrew women in future generations. Of course, while I am willing to make the sacrifice, I cannot demand it of anyone else."

"I made the suggestion," Noah said, "you can count on me."

"I am willing to put it off for ten years and then reevaluate," Milka said. Hogla and Tirza went along and the die was cast.

"I suggest," Milka offered, "that Noah draw up a banner proclaiming our struggle, and we will parade through the camp with it every day. How about 'NO LAND, NO MEN?'"

"Leave the jokes to Noah," Machla said sternly. "This will be a silent protest, and we will maintain our dignity at all times."

"No comedy now, this is serious," Noah said. "Five of us walking back and forth to the Tribal Center each day will attract sufficient attention. Of course we have to have a legitimate reason to go there. Since none of us are doing any public service now, I would suggest that we undertake a project to visit and help sick people in need of assistance. When people ask us why we are not married, we will tell them and word will rapidly spread."

"I think you are all stark, raving mad," Achla shouted. "You will be left a bunch of old maids and spinsters. Women who turn down men when they are young find that no one asks them to get married when they are old." Achla, of course, was speaking for the record. Deep in her heart, she felt that as soon as some really attractive men came along, the girls would forget all about their reform movement.

Without revealing their motivation to Barak, Machla requested and received a tent in the Tribal Center to meet a pressing social need in the area of tribal health. Barak made an announcement at the next council meeting that a volunteer visiting and health service would soon be available in Menashe. Since all commanders of 1,000 were officers of the council, he requested them to tell their subordinates of the new project and spread the word throughout the tribe.

The program started a week later and filled a long-standing need. Word gradually filtered down to the families of the tribe as to the motivation for the project. Each day, the daughters of Zelaphchad chose a different path to walk to the center. They also chose a new path on the way home. Along their path they paused to greet the families who wished to talk to them. Noah was especially helpful because she had hosts of friends to whom the word was quickly passed. For the next two years, the project continued and succeeded in all its goals. People became aware of the problem of the daughters of Zelaphchad. They sympathized with the cause and offered words of encouragement. The health care activities were well received and brought much aid and comfort to those who were sick.

Machla was twenty-three when Eliav reached his twenty-first birthday. He was a handsome man and quite mature for his age. He followed the project of the daughters of Zelaphchad closely and their actions caused him much distress. On several occasions he conveyed his feelings to Machla that what she was doing was not only futile but morally wrong. Machla responded gently but firmly. "I am always receptive to moral judgments about my behavior, especially when I respect the source. In this case, however, there are clearly conflicting interests. If I persist in my cause and win, it will be largely at your expense. Your inheritance will be diminished to satisfy the needs of your cousins."

One night in late spring, Eliav asked Machla to walk with him along the moonlit path. It was there that Eliav proclaimed his love for her. "Machla, you are the woman I always dream about, the one I love more than anyone else on earth. I am asking for your hand in marriage."

This time Machla was not caught by surprise. She knew how Eliav felt about her and was anticipating a proposal. "I am greatly flattered by your words, Eliav. You are a dear friend and the only one who has professed his love for me. Nevertheless, I am not ready to accept the proposal, primarily for reasons which do not relate directly to you."

"I am fully aware of the situation," Eliav said, "but I cannot believe that a woman such as you, so devout and so learned in the Torah, would put concern for a piece of land ahead of her religious obligations. Your duty as a Hebrew woman lies in marriage, motherhood and family. Having made a serious proposal, I deserve a better explanation of your objections so that I may have a chance to overcome them."

Machla sat down on a rock outcropping and signaled Eliav to do the same. As they were getting comfortable, she had a brief vision of a green and beautiful land beyond the horizon. The land was rightfully destined for her and her sisters. "Eliav, my sisters and I have decided to defer marriage until our inheritance problem in Canaan is resolved. It concerns you in the sense that if we get our father's property, it will come from your future land. I assume that if we win, that will not affect your love for me, so I will put off the discussion of that barrier to marriage until afterwards.

"Let us assume for the moment that no external problems exist and that you made an honorable proposal to me. Even in that case, the answer would be 'no.' I am now twenty-three years old. Although my mother already had four children at this age and your mother had two, each case must be judged individually. I spent my teen-age years taking care of my sisters and teaching them. I devoted every spare minute of my life to Torah.

"Two years ago, when I started to enter the real world, the matter of Canaan came up. Once more, my social activity became dormant. You are actually the only man I have ever spoken to socially. It is not fair to expect me to make a decision for life based on a single case. I would not even buy cloth without making comparisons and I certainly would not accept a husband on that basis."

Eliav was not happy with what he was hearing but, as usual, he was overcome by the way she made her presentation. Her logic and intelligence were her best qualities and he respected her for them. For Machla, the dialogue was even more difficult. She cared for Eliav and didn't wish to inflict pain upon him. Nevertheless, she could not refrain from telling the truth.

"I can tell you, Eliav, that you are a handsome and civilized man. You get along well with people and have shown kindness for others. You are intelligent and have a good foundation in Torah. I know that you will keep the laws and observe all the commandments.

"In two areas, however, I am hoping for something a little different. For one, I dream of being wed to a Torah scholar of the highest rank. One at whose feet I would sit and learn the wisdom that has so far eluded me. The Torah is as vast as an ocean. No one ever masters it all but there are some who venture in much deeper than others.

"The other aspect is something that I am almost ashamed to speak of. It has to do with the physical aspects of love and marriage and this I have learned from my sisters. When they see certain men, their hearts flutter, they get aroused and their bodies react. They are physically drawn to the man and want to be in his arms. I do not feel these impulses with you. It is as if you are my brother or a female friend. I know that many women do not concern themselves with these matters. They marry for security or because they respect the general qualities of the man. There may come a time when I will also feel that way. But, right now, the question of my emotional responses is still of major concern to me."

Eliav answered somewhat sadly but with great perception. "I have been aware of the first problem since I was sixteen. It was then I decided to do something about my Torah knowledge. As you know, I attended your class faithfully. What you may not know is that I have frequent supplementary sessions with Meir and his father and I review my lessons on a regular basis. Clearly, the knowledge is enough to observe the commandments and educate our children even though it does not compare with those who have reached more advanced levels.

"Let me tell you something, Machla. The only place where you will find Torah scholars on your level is among the commanders of thousands, judges of tribal courts and members of the High Court. We are dealing with about 300 tribal judges, 600 commanders and seventy elders. Give or take a few, we are talking of about 1,000 men. There may be a handful of these men under thirty, but virtually all of them are in the late thirties for commanders and late forties for judges. Positions of this nature are given only to married men. That means you will not be able to find any single men who meet your needs. When it comes to second marriages, the problems abound. You will have to confront wives who are jealous and resent your presence or men who have insufficient wealth to support two households. I don't think that you will ever find what you are looking for.[5]

"Furthermore, many Torah scholars are not interested in wives who are learned. They look for women who can cook and take care of children. They are loyal to the tradition that Torah is for men only. Now, let us look at it from a different vantage. Suppose you marry someone who is less learned than you. You might run into problems there as well. You cannot hide your knowledge and many men resent a wife who is ahead of them intellectually. With me, you have no cause for concern. I love you because you are learned, not in spite of it. I accepted you as my teacher for two years, and I was proud to be your student."

Machla's eyes were tearing up. "I concede that I could in time come to realize that my dream is an idle one. Go on Eliav."

"As far as being swept off your feet emotionally, that is a product of sleeping in one tent with Noah. She has a right to be childish at seventeen. You are twenty-three, Machla, and should know better. Infatuations do not last long. The important thing in a marriage is the quality and character of the partners. At your age, you should be judging candidates with your head and not your heart."

Eliav's arguments were quite persuasive and Machla had to concede their inherent merit. "Again you are probably right, Eliav. If great Torah scholars who make my heart throb are not readily found, your chances are good, very good indeed. Now that we've taken care of the personal area, let's go back to the group problem. My sisters and I are determined to secure our family inheritance in Canaan before any of us considers marriage."

Here, also, Eliav was not at a loss for words. He had given the problem much thought and had discussed it with others. "As matters now stand, I will inherit about a quarter of what would have been your father's property. If you were to marry me, I would be willing to build the family home on that section and you will be able at least to live and work on that land. Do not forget that if we are married we are considered one flesh. If I own your father's property, then you own it, too. I think that that is a far more rational approach than your present course of action. Do you know what will happen to you if you continue what you are doing? You will end up without land, without children, without a husband and, above all, without food. You will be scavenging in the fields for morsels to eat and be dependent on the charity of others."

Machla had heard such arguments from others, including her mother, and her mind was not receptive to them. "You are entitled to make these dire predictions, Eliav, but I am equally entitled to ignore them. I trust in the Lord and he will be my savior. If matters change in any way, I will advise you at once. In the meantime, we will have to stay just as friends. If you choose not to wait for me, Eliav, I will understand. I will not hold you to a rejected proposal."

The smile faded from Eliav's face and was replaced by a grim and determined look. "Until you are married to another man, Machla, I will not give up or even look at any other woman. You are the one I love — no one else but you. If you can defer marriage until you get your way, so can I. This is a game we can both play." They walked silently back to their tents, each as stubborn as the other.

Machla didn't sleep well that night and looked very tired in the morning. Noah was quick to get at her. "If you are going to carry on like this Machla and come home after me, you are going to have to move to the front of the tent. You almost stepped on my head. What happened? Eliav proposed?"

"You know too much and you talk too much, Noah." Machla couldn't resist having fun at Noah's expense. "If you must know, he did propose and we are getting married."

Noah let out a shriek. "Traitor. Unholy wretch! Here I've turned down scores of men for your Land in Canaan Policy, and now you say you are quitting the campaign to marry a young boy."

"Take it easy, Noah. I neither gave him a final 'no' or a final 'yes.' I was flattered that he wants me and a very small possibility exists that in the distant future we may get married. For the moment, though, you will have to control your impulses and continue breaking hearts."

"Yes, Master," Noah said, greatly relieved.

Machla regained control of herself and led the march to the Tribal Center. Requests for assistance to the sick kept increasing and Machla had to put out a call for additional volunteers. Other women responded and Machla arranged for them to be trained. Each new volunteer went out with one of the sisters for a period of time until she had mastered the basic skills.

Eliav kept in close contact with Machla but did not bring up the subject of marriage or Canaan. As long as they avoided these topics the relationship was pleasant and Machla appreciated his companionship. Nothing changed until Eliav's father, Shafat, asked to meet with her. She arranged to see him the next day after work at the Tribal Center. The fact that her four sisters walked home without her was not unusual. It frequently happened that one or more of the sisters were involved with very sick people who couldn't be left alone. In such cases they stayed on as long as they were needed.

Machla had mixed feelings about Shafat. He certainly was not a scholar and was far less refined than Azriel. Still, he was basically a decent fellow and very loyal to his family. He wasn't as well-built as Zelaphchad, but he was heavier and more muscular than Azriel. The long hours he spent outdoors were reflected in his complexion. He had never conversed seriously with Machla until this meeting at the Tribal Center.

Shafat sat down on a bench next to Machla and spoke to her gently. "You probably know why I asked to speak to you. In normal cases, if I wanted to arrange a match for my son, I would speak to the girl's parents. That is the traditional way of doing such things. In this case, my brother is dead and Achla despises me. That leaves me with no recourse but to speak to you directly."

Machla asked him, "Are you aware that Eliav has already proposed to me?"

"Of course I am aware of it. I've known for many years how he feels toward you. In fact, I released him from shepherding work so that he could pursue the dictates of his heart. I would be happy if you were to respond to his proposal for you are a pious and learned woman. He told me that he stated his intentions to you but your answer, if not a definite no, was quite negative."

"I wouldn't consider it very negative but I must admit that it was not encouraging. I want you to know, however, that my action in no way reflects on Eliav's character. He is a very fine man and quite sincere. Even though I am not in love with your son, I am still quite fond of him."

"I appreciate your words, Machla, and understand your feelings. Ordinarily, I would not intervene in your personal matters. A man cannot expect his father to do his courting for him. Parents are there only to advise and consent. If a woman is not convinced in her heart that she wants the man, the marriage will not be blessed with happiness and should not take place. The reason that I have asked to speak with you is that in this case there exists a certain circumstance which I feel prevents you from being more receptive to Eliav. It is an external problem for which my son is not at all responsible. This factor not only distances you from Eliav, but from all other men, as well. I feel that I should address myself to this subject. I may not have shown sufficient interest in your welfare in the past, but I am still your uncle and very concerned about you. This is a matter where my intervention is necessary and justified."

"I am not questioning your right to offer advice, Shafat, and I will listen to what you have to say. You know the problem, so please feel free to offer any suggestions."

"As a matter of fact, I have a few ideas that I would like to convey to you. Specifically, I have a plan that would be worthy of your full consideration." Machla paid close attention because she sensed that Shafat's advice would be accompanied by some offer or dowry.

"As you know, Machla, your father stood to acquire a very substantial estate in Canaan. Azriel and I will share equally in his property. My half of it will be passed down to my two sons, Azriel's half will be divided among his three. Of course, I speak for myself and my children and not for him. I have discussed that matter with my two sons and we have agreed to the following on condition that you marry Eliav. I will leave instructions that all of Eliav's share and half of Baruch's land should be sold to you and your four sisters for a nominal price.

This will mean that you personally will live and work on your father's property, and that the daughters of Zelaphchad will be the actual owners of the land."

"What will happen in the Jubilee year?"

"In that year, when the land lies fallow anyway, it will be returned to my sons. Immediately after the Jubilee it will be sold to you again for a forty-nine year period. We could give it to you as an outright gift, but you would be better protected if there were a recorded transaction and a legal bill of sale."

Machla pondered the offer for a minute. Her mother had certainly not expected any such generosity from Shafat. She herself was pleasantly surprised. She was careful, however, not to reveal her inner feelings. "That is a very generous offer, Shafat. One of the possible goals of our campaign was actually quite similar to it. It is, of course, not the ultimate goal. This proposal would give us our father's land in Canaan but not by inheritance. It would come to us by purchase conditional upon marriage. It would also keep the Zelaphchad name on the property for only two generations rather than in perpetuity. Nevertheless, it is a substantial offer. Our material well-being will be secured and some association with the Zelaphchad name will be achieved.

"Since my sisters are involved in the action and will be affected by your generosity, I will advise them of the plan and seek their opinions. Incidentally, for how long is this offer valid?"

"I would like to extend it indefinitely but I would have a problem if I were to do so. Eliav will not marry anyone else in this world but you. That in itself would be serious but not overwhelming. The real difficulty is with my three younger children. They will not enter into marriages because they have been taught that it is not proper for younger children to get married ahead of older ones. While my children remain single, Azriel's children will start building families. Meir is already spoken for and Azriel is currently seeking a match for Yakira. I guess we can wait a couple of years until Baruch is twenty-one and Bracha nineteen. Waiting any longer than that would limit their marriage possibilities."

"What would you do if after two years we still have not accepted your offer?"

Shafat answered sternly. "It would not be a wise thing to do, Machla. You will never be able to buy the property at the regular price. True, the nominal sale is conditional upon your marriage to Eliav, but that is the only way that you can ever hope to acquire your father's land. Aside from that, Machla, if you and your sisters do not give up your ridiculous action by then, Azriel has agreed to join me in a formal complaint to the tribal council about your behavior."

"On what grounds could you do that?"

"We would file a complaint because, as your uncles and closest relatives, we are being exposed to ridicule by your errant behavior. Your actions may very well have a negative impact on the chances of our children to secure the best possible candidates for marriage. Many people are reluctant to let their children enter a family that has achieved notoriety."

"I know why you would do such a thing. What I was asking is what accusations could be filed against us."

Shafat did not hesitate. "Among other things, you would be accused of acting contrary to the law and spirit of the Torah, acting immodestly and presumptuously, contributing to the deterioration of tribal values and conducting yourselves in a way that might lead you and others into immoral behavior." Such a detailed list of charges could not have emerged from Shafat's mind alone. The stated grounds for the case clearly bore the imprint of Azriel's analytical mind.

Machla's face was flushed with anger. Shafat had started out speaking softly but was holding a heavy cudgel behind his back and he would not hesitate to use it. "I thank you for original offer, Shafat, which I shall relay to my sisters. I will also tell them about the dire fate that awaits us if we do not accept your offer," she added with sarcasm.

The family was eagerly awaiting Machla's return because they knew that she had important news. After dinner, the family distanced itself from the tents and Machla delivered the full report.

"I would like to point out," she said, "that this offer meets or exceeds some of the goals that we have set for ourselves. It would, of course, be better if the tribe took all of our father's land away from our uncles. Shafat's willingness to sell three quarters of his land for a token, is a step in the proper direction."

"It would be fine if we could get the land for a few shekels, but you are being asked to pay for it with your body and soul," Noah protested.

"Thank you for your sincere concern, Noah. Of course, only I would have to sell my body and I will receive some real property in Canaan for it. The rest of you will donate your bodies to men in the name of love." •

"Different things make different people happy," Noah said, because she had to have the last word. "Are we voting on the offer?"

"Yes, but not openly," Machla said. "I will distribute a coin to each of you. If you mark the coin with lampblack or charcoal it means a 'no' vote. I will collect the coins in a jar." Some five minutes later Machla emptied the jar in front of her curious sisters. Four of the coins had discreet black stains upon them. The fifth was smeared with black soot all over on both sides. "That's mine," Noah announced proudly, "I am not going to let those reprobates threaten to put us in jail."

The next evening, Machla saw Eliav leave the tent and walk down the path, so she used that opportunity to speak to Shafat. "My sisters have asked me to convey their sincere appreciation for your generous offer, Shafat. Unfortunately, it falls short of the goals that we think we can achieve by our present efforts. For the time being, then, the offer is unacceptable." Shafat was very disappointed but not surprised. He knew that Machla, the daughter of Zelaphchad, was even more strong-willed than her father had been.

"You told your sisters where this behavior might lead?"

"Certainly, I did. They all look forward to seeing you at the tribal council in due course."

The next two years went by quickly. There were no major changes on the national scene as the children of Israel continued to wander in the desert. Several important events, though, occurred within the family. Azriel's two children got married. Meir wed a girl, Nechama, and his sister married Ekron. Shafat's children waited patiently for Eliav to make a decision. Since none was forthcoming, they delayed entering into marriage.

A few days past Machla's twenty-fifth birthday, the secretary of the tribal council greeted her and her sisters as they arrived for work. He had been waiting at the tent from which the sisters conducted the health care services. Achla was at the center earlier because she made a point of not walking with her daughters when they strode through the camp as a group. She did not want anyone to think that she was endorsing the action of her daughters.

"Daughters of Zelaphchad," he chanted in a loud voice, "please gather together with your mother and stand before me while I read this summons to you." The secretary had to read it for the women because no members of the family had learned Hebrew script.

> "The council of the tribe of Menashe, acting on a complaint filed by Azriel ben Chefer and Shafat ben Chefer, herewith summons:
>
> Achla, widow of Zelaphchad ben Chefer
> Machla, the daughter of Zelaphchad
> Tirza, the daughter of Zelaphchad
> Hogla, the daughter of Zelaphchad
> Milka, the daughter of Zelaphchad
> Noah, the daughter of Zelaphchad
> to appear before the Council at a special meeting, on the first day of the next week, the tenth day of the second month of the twenty-first year after the departure of the children of Israel from Egypt."

In a fierce rage, Machla shouted, "What is our mother being charged with?"

The secretary calmly answered, "She is being charged with failing to rear her children according to the spirit of the Torah and aiding and abetting sinful behavior on the part of her daughters."

White as a sheet, Achla screamed, "How can they say that? I told my daughters they were all stark, raving mad."

CHAPTER

SIX

"THERE IS NO REFUGE FROM THE DAY OF JUDGMENT"

The Tribal Center was a flat, rectangular area, about 100 cubits square, with two large tents situated at opposite corners. One tent served the tribal court while the other was used by the tribal council. Each Hebrew tribe had a twenty-three judge court of its own, a formal body with authority to rule in major cases. All tribal courts were subordinate to the High Court in the main camp. That court consisted of seventy judges, serving under the direction of Moses and Aaron.

The tribal council conducted the civil affairs of the tribe. As opposed to a judicial body, it limited itself to administrative problems. Its duties included keeping the peace, enforcing judicial orders and resolving matters affecting tribal welfare. Typically, if families began to feud over a matter of location, it would come to the attention of the council. If the council determined after a hearing that there was a violation of law, it could seek a judicial review and an order authorizing punishment of the offender. In routine cases, the council was not bound to follow the judicial procedures of the tribal court. It did, however, make a determined effort to abide by the courtroom model wherever possible.

The council was composed of the president of the tribe and all commanders of 1,000. In Menashe, it was Gamliel who presided over the body. When the council was inaugurated in the year of the Exodus, there were only thirty-two commanders in office. As the tribe expanded, so did the number of commanders on the council. There were forty-two of them at the time that the case of Machla and her sisters was considered.

In addition to voting members of the council, there was a secretary and a legal advisor. The advisor — an alternate judge of the tribal court — guided the council on points of Torah Law. The president voted only in cases of ties. In the event that some commanders were absent from a meeting, a majority of those present and voting could act on council business. A quorum comprised twenty-two voting members.

All of the commanders were present for the Zelaphchad hearing, as the subject was unusual and the protagonists were well known. Not only were the commanders on hand but several hundred spectators clustered on the Center grounds waiting to hear the proceedings. Some sat on the benches that were placed between the big tents while others just stood around. The benches were there for the convenience of those who had business in either of the larger tents or in one of the eight smaller tents in the rectangle. The latter tents were for service programs and special classes.

Of the eight tents, Achla had one for her sewing classes and her daughters had one for the health service. Two tents, somewhat larger than the other six, were used for advanced Torah instruction of young men. The tribal president had a tent in which he received visitors. The remaining three tents were used for tribal functions as needed.

When the children of Israel moved from one encampment to the next, a crew of volunteers dismantled the tents of the Center. At each new location, the same volunteers reassembled the structures. In some tribes, the Centers were quite elaborate. Although Menashe was a relatively small tribe, its tribal organization and administration were above average.

On the tenth day of the second month, Achla and her daughters arose early, donned their Sabbath clothes and headed for the council tent. Along the way they were warmly greeted by families extending good wishes. At the Tribal Center, they were hailed by loud cheers from the assembled crowd. The reception helped lift their spirits and dispel some of their anxieties. It was, after all, a summons to a trial in the presence of the tribal leadership, a situation bound to cause trepidation. The welcome accorded to the Zelaphchad family was in marked contrast to the stony silence which greeted Azriel, Shafat and their children, when they arrived for the hearing.

Machla perceived that public sympathy was overwhelmingly on her side. She recognized, among those on hand, families who were helped by the health service and others who had benefited from Achla's classes. Some of those present were not even familiar to her. By far, the largest contingent was made up of Noah's friends. Noah had given strict orders that they should all be on hand but stand segregated by sex. She wanted to be sure that no one would find fault with her supporters. Women were stationed in a group to the left of the entrance to the council tent. The men congregated on the right.

Machla was pleased by the large public turnout. What troubled her was that many of those in the audience came out of indebtedness to her family or in sympathy with people in distress. A council summons was regarded by many as a sign of serious trouble. What Machla was looking for were newly won adherents to the cause of inheritance rights for women. She could not determine whether those present were true believers. When she looked at them, however, she sensed that they were more than idle curiosity seekers.

Her sisters had appointed her to take care of the defense at the hearing, with Noah as an alternate. In planning her strategy, Machla analyzed the charges very carefully. Three of them were clearly trivial. As all of the sisters were extremely observant, the prosecution could in no way sustain a charge of immoral behavior against any one of them. Equally far-fetched was the charge that the sisters might encourage others to sin. Even if such a charge were true, Hebrew law held that only the sinners themselves could be punished and not those who requested of them to transgress. In the final analysis, the Torah held each individual responsible for his own deeds.[1] That approach was in effect even before the Torah was given. Thus it was that the Almighty wouldn't allow Adam to blame Eve for tempting him to eat the forbidden fruit. As to the charge of debasing tribal ideals, it had little credibility in the light of the record of tribal service by the Zelaphchad family.[2]

Based on her religious knowledge, Machla was convinced that their campaign had not violated any specific Torah laws. She would have to prove her opinion in court, but she was confident in her ability to do so. What worried her was the charge that the daughters were not acting in keeping with the spirit of Torah. Such an accusation was both broad and vague. It could be leveled against almost any innovative behavior that departed from existing customs and norms.

She would simply have to wait for the prosecution to define this charge before she could develop a defense against it.

Before fighting any of the charges, she planned to take certain procedural steps. The first of these steps would be to sever her mother from the case. The charges against her mother were without real substance and were submitted maliciously by her uncles to torment Achla. Machla would next try to dismiss charges against her middle three sisters who, to the best of her knowledge, had never enjoyed being the recipients of marriage proposals. She assumed, with good reason, that one who has never received a marriage proposal cannot be accused of turning it down in a manner contravening the letter and spirit of Torah Law. That left her and Noah alone to face any censure. In her case, Eliav had proposed to her and both he and his father had heard from her own mouth that there would be no consideration of marriage until the inheritance problem was resolved.

Noah's case was hopeless. She didn't know how many direct proposals the girl had turned down but, ever since she was seventeen, the family had been receiving requests for Noah on behalf of eager swains at an average rate of one a month. Some came from very distinguished families, often with offers of large dowries. To all of them, Noah replied that she would be delighted to consider the proposal after the daughters of Zelaphchad were given their inheritance in the Land of Canaan.

As they were entering the tent, Noah whispered to Machla, "Try to get the case heard outside. Audience support is very important."

The moment Gamliel called the meeting to order, Machla rose for a procedural motion which took precedence over other matters. "If it please Your Excellency, we request that today's session of the council be held outdoors. Many people are gathered outside who have a great interest in these proceedings. They certainly should not be deprived of the opportunity to hear them. May I point out that all trials of the High Court are held outdoors. All trials of the tribal court are also open to members of the public, or at least those who can fit into the court tent."

"We are not a court of law," Gamliel answered. "However, I will ask our legal advisor to rule whether it is permissible and I will ask the plaintiffs if they have any objections."

"We do object, Your Excellency," Azriel said, "on the grounds of propriety. The public has a right to learn of the proceedings after the fact. During the hearing, they may interfere with the deliberations of the council." Azriel sensed the mood outside and felt that some of the commanders might cater to sympathies of the crowd.

Gamliel turned to the legal advisor and held a whispered conference. After the consultation was completed, he stated, "I am advised by our counsel that council regulations provide for all sessions being open to the public unless notice of an executive session, closed to the public, has been posted. No such notice has been filed in this case. He has further stated that moving the case outside would be unduly cumbersome and possibly disruptive to the deliberations. To satisfy the needs both of decorum and the right of the people to hear, I rule and order that we pull back the front curtains of the tent to expose ourselves to public view." Some of the volunteers who attended council meetings quickly opened the curtains. It was easily done, because the tent was designed for rapid disassembly in preparation for tribal movements.

"If there are no further procedural motions, we shall get the session underway." At this juncture, Gamliel began the hearing officially in a loud, booming voice. "The order of the case shall be the reading of the charges against the daughters of Zelaphchad and their mother, opening statements by the prosecution and the presentation of prosecution witnesses. Thereafter, the defense will present statements and witnesses. We will then hear rebuttal witnesses, if there are any, and closing arguments. Since the issue of today's meeting does not involve a capital case or a monetary matter, we are actually free to follow any procedural order that we wish. Am I right, counselor?" The legal counsel nodded his consent and Gamliel continued.

"Before I call for the charges to be read, it is proper to introduce the attorneys for both sides and determine whether there are any commanders who wish to disqualify themselves." Turning to the rows of the commanders, Gamliel inquired, "Are there any of you who feel that you cannot properly sit in judgment on this case? If so, please rise and state your reasons." Barak and three others stood up. Machla had expected Barak to withdraw. She regretted the loss of a supporter but she realized that it was the only honest path for him to follow. She was surprised that three other commanders were asking to be excused.

Gamliel recognized Barak and asked him to explain why he could not sit in judgment. Barak answered, "Aside from the fact that I am the commander of the families on both sides of the dispute, I am the teacher of Meir, a son of one of the plaintiffs. Additionally, one of the defendants, Machla, the daughter of Zelaphchad, worked for my family for five years without charge. Without prejudicing the outcome of the case, I believe I can say that I am terribly grieved that such a dispute has arisen among the families that I supervise."

"You are excused, Barak. Nimshi you are next."

Nimshi was a cheerful, heavyset man, who spoke in a low pitched voice. "I am prejudiced against Noah, the daughter of Zelaphchad, and her mother. When my son, David, was of age to be married and — may I say, he is a fine young man — when I was looking for a bride for him, I heard the most glowing reports about the young woman, Noah. I then sent a very distinguished intermediary to speak to the family on his behalf. The offer was rebuffed without anyone even giving David a chance to present himself. I think it was an ill-mannered action on their part and I can no longer vote impartially."

"Excused, Nimshi. The next request is from Chanan."

Chanan was a young commander below the age of thirty. "If it please Your Excellency, I think Nimshi was more fortunate than I was. I sought Noah not for my son but as a wife for myself. As you know, my first wife died in childbirth five years ago and left me with a boy to raise. I spoke to Noah's mother about my interest in her daughter and she told me, in so many words, that I was wasting my time. Her daughter would not see anyone, even me. I feel offended that a mother should seek to prevent a daughter from getting married."

"What prompted you to seek Noah?" Gamliel asked.

"I heard that she came from a very distinguished family," Chanan said with a straight face.

From the defendants' area there were peals of laughter. Even Gamliel was smiling. "There are some very obvious reasons why men would seek this young lady," he said, "but I doubt that lineage is one of them. In any event, I understand your feelings and you are excused. I am ready for the last request for withdrawal."

Zeldan spoke in a strong voice that was quite audible outside the tent. "Fortunately, Your Excellency, I am neither a rejected suitor nor the father of one. I am indebted to Tirza for saving the life of my son, Oran, who was stricken with a severe illness. Oran hovered between life and death for two days, and it was the devoted and extraordinary care that Tirza gave him that helped save his life."

"Does that make it impossible for you to judge fairly in this case?" the chair asked.

"Yes it does, Your Honor. The woman is saintly and there is no way in the world that I would vote to condemn her."

"Very well, then, you are also excused. We are now free to turn to the question of counsel for the plaintiffs and the defendants. When the council accepted the plaintiff's action, it agreed to provide a prosecutor. We designated Abba, the commander, to serve in that capacity. Our choice was subsequently approved by the plaintiffs. Since Abba cannot serve as judge and prosecutor simultaneously, he will be deprived of his right to vote."

As the preliminaries were drawing to an end, interest among the spectators began to pick up. While they realized that certain matters had to be resolved before a hearing, they were anxious to get to the actual case. There was now only one additional task confronting the presiding officer. Whispering and movement stopped as Gamliel continued.

"The council has a moral obligation to provide the defendants with counsel. The Zelaphchad family may choose one man from among the commanders present to defend them. He, too, will forfeit his voting rights. What is the defendants' pleasure?"

Machla didn't hesitate for a minute. "If it please Your Excellency, we prefer to act in our own defense."

"You are within your rights, but it pleases me not at all. What do you stand to gain by refusing to have a distinguished scholar help you with your case?"

Machla had anticipated some objection to her course of action and was well prepared. "We stand to lose because we have not found, among the learned gentlemen of this tribe, any men who fully understand the problems of women and, especially, their inability to get fair treatment in the area of inheritance. What we may gain in scholarship from a male counsel, we will forfeit in prejudice." This assertion caused a loud buzz in the audience. None of them had ever seen or heard of a woman defending a case at the council. It took several moments for the audience to quiet down.

Gamliel was clearly upset by Machla's response but, from his position, he couldn't argue. "The secretary will note for the record," he said, "that the defendants declined the offer of counsel. The preliminaries have now been concluded. With four withdrawals and one commander serving as prosecutor, we are left with thirty-seven voting members of the council. The prosecutor will now read the charges and make his opening statement."

The choice of Abba to conduct the complainant's case was a wise one. Azriel had readily agreed to the designation because, in addition to his scholarly reputation, Abba was a mature man in his middle fifties. Azriel had assumed that an older man would be more conservative and look unfavorably upon attempts to upset the prevailing social status quo.

Abba held a copy of the summons in his hand and read slowly and deliberately. "Members of the council," he declared, "our body has agreed to consider a complaint filed by Azriel Ben Chefer and Shafat ben Chefer against the five daughters of Zelaphchad and their mother, Achla. The charges against the daughters include violation of Torah Law, violation of the spirit of Torah Law, haughty and immodest behavior, debasing tribal ideals and behaving in a way that could cause them and others to pursue immoral behavior. The charge against their mother is that she did not rear her daughters properly and did nothing to prevent them from acting as described in the charges just stated." Abba paused at this point to let the commanders and the audience grasp the broad scope of the case. It was clear to all that the Zelaphchad family was being charged with major infractions of the Torah Law. Before opening the actual case, Abba took a drink of water and stroked a beard that was more than half gray.

"All of those present today are aware that the very first commandment given to man is: 'Be fruitful and multiply, fill the earth and possess it.' It is under terms of this Torah law, that men and women get married and bear children. Before the first woman was created, the Lord said of Adam, 'It is not good for man to live alone.' Of course, if it is not good for men to be alone, it is certainly not good for women, who need support and protection, to remain by themselves.[3]

"The daughters of Zelaphchad are unusually well-versed in our traditions, yet they choose to ignore these basic teachings. Four years ago, they entered into a conspiracy to shun marriage. Their justification for this behavior is that it would further their campaign to inherit their deceased father's land in Canaan." Here Abba raised his voice and adopted an accusatory tone. "They did this in the face of established traditions amongst our people that women do not inherit property. They disregarded the fact that the proper place for a woman is on her husband's land. After four years, many people have learned of their cause but, in a practical sense, these women have violated the Torah without advancing their goals in the least.

"As part of their campaign, they paraded as a group through the various areas of our tribe in order to call attention to themselves. I submit that this behavior is immodest and not in keeping with the humility incumbent upon Hebrew women.

"It is well known that the tribe of Menashe is dedicated to marriage and family. We believe in large numbers of children, for they are our future.[4] These defendants not only deny the tribe the children that they might bring into the world but they also may encourage others to abandon motherhood for selfish, material causes.

"The last charge follows logically. If women are not married in an agricultural society, they will have no means of support. In their desperation, they may turn to prostitution. That practice, which is forbidden by the Torah, poses a severe threat to familial values.[5]

"We hold the mother of these sinful women fully responsible for their wrongdoing. If she had inculcated true moral values in their hearts, they would not behave improperly. Even now, she should be able to control them and insist they abandon their actions and get married.

"To verify that the daughters of Zelaphchad are guilty of the charges made against them, we will call a number of witnesses. Our first witness is Eliav, son of Shafat."

Eliav walked forward to the Center of the tent and took the chair reserved for witnesses. His usually cheerful face was now tense. This was the first time he had ever testified in public and his appearance revealed his anxieties.

"What is your age, Eliav?"

"I am twenty-three years old."

"How are you related to the defendants?"

"The daughters of Zelaphchad are my first cousins. Their mother is my aunt."

"Do you have more than a familial interest in any of the daughters?"

Eliav felt that he had nothing to hide. "Yes, I do. I have the deepest regard for Machla and I love her very much."

"How long have you felt this way?"

"Since I was sixteen."

"How did you pursue your interest in this woman?"

"I attended her Torah class and frequently engaged her in conversation."

"You attended her class? What Torah could you have learned from a woman that your father did not already teach you?"

"My father did engage a tutor for me when I was young. Here we are talking of advanced Torah study."

"You gained advanced Torah knowledge from a woman?"

"I did indeed. I would venture to say that all of those assembled here could learn from Machla."

Abba expected some catcalls or protest from the commanders but none were forthcoming. Most of them were fully aware of Machla's knowledge of Torah. When nothing was heard, the prosecutor returned to his main point.

"Did you propose marriage to Machla at any point?"

"I did so two years ago."

"What happened?"

"She declined my proposal."

"On what grounds?"

"She said that she wasn't ready to give me a definite answer because she had no other suitors to compare with me. She further stated that even if she did conclude that I was the right man for her, she would not consent to marriage. This was due to the decision that she and her sisters made to defer all marriage proposals, in the hope that such actions would further their cause."

"Do you feel that if it weren't for this outside factor she would marry you?"

Machla jumped to her feet quickly. "The question is pure conjecture and the witness is not in a position to answer it."

Abba argued for his right to ask the question. "If the answer is yes, it would show that the only factor preventing marriage on Machla's part is the conspiracy."

"It would show no such thing," Machla retorted. "What the witness may feel does not say with any certainty what someone else would do."

Gamliel ruled in Machla's favor, but Abba was not overly upset with the ruling. Having shown that Machla deferred acting on a marriage proposal was sufficient to suggest that she was part of a concerted action restricting marriage. Abba thanked the witness and was ready to dismiss him. "Do you wish to question the witness, Machla?" Gamliel asked.

"No, Your Honor." Machla saw nothing to be gained by annoying Eliav. He looked frightened enough as it was and she never felt anything but kindness toward him. He certainly was not responsible for her troubles.

Abba next called upon Shafat to testify. Shafat walked slowly to the center table and answered some preliminary questions about his identity and relationship to the defendants.

"Were you aware before Eliav's testimony that your son had proposed to Machla?" Abba asked.

"Yes, indeed."

"You were satisfied with his choice?"

"I most certainly was. Eliav sees in Machla lofty spiritual and intellectual qualities."

"Did Eliav advise you as to why the proposal was rejected?"

"He did and I felt badly on his behalf."

"Would you still want him to take to himself a wife against whom you and Azriel filed a complaint with this council of improper behavior?"

"Our motive in filing the complaint was not punitive but corrective. Machla is a highly educated and pious woman. She has unfortunately become obsessed with owning her father's land in Canaan and this obsession has caused her to go astray as it did to my two brothers, of blessed memory. It is my sincere hope that action by the council will cause her to see the error of her ways and encourage her to walk in the path of righteous Hebrew women."

"Did you do anything else to help your son with his problem?"

"I did. I had a talk with Machla at the Tribal Center. I told her that if she would marry my son, I would make her an offer with regard to owning property in Canaan."

"You did? May we know what that offer was?"

All eyes focused on Shafat. This was new information that no one had heard before and it was of critical importance to the case. "I have inherited half of the property of Zelaphchad, the land to which he was entitled in his own right and that which he inherited from Chefer and Ram. Following my death, my rights will pass to my two sons. With their consent, I offered to sell to the daughters of Zelaphchad most of our share of their father's property for a nominal amount. We also agreed to sell it to them again for the same sum after it reverted to us in the Jubilee year. In that way, they would legally own their father's land in Canaan during their lifetimes."

A buzz of conversation spread through the tent with this disclosure. Gamliel had to restore order before Abba could continue.

"Did they accept this offer?"

"No. They remain convinced that they can change our traditional inheritance laws so that women will inherit land directly, rather than by purchase or marriage."

"One more question if I may? Do you feel that Achla, the widow of Zelaphchad, is fulfilling her responsibilities as a Hebrew mother?"

"It is obvious from the complaint that we filed that we are not of such a mind."

"What should she do?"

"It is not for me to review past errors. If I were her, I would abandon my volunteer work and concentrate on getting my daughters married."

"Thank you Shafat, no further questions."

Machla felt that it wouldn't hurt to weaken the aspersions that Shafat cast on her mother. "From your testimony, it would appear that you think parents should encourage their children to get married. Did you tell Eliav to forget about me and find someone else with whom he can be fruitful?"

"No."

"How many other children do you have that are of marriageable age?"

"Two, Baruch and Bracha."

"Are they married?"

Machla had hoped to score points with this question. She didn't anticipate the answer, though, because she had not kept up with family events.

Shafat knew that Machla had made a slip. He answered in a strong voice, "I have successfully arranged marriage partners for both children. We have given Eliav till after this hearing. If there is no change in your attitude within the next few weeks, Machla, we have Eliav's permission to allow the marriage of the younger children to take place ahead of his own. Let us not forget for a moment that in the case of your mother, there are still five unmarried daughters at home."

Machla was unhappy to lose a point but she took her setback with grace. "My best wishes on the engagement of your children. I have no further questions."

Abba called a few additional witnesses to verify that each of the daughters of Zelaphchad had at one time or another revealed the reason why they were not getting married. He then called on Zila, the daughter of Patar, to testify. Zila, a woman in her sixties, had a wizened face lined with deep wrinkles. She was a first-class busybody who had appointed herself as keeper of the morals of the tribal women.

"Zila," Abba asked, "have you noticed the daily procession of the daughters of Zelaphchad to the Tribal Center?"

"Yes I have."

"Do you find it offensive?"

"I certainly do. I think that it is wanton and indecent. Young women should not attract attention to themselves. When a group of five women parade single file, it is haughty and immodest."

"How should they get to work?"

"They should walk together sedately and keep their eyes down. This upstart, Noah, waves to people and returns everyone's greetings. She is laughing and smiling all the time."

"Thank you, Zila," Abba said. "Your witness, Machla."

Machla couldn't resist. "Are you married, Zila?"

"No."

"No further questions," Machla said, getting a laugh out of the audience.

Zila, of course, was not one to let herself be victimized by Machla. On the way back from the witness stand she passed near the defense table and whispered in a voice filled with hate, "sluts."

Abba then called upon the council secretary. The latter was not asked to testify but to provide data.

"Honored secretary, can you tell us how the tribe of Menashe fares in comparison with others in matters of population?"

"We have not had a national census in twenty years but it is obvious that Menashe is growing faster than all others. This we know from the fact that we have gained more officers of thousands than any other tribe since the last census."

"Would you say our tribe is dedicated to fruitfulness?"

"Yes, this tradition harks back to the days of Jacob who blessed Joseph, the father of our tribe, with blessings of the womb."

"Based on our current birthrate, how many children would you expect five healthy young mothers to produce if they were married?"

"Between twenty and thirty offspring at the very least."

"Then you would say that the behavior of the daughters of Zelaphchad, who are deferring marriage, affects tribal values?"

"It most certainly does."

When Abba finished with the secretary, Machla asked him, "Do you keep records of tribal services?"

"That is part of my responsibilities."

"Do you keep track of how many people have availed themselves of the tribal health care service?"

"We have a slate and we enter a mark for each request."

"Do you have any idea how many lives were saved by this service?"

"We don't have an exact count but, based on comments and reports, I would say in excess of 100."

"Would you say that saving 100 lives of people does more for the tribal population than not giving birth to twenty or thirty children?"

"From a statistical point of view, the population grows either by increasing the birth rate or decreasing the mortality rate. I don't think it is fair or correct to link the two."

"You are probably right, honored secretary, although the fact still remains that if my sisters and I were married we would not have had the time to develop and maintain the health service. Of course, that is not our reason for deferring marriage. I mention it to show that the daughters of Zelaphchad are not indifferent to the value of life."

Machla could tell from the audible audience response that she had made a winning point. She allowed Abba to continue. "While reserving the right to call rebuttal witnesses and make a summary at a later point, the prosecution rests."

Machla stood up and waited for the attention of the audience. Abba had made a very good case and she would have to present a strong defense to overcome it.

"Members of the council, first let me commend you for your concern with the moral values of our tribe. In connection with our case, I wish to introduce several motions. I will also ask for consideration of one motion that is not directly related to the charges against us but will help us in our cause.

"At the outset, I move that the council dismiss all charges filed against our mother, Achla.

"Secondly, I request that all charges against those of my sisters who did not receive proposals of marriage be dropped.

"Thirdly, I urge the council to vote for the dismissal of all charges against the other members of my family on the basis of the arguments that I will present.

"Finally, although not related to the case at hand, I would like the council to take action on the problem of our inheritance in the Land of Canaan and see what can be done to help us.

"As my first witness, I call upon my revered mother to testify."

As Achla walked to the witness table, all of the daughters stood up as a mark of respect. Achla knew that Machla would be protective of her during her testimony and she was not unduly concerned. The pre-trial anxieties had subsided and were replaced by pride in her daughters. She was happy with the way Machla was conducting herself and with the respect shown to her children. She could not hide all the signs of middle age but she dressed and stood with confidence. Her clothing, which was all sewn by her own hand, reflected both great skill and good taste.

"Mother, did you receive a religious education of your own?"

"I was never given a formal education in the Land of Egypt. My parents, by example, taught me the basic values incumbent upon a Hebrew woman. When they were teaching my brothers about the history and traditions of the Hebrews, I listened in. There was no formal education for women at that time."

"Did the lack of Torah education of your children cause you concern?"

"Of course it did. I was so busy taking care of five young daughters by myself that I had very little time to devote to the problem of their education. I was greatly concerned, however, that they were not getting any."

"Did you make any efforts to do something about it?"

"I tried very hard to secure a father for my daughters. I applied for a Levirate marriage and I was open to proposals."

"Did you feel that your daughters were under control?"

"With the exception of Noah, who was born after Zelaphchad died, I never had disciplinary problems with any of my children." Noah gave a weak smile when reflecting upon her childhood sins. Many of those in the audience smiled broadly.

"Did your children finally receive a Torah education?"

"It is well known that my daughters are the most learned women in Torah, not only in Menashe but probably among all the tribes of Israel. All of them can recite the entire Torah by heart from the words 'In the beginning,' onward. For this I have to thank you, Machla. You devoted five full years to teaching your sisters. Even now, you are constantly adding to your own knowledge and to theirs as well."

"Are all of your daughters strict observers of the Torah?"

"Yes, indeed."

"Did you in any way encourage them to defer their marriages and reject proposals?"

"Not at all. I pleaded with them to forget about land in Canaan. That passion already caused the loss of my husband and I am terrified that my daughters will abandon their lives for the same cause."

"What did you say when you heard of their plans?"

"I said they were stark, raving mad. They should forget the nonsense and get married as Hebrew girls should do."

"Do you, personally, believe in the traditions of marriage and family?"

"Very much so. I stress these values over and over again."

"Thank you, mother." Machla was quite pleased with the competent way in which her mother had testified. "I will not ask you any additional questions, mother, but is there a statement that you wish to make to the council?"

"There is something that I have to say to these worthy gentlemen." Achla's voice was clear but a touch of sadness could be detected. "After I failed to persuade my brothers-in-law to participate in Levirate marriage, I petitioned the council to help me find a husband so that my children would be brought up properly. This council did not act on the petition and was utterly indifferent to the plight of a widow with five daughters. Now, all of a sudden, they are concerned with finding marriage partners for five beautiful women who do not need their help in the least. My daughter, Noah, has received more than twenty valid marriage proposals. I cannot see why the council has to waste its precious time worrying about her instead of helping those who are truly in need."

The revelation that her mother had sought the help of the council to find a husband, came as a shock to Machla. She had had no idea how desperate her mother was to remarry.

Abba chose not to ask Achla any questions. For the next phase of the defense, Machla's plan was to call her three middle sisters one by one and get the cases against them dismissed on the grounds that they had not rejected marriage proposals.

"If it please the court, I will seek to separate from this case those who should not have been charged. I am sure that the learned gentlemen are aware that the elders have taught that mere intent to violate the law of the Torah is not punishable."[6]

So saying, she called Tirza to testify. Tirza walked briskly to the witness stand. She was the most physically fit of the daughters. Almost as tall as Machla, she was somewhat trimmer. She regularly walked to many different places, both in and out of the tribe, for the purpose of doing good deeds. "Tirza, please do not be offended by my inquiries. I will ask all my sisters a series of questions to prove that they are not guilty of haughty or immodest behavior, one of the charges in the case."

"Do you observe all of the commandments of the Torah?"

"All that I am aware of."

"Do you dress in keeping with the traditions of modesty of Hebrew women?"

"Yes."

"Have you ever had any physical contact with a man?"

"Other than with my father, no."

Machla was now going to ask the key question about proposals. She had already lost one point in the trial by not knowing details of family events. In the case of her sister, she couldn't imagine that Tirza would have received a proposal without telling her.

"No gentlemen has ever proposed to you, has he?"

Abba was on his feet in a flash. "Counsel is guiding the witness in her response."

Gamliel ruled in his favor and told Machla to ask the questions directly.

Machla responded, "I am sorry. Tirza, has any gentleman ever proposed to you?"

Tirza hesitated for a second, and then asked. "Am I required to answer the question?"

Abba, realizing that Machla had again fallen into a trap, took advantage of the situation. "If she doesn't answer the question that has been posed, I will ask it myself later. It is very relevant to the case."

Gamliel ruled that Tirza could wait until Abba asked her the question. She could also elect to answer it voluntarily.

"There was one gentleman who asked for my hand in marriage," Tirza conceded.

"Was it a serious proposal?"

"Yes."

"You did not tell your family about it?"

"Since the proposal was not accepted, I did not see the need."

Machla did not want to ask her why she turned the proposal down as there was no point in having Tirza incriminate herself. She was quite sure that Tirza had done so in conformity with the plans of the sisters to defer marriage and she was equally sure that Abba would catch her on it.

As soon as she released her sister, Abba asked her why she had turned down the proposal and Tirza said wisely, "I did not give the proposal full consideration because, at that time, my sisters and I were deferring marriage. I do not know what my decision would have been had there been no external factors."

Machla was going to call Hogla next and was fearful of another surprise. Nevertheless, she felt compelled to establish her sisters' moral behavior and she had committed herself to calling them all. After Hogla answered all questions regarding religious behavior in the affirmative, Machla asked her about proposals. Hogla clearly didn't want to show that she was not as desirable as the others.

"Well," she said, "there was this one man I knew who did say that if he were to get married he would choose someone like me."

"Sorry, Hogla, that's not enough. Was there an actually serious proposal or not?"

"No."

Machla then called on Milka and she expected no trouble because Milka was not even twenty-one.

"Have you had any proposals?"

"Yes."

"Not more than one?" Abba objected at once and the chair again cautioned Machla on making assumptions. Machla rephrased the question. "Was there more than one?"

"Yes."

"I do not have to ask you how many and I don't imagine that Abba will." Again Machla misjudged. Abba did ask her how many. When Milka sought to elude the question, Abba pointed out to Gamliel that repeated violations of the law were significant and Milka should answer. The chair ruled in his favor.

"I have had three proposals of marriage and I did not accept any of them."

The last of the sisters to testify was Noah. After completing the religious behavior questions, Machla took a fresher approach. She had stumbled twice and was not going to do it again.

"Noah, are there any eligible gentlemen in this tribe who have not asked for your hand in marriage?"

"Not too many," Noah answered with a dazzling smile. "I told those who approached me directly that I was too young. I told my mother to say the same thing. A girl of nineteen is not really ready for marriage." She gave Machla a knowing look that indicated it would be wise not to ask her any further questions. Machla took the hint.

Abba didn't even question Noah because her answers would have been as anticipated. Given her vast popularity, he didn't want to take a chance of offending her in any way in front of the audience.

Machla quickly reviewed where she stood. She was sure, that her mother and Hogla would be exonerated. That left her and three sisters subject to the council's censure. She would have to attack the substance of the charges in order to acquit the four of them. At that point, she realized that she herself had not yet testified.

"If it please the council, I am scheduled to testify next. Since I am counsel for the defense, I cannot do both at the same time. I will ask my sister, Noah, to act as defense counsel and call me as a witness." Noah had been waiting for the moment all morning.

"Your Excellency, am I now acting as defense counsel?"

"You are, Noah," Gamliel responded.

"In that case I have a motion to make. I move that the charges against me be dropped on the grounds that, although I committed the behavior in question, I did so under coercion."

Machla turned pale when she heard what her sister was trying to do. For the first time her self-confidence at the trial was shaken. Ruefully, she thought that her sister might do their case more harm than all the learned scholars in the tribe who were prosecuting them. What hurt most was that Noah was the one who had first dreamt up the plan of deferring marriages and she, herself, turned down more proposals than all of the other sisters combined. Now she was trying to escape any censure and leave the onus upon her sisters. Noah started to question Machla.

"I know that you are observant but, for the record, I will ask you to affirm it."

"I keep all of the laws of the Torah to the best of my knowledge and ability."

"Is it true that you have a violent and aggressive nature?"

The question caught Machla completely off guard. After reflecting for a moment she responded, "Perhaps I may be aggressive in certain areas but definitely not prone to violence."

"Are you sure?"

"Yes."

"Would you mind if I refreshed your memory?"

"I guess not." Machla was reviewing her relationship with Noah but could not think of any behavior that could be considered violent. Noah was devious, however, and might come up with something.

"Do you remember an incident when I repeated a nasty remark to our mother? You wanted to know where I had heard it and I wasn't inclined to tell you." Machla frowned. She could not believe that Noah would use this occasion, so critical to the cause, to dredge up an altercation that should have been ancient history. Apparently, after eleven years, Noah was going to get even for the time that Machla brought her into line.

"I remember the incident."

"Do you remember what you threatened to do if I would not tell you?"

"I said that I would break you in two or words to that effect."

"Did you grab my arm and twist it behind my back hard enough to almost break it?"

"I guess I did."

"On certain mornings when I overslept and did not get up to gather the manna, did you wake me up in a violent manner?"

"I wouldn't say violent."

"Did you brutally kick me in a certain part of my anatomy?"

"On one occasion."

"Did you pull my hair?"

"On several occasions."

"No further questions to the witness but I would like to ask the legal advisor a question. Your Honor, if a person commits a wrongful act under duress, is he subject to censure?"

The legal advisor proceeded cautiously. He knew that Noah was almost as well-versed in Torah as Machla and he did not want to make any errors.

"In general terms, a person is not excused for wrongful behavior because of coercion. Each person is responsible for his own behavior and, if someone tells him to act wrongfully, he is supposed to say no because he is already sworn to correct behavior at Sinai."

"What if someone threatens that person's life?"

"In that case, there are only three commandments for which one has to yield his life rather than violate the Law." Noah knew the three commandments but wanted the counselor to recite them.[7]

"What commandments are they?"

"A person has to sanctify the name of God and yield his life rather than violate the laws of murder, idolatry or immorality."

"Will you agree that none of these laws are involved in the case before the council?"

"I think that is obvious."

"Then I would have been permitted to join my sisters in their behavior?"

"I hardly think that you were in a life-threatening situation that would have exempted you from observing the laws."

"How would you like to be told that you will be torn in two? How would you like to have your arm twisted to breaking point and be subject to constant violent physical and verbal abuse?"

Noah was the consummate actress and put on one of the best theatrical performances ever seen in the tribe. With tears in her eyes she told the court that she was deathly afraid of defying her sister and that she had to go along under complete and total duress. She stressed that she was only fifteen years of age when the plan was undertaken. She claimed to be absolutely terrified of Machla and fearful for her very life.

The legal advisor was unmoved and remained skeptical. He was suspicious that Noah was up to some mischief and he directed some pointed questions to her.

"Don't you think that Machla was using nothing more than regular discipline in handling one who was known to be an unruly child?"

"Do I look like an unruly child?" Noah smiled in glorious innocence.

"I cannot tell by looking at you but so I have heard."

"A learned man such as you should not believe everything that he hears."

"Tell me, Noah," he persisted, "if you had no reason to be afraid of your sister would you have joined the plan? Before I can offer legal advise to the council on your motion, it is important for me to have your answer."

Noah responded in all innocence. "Who, me? I love children and I love to cook and I dream of keeping a tent in sparkling order. I can think of nothing better than marriage."

Her sisters struggled to contain their laughter. Noah carried on for another few minutes extolling marriage and family.

When she finished, Machla completed her testimony and left the witness stand. Noah then returned to where the family was sitting, winked broadly at Machla and relinquished the role of defense counsel. Noah, with her acting, had established a defense of coerced behavior that would get her excused from the censure that might be imposed on the daughters of Zelaphchad.

Machla called several witnesses including Barak to prove that she and her sisters were modest and observant. She then addressed the legal counselor.

"Since we are accused of violating a law of the Torah, can you tell the council which law is involved?"

"In drawing up the charges, the council was referring to the very first command of the Torah to be fruitful and multiply." Machla was weaving a net that would produce critical admissions on the part of the counselor.[8]

"Can a man ever be accused of violating this law or be punished for doing so?"

"Possibly in extreme circumstances, he might be."

"Would you care to explain?"

"A person cannot be punished for breaking a law that extends over a period of time until the given time is passed. Let us say, for example, that a man has a week to perform a certain task. He cannot be punished until the week is over. In the case of being fruitful, a man may be fruitful to the very end his life so there is always a chance for him to observe the commandment. Of course, if he had himself castrated so that he could not perform the law, or if he took a vow in God's name that he would not do so, there might be some grounds for censure." At this point Machla closed the trap.

"Are you aware that being fruitful and multiplying is a positive command?"

The legal advisor realized his error. "I am aware," he said with some embarrassment, "that it is a positive command and that there are only two positive commands in the Torah, that of Passover and circumcision, which are subject to punishment. The example I gave would apply only to negative commands. It is still possible, however, that council censure might be appropriate in such a case even though no punishment prescribed by the Torah can be imposed."[9]

"Is a woman subject to the commandment, 'Be fruitful and multiply?'"

"A woman is not so commanded because it is not in her control to execute such a command. It is the man who takes the woman in marriage."[10]

"If a woman never got married then, she would not be in violation of the command?"

"There is talk among the elders to create a prohibition against women who choose to remain single throughout their lives."

"Has such a prohibition ever been adopted?"

"No, and I am not sure that it ever will."

"In any event, you admit that under the Torah Law a woman cannot violate this commandment?"

"You are correct."

Winning this point gave Machla a lift because it seriously diminished the case against her and her sisters. She also picked up the feverish whispering in the audience which indicated admiration of her knowledge and performance.

Addressing the council, Machla continued in a strong voice. "It has now been established that we did not violate the law of the Torah. To claim that we violated the spirit of the Law is a very complex matter. If we had prevented all men from getting married, it might have been said that we acted contrary to the spirit of the Law. It so happens that there is a large surplus of women in the tribe due to the untimely death of so many men in the desert. There are actually enough women for many men to enjoy plural marriages. The fact that a mere five women are not available for marriage, when thousands are willing and able to do so, means that we are not endangering the observance of this commandment in any significant way. Remember that we are not opposed to the concept of marriage and the birth of children. We totally support such institutions and we hope to participate in them ourselves as soon as we resolve our inheritance problem."

Machla paused for a deep breath and then continued. "We have earlier established that our behavior has been modest and that we did nothing to undermine tribal values. There remains only the suggestion that those who avoid marriage might become destitute and be forced into prostitution. Let me assure the council that having been proven to be women of modesty, we ourselves will not be guilty of immoral behavior. If we were ever confronted with such a choice we would immediately elect to get married. As for other women, it has been established by the alternate defense counsel that each person is responsible for his own behavior. In no way can we ever be held to blame for what others may do.

"In the light of this presentation I request that my third motion, which called for dismissal of the charges, be accepted by the council." Thereupon, Machla rested the case for the defense.

Abba took stock of where the prosecution stood and was not at all pleased. Clearly, he would not secure a majority vote on four of the charges and the vote on the fifth, the one dealing with the spirit of the Law, was very much in doubt. He had prepared a contingency plan that he now found necessary to invoke. The plan would abandon the four charges, which he deemed lost anyway, and would redefine the fifth charge so that it would have a much better chance to survive. Turning to the chair, he used his privilege to call additional witnesses. "I have a pair of witnesses whom I wish to call in rebuttal to Machla's argument about the spirit of the Law. I ask that Simon, the son of Hosea, and Benjamin, the son of Michael, be summoned to testify." Two mature, middle-aged men walked to the witness table. Simon, in the lead, seemed the more sedate of the two. His beard was longer and grayer and his brow more furrowed. Benjamin had a more rugged appearance and a heartier look.

"If this were a regular court," Abba said, "we would have the witnesses questioned separately. Since we are only a council, I will take the liberty of letting them testify as a unit."

"No objections," Machla said. She was deeply concerned as to what the pair would have to say.

"I will ask Simon to speak for both of you. Will you please tell the council, Simon, what assignment you were given?"

Simon spoke slowly to the council. "In preparation for this case, we were asked to travel to the tribe of Judah to seek a legal opinion on the issues before the council from the most learned legal advisors available. We did travel to Judah and were directed to an outstanding scholar, Elchanan ben Uriah."

"What is his capacity in Judah?"

"He is the legal advisor to the tribal council. He sits as an alternate judge on the tribal court and is in charge of all programs of higher Torah studies in the tribe of Judah. He enjoys a reputation of being a profound scholar in a tribe that is known for its Torah studies."

"Can you tell us why the council sought an opinion from a scholar outside of the tribe?"

"The council felt that in a matter where the issues were so complex and the ramifications so far-reaching, an outside opinion was fully warranted. The council action today may set a precedent for all the tribes of Israel."

"Were you successful in securing his opinion?"

"Yes. He gave us a great deal of time and spent an even longer period studying the case before reaching his conclusion."

"And what was that conclusion?"

"He told us that based on the facts of the case as we related them, the women were not directly in violation of the first commandment of the Torah. He then explained what a violation of the spirit of a law means. Where a person is subject to a law, yet manages to circumvent the law in a way that technically does not violate it, he may be charged with acting contrary to the spirit of the law. Take, for example, the case of a man who reaps his field and leaves the droppings for the poor, as required. If the man then stations a lion in the field to prevent the poor from reaching their food, he has violated the spirit of the law but not the letter. The spirit of the law is to help the poor and he has defeated the intent of the law. Since the commandments to leave parts of the harvest for the poor are stated in both positive and negative terms, he is subject to censure for his behavior.

"Judge Elchanan then added the following: 'In a case where women are not subject to the letter of a law in the first place, they can not ever be charged with violating the spirit of that law. If there were only one man and one woman in the world, and the woman did not permit the man to cohabit with her, there might be some room to maneuver. It could possibly be argued that she is violating the spirit of the law by preventing the man, who is subject to the law, from observing it. At the present time, however, if a woman does not accept a man for marriage, he has ample opportunities to approach other women. The woman who refused the man did not prevent him from observing the law and does not deserve censure.

"The council should not have charged these women with conspiracy to violate the first commandment, but with conspiring to endanger the survival of the Hebrew nation.

"A conspiracy may be defined as a concerted action by a group of people to do evil. It must involve more than one person but does not require many. It could involve a commandment, as in the case of those who urged worship of the golden calf, but even that is not obligatory. The conspiracy of Korach against Moses or the spies against the Land of Canaan did not involve commandments, yet posed a direct threat to national survival. The Lord dealt harshly with all of these evil actions.

"If the action of the daughters of Zelaphchad were widely imitated and other women started avoiding marriage for various personal causes, it would have the potential of destroying the Hebrew nation. In fact, there is an historic precedent in the area of limiting procreation. When Amram, the father of Moses, and his rabbinic court suspended cohabitation in the face of Pharaoh's decree to kill all male children, Miriam said that his edict posed a greater threat to the Hebrew people than Pharaoh's decree. While Pharaoh's law would only kill the male children, Amram's ruling would destroy the entire nation. Amram reconsidered and rescinded the ruling.

"Before our nation enters Canaan, the Torah will certainly instruct the courts how to deal with conspiratorial behavior. For the moment, the judicial and legislative bodies of the nation must deal with such actions under the powers inherent in the laws of the 'Rodeph', the pursuer. If one sees a man pursuing another person with the intent to kill, or pursuing a woman with the intent to rape, he is required under Torah Law to intervene and attempt to save the victim. The daughters of Zelaphchad in this conspiracy may be deemed 'pursuers' who threaten the survival of the tribe. The council, whose duty it is to protect the interests of Menashe, must therefore intervene. If a censure is sufficient to disperse the conspirators, it should issue one. If more than that is required, it should refer the matter to the tribal court."

Abba was very pleased with the report and said to the witnesses: "On behalf of the council I thank you for the testimony you have given. Your Excellency, I request that the charge against the daughters of Zelaphchad be understood by the council in the light of the testimony just offered. Since the Torah was given to protect the Hebrew people, actions which threaten the survival of a tribe, as part of a nation, are contrary to the spirit of the Torah and justly deserve to be censured."

Gamliel waited patiently for conversation about the report to subside. Slowly turning to Machla he then said, "You may question the witnesses now."

Machla was not fully recovered from the impact of the testimony. The clarity and power of the ruling was far above anything she had ever heard in Menashe. The grim realization set in that the scholars of her tribe were mediocre in comparison with what was available elsewhere. What Elchanan Ben Uriah had done in one stroke was to give the right to future courts and councils to undertake wide-ranging actions within the framework of protecting the welfare of the nation. Although it was a concept that broke new ground, it was a very sound idea and rested on a strong rational foundation. No society can long permit any sector of the population to undermine its existence and must adopt defensive measures. It would, however, be more than twenty years before this concept would be formally defined in Torah laws relating to kings and courts in the Land of Canaan.

Machla was not prepared to offer a defense against this new testimony and she realized, sadly, that she and her sisters would not emerge unscathed from the council hearing. She felt that it would be futile to ask for a delay to study the opinion or to claim that the new approach went beyond the original charge. The council was now convinced that the daughters of Zelaphchad posed a mortal threat to Menashe and that it was their sacred duty to protect the tribe. The commanders would certainly not be moved in such a situation by legal technicalities.

She addressed the witness hoping to salvage what she could. "I would like to summarize your testimony if I may. You did say that your authority ruled that we were not in violation of the first commandment of the Torah, even though we acted as a group?"

"Yes I did."

"You did say that if we had done what we did as individuals and not in a group, we would not have posed any threat to the tribe?"

"Yes I did."

"Did Elchanan ben Uriah feel that we acted immodestly?"

"He said that no actions reported to him appeared to be of an immodest nature."

"Did he feel that we were undermining tribal values or leading women into sin?"

"He made no comment on those points."

"I have no further questions."

At this point Abba concluded his case by saying that the facts and the testimony spoke for themselves and that the council should vote to censure the daughters of Zelaphchad for violating the spirit of the Torah. Other than that they could vote on the various defense motions in accordance with their consciences. Abba apparently now felt that if even if one of the charges stood up, the daughters of Zelaphchad would have to alter their behavior.

Machla had no further statements to make.

Gamliel then called for a recess to allow for the council members to consider the evidence and vote on a verdict. Members of the Chefer family on both sides of the case stepped out of the tent to allow the commanders to proceed with their deliberations.

Several anxious hours passed before the verdict was announced. When the council was ready with its decision, the plaintiffs were asked to return and enter the tent. The defendants were requested to remain standing and hear the verdict. With a silent prayer in their hearts that the council would act in a reasonable manner, the daughters of Zelaphchad and their mother rose and listened intently.

Part 2

THE DESERT

*"THE DAUGHTERS OF ZELAPHCHAD
WERE WISE"*

Gamliel rose to his feet and surveyed the audience. After a pause to heighten the suspense, he announced the verdict in his ponderous voice:

> "After due deliberation, the council of Menashe finds as follows:
>
> "Achla, the widow of Zelaphchad, is not considered derelict in the upbringing of her daughters or responsible for their misdeeds. Charges against her are dismissed unanimously by the council."

Although this part of the verdict was expected, the daughters breathed a sigh of relief when their mother was legally exonerated.

> "By unanimous decision, charges against Hogla, the daughter of Zelaphchad, are dismissed.
>
> "By majority vote of the council, the charges against Noah, the daughter of Zelaphchad, are dismissed. The council commends her for waging an outstanding defense to prove her innocence. It accepts her claim that forces beyond her control exerted an undue influence upon her behavior.
>
> "By unanimous decision of the council, four of the five charges against the remaining defendants are canceled. By a majority vote, the council herewith censures the

daughters of Zelaphchad, Machla, Tirza and Milka, for acting contrary to the spirit of the Torah in endangering the survival of the tribe of Menashe. We call upon these women to immediately cease their improper actions. We feel that this censure will be sufficient to cause these women to abandon their conspiracy and live in keeping with the traditions of Israel. In the light of this hope, the council does not find it necessary to forward this verdict to the tribal court for further action.

"With regard to the additional motion of the defense, the council will appoint a committee to look into the problem of inheritance rights for women and consider what can be done to assist the daughters of Zelaphchad in their cause."

Pandemonium broke loose in the tent. Noah's friends outside cheered loudly and Noah waved a victory signal which caused them to further amplify their support. Machla signaled Gamliel that she wished to make a statement. When the chair quieted the audience, Machla addressed the council.

"We wish to thank the council for dismissing charges against my mother and two of my sisters. We regret the censure of the remaining sisters on one of the five original charges, but we will not ignore its message. From this day on, we shall not act as a group in the matter of marriage. We will hold no meetings or discussions on the subject and we will not coordinate our activities. Each sister will act individually according to the dictates of her heart and treat marriage proposals on their merit. This decision will by its nature prevent us from marching in a group in order to attract attention. In this connection, we thank the council for ignoring the testimony of those who deem themselves paragons of virtue." Although Machla did not harbor any bitterness against the council, she was angry with herself for losing the case.

Gamliel was pleased with the statement. "That is a wise decision on your part. Despite my reservations about you serving as a defense counsel, I must admit that you performed in an acceptable manner. With more experience, you might compare favorably with the male attorneys in the tribe. In the near future, I hope to dance at your wedding. This hearing stands adjourned."

Noah smiled at Machla. "Remember that your defense was only termed acceptable while mine was considered outstanding." So saying, she disappeared quickly to join the crowd of her well-wishers.

Machla and the three middle sisters walked back to their tent area after hearing the verdict. It was already late in the afternoon and there was no point in returning to work. They had arranged substitutes for the full day, not knowing how long the hearing would last. Achla tarried a while because she was still determined not to walk through the tribe in her daughters' parade. This was the last time the sisters would walk in a group. In fact, they already started walking side by side instead of single file. For a long interval after reaching home, there were no signs of Noah.

They hadn't eaten during the proceedings and were quite hungry. "Where is Noah?" Machla wondered aloud. When the sisters failed to answer, Machla suspected something. "All right, where is Noah?" she demanded.

Finally, Milka, who was closest to Noah, volunteered. "She went into hiding. She was afraid that you were going to break her in two and torture her with indescribable savagery."

Machla laughed aloud, "Does she think I'll be mad at her for stealing the show and outsmarting us all?"

"Yes!" the sisters shouted in unison.

"Do you all think the same way?"

"Yes," they chanted in chorus.

"Listen girls," Machla pleaded in exasperation, "I am a gentle soul, I wouldn't hurt a fly. Furthermore, I love my sister, Noah, despite her miserable behavior."

Milka went into a superb imitation of Noah at the council. "Is it true, Machla, that you once spilled a pitcher of ice-cold water on my poor little head?"

Machla realized that she would be the butt of jokes about her tyranny for many months to come. "All right," she said. "Whoever knows where Noah is hiding, send this peace offering to her. She's probably very hungry." Machla raised some manna cakes but no one took them from her.

"If I bring her anything from you she will make me taste it first," said Milka. "Anyway, her girlfriends gave her a victory party and she's certainly not hungry."

Machla was getting a little frustrated. "Listen girls, someone tell me where she is hiding and I will talk to her myself." Machla was greeted by loud silence. Beneath all the jesting, Machla realized, there was an element of truth. Since taking over for her mother, she had ruled over her sisters very strictly. It was a necessity with Noah because she could evade any control or management. The other sisters didn't need such strict supervision but Machla couldn't make any exceptions.

"Well, then," Machla said in defeat, "tell Noah to come back and tonight I will emancipate all of my sisters from supervision and control." The sisters cheered loudly and went out to fetch Noah who was sitting behind one of the tents listening to the conversation.

"Welcome my abused and tormented sister," Machla said. "You have no doubt returned to apologize to me for besmirching my good name and to us all for escaping the censure at everyone else's expense."

Noah pretended full innocence. "I really had no choice. A public censure would have hurt my chances to find a qualified partner in marriage. You know how careful a girl has to be about her reputation."

Machla raised the manna cake and was about to throw it at Noah when her sisters started yelling, "Violence! Violence!"

Machla quickly dropped the cake but said to Noah, "Nothing can possibly hurt your chances in marriage. For reasons which I cannot fathom, there are hosts of men who want you."

"Lineage, that's what it is."

"Don't I have the same lineage as you?"

"I guess there is a black sheep in every flock."

Machla gave up the bantering because she was no match for Noah in repartee. Instead, she made the announcement that her sisters were anxious to hear. Machla called her mother, who had arrived at the tent, to join the discussion.

"From this day on," Machla declared, "I consider all of my sisters fully grown up and emancipated. I am no longer responsible for any of their deeds or misdeeds. Never again will I beat, kick, yell, cajole or otherwise abuse them in order to make sure that they act in a civilized manner. Is my message clear?"

Noah organized the four younger sisters in an impromptu freedom dance.

"We shall sing to the Lord," she chanted, "for He has wrought great deeds. He has brought us forth from bondage once more."

"Why are you turning them loose?" Achla demanded to know.

"So it should not be said by anyone that by my fearsome personality I kept our illegal conspiracy in force. I plan to abide fully by the decision of the council."

"You plan to get married?" her mother asked hopefully.

"The council didn't order us to get married. All they wanted was that we consider proposals on their merits. That I intend to do and I guess that my sisters will do the same."

"Well, I hope that the new behavior will be an improvement. Sooner or later, if the girls don't have to worry about you, one of them will give in and get married. When that happens the rest will follow."

Eliav called on Machla a week later to see whether his chances had improved as a result of the case. "I'm sorry my father and uncle dragged you through the hearing," he said. "I couldn't prevent them. But I want to tell you that you were wonderful. I savored every word and admired your poise and self-control."

"Thank you, Eliav, you say the nicest things."

"Machla, I still want to marry you. Do you find it in your heart now to say yes?"

"No, Eliav, I am not ready to accept. You are still the only one in this world who loves me the way I am, but I do not want to enter a marriage on that basis. I want to remake my personality so that I will become a warmer person, more human, more sensitive. I can only do so by developing friendships and communicating with others. I took the first step by giving up responsibility for my sisters. This will give me more time to work on self-improvement."

Eliav was not at a loss for his response. "I am not unaware of your problem, Machla, and I know of these faults. They stem from the fact that you and your sisters were orphans and that you found it necessary to assume the role of their father. They are well adjusted now but you are still fighting the wars. You want to be a great scholar who will change the world and its traditions. You are so driven that you cannot relax and take life a little easier. I think that marriage will settle you down. You have achieved more in your youth than most women achieve in a lifetime. Isn't it time to curb some of the ambition that makes you frighten others away?"

"How come it doesn't bother you?"

"I could say that love, like bribery, 'blinds the eyes of the wise,' but that is not the case here.[1] Do you remember teaching us why the holy ark was plated with gold on the inside as well as the outside even though no one can see the interior gold? It was to teach us to look into the hearts of people, for that is what counts. If a person has a golden exterior, but a wicked heart, there is no hope for him. In your case, the exterior is rough but I have looked into the heart below it and I see pure gold."[2]

Machla turned aside so Eliav wouldn't see her tears. She regained her composure in a few seconds.

"I hope what you say is true. I am going to try to become a complete person in the next few years. Listen, Eliav, I don't want you to waste any more of your time on me. A man of twenty-three needs a mate, and you should not delay marriage waiting for a confused woman who doesn't know what she wants or needs. Join your brother and sister in getting married. If I can't find someone who loves me as you do, it will be my misfortune. I will blame no one but myself."

"We have had this discussion before, Machla, and I am not ready to change my mind. My brother and sister have no reason to delay their marriage, but I do. I will wait for you as long as you are not married to someone else, even if I have to wait until our nation enters Canaan. I will not enter the Holy Land without a wife because it is not proper for me to do so. Until that day, though, as long as you remain single, I will, too."

Machla had a look of acute despair on her face. "I cannot prevent you from doing so, Eliav. As you heard at the hearing last week, a man cannot be punished for violating the first commandment of the Torah until his dying day. As for me, I, too, will not enter the Holy Land without a husband as long as anyone is willing to marry me." The conversation ended on that note.

The years passed by and, contrary to everyone's expectations, the daughters of Zelaphchad, acting individually and for various reasons, chose not to get married. When they received proposals, they acted on the basis of the worthiness of the candidate. Of course, the main test of worthiness related to the man's views on property ownership by women. No men passed such a test to their satisfaction and thus the sisters remained single. They still worked on the health care project but only on an occasional basis. They had trained enough volunteers to assume most of the work. Achla divided her time between teaching her sewing class and bemoaning the fact that her daughters were still unmarried.

With the exceptions of Eliav and Meir, all of Machla's cousins were building large families. Eliav remained single by choice. Meir had been married but his wife suffered severe complications during the course of the birth of her second child. Neither the mother nor the baby could be saved. Childbirth under desert conditions was very hazardous and both infant and maternal mortality were high. To avoid additional risk, the sacred Hebrew practice of circumcision was suspended in the desert. That helped more male children survive but little more could be done for the mothers and daughters.[3]

The Lord did not shorten the period of wandering in the desert for the children of Israel. Rather, He fulfilled his pledge that none of the men who left Egypt beyond the age of twenty would live to enter Canaan. Most of the generation died of natural causes, but Moses did reveal at a later time that the hand of God was at work in hastening their deaths. Machla was saddened by the death of her uncles Shafat and Azriel. She also mourned the death of Gamliel, the tribal leader. Barak was still alive but now served as a judge rather than as a commander — a change made necessary by his failing health. Despite his weakened condition, he still kept Machla informed of new Torah laws and court precedents.[4]

With decreased responsibilities at home and in the tribe, Machla had more time to devote to herself. As she aged, her personality mellowed. Gone were the angry outbursts and the rampant aggressiveness. Her appearance also took on a softer look. She occasionally spoke to single men and widowers but no deep relationships developed. Some married women still viewed her with suspicion while others befriended her. Her social life was satisfactory, albeit relatively limited.

Noah never had any social problems but, as she approached the age of thirty, the number of potential suitors declined. Heads still turned when she walked by, but it was a mature type of beauty that the viewers admired rather than a youthful one. The other sisters led a full, if not exciting life.

The sisters did not abandon their dream of land in Canaan but the goal survived only in a dormant state. The council committee appointed to look into the question reported back that it could not change the inheritance laws. If the daughters brought the case to the High Court, the council would submit a supporting brief. If all else failed, the council stood ready to award the Zelaphchad daughters some publicly held tribal land. This would not be a general policy for all women in a similar situation, but special compensation for the years of tribal service contributed by an outstanding family.

Machla was determined that the family would try its case in court before the tribes entered Canaan but she put off any action for lack of confidence. Her experience in the council case convinced her that knowledge of the Torah in itself was insufficient to win cases in court. There was an art to conducting a case but it only came with practice. She felt that she couldn't adequately present the case by herself, nor could the family hope to find high-ranking scholars who would volunteer to help. There were no funds available to the family to engage such scholars. All the work they had done for others was on a voluntary basis and no compensation was ever received. She reviewed the mistakes she made at the council hearing hundreds of times. At night, as she lay in her tent, she would replay the scenario wondering whether a word here or there would have made some difference. Even though her sisters never criticized her performance, she herself, could never rationalize her failure to do better.

The situation took a turn, however, one fall day in Machla's thirty-fourth year. An event occurred that would lead to a change in the destiny of the daughters of Zelaphchad, especially Machla, and the history of the children of Israel.

Machla awoke early that morning with nothing special planned for the day. The Sukkoth festival had passed and she wasn't on duty at the health care tent. One idea that came to her was to attend the morning services in the center of the camp. She enjoyed the services but not the long walk alone from her tent to the worship area. She heard Noah stirring on the other side of the curtain and thought that maybe she would accompany her. Noah's habits had improved slightly since she was on her own, free of Machla's stringent supervision.

"How would you like to take a walk to the Tent of Meeting?" Machla asked her.

"Not a bad idea," Noah said, stretching. "Very little else doing around here."

The women got dressed and walked down the path leading to the main camp. The children of Israel had moved to a new encampment just before the holidays and the terrain was still somewhat unfamiliar. Even though the travels were in deserts, each location had a geography of its own. The land was rocky here and the soil was rough. Difficulties had been encountered in assembling the Mishkan and the larger Tribal Centers. The Levites, of course, were up to the task and did their work diligently. Once their tasks were completed, most of the Levites were not burdened by very strenuous work.

The crowds were sparse near the Tabernacle in the aftermath of a major holiday and the women's section was virtually deserted. The daily ram had already been offered on the altar and now the priests were sacrificing voluntary offerings.[5] The sisters were in a state of ritual purity and could enter into the worship area as far as women were allowed to go. From that vantage point, they observed the priestly rituals for a long period of time. Thereafter, they slowly walked toward the main entrance. Near the main gate, a cloth attached to the perimeter curtain obviously served as a notice board. Neither of the two were able to read the Hebrew notices but Noah glanced at them anyway. One of them attracted her attention. "That one looks important," Noah said, pointing to a neatly cut square of papyrus. "I have never seen writing like that."[6]

"It looks like an alphabetic script rather than picture writing," Machla said. "I have heard that the tablets of the ten commandments are written in real letters."[7]

"Can you read any of it?"

"No, not a word. I wish I could."

"Leave it to me," Noah said, "I will take care of it."

She returned several minutes later with a senior Levitical official in tow, who was more than willing to assist her.

"Can you read this notice to us?" she asked him. "We are unable to make it out."

"I would hardly think you could. That notice is written in Torah script."

"What does it say?"

"It should not be of much concern to you. It is not a lost and found notice like the others."

Noah was persistent, "Well, then, what is it?"

The Levite answered, "It is a request from Elchanan ben Uriah from the tribe of Judah. He is in charge of the Torah schools in that tribe and he is looking for teachers. He knows that there are many learned Levites who have some spare time now and he is hoping that some of them will volunteer to teach. He has posted such notices before."

Machla's ears perked up at the mention of the name Elchanan ben Uriah, the scholar from Judah who earned her a council censure with his legal opinion. "Can you read the actual text for me? I would very much appreciate it."

The Levite was skeptical but finally said, "If it will make you happier to know, the text reads as follows:

Volunteer Teachers Needed
For Advanced Torah School
See Elchanan Ben Uriah
Tribal Center — Judah

"Thank you very much," Machla said, studying the words intently. "Can you tell me which word spells Elchanan?" The Levite pointed to a five-letter word in the third line. Machla reasoned that two letters would be required for the consonant sound "EL," and that one letter could take care of the consonant "CHA." That left her with two letters for the final "NAN" sound. Both "N" letters should have been the same but were apparently different.

"Why are the two 'N's' different?" she asked.

The Levite was delighted to explain. "When the letter 'N' comes at the end of the word, it changes form. It becomes what we call a final 'N.'"

"Does that mean that I will have to learn two versions of each letter in Torah script?"

"No," he said. "There are only five letters that change at the end of a word. With twenty-two regular letters, you will only have to learn twenty-seven letter forms to master the entire alphabet."

"How long has this script been in use?" Machla wanted to know.

"It was given to Moses on Mount Sinai. The ten commandments which he received there were carved in Torah Script and Moses used the same alphabet to write the remaining parts of the Torah."

"That is truly wonderful," Machla said, thanking the Levite once again for his time.

On the way back to the tents, Machla was in a reflective mood. "I know what you are thinking," Noah said, "and the answer is no, emphatically not."

"It would only take some forty minutes to get to the Tribal Center in Judah. What do you stand to lose?"

"I will tell you what. You have some hare-brained scheme to apply for the teaching job but you are afraid to go by yourself and you want me to hold your hand."

"Is that too much to ask from a devoted sister?"

"It most certainly is. Mind you, it's not the walking or a couple hours of time. Elchanan takes a look at me and right away he offers me a job. 'A big Mitzva' is what he calls it. And for the next five years, I'm walking my feet off running to Judah each day to teach kindergarten."

"You have something better to do?"

"I most certainly do."

"You know Elchanan can't possibly be a young man anymore, given the high positions he held years ago. At our council hearing, our legal advisor was almost fifty and most of the tribal judges are well over that. I picture Elchanan as a short, heavyset man. He probably has a long, gray beard, deep furrows in his brow and is stooped over from years of study. He is surely not the type to be attracted to a pretty face."

"They are never too old to notice, Machla, never too old. You want to have some fun? More power to you. I like adventure, too. But adventure takes courage. I'll lend you my blue dress. If you go easy on the manna tonight, you might just squeeze in."

"No thanks. I want to look staid and mature, not like an overgrown child."

Aside from general boredom, Machla was motivated by two factors in seeking her new adventure. She missed the teaching that was the center of her life when she was young. The teaching forced her to organize and clarify her Torah knowledge. It gave her an opportunity to answer questions that would otherwise never occur to her. She also derived a sense of fulfillment from encouraging students to live a Torah life.

The other factor was Elchanan ben Uriah. She never lost her admiration for the way he rendered a legal opinion. It didn't matter that she was the victim of his Torah insights. What was important was that she would meet such a profound scholar in person and perhaps have a chance to discuss Torah subjects with him.

The next morning, Machla awoke early and washed herself. She then chose her Sabbath clothes and dressed carefully. She had no jewelry to put on, but the garments, long and elegant, were the best her mother could sew. It was the first day of the eighth month and special services were conducted at the Tabernacle to honor the new moon. Machla took the time to observe the sacrifices because the Tabernacle was on the way to the tribe of Judah. Elchanan's notice was still posted near the gate. After leaving the temple, she walked eastward to the tent area of Judah. Asking directions from a number of people, she arrived at the Tribal Center of Judah a little after nine in the morning.

She wasn't sure where Elchanan would be at that precise moment. In Menashe, the court sat daily and the council met weekly unless a matter of special urgency arose. She imagined it would be similar in Judah and, as it turned out, she arrived at a fortuitous time. The council was not in session and the court, with a full complement of judges on hand, did not require any alternates. When she inquired as to the whereabouts of Elchanan, it was suggested that she try the middle-sized Torah-studies tent.

"Will I be interrupting a class?" she asked.

"No," she was told, "the tent is used for advanced students whom Elchanan teaches by himself. He lectures from eleven to one on those days that he is free to do so. The students remain in the tent thereafter to review. If he is in the tent now, he may be meeting with students or parents or responding to inquiries from other tribes."

Machla was pleased that Elchanan was still issuing legal opinions and that other tribal councils were soliciting his advice. She approached the tent and lifted the flap. Inside she saw only one man standing next to a lectern, apparently reviewing his studies in a low, but audible voice. She decided that the man could not be Elchanan. He was tall with well cut features and piercing brown eyes. He wore a trimmed beard, rather than the more common loosely flowing ones. His hair was completely black, no gray at all. He swayed slightly as he was reciting but the posture was correct and the bearing aristocratic.

All told, Machla was looking at one of the most handsome men she had ever seen. She estimated his age as slightly beyond the middle thirties. If he were Elchanan, it would mean that the legal opinion he sent to her hearing was composed by a man in his twenties. She gravely doubted that such powerful thoughts could have emanated from a young man.

"I am looking for Elchanan Ben Uriah," she ventured when he noticed her. "Would you know where he is now?"

"You have found the man you are seeking. I happen to answer to that name."

"Oh, Your Honor, I am sorry," Machla said with some embarrassment. "I could not imagine that you were the judge himself."

"And why not, pray tell?" he inquired, with a broad smile.

"Based on his reputation, I sort of expected an older man with a flowing gray beard."

"Quite flattering." Elchanan was intrigued by Machla's poise and the smoothness of her speech. This was no ordinary woman standing before him. She was extremely attractive, if not outrightly beautiful. The salient feature of her appearance was the determined look on her face. "May I know from whom I have received such a compliment?"

"I am Machla, Your Honor, from the tribe of Menashe."

Elchanan was speculating as to the purpose of her visit. She was wearing very traditional dress but her hair was uncovered. That meant she was not married and obviously not coming in connection with an educational problem of a child. He also ruled out marital discord on the same grounds. Arranging marriages was in the province of local commanders and did not require inter-tribal intervention. He decided not to waste time in guesswork.

"What can I do for you, Machla?"

"Your Honor..."

"You may call me Elchanan. I'm not in court or at the council now."

"Thank you, Elchanan. I did come, though, to see you in one of your official capacities, that of director of Torah studies for the tribe of Judah."

Elchanan waited for her to continue.

"I have come in response to the notice you posted near the Tabernacle gate."

Elchanan looked at her strangely. "You were able to read the notice?"

"My sister, who was with me, found a Levite who read it to us. It is in such a beautiful script."

"You have someone to recommend for the position?"

"Yes, indeed."

"May I ask who he is?"

"You may ask who *she* is," Machla corrected, emphasizing the pronoun.

"She, you said?

"Yes, the applicant is a woman."

"You are applying in your own name?"

"I am, indeed."

Elchanan burst out laughing. "How can you apply to teach Torah when you don't know any? These students are men between the ages of fifteen and twenty who are in training for future positions as commanders and judges."

"Listen, Elchanan," she said sharply, "If it were a 'Machlon' sitting with you, instead of a 'Machla' would you blithely assume that he was ignorant of Torah?" She was using the masculine equivalent of her name. "Do me a favor and for the next fifteen minutes make believe that it is Machlon conversing with you."[8]

"That is not too easy, given the attractive features with which the Lord has endowed you."

Machla would not be patronized and Elchanan continued.

"If a man came to see me about a teaching position, I would take it for granted that he was not playing games and that he must have some qualifications to support his aspirations. The remaining question would be whether his knowledge and ability of expression were sufficient."

"You would undertake some form of testing, I presume?" Machla was fully confident that her knowledge was sufficient to cope with any test that Elchanan could improvise. She had an excellent foundation in Torah and was continuing to receive instruction from Barak.

"Well, I would talk to him about Torah. You can determine the Torah level of a person rather quickly."

"Please talk to me then."

Elchanan was not one to avoid a challenge of that nature. Nevertheless, he wanted to avoid humiliating an attractive woman. He would ask her a preliminary question that some women might answer and would end the charade with the next one. He was absolutely certain that there were no women in any of the tribes with more than a smattering of religious education.

"Can you recite some passages from the Song of Moses?" [9]

Machla started from the beginning:

> "I will sing to the Lord,
> For he has triumphed gloriously:
> The horse and the rider has he thrown
> into the sea.
> The Lord is my strength and song
> and he is become my salvation.
> He is my God and I will praise him..."

Elchanan did not require more of the Song of Moses. "How about Jacob's blessing to the tribe of Judah?"[10]

Machla replied at once:

> "Judah, thou art he whom thy brethren shall praise. Thy hand shall be on the neck of thy enemies; thy father's children shall bow down before thee. Judah is a lion's whelp: from the prey, my son, thou art gone up: He stooped down, he couched as a lion, and as a lioness; who shall rouse him up? The staff shall not depart from Judah..."

"Very good," said Elchanan. "Let us move from the beaten track. Can you list the generations of Esau?"[11]

"From which wife?" Machla snapped back.

Elchanan admired her precision. "Ahalivama," he ventured.

Machla recited the proper verse.

"And these were the sons of Ahalivama, the daughter of Ana, the daughter of Zivon, Esau's wife: and she bore to Esau — Yeush and Yalam and Korach.

"You need not pursue questions of memorization, Elchanan. I can stand here and recite the whole Torah from 'In the beginning' and not miss a word. Perhaps you should try some questions of meaning or interpretation."

Elchanan had some colleagues who were good at rote memory so he varied the task somewhat.

"Can you list all occurrences of the verb 'Vayashkem,' to rise up, that appear in the Torah?"[12]

Machla didn't hesitate for a second.

> "In the past, singular form, there are eight occurrences:
> Three for Abraham:
>> once to inspect the ruins of Sodom,
>> once to discharge Hagar,
>> once for the binding of Isaac.
> One for Abimelech after the kidnapping of Sarah.
> One for Jacob when he made his vow.
> One for Laban when he parted with his children.
> Two for Moses:
>> once when he built an altar at Mount Sinai,
>> once when he went up to for the second tablets.
> In the past, plural form it occurs three times:
>> once at the treaty of Isaac and Abimelech,
>> once at the worship of the golden calf,
>> once...."

Here Machla hesitated and her voice cracked. She fought to regain control and hold back tears. "Once where certain Hebrews ascended Mount Paran to attack the Canaanites."

Elchanan noticed the pause and the emotions it engendered, but couldn't understand why one verse affected her so. Before he could respond, Machla continued. "The verb also occurs once in the future, imperative plural." Elchanan could not recall the occurrence for a moment.

"Where is that?" he asked.

"Lot told the Angels that they were to arise in the morning."

"Very well done, Machlon," Elchanan smiled. He realized he would have to raise the level substantially to put this woman in her place. For the next thirty minutes, he covered some of the most complex areas of Hebrew Law and asked questions of logic and interpretation. Machla answered directly and did not make a single error. In desperation, Elchanan chose to ask about passages of law that were revealed only a few days earlier at the High Court. Elchanan had attended the session with the judges of Judah. These laws were not yet released even to the commanders of 1,000.

"Let us say a man was tithing animals. You know how it's done. The animals proceed in single file and every tenth one is sanctified. What if the tither wants to exchange the chosen animal with a better one, so that he can make an offering of superior quality?"[13]

Machla answered quickly. "The choice of the tenth animal must be random. The tither may not inspect it to see whether it is good or bad. Nor may he exchange an animal after he has selected it in the usual manner. If, in fact, he does so, both the original animal and the intended replacement become sanctified."

Elchanan paled. "Where did you hear that?" he demanded.

"Is it not so written in the Torah?" Machla responded innocently, trying to control a self-satisfied smile that was spreading across her face. She had no intention of disclosing that she had visited Barak on the previous Sabbath and had heard the instruction from him.

Elchanan remained silent for a moment. "Please tell me that I am not dealing with the supernatural here — prophecy or magic or mind-reading."

"Nothing out of the ordinary."

"You have someone in the High Court or some high ranking tribal judge teaching you," he said in an accusing voice.

"And, if I do, is there anything wrong with it? The Torah is the inheritance of all the children of Israel. In fact, we learned that it was revealed to women first for it is written, 'Thus shalt thou say to the House of Jacob,' meaning the women of Israel."[14]

Elchanan had heard enough. "Let me think for a minute," he pleaded. There were thoughts deep in his mind that were struggling to come to the fore, to become coherent.

"You say that you are from Menashe?"

"Yes."

Mentally, Elchanan reviewed his contacts with Menashe. He suddenly recalled an unusual instance where two men from Menashe sought his opinion on a case which dealt with five women who were deferring marriage to further their claim to inherit property in Canaan. The father of the five had no sons and had died from injuries incurred in the attack on the Canaanites on Mount Paran. The minute Elchanan thought of Mount Paran, he made the association. Machla's voice had cracked when she was reciting the verse that told of the attack on Paran that had cost her father his life. The details of the case came back to him. Machla was the older sister and the men who had came to see him had also mentioned Noah.

"How is Noah?" he asked, with a twinkle in his eye.

Machla realized that the game, pleasant while it lasted, was over. "Noah is fine, but she was afraid to come."

"Why is that?"

"She was certain that you would put her to work for the next five years and she relishes her freedom."

Elchanan reflected for a minute. "Whatever happened in the case? The men solicited my opinion but never apprised me of the results."

"Before the prosecution got to your opinion, I had already exonerated my mother and one sister who had never been asked to marry. Noah was able to exonerate herself and the prosecution had conceded defeat on four of the five charges. After your opinion was offered, I and two sisters were censured by the council."

"How did Noah get off?"

"She claimed that she was coerced, intimidated and forced into sin by her oldest sister."

"Surely her life was not threatened by a peaceful woman such as yourself."

"The way Noah told it, she had the judges convinced that I was King of Sodom and a personification of Satan."

"Did you ever abuse her?"

"Are you jesting? I gently admonished her on several occasions for staying out late, oversleeping in the morning and failing to get the manna."

"She was the defense attorney in the case?"

"No, I was. When I was testifying as a witness, though, she took over the defense and that was when she put on her performance. She had the commanders in tears."

"We could use such defense attorneys here. How come you didn't challenge my opinion?"

"I have often asked myself that question. Gamliel put his finger on it when he said that I was learned, but inexperienced in court procedures. I feel that I did well for a beginner but I made certain elementary mistakes. I led the witnesses, I made unwarranted assumptions and, in certain areas, I wasn't sufficiently prepared. As for your opinion, it was quite exotic and theoretical. I should have challenged it and made a distinction between our conspiracy and the ones which were cited. Ours was indirect. The consequences of our action were neither immediately apparent nor inevitable. I guess I was overawed by the quality of the opinion and the scholar who authored it."

"That does reflect some inexperience. What happened after the censure?"

"We abandoned the concerted action and the public acts of protest. We now act on an individual basis and weigh each marriage proposal on its merits."

"Are any of the sisters married?"

"No."

"I see," Elchanan said, "an interesting case indeed. I concede your vast knowledge, Machla. I also remember that you had many years of teaching experience but, even if I were inclined to let you teach our young men, the parents would never agree to it."

"Why is that?" she asked.

"The young men might be distracted by your appearance."

"Is it not written in the Torah, 'You shall not stray after the sight of your eyes?'"[15]

"Listen, I am twice as old as the students, a married man with four children. It is taking a lot of will power on my part to abide by the commandment. The evil inclination is very strong in young men."

Machla was of course pleased that someone regarded her as attractive, particularly when the judgment came from a man as handsome and distinguished as Elchanan. She was sad, however, that the very quality which had earned such praise might be the factor that would deny her an opportunity to gain a position.

Elchanan was thinking rapidly. He didn't want to chase this saintly woman away. "You know," he said, "I have a twelve year old daughter, Dina, and I would be the proudest father alive if she had a tenth of your knowledge." A plan was beginning to take shape in his mind but it wasn't fully thought out.

Machla encouraged him because she enjoyed being in the presence of a man of such scholarship and achievement. "I cannot volunteer to teach just one student. Could you perhaps organize a group of five or six young women? I would be happy to start with them."

"Yes, but I cannot announce it as a Torah class. There might be some objections from certain members of the tribe."

"You could precede the class with instruction in some domestic skill and call the class 'Preparation for Torah Womanhood.' The title is not as significant as the contents."

"You are a real veteran of these wars, I see. What sort of skills do you have in mind?"

"You could try sewing or food preparation or child care. It doesn't matter much."

"That is an excellent idea. I know many women who boast of their domestic skills and now have time to teach. I will recruit one to start. Let's see. We cannot teach in the mornings because girls of this age have responsibilities at home. We could start the skills class at one-thirty and run your class from three-thirty to five-thirty, if that meets with your approval."

"That is fine with me. Do you supervise all of your teachers personally?"

"Yes, I do. I meet with them at the start of the week and they present an outline of the material they plan to cover during the next few days. Once a week, I visit each class and examine the students orally. At the end of the week, I meet with the teacher for an evaluation of the teaching and the progress of the students. At that time we also consider problems with given students or parental complaints."

"When can my class get underway?"

"I will announce the program at the council meeting tomorrow and the commanders will brief their subordinates immediately thereafter. We can start the class on the first day of next week. I am sure that everything will be in place by then."

Machla admired his confidence and self assurance. "Everything suits me well. I will present my teaching plan to you next week on Sunday at two. Now there is only the matter of compensation to resolve."

"Compensation! What compensation? Surely a woman with your knowledge knows that one may not receive payment for providing Torah instruction."

"We are not talking about money. We are talking of a kindness that you could do for me in return for working in your tribe as opposed to my home tribe."

"And pray tell me what that may be?"

"I need someone to teach me Torah script."

"That is a small price to pay. We actually have samples of the script on papyrus in our library and we teach Torah script to our advanced students. With a little help, you can master it on your own. I am now beginning to understand how you accumulated your Torah knowledge. You trade favors for wisdom."

"In general terms you are correct. One must makes sacrifices to learn Torah."

With the interview over and agreement reached, Machla took leave of Elchanan. She was elated at her achievement and her spirits were high. But the emotions that were generated were not entirely of the purest kind. Eliav had told her that women of her age no longer experience heart-throbbing at the sight of handsome men. In her naiveté she had believed him. Now, in the presence of Elchanan, she realized that she had been misled. When Elchanan's eyes looked into hers they stirred her up in a way that Eliav's never could. She was excited just sitting and talking to him and the feelings were quite intense.

She had no intention of revealing that aspect of her encounter to Noah, and certainly not to the others. She merely told them that she wasn't accepted to teach males but that she was invited to teach a class of young women and had accepted the offer. Achla was glad to hear the news because it meant that Machla would be in a tribe where she might meet new men. Also, her sisters would be a little freer to socialize, if Machla were distracted elsewhere.

Noah was somewhat more suspicious. Machla didn't look like a woman who had accepted a difficult task. She looked rather like a woman who had discovered a whole new world and who was about to embark on an adventure. There was almost an idyllic look on her face that reminded her of the look on the face of a cat who discovered a huge supply of cream. "Tell me about Elchanan," she probed. Machla related the interview in detail and how she had surprised Elchanan with her responses to his questions.

"What does this Elchanan look like?" Noah persisted, because she felt instinctively that Machla was holding back some information.

"Nothing special. He's married, has four children and looks like a judge is supposed to look."

"Does he have a son, perhaps?"

"Three of them, but not quite our age. Why do you keep looking for a romantic aspect to everything?"

"There is something here that doesn't quite mesh. I am sure it will emerge soon enough."

Machla ignored her and went about her business. She spent the next few days preparing for her new position.

Elchanan, for his part, was buoyed by the meeting with Machla. She was the most unusual woman he had ever met; smart, attractive and dedicated. If she succeeded in her work — and he had no doubt that she would — it would reflect very well upon him and enhance his stature in tribal circles. It would also add some spice to his life because here was a person with whom he could match wits. She was not at all intimidated by him as were others. What is more, he suspected that she possessed even more knowledge than she had displayed.

His announcement at the council evoked considerable interest. He had explained that many young women were growing up without a solid foundation in traditional knowledge and customs. It was not a severe problem in the desert, where matters were tightly controlled, but these women would someday be raising their families in Canaan. In a large country, the households would be widely spaced and the responsibilities of each mother would be far greater.

He described the program as planned and cautioned that it was strictly experimental. Only very bright girls between the ages of eleven and thirteen would be accepted in the first group. He added that the teachers would be pious God-fearing women and that he would personally supervise the program. Caleb, the tribal president who had succeeded Nachshon, was most pleased. As one of the spies who had reported favorably on Canaan, he was very concerned with preparing the children of Israel for life in the Promised Land. Any program that would further this goal was desirable to him. Furthermore, it would extend the educational programs for women first initiated by his wife, Miriam, for the daughters of Israel. Elchanan was related to Caleb who was extremely satisfied with the work that he was doing for the tribe.[16]

Elchanan encouraged the commanders to recruit students and by the time the class started, Elchanan had accepted eight girls including his daughter, Dina. His wife, Batya, was very happy with the idea of Dina going to school. Elchanan was too busy to teach her much and she herself did not possess sufficient knowledge to do it. She asked Elchanan about the teacher, but he was very sparing in details. He told her the she came from the tribe of Menashe and had teaching experience with young women. He had interviewed her and found that she was a mature woman with qualities equal to or in excess of expectations. Batya automatically assumed that the teacher was married because Elchanan had used the term mature and all the mature woman she knew were married.

The other class was a general course involving all domestic skills and an experienced homemaker was engaged to teach it. Elchanan had no trouble persuading Dina to attend because basically she was an obedient girl. He convinced her that learning Torah was a pleasure and that it would give her a great advantage when it came to finding a marriage partner.

When Machla arrived on the first day, Elchanan was waiting for her with great anticipation. She described her teaching plans to him in detail. She would try to teach the Torah in the order that it was written but would feel free to cite passages from other sections if they were logically related. She would stress history at the start as it would hold student interest better than law. Of course, she would present the moral implications of the stories as well. The first week of studies would be devoted to the creation of the universe and the second week to events in the Garden of Eden. She would then spend two weeks on Noah and the flood and three to four weeks on Abraham. Elchanan accepted her outline and made a few suggestions of his own.

The question of a teaching location was considered next. Machla told Elchanan that she realized the difficulty of locating a class for pubescent girls in the midst of the Tribal Center tents occupied by teenage male students. Such an action would surely generate a storm of parental protest and might possibly lead to undesirable situations. Since she preferred to teach out of doors in any event, all he had to do was find her a teaching location somewhat removed from the

Center. At the site, she would need a small tent to store supplies and conduct private meetings with students or parents. Elchanan agreed and made the necessary arrangements. Before Elchanan left her on her own, he told her that all of her eight students were fully qualified with one possible exception. There was a girl by the name of Malka, the youngest in the class, who was accepted for reasons that had as much to do with compassion as ability. She was bright but shy, withdrawn and physically small. Her mother was a young widow who had four other children younger than Malka.

Machla hadn't expected as many as eight students but she had no trouble with the number. The class was attentive and the students were taken with her professional ability and dramatic appearance. They had never experienced a woman Torah teacher whose knowledge was on such a high level. The two hours passed quickly and the students were encouraged to review their work thoroughly.

Elchanan walked Dina home after class and she reported to him that she enjoyed the class very much. Dina, who already knew of such things, told her father, "Our teacher is a beautiful woman and has a perfect figure. How come she isn't married?"

"You should think of teachers only in terms of wisdom, not beauty. You would be well advised not to speak of such things to your mother because she might feel that you are making unfavorable comparisons with her. In your eyes, your mother must remain the most beautiful woman in the world. Let your teacher's appearance remain our secret. Just tell your mother how much you enjoyed the learning and that will make her happy." Dina was smart enough to realize what her father was really concerned about and didn't say anything further for fear of endangering a marital situation that, at best, left something to be desired. She was of an age where she understood domestic problems and was able to compare her family with others.

Machla walked home at a leisurely pace and reviewed her first teaching effort. She was satisfied with it but, always self-critical, found room for improvement. The important thing was that she had established a good rapport with her students and that none of them, even little Malka, presented any unusual problem. The next two days passed quietly.

CHAPTER

EIGHT

*"THE WORLD EXISTS BECAUSE OF
THE VOICE OF CHILDREN WHO
STUDY TORAH IN THEIR MASTER'S
HOUSE"*

It was after class on Tuesday when the woman came to see her. She was in her early thirties, of fair appearance. With her was a girl of twelve who must have been crying for at least several hours. She introduced herself as Yafa and her daughter as Aviva. Machla took them into her tent because she sensed that the matter was of a private nature. "Teacher Machla," the woman said, "I want you to talk to my daughter, Aviva, for a few minutes."

Machla spoke to the girl and found her to be intelligent and well-spoken. When she asked her if she knew why her mother had brought her to be interviewed, she answered that she desperately wanted to learn Torah. However, she was not accepted into the class even though her closest friend was. Machla was shocked because she was under the impression that Elchanan had made a heroic effort to recruit the first eight students for her class.

"If Aviva has to start a few days late," Machla said, "it would not be much of a problem. I can help her make up the work she missed. Have you spoken to Elchanan ben Uriah?"

Yafa stared at her in total disbelief. "You mean you don't know what has been going on here since Elchanan announced the class last week?"

"I have no idea."

"Let me tell you. The commanders spread the word on Tuesday. By Wednesday, there were more than 100 requests. Parents have been waiting for years to get help in teaching their daughters values of the Torah. Elchanan rejected half the requests by that afternoon on various grounds and scheduled personal interviews with girls for the next two days. While I must give him credit for hard work, the fact remains that my daughter, who was interviewed on Thursday, was not chosen."

"I'm sorry to hear that," Machla interjected.

"Aviva hasn't stopped crying since then. Would you believe that of the fifty candidates only two were chosen?"

"What do you mean, two? I have eight students in my class."

"I mean two girls from ordinary families without rank or privilege."

"I do not understand."

"Let me explain. You have eight students in all. Three are the daughters of commanders of 1,000, one is the daughter of a judge, one is the daughter of Elchanan himself and one is a poor orphan girl. That leaves only two for the common people."

Machla felt both surprise and pain. "Why was the class limited to eight girls?"

"Some of us asked Elchanan that and he said that the class was only experimental. He was afraid that a larger class would endanger the results. 'Success of the program is critical,' he insisted, 'or, the council will not support similar ventures in the future.'"

Machla felt sad that she had underestimated the potential of her undertaking. She didn't know how to resolve the problem but she felt it would be wrong to sit idly without trying to help. "There is probably some room to add a few students to my class," she said. "Would you like me to bring it up to Elchanan?"

"It can't hurt, although he seemed rather adamant on the point. I came to see you in the hope that you might have some alternative suggestions. My husband knows virtually no Torah at all."

Machla suddenly had a vision of herself hiding behind Azriel's tent, a thirteen year old girl yearning for Torah. "I have one idea but I have to ask Aviva something first."

Aviva looked at Machla hopefully. "Tell me the truth, Aviva. Do you really want to learn Torah or do you just want to be together with your friend?"

"I really want to learn, Teacher Machla. I asked my mother to get me into the class on my own. My friend didn't even know about the program till afterwards."

"Would you make a real sacrifice to learn?"

"Yes."

Machla told Aviva how she had started her Torah studies. Mother and daughter listened in rapt amazement. "Hear me out carefully," Machla said. "You know that I teach out in the open. The area is surrounded by a rock ledge on which there are a number of places where Aviva can sit without being observed. I will take no notice of her and, if any of the girls in the class object, I will tell them that the Torah is open to all. The only condition I impose is that Aviva not tell anyone what I said or what she is doing."

Yafa thanked Machla for the suggestion. Until Aviva was formally admitted to class a month later, she faithfully sat on the ledge and audited the class. Occasionally, passers-by also stopped to observe the Torah class. At other times, a few young girls actually listened in. Machla never objected to an audience as long as it did not disturb her class or distract her students.

On Thursday afternoon, a half hour before the end of the instruction period, Elchanan visited the class. As soon as he approached, the girls rose in respect. Elchanan appreciated the gesture as it did not always happen in the boys' classes. "You may be seated, my daughters," he said. "Would anyone like to tell me what subjects were covered in class this week?"

Eight hands were raised in unison and Elchanan picked a student at random. "We learned that, in six days, God created the world and all that is in it."[1]

"Very good, but why did it take Him so long?" That was a question that Elchanan frequently used in beginning classes to show that learning was a matter of thinking rather than rote. Again, the hands started flying. In other classes Elchanan never drew more than a hand or two for a question of that nature.

"The Lord could have created the world with a single word," the chosen student answered, "but He decided to use many steps so that the wicked people, who destroy the world, will be punished for breaking something that took a long time to fashion. The good people, who preserve the world, will be rewarded for saving a very complex creation."

Elchanan was pleased with the response and Machla was happy that her students were not rattled by a surprise question. Elchanan continued the examination in a systematic way as the girls answered each of the questions. He was looking for a question that, when answered, would allow him the opportunity to say a few words of original instruction to the children. He finally asked the class, "Why is it that the Almighty created the insects and the crawling things before He created man?"[2]

From a sea of hands he picked one who said, "That is to teach man humility. If ever man thinks he is very great, he can be told that even a little ant preceded him in the order of creation."

"That is correct. Now tell me children, why should a man be humble? What does he stand to gain by it?"

Here a strange thing happened. Five or six of the children raised their hands at the start of the question but all of them dropped their hands when the examiner started to qualify it. He was at a loss as to what went wrong but the situation gave him a chance to provide an answer by himself. To make doubly sure that he would not be repeating something the children had already heard, he called upon little Malka, even though she had not raised her hand. During his original interview with her, Elchanan had sensed that the girl was very intelligent. Even if she knew the answer, however, she might be too shy to volunteer. Calling on her would give her a chance to overcome her shyness.

"Why should man be humble, Malka?"

His intuition was quite correct as Malka did have an answer for him. "Man was created in the image of God. This does not mean that man looks like God but that he must behave like Him. Since God is merciful, he must be merciful. As God is kind so must he be and, since God is humble, man has to be humble too."

Elchanan hadn't expected such a perfect answer. "Malka, why didn't you raise your hand if you knew the answer? It is important for you to show your teachers that you are able to follow the work."

"Knowing the answer is not enough," she responded. "Teacher Machla requires us to ask ourselves the questions and rehearse the answer several times before we venture to speak about Torah."

"You hadn't rehearsed this question and answer?"

"No, Your Honor, I work at night to help my family and sometimes I cannot rehearse all the teachings."

"I see," said Elchanan, "for an unrehearsed answer, your response was extremely accurate. I agree that we were created in the image of God and that we must behave like Him, but what makes you think that God is humble?"

"Don't you know that God is humble, Your Honor?" she said, tears starting to form in her eyes.

"I know that, Malka, I was asking you how you know it. It will be all right if you just say that your teacher taught you that."

"She didn't, Your Honor. She just told us that when God was about to create man he consulted with the angels although he did not have to. Anyone who asks advice from people who are below him must be very humble and that is how I know that God is humble."[3]

Elchanan smiled broadly. "That is an excellent proof. Now can anyone tell me what we stand to gain by being humble?"

Again the hands stayed down. Elchanan was too wise to think that Machla would have missed so basic a point. Frustrated with the silence, he turned to his daughter. "Dina, why is no one answering my question?"

"With all due respect, father, Teacher Machla forbids us to answer unclear questions. She feels that if we do not understand what the questioner is driving at, we will most certainly offer the wrong answer. The problem here is that no one has the courage to request you to rephrase the question."

"How should the question be asked?"

"You have to explain whether you mean 'gain' in the sense of Divine reward, 'gain' as it concerns the human personality or 'gain' as it relates to relations between men."

"I see," said Elchanan, who 'gained' a lesson in humility himself, "How does a man become a better person by being humble?"

The hands flew up at once. Elchanan chose girls who had not spoken before.

"A man who is not humble thinks he knows everything so he will not be willing to learn anything new."

"A man who is not humble thinks he is perfect so he will not be willing to improve in his ways."

"When a man is vain, he antagonizes other people and loses his friends. Without friends, a man's personality suffers."

"Children," Elchanan said, "You have made me very proud of you. Keep up the good work." Turning to Machla, he said, "I will see you right after class."

Since class time was up, Machla dismissed all the children but Malka. She took the girl in her arms and hugged her. "You were very smart today, Malka. Both I and the judge are very proud of your work."

"Thank you, teacher," Malka said. "I love you."

Elchanan returned a few minutes later. "I have never seen a better prepared class than yours and that you did it all in a few days is utterly amazing." Machla thanked him for the compliment.

"There is a matter I would like to discuss with you, Elchanan," Machla said. "I am concerned that so many girls were denied admission to the class. I am even more concerned that of those admitted, most are from distinguished families."

"There was some favoritism, Machla, but, if it will make you feel better, it was not done out of fear. I turned down a large number of daughters of commanders and judges as well as daughters of commoners. This is an experimental program. If it succeeds, the commanders will vote to continue and expand it. If they have some personal experience with the program, they will support it and protect it from those who find it objectionable. I did not tell you which children are the daughters of commanders because I wanted you to treat all students alike."

"I did not ask any children what their fathers do and I am glad I didn't. It is a very unhealthy situation, though, when so many girls want to study Torah and so few are allowed to do so."

"Do you have any ideas as to what I can do about it?"

"As a start, we could enlarge my class a little."

"I won't do that unless you are absolutely certain you can handle additional students without compromising the results."

"I can take four more."

"That will help but I turned away more than forty girls of those who had interviews, and many others were rejected without interviews. My problem is in finding women who can teach Torah. Now, if you could somehow convince your four sisters to come down and teach we would be able to meet much more of the demand."

"You will generate a civil war if you tried that. The daughters of Zelaphchad are the tribal treasure of Menashe. Our tribe will never give us up to Judah. How about finding a few men teachers?"

"We are thinking about it. No men will consent to do it full-time. The best we can do is request each commander to devote at least one afternoon a week to girls. If they look upon it as a universal chore rather than as an individual assignment, they might be more inclined to do it."

"I would hope that you could come up with a better solution than that."

"In time, I am sure we will."

"Oh, yes. What about my compensation?"

Elchanan had not forgotten. He gave her a papyrus with the Torah script alphabet written out. He then had her memorize a verse which contained words starting with successive letters of the alphabet. As she chanted the verse over and over again, she pointed to the matching letter of the alphabet. On her way home she committed the verse to memory.

Machla was elated with the performance of her students, particularly with Malka. From her own experience she knew what it meant to be an orphan. She resolved not only to teach Malka, but to continue giving her added attention and affection to compensate for her lack of it at home. As far as recruiting her sisters to teach, she had absolutely no intention of doing so. To herself, she had to admit that a good part of the reason was her reluctance to share Elchanan with anyone else.

The class went along well during the next two months. Enrollment reached twelve, including Aviva, who came down from her perch to join the class. Elchanan tested the class every Thursday afternoon. The children could not sustain perfect results but they acquitted themselves admirably. After one such evaluation, Elchanan confided to his wife that there was a great change in Dina. She was more obedient and more interested in learning. At times, she questioned him so much that he found it hard to study. When he complained, she said that it was more important for him to teach than to study. When he asked her why, she said, "a scholar saves only his own life when he studies. A teacher saves many lives."

Two months into the semester, Elchanan brought a visitor to the weekly examination — the tribal president, Caleb, the son of Yefuneh. The distinguished man, already seventy, was an historic figure among the Hebrews. The students did not have to be taught how to react to his presence. Immediately they rose and bowed. Machla herself bowed hoping to cover the fact that she was trembling and in a cold sweat. Here was a national hero, a brother-in-law of Moses, coming to visit her class. He was one of the elders of the people of Israel and, by Divine promise, he and Joshua were guaranteed to enter Canaan. As such, they were the only men who left Egypt between the ages of twenty and sixty who would survive to enter the Promised Land. Caleb bore his age well. He had an aristocratic appearance and commanded respect wherever he went.[4]

Elchanan introduced Machla to him and mentioned her father's name.

"Zelaphchad? I remember him. He was the officer who remained loyal to Moses in the presence of Pharaoh." He didn't add anything further because he also knew how Zelaphchad had met his death. "We are delighted to have you with us and I have already heard some wonderful tidings about your work."

With the introductions out of the way, Elchanan put some heavy questions to the class. He no longer worried about the level of questioning because he had absolute confidence in Machla. The class had completed the study of Abraham and the questions related to that historic figure. Wishing to please Caleb and relate something about him to the students, Elchanan asked, "What was Abraham asked to do when Lot had departed from him?" Every last hand went up for the question. "Abraham was told to rise up and walk across the length and breadth of Canaan in order to acquire possession of it," one girl answered. The response provided Elchanan with the lead he needed.[5]

"Of men living today, who else among the children of Israel was privileged to walk across the entire Land of Canaan?"

Elchanan didn't expect any hands to go up because the answer was much further in the Torah and Machla had presented her weekly outlines without any such linkage. Little Malka, however, had taken Elchanan's instructions about not withholding answers very seriously. She raised her hand and Elchanan had to call upon her. "There are two Israelites who were so privileged: His Excellency, the President of Judah, and Joshua, the son of Nun."[6]

Elchanan was upset because he thought that Machla had gone beyond the limits of the curriculum she had presented. "Did your teacher teach that in class?"

"No," Malka said. "That is from teachings found elsewhere in the Torah."

"So how did you know the answer?"

"That was my extra credit question."

"What does that mean?"

"Each night before we go home, our teacher gives us an extra credit question and we have to try to found out the answer."

Elchanan looked sharply at his daughter, Dina, who had never said anything about extra credit work. Malka noticed the look and quickly came to Dina's assistance.

"Of course, we are not allowed to discuss the question with our fathers."

"Why is that?"

"It would not be fair. Some of us have fathers who are not learned in the Torah. In my case, I have no father. I got the answer from the man whom I work for at night to help my family."

"How does your teacher reward the extra credit work?"

"She kisses me and hugs me," Malka said, innocently unaware that Machla was giving her special affection. The other students smiled but did not laugh.

"Does she give any other reward?"

"Yes, she has a slate and makes a mark on it every time we get the answer right."

"May I see the slate, Machla?"

Machla lifted up the cloth on her table and handed Elchanan the slate that was under it. In the right hand column, were the names of each of the girls in the class written in beautiful Torah script. In a second column, to the left of the first, were the names of the twelve tribes of Israel, also written in the same script. White dots were then entered in each row for correct answers. Malka's row was filled to the end with dots. Dina's row, Elchanan noted, had at least a respectable number.

"I am the tribe of Menashe," Malka said proudly, "because Menashe is a very small tribe in Israel and I am the smallest girl in my class."

Caleb, who was very wise, did not for a moment believe that he was hearing a routine class examination. He said to Elchanan, "You did not have to prepare a staged examination for my benefit." Machla heard the remark and did not let it pass.

"If it please His Excellency, the children had no prior knowledge of the questions to be asked and they had no advance word that His Excellency would honor us with his presence. I would be most pleased if His Excellency would himself conduct the remainder of the examination."

Caleb accepted the challenge and asked many questions. The results were the same as those for Elchanan's series. The children simply did not miss any. It was then that Caleb asked how many times God tested Abraham. When the students completed listing the ten occasions, Caleb asked, "Why did God test Abraham at all?"[7]

He was greeted by a stony silence and not a single hand rose up. Elchanan, who was a veteran of examinations in Machla's class, knew from experience that when the entire class kept its silence it was not because the students did not know the answer but because they found the question improper. On those occasions he would have Dina explain what was wrong with the question. He realized that no one was going to correct the president, so he asked Dina what the problem was.

"We are not encouraged to venture opinions on God's actions or the reasons for them. Such expression may lead to us criticizing God's works or pronouncing judgments upon them. That may lead to terrible consequences."

"I see," said Caleb, "I will rephrase the question. Without saying for certain, what may be one possible reason why God tested Abraham?"

The students still held back. "Call Malka," Elchanan said. "She will tell you." Caleb asked Malka to do so.

"God tested Abraham for the same reason His Excellency is testing our class. His Excellency loves us and wants to reward us with praise but there must be a reason for the praise or else it would not be deserved. So he asks us very hard questions and, when we answer them correctly, he rewards us. It is the same with God. He wanted to reward Abraham but needed a reason to do so. He therefore gave him a very hard test, to sacrifice his only son. When Abraham passed the test, God rewarded him with a promise of victory in the Land of Canaan. As it is written in the Torah:

"Because thou hast done this thing and hast not withheld thy son, thy only son: That I will exceedingly bless thee, and I will exceedingly multiply thy seed as the stars of the heaven, and as the sand which is upon the sea shore; and thy seed shall possess the gate of its enemies; and in thy seed shall all the nations of the earth be blessed; because thy hast obeyed my voice."[8]

Tears came to Caleb's eyes as he heard the young girl recite the original Torah text so beautifully. "God bless you, Malka," he said with emotion, "and God bless your teacher, the daughter of Zelaphchad. I survived a generation that did not respect the Torah and now I have lived to hear the words of our holy Torah coming even from the mouths of young girls."

Elchanan and Caleb took their leave and Machla dismissed the class. Everyone left but Malka, who knew that her reward today would be the best ever.

Elchanan was unstinting in praise of Machla's efforts during the examination. "Caleb was truly proud of you and I am impressed by your methods and dedication. By the way, your Torah script was not only beautiful but absolutely correct. Beginners often spell incorrectly but you don't."

"Thank you Elchanan. My sisters and I wanted to show our appreciation for your teaching us Torah script. We have embroidered this cloth with Torah lettering as a present to you. She presented him a cloth with woven letters which read:

ELCHANAN BEN URIAH
JUDGE AND LEGAL ADVISOR
IN THE TRIBE OF JUDAH

Elchanan accepted the gift with profound thanks. "I hope you won't mind if I hang this beautiful cloth in my tent at the Tribal Center. I think more people will appreciate the quality of the art that way."

Machla realized that what Elchanan meant was that he didn't enjoy the prospect of having to explain such a gift to his wife. "It is your cloth, Elchanan, display it as you see fit."

As time passed, Machla's fame spread throughout the tribe of Judah. Her students had learned about Joseph and bondage in the Land of Egypt. Elchanan still tested the class, not out of need but because he enjoyed being in Machla's presence. A month before Passover, Machla found Yafa waiting at the tent after class. This was the first time that Yafa had come to see to her after Aviva was formally admitted.

"How are you?" Machla asked. "I haven't seen you for quite a while."

"All is well with us and Aviva enjoys her studies immensely. Since she entered the class she has changed a lot and is more popular among her friends. It seems that girls who study Torah enjoy a special status."

"That is good to hear. Did you just drop by or is there anything you wanted to see me about?"

"There is a matter I would like to discuss although it concerns you rather than me."

Having indicated the subject of the conversation, Machla invited her into the tent. She didn't want anyone listening to personal matters. She hoped that Yafa wasn't a matchmaker on the side with some widower to recommend.

"I have something to tell you which may be of serious concern. You were very helpful to me so I thought I might be able to return the favor."

"I am listening."

"I am not sure how to phrase such a very delicate matter but I will do my best. Yesterday I overheard my daughter talking with one of the girls in the class, and I didn't like what I heard. It seems that the girls think that Elchanan has certain feelings for you that go beyond a professional relationship."

"You certainly have no problem phrasing things in a very refined way."

"My daughter learned from you and I learned from her to rehearse things before saying them. I did rehearse this conversation to some extent."

"Can you elaborate a little?"

"Yes. Apparently the girls are debating whether Elchanan has fallen in love with you or is just attracted to you in a physical way."

"Whatever gives them such silly ideas?"

"I think they see it in his eyes, in his rapt attention and respect. The two of you make such a handsome pair that it is not hard to project that something exists between you."

"I certainly value Elchanan's attention but I am not in a position to judge whether there is anything more than professional courtesy involved. You've spoken to Elchanan a number of times and you are quite attractive. How does Elchanan look at you?"

"Like a worm in his manna cake. Of course, I am a married woman and that may have some bearing on the case. Still he does not look into my eyes nor, for that matter, at any other part of me."

"See, he must be a saintly man."

"Let me assure you that he is no saint. He is an ambitious person who aspires to reach the highest levels. Your presence has boosted his popularity and that might be why he treats you in a special manner. I, however, choose to believe that he is driven to some degree by the evil inclination."

"All men are, Yafa. Without the evil inclination we would not reproduce and multiply. What the good inclination must do is channel the physical drives into paths that are not sinful. If, indeed, Elchanan is driven towards me from that source, I would be both honored and flattered. As you know, I am permissible to him if he wishes to have me in a licit manner."[9]

"I don't think you understand the problem that exists. You are both public figures and extremely vulnerable. Let me give some examples of trouble that may emerge. Suppose people start saying that Elchanan is sponsoring the program for girls because he is interested in procreation rather than education. Suppose some of the girls in the class talk in Dina's presence and she repeats the insinuations to her mother. Batya could make such a fuss that you would have to be asked to leave. The class will not survive without you for there are no other women in our tribe who can teach Torah."

The truth began to dawn on Machla. Yafa was not trying to protect her from Elchanan at all. Yafa's concern was the continuation of the class and the education her daughter loved and needed so desperately. "You have every right to be concerned about the class. If I had a daughter, I would fight like a lion to protect her education. Do you have any suggestions that I might consider?"

"As a matter of fact, I do. If I were you, I would hold the professional conferences at the Tribal Center rather than out here. People realize that meetings held at Center are for business only. Seeing you out here, they may get other ideas. Secondly, when Elchanan is testing the students maybe you can distance yourself from the class area and let him and the girls concentrate on the work. I've already ordered Aviva not to talk about such things and told her to make sure that no one says anything to Dina."

Machla thanked Yafa for her advice but she did not commit herself to any course of action. Under ordinary circumstances she would have told Yafa to stay out of her affairs. Here, however, there was Torah education at stake, and she could not treat lightly what to other people was a matter of life and death. She also realized that Yafa's observations were made with good intentions. The following week, without explaining why, she asked Elchanan to meet with her at the Tribal Center rather than in the area designated for her class and tent. He agreed because it made no difference to him. During class examinations she usually stood behind her students facing Elchanan. Bit by bit she moved to a location behind Elchanan, which forced him to choose between looking at the students or looking at her. He was unhappy at being deprived of his visual pleasure and he asked her about it. "I will give you a hint but I cannot elaborate. I made some changes to protect you from the evil inclination and the Torah program from wagging tongues."

Two weeks after Passover, Elchanan visited the class again to test the students. After the examination he asked Machla to come to the Tribal Center and wait a few minutes for him, as he had to find out whether his presence would be required in court the next day. The court did not usually sit on Fridays, but an emergency had come up and there was a possibility that some judges might not be able to attend on the eve of the Sabbath.

When Machla arrived at Elchanan's tent, she noticed a woman waiting nearby in what was obviously a very agitated state. The woman was about Machla's age or maybe a little bit younger. Her clothes were not in order and everything about her seemed in disarray. She was an average looking woman but her figure was not well proportioned. Her hair was covered in a manner which indicated that she was married.

"By any chance, have you seen Elchanan ben Uriah?" the woman asked as Machla paused near Elchanan's tent.

"I am waiting for him, too. He told me that he would be here in a few minutes after he talks to the secretary of the court."

The woman eyed Machla with curiosity. Machla always dressed in her finest clothes on Thursdays for the examination and evaluation. She was looking particularly good and was in high spirits because her students had performed in an excellent manner.

"And pray tell why are *you* waiting for Elchanan?" the woman asked. There was some stress on the word 'you', which Machla didn't like, but she restrained herself and answered politely. "I work for Elchanan and we have a conference scheduled."

"What do you do for Elchanan?" the woman asked.

"I teach a class."

"Elchanan wouldn't let a woman who looks like you teach men. They have only one class for girls and you couldn't possibly teach that group."

"Why not, may I ask?"

"Well I know the skills teacher personally and the Torah teacher is old and married. You obviously have neither of those attributes."

"I have no idea where you got your description of the Torah teacher but the fact remains that I have been teaching that class since after Sukkoth."

"You are Machla?" the woman asked, anguish clearly visible on her face. "My daughter did not tell me the truth about your appearance."

"I do not believe for a minute that any of my students would lie," Machla said angrily.

"She didn't lie. She just neglected to tell me the whole truth."

Machla quickly deduced that she must be facing Elchanan's wife. Dina might not have described Machla properly to her mother, either because Elchanan had requested her not to or she had enough sense on her own. No other student had any reason to distort her appearance and, anyway, she had met the parents of most of the girls in the class.

"You are Batya, then. I am very glad to meet you. Your daughter gives me great pleasure in class."

"Thank you."

"You seem very upset, Batya. Is anything wrong?"

"It's my son, Avi. He's running a very high fever..." Just then Elchanan came along and saw his wife talking to Machla. "Do you women know each other, or shall I introduce you?"

"We know each other already. Listen, Elchanan, Avi is very sick. He has a high fever and hasn't eaten all day. You have to come home and get some help."

"Have you tried getting a midwife?" The midwives knew a little about health matters and were frequently called in to help with children's illnesses.

"They are all out delivering babies and I couldn't find anyone," Batya answered.

Machla felt that she had no choice but to offer assistance. "Listen," she said to the both of them, "I can help you with Avi."

Batya was doubtful. "What can you do?"

"I have been a nurse for more than ten years. My sisters and I train and direct all the health care workers in the tribe of Menashe."

Elchanan gasped in amazement. "Is there anything you can't do?" He paused quickly because he realized he had said too much. He continued in a more composed voice. "I would greatly appreciate your help, but do you have any equipment or material with you?"

"I have it all in my tent. I keep it there in case any of the students take ill. We pass the tent on the way to your home."

The three of them started walking to Elchanan's tents. Machla ran ahead and scooped up a cloth bag which contained all of her creams, ointments and assorted supplies. Along the way she got a more detailed description of Avi's symptoms and did her best to calm Batya's fears. It took the group about ten minutes to arrive at the location. Batya had moved Avi to the larger tent, occupied by her and Elchanan, so there was enough room to work inside the tent.

Dina was home already and was very surprised to see Machla. She was even more surprised when told that Machla was a trained nurse. Machla asked her to first get a basin of water and then to prepare candles in case they would be needed. Meanwhile, Machla pulled out a white smock to cover her good clothes. The smock had a wild ox embroidered on the back, a touch which only Elchanan appreciated. Although the tribal symbols were not yet officially recognized by Moses, the tribe of Menashe had adopted for itself the symbol of the wild ox. It appeared on the flags of the tribe when Menashe was marching in the desert. Machla had ordered that it also be put on the clothes of the tribal health care workers.

Avi was about four years old, a well-developed child, but the high fever left him listless and unresponsive. At intervals, he whimpered and cried. Machla examined him thoroughly trying to eliminate the more severe diseases. She was relieved that there were no abdominal pains which usually indicated a fatal disease that could not be cured. She also inquired about blood in the urine or stools and got a negative answer.

After eliminating the more serious diseases, she listened to the pulse and heartbeat and they seemed in order except that the pulse was rapid. She felt for swollen glands and checked to see if Avi's tongue was coated. She was relieved that neither symptom was present.

Machla concluded that the boy had a childhood disease that started with high fever and ended with a rash. When Machla made her diagnosis known, the family felt less concerned. She then went to work on the child seeking to reduce the fever by sponging and bathing him. As the fever went down, the child perked up. Machla continued working very skillfully as the family watched in admiration.[10]

She then showed Batya the first signs of the developing rash. The rash was very faint but she said that it would become more pronounced in the next few days. To treat the rash, she gave her an ointment that was to be applied every few hours. She also instructed her to provide Avi with as much liquid as possible to replace fluids lost during the period of high fever.

"How many nurses do you have in the tribe of Menashe?" Elchanan asked.

"Over 100 are trained, but not all of them work full-time. Most important is the fact that we do not wait until children are ill before training mothers. As soon as a woman is pregnant with her first child, she receives instruction in child care at the Tribal Center. I believe that our tribe has a significantly lower rate of child mortality than do the rest."

"How did you get into this field in the first place?" Dina asked with some curiosity.

"It's a long, personal story," Machla answered. "I do not think that this is the time or place to talk about it."

It was now about eight in the evening and Machla was anxious to get home because her mother might be worried. Elchanan asked Batya to serve Machla some food and Batya did so.

"Are you sure you will be able to go home by yourself at this hour?" he asked in a solicitous manner.

"I should have no problem," she answered.

"Let me introduce you to my other two boys before you go. He called the boys out of his children's tent where they had been instructed to stay. Achituv was about ten and Michael about six. Unlike Dina, they had a strong resemblance to their mother. "This is Teacher Machla," he said, "and she is also a nurse."

"She is also very pretty," Achituv said, much to his father's obvious dismay. Batya sensed an unfavorable comparison and was unhappy about it.

Machla took her leave and headed home. On the way she dropped her bag at the tent and put her smock into it. She then reached the border which separated the tribe of Judah from the northern side of the tribe of Levi. It would have been easier for her to traverse the Levitical area and reach Menashe, which was on the southern border of the tribe of Levi. She didn't feel that it would be proper, however, to exploit the holy ground of the Levitical camp as a short cut if she were not intending to attend a religious service. It would, of course, be safer because Levites were on duty around the clock. Nevertheless, she chose to walk the perimeter of the Levite encampment, where, on the western border of the tribe of Levi, she would find herself in the tribe of Dan.[11]

Since it was at the beginning of the second month, there was no moon overhead. Ever since the tribes had been traveling in the desert, there was a pillar of Divine fire illuminating the way. The pillar, though, hovered over the center of the camp and, on the far side of some hills, there were shadowy areas. It was in one such deserted area that she was accosted by a young Danite who mistook her for a lady of the night. He approached her and asked, "And how much would my pretty lady charge for a few hours of pleasure?"

Machla didn't scream because the man didn't seem like someone who would attack her forcibly and she doubted that anyone would hear her. Instead, she faced the man with a withering look. "Young man, I know that the tribe of Dan stood with the rest of the children of Israel at Mount Sinai. How come the commitment made by the parents to uphold the Torah was not passed on to the younger generation?"

The man, unprepared for a literary and aristocratic response from a woman he imagined to be a lady of the night, slunk away to look for other game and Machla continued along her way. She was greatly relieved to reach the friendly confines of Menashe where she was known by everyone in the tribe. Her family was out waiting for her and, in fact, they were just about to dispatch a couple of the sisters to look for her. She was in no mood to tell them that Elchanan had young children so she simply said that the brother of one of her students was ill and that she went to his tent to attend to him. She avoided any mention of her accoster in Dan because she was afraid that her family would forbid her to travel alone in the future.

Back at Elchanan's tents, Batya had a few accounts to settle. She took Dina for a walk and spoke to her sharply. "Why did you hide from me the fact that your teacher was young, single and beautiful? Did your father order you to keep quiet in this matter?"

Dina had to be very careful because she didn't want to get on the wrong side of either parent. "My father did not forbid me to say anything. He did, however, teach me that a child must feel that her mother is the most beautiful woman in the world. I took that to be part of the honor that a child must give to her parents."

"Do you really feel that way about me?"

"The same law that teaches us to honor our parents also instructs us to honor our teachers. I believe that I am allowed to feel that my teacher is as beautiful as my mother. I never said so because you would think that I love my teacher for her appearance rather than her wisdom."[12]

"You do consider her as beautiful as me then?"

"Yes, mother."

"You are a smart girl, Dina, and you have learned to lie as tactfully as your father. Only an idiot would fail to realize that your teacher is incredibly gifted and one of the most stunning women among the children of Israel."

"Wait till you see her sister, Noah," Dina said when her mother finally accepted the truth. "Word is that Machla pales in comparison to her."

"It is enough that I will have to contend with one," Batya said with resignation.

Elchanan got his share when he and Batya retired for the night. "I see that you employed a very attractive teacher for our daughter and didn't bother telling me that she was single."

"I employ teachers only on the basis of their knowledge."

"You didn't notice her looks?"

"I do not pay attention to such details where my teachers are concerned."

"Elchanan, you are a scholar and a pious man. Some mothers even consider you a saint. But you are no angel. You had a mighty strong evil inclination when we were first married. It may be dormant as far as I personally am concerned but it is not dead. It only needs a woman such as Machla to wake it up."

"I have won a complete victory over my evil inclinations, my dear."

"You are a consummate liar, Elchanan. Are you in love with Machla?"

"I love only you, darling."

"Listen to me carefully, Elchanan. You are a great man, a true prince. Everyone considers you the second most important man in Judah and I bask in your glory. For me, a woman from a middle class family, it is an honor to be your wife. Every day, I thank God for the privilege. I raise your children while you are involved in your work. I am loyal and obedient to you and you have never heard a complaint escape my lips.

"I know that a man in your position is entitled to a second wife and you can easily support a larger family. All I ask is one thing. When you do take another woman, don't cast me out entirely. Keep me, the mother of your children, as your first wife. I would be content with my status as long as I could be near you and enjoy the minimal cohabitation that is required. I promise that I will cause no strife between me and my nemesis."

"I have no plans at the moment to take a second wife. It takes all of my energy to keep one wife happy. As for Machla, you have no cause at all for concern. Even if I were to consider her in a romantic way, Machla and her sisters are deliberately not getting married for reasons that I consider misguided. Someday I will tell you all about her cause. Rest assured, though, if ever I am dumb enough to get involved with another woman, I will keep you around for security. If a man has only one wife, he is at her mercy. If he has two, and the second wife tires of him, he can always return to the first one."

Batya delivered a good kick to Elchanan's backside. "You are not even a saint. Just a devil. But I love you, anyway. Come closer to me and I'll show you that one woman is all that you will ever need."

On Sunday, Elchanan was waiting for Machla to arrive with her lesson plans.

When she came in, he told her that Avi was much better and that the rash was beginning to subside. He conveyed Batya's thanks as well.

"By the way," he asked her, "did you get home safely Thursday night? I was worried about you and forgot to tell you to cross through the Levitical camp."

"I chose not to use the camp as a short cut."

"The priests put offerings on the altar all night. You could have watched the sacrifices. Better yet, you could have offered a personal prayer. Such a prayer can be recited at any time. Once coming into the Tabernacle for a legitimate reason, you are free to leave in an opposite direction."

"That is something I didn't know and I will keep it in mind. It is, of course, the custom in Menashe to offer all personal prayers at the bier of Joseph, the father of our tribe. Incidentally, Elchanan," she added, "do I look like a lady of the night?"

"I cannot say one way or another," he replied cautiously. "It is not my practice to associate with loose women and I am not exactly certain how they look. Why do you ask?"

"On the way home Thursday night, a man of the tribe of Dan accosted me and asked me what I would charge for a few hours and I didn't even know the prevailing rates."

"Judging by your appearance, Machla, I would say that you could command a very hefty fee."

"Don't be funny, Elchanan. It could have been a very serious business."

"What did you finally tell him?"

"I told him that I didn't know why the parents of the Danite tribe did not properly educate their children in the values of the Torah."

"A very appropriate response. I agree, however, that it is no laughing matter. In the future, if ever your work keeps you here after dark, I will personally escort you home."

"I think I would be safer with the men of Dan," she teased him. "At least they would pay for my services. Seriously, though, its a very generous offer and I appreciate it."

CHAPTER

NINE

"TALMUD TORAH IS EQUIVALENT TO THEM ALL"

In the late spring, the tribal council of Judah began to exert pressure on Elchanan, demanding a comprehensive report on the class for teen-age girls that he had inaugurated. Elchanan had not kept the council abreast of developments in the project. He was afraid that if he accurately reported the spectacular success of the undertaking, the council would demand its expansion. While not opposed to additional classes, Elchanan had no idea where to find teachers for the new students. The commanders who had children in the class, however, would not let him evade his responsibilities and play down the achievements of the venture.

One of the commanders took the floor and stated that girls in the tribe had never reached the level of Machla's class at any other time in the history of Judah. What is more, the commanders were besieged by irate parents demanding advanced studies for their daughters. "Your daughter is learning, Elchanan," he said. "What about the hundreds of others?" The members of the council turned to Elchanan to see how he would defend himself against the commanders who were attacking him.

"The demand is highly vocal," Elchanan answered, "and quite exaggerated. Certainly there are not 100 qualified girls in the tribe who can cope with higher Torah studies."

"The commanders sitting here, have at least thirty daughters who would be happy to enter Torah classes," the commander retorted. "Just to prove my point, let me ask the commanders who have received five or more requests from parents, to so indicate." About forty of the seventy-five commanders raised their hands.

"That alone represents some 200 students. Add the commanders who have received a smaller number of requests and those who have received well over five and we are talking of close to 400 students. Remember that there are some 7,500 girls in our tribe between the ages of eleven and thirteen.[1] I suggest that we appoint a committee to look into this problem and come up with a solution. If you have no answers, Elchanan, the committee can always interview Teacher Machla and get her ideas."

Elchanan lost his temper and countered angrily with vehemence. "For all these years, the council didn't do a thing to further Torah instruction for women and left us in a situation in which we had to import a teacher from Menashe to teach our children. Where does the worthy commander expect me to find thirty women in the tribe who can teach Torah? Forget about men, because I have not been able to induce any men to teach women on a regular basis. They are willing to offer a few hours a week but classes cannot be maintained with such limited teaching resources."

At this point, Caleb intervened in an attempt to cool the debate. "I personally had the pleasure of visiting the class of the daughter of Zelaphchad and it was a very moving experience. You cannot believe how well these girls do until you hear them quote the Torah. I asked them questions that many young men would find difficult and they answered without any hesitation.

"As chairman of the council, it is within my power to appoint committees and I will do so shortly. I want this committee to work with Elchanan because he is not to be blamed for our neglect during the last two decades. It is, in fact, his success that made us aware of this urgent need." Caleb then named a committee of seven commanders and instructed them to report back to the council within two weeks.

When Elchanan met with Machla after class, he complained bitterly about the treatment he received at the hands of the council. "Instructing women without teachers is like making bricks without straw," he lamented.

Machla thereupon gave Elchanan a lesson from her family history in the art of making bricks without straw. She told him how Ram and Zelaphchad coped with Pharaoh's decree. "I tell you this, Elchanan, not to boast of family heroism but to show you that even the most difficult problems can be solved when there is a will to do so."

"You have a solution in mind?" Elchanan asked, enjoying the way her mind worked and feeling certain that she would suggest some new ideas.

"I do, but first I want to give you a lesson in politics. When the council started harassing you, your reaction was only defensive. You spent undue effort trying to exonerate yourself from blame for the problem. You didn't succeed too well and, if Caleb hadn't intervened to save your neck, you would have been entirely ignored by the committee. The fact remains that you, as director of religious education for the tribe, should have done much more to train women. What the council wants now are plans and action, not excuses."

"From you, Machla, I am willing to accept the harshest criticism. I admit my failures. Tell me what can be done?"

"If you will dispense with the class review for today, I am willing to spend the time needed to work out a program with you."

"It might take several hours and you will have to walk home after it gets dark."

"I have no problem with that because, if memory serves me right, you personally promised to escort me home on such occasions."

"It will be my pleasure. Do you trust me?"

"Of course I do. I am protected by the Torah."

Elchanan understood the full significance of the reply. Although Machla was single, and could in time get married to him, he was not at liberty to touch her now. Because of her regular menstruation, Machla might be in a state of ritual impurity. To purify herself from the menstrual blood she would have had to immerse herself in a pool of water called a Mikva. Although the Mikva was a pool, its purpose was not to provide physical cleanliness but rather spiritual purification. Single women, as opposed to married ones, were not required to perform such immersions on a regular basis.[2] Only if they were members of priestly families who ate sacred foods or if they planned to view religious services in sanctified areas of the Mishkan, were they required to be in a state of ritual purity. Before Elchanan could come into physical contact with Machla he would have to determine her purity status. Given Machla's modesty and piety, she would never reveal such information to any man other than her husband.

Elchanan, who was a strict observer of these purity laws in his own home, decided it would be wiser not to pursue the matter any further despite his feelings for her.

"Well then, let us get to work," he said to Machla.

Machla started by outlining the three phases of the solution. "Firstly, we must clarify our needs. Secondly, we must outline steps to meet the needs and, finally, we must determine the best way to present our plans to the council. What are the needs, Elchanan?"

"The need is to provide enough qualified teachers to instruct three to four hundred teen-age girls in Torah for two hours a day."

"How many teachers are we talking about?"

"Well, setting a class limit of fifteen and allowing a few replacements for teachers who drop out because of health or unsuitability, thirty teachers should be sufficient."

"What period of grace do you think the council will grant you in this matter?"

"If I don't have three or four classes going by the time the fall holidays are over, I will be in serious trouble."

"So you plan to find three or four teachers and recruit about fifty students by the end of the summer?"

"I guess that is what I should try to do." Elchanan said dejectedly.

"Your approach may be somewhat shortsighted, Elchanan. You won't find three knowledgeable woman who are willing to teach and, if you tried to select only fifty students out of 400 applicants, you will have an uproar on your hands."

"I am well aware of the problem," Elchanan responded, imagining himself being bombarded by a horde of angry mothers and daughters. "I thought you were ready to offer a solution."

"Be patient, please, and listen. Your goal must be to accept all 400 students and not waste time looking for experienced teachers. If you promise the council to provide classes for all 400 students, will the council grant you six months to start the program?"

"They most certainly will."

"Now for the teachers. I am convinced that if we are allowed six months, we can train thirty teachers to the point where they will be able to start teaching classes."

"Just a minute, Machla. Remember that you are talking about women who have no Torah background and no teaching experience."

"I am fully aware of that. I started teaching my sisters when I was only fourteen and had been eavesdropping on my cousins' Torah lessons for only a year. Believe me, I wasn't far ahead of my sisters and I had no special training in teaching."

Elchanan's mood became a little less somber. "You will have to tell me more about your early years at some other time. Go on with your teacher-training plan. It may have some possibilities."

Machla replied at length. "There are two parts to teacher training. One is having the trainees learn the subject matter and the other is instructing them in teaching methods. What I am suggesting for the knowledge part is an abridged summary of Torah as a whole. I would not want students asking teachers questions on religious matters and find that the teachers do not even know that the answers are somewhere in the Torah. The summary should take about five months. A month before the classes, we should start teaching the first month's lessons in painstaking detail and demonstrate to the women how the lesson should be taught. We would let them observe existing classes and even give them practice teaching. After the classes start, we could keep the teachers sufficiently ahead of the students to make the system work."

"The plan sounds good, Machla, but it entails a lot of risks and many loose ends. Do you mind if I ask several questions?"

"Go right ahead."

"Who will recruit the trainees?"

"That is your responsibility, Elchanan. I would suggest that you seek women in their forties, with grown up children, who are looking for something to do."

"Who will write the Torah outline?"

"I will be happy to."

"Who will design the model lessons?"

"I will be happy to."

"Who will arrange for observation and practice?"

"Next month, I will start allowing a small number of the women to sit in my class every day. For practice they can use each other or we can round up some test students. Each woman will have to demonstrate a lesson in front of a class and be subject to criticism and review."

"I have hesitated to ask the last question until now because I have a terrible premonition that I will be unhappy with the answer. Who will train the teachers?"

"Life was never intended to be easy, Elchanan. We do not ask to be born and we do not determine when we die. We are simply here to serve our Creator."[3]

"Break it to me gently, without the preaching."

"All right, then. There will be thirty or more trainees who will require two teachers. I am willing to teach one section and stay later than usual. You are assigned to teach the other section and walk me home if I have to leave after dark."

"I cannot teach females."

"You most certainly can. The reason you have not been able to recruit male teachers is that you were not willing to set an example yourself. If you were to teach, they would do so as well. Remember, these are older women who do not bite. In fact, I'm sure most of the women would prefer your class to mine."

"What would Batya say if I taught fifteen women?"

"She would much prefer it to having you deposed by the council. In fact, if it weren't for your younger children, I would recruit Batya for the class and that way she would be able to keep an eye on you."

"Sometimes I wonder whose side you are on."

"I am on your side, Elchanan. I want you to succeed but success derives only from hard work. We will teach the women from the hours of two to four each afternoon. I will offer my regular class a half hour later than usual from four to six."

"How do we present this to the council?"

"Ask the committee chairman to gather his committee one night next week. We will have to schedule another meeting before then to rehearse the presentation."

Machla and Elchanan worked for an additional hour planning the curriculum and sorting out details of the program. When they had enough, Machla asked Elchanan to escort her home. They left the Tribal Center and walked west to the border of the Levite camp. Elchanan was well known throughout the tribe and people greeted him along the way. By the next day, Batya would certainly know that Elchanan was walking with another woman but he no longer was concerned. Enough people recognized Machla so Batya would readily learn the identity of the woman involved. Since Batya had already spoken to him on the subject of Machla, he had nothing further to risk.

When the pair reached the Levitical camp, Machla still did not want to cut across the area. Subconsciously she may have wanted to lengthen the walk so that Elchanan would have more time to talk to her.[4]

"On the way back," she said to him, "you may cut through the Levitical area if you so wish."

Ten minutes were spent walking through Judah to the tribal border. Walking to the border of Menashe around the perimeter of the Levite camp took about thirty minutes. All told, it took Elchanan forty minutes to walk Machla home and twenty-five minutes to return. Machla didn't allow Elchanan to walk with her in Menashe because she didn't want her sisters to know that a man was escorting her home.

As the two walked, Elchanan made a suggestion to which Machla responded with a warm glow. "Let us not talk about work during these walks. I want to relax and enjoy your company."

The chill of the early spring nights had abated and the weather was mild. It was a starry night in the desert with virtually no wind. They talked mostly about themselves, their hopes and aspirations. At times they ventured into politics, current events and the arts. They found it easy to communicate and the walk left Machla excited and elated. She was becoming increasingly fond of Elchanan and the time she spent privately with him heightened her feelings. Elchanan, for his part, enjoyed seeing Machla in a somewhat lighter mood when she was not carrying the weight of the world on her shoulders. Up to now, he hadn't even known that she had a lighter and more human side.

Upon returning home, he started planning the new venture and he arranged a meeting with the council committee for the following Wednesday. After class on Tuesday, he met again with Machla to complete work on the presentation. During the walk home he asked her to attend the committee meeting with him.

"Why do you need me? The details are all worked out."

"You inspire me and give me a measure of confidence I would otherwise not have."

"Someday you will have to cut the apron strings and stand on your own feet, you know."

"Yes, mother. But, for the time being, I would feel better with you present."

"I will have to tell my family that I will be late. They only expect that sort of thing from Noah." Machla did not seem unduly disturbed by the prospect. Elchanan, in fact, thought that he detected a gleam in her eyes but he couldn't be sure.

"Tell them you are working on a new project."

"I will," she said and bid him farewell at the border.

When she told Noah that she would be out late the next evening, Noah thanked the Lord that she had the foresight not to get involved in the project at Judah.

"Congratulations Machla, you are the first Hebrew woman to go back into bondage after the Lord delivered us out of slavery."

"It is all in a good cause," Machla answered. "Don't wait up for me."

The committee gathered in the Tribal Center the next night. Elchanan studied the men carefully and quickly realized that the group was heavily weighted with younger captains, parents of teen-age children. Their mood was not light and undoubtedly reflected some uncertainty about the outcome of the session. Having heard Elchanan state his rather rigorous position at the council meeting, they were expecting Elchanan to come up with various excuses for not being able to do anything about the situation. Instead, they heard an optimistic and detailed plan to start the teaching of 400 girls within six months.

"Who is going to train all the teachers?" the chairman wanted to know.

"Machla has volunteered to teach one section of the teachers and I myself will teach the other group."

"Are you serious, Elchanan?" the chairman asked in total surprise.

"Of course. Have you ever known me to shirk my responsibilities?"

"Not really. What you are doing will set a good example that others may follow. What will you need in the way of help from the council?"

"Our first task is to find candidates for teacher-training. The qualifications are not overly severe. We are looking for mature, pious women, who are willing to work hard. They need not have an extensive background in Torah but they must be willing and able to learn. It goes without saying that they should be reasonably free of domestic responsibilities. I would like each commander of 1,000 to recommend at least one candidate to us. Time is of the essence here."

"What else will you need?"

"We could certainly use some clerical help and the council will have to find an area for thirty classes to meet."

"I would like to ask Teacher Machla a few questions, if I may," a committee member ventured. "As a teacher of women, do you really feel that a woman can be trained in six months to stand in front of a class and offer Torah instruction?"

Machla answered with confidence. "If the women are carefully selected and trained, I feel that at least two thirds of them will complete the training course and be qualified to teach. A few more may drop out for various reasons after they start teaching. If we start with forty, we should end up with twenty-five reliable and effective teachers."

"Have you ever taught adult women?"

"No, but I see no reason why they should present any special difficulties."

Each member of the committee felt that he should ask a number of questions to justify his presence on the body and have something to say at the council meeting. Elchanan was impatient, but Machla took her time and answered each question at length. As a result, it was late in the evening before the committee adjourned, tired perhaps, but very satisfied with the plan.

The full council was even more satisfied a week later and voted to approve the proposal. Machla was again requested by Elchanan to attend and she answered many questions that were put to her. Since the council meeting took place in the morning, she had to leave for Judah very early so Elchanan made arrangements to provide her with lunch.

Batya followed developments closely and had very mixed emotions about the situation. She was happy that Elchanan was undertaking a project that would further enhance his status in the tribe. On the other hand, she was well aware that Machla was making major contributions to the planning and implementation of the program, a fact that would make Elchanan even more beholden to her. Batya had heard very quickly that Elchanan was walking

Machla home on a frequent basis and she found it hard to restrain herself. "Don't you find it burdensome to have to walk your teacher home so often?"

"Very burdensome, my dear."

"I know that you can't afford to let anything happen to your beloved teacher but could you not delegate the onerous work to some younger man who is not as busy as you?"

"I am not the type to impose such things on others. In any event, the walk is healthy and I feel very refreshed thereafter."

"Of that I am certain. Would it not be nice if you were to walk with me occasionally?"

"It would indeed. This Sabbath, we will take a nice long walk together."

"I thank God for small favors. What would I do if Machla lived in Judah?"

"In that event, I would not have to walk her home at night."

Batya could not resist a parting shot. "In that event, you would not even come home at night."

Elchanan did not let Batya upset him. He knew that all women were jealous of rivals, and he was thankful that Batya was fairly restrained and would not trouble him too much. He made a firm resolution to treat her with kindness and devotion to offset his ever increasing affection for Machla.

About seventy women responded to the invitation to train as teachers. Four of them came from the neighboring tribe of Issachar, after one of the commanders spoke to a colleague there about the program in very glowing terms. His friend described the project in an announcement made at the Issachar council meeting. Issachar had a reputation for scholarship and even some of the women wanted to learn. Their primary interest was studying rather than teaching but they were willing to teach in return for the Torah knowledge. All of the women who belonged to other tribes were readily accepted.[5]

At Machla's request, she conducted the interviews with Elchanan and a commander representing the council. Machla was teaching Elchanan the basics of dealing with a governing body. The commander did not speed up the proceedings, but it was politically important for the council to feel involved in the selection process. The procedure was fairly simple. Any applicant who was passed by all three interviewers was immediately notified of her acceptance and was told to report the following Monday. Those who received two favorable votes out of three were left pending until it would be determined whether they would be needed. Candidates who received one vote or no votes at all, were gracefully rejected.

Yafa was among the applicants. To say the least, she and Elchanan were not at all fond of each other. It was not only because he had turned down her daughter, Aviva, for Machla's program, but also from earlier friction in connection with the education of her sons. She was a very determined woman when it came to religious training. Elchanan rejected her as a teacher trainee because he felt she would be too aggressive for the students. Machla also had her doubts, but when she considered the fierce desire for Torah that Yafa had given her daughter, she felt that she had to vote yes. She was hoping that the commander would be the one to say no and thereby terminate the application. Much to her surprise, however, the latter had no objections to her.

With only about half the candidates being selected on the first cut, Yafa managed to get in from the remaining group. The trainees were younger than expected due to the presence of widows whose husbands died without leaving large numbers of children. Overall, the interviewers were satisfied with the quality of the trainees and their willingness to work hard.

With the exception of Yafa, the trainees were divided at random between Elchanan and Machla. Elchanan wanted no part of Yafa on general principle, and Machla felt that it was wrong for her to teach a mother and daughter simultaneously.

"What can I offer you," Elchanan asked her, "to overlook principle and take this burden off my hands?"

"I am willing to strike a bargain with you," Machla answered. "My patron who has been keeping me current in new Torah passages is now too ill to continue. All you have to do is keep me posted on new Torah sections and court rulings that relate to them."

"That is absolutely out of the question," Elchanan answered. "I cannot teach court rulings to a woman," he responded emphatically.

"You are already about to teach twenty women. Why would it hurt to add one more?"

"The level is not the same. If I made the effort, I could manage to teach women about Abraham and Isaac. Court rulings are of a different nature entirely."

"Do you feel that I would have difficulty following judicial reasoning?"

"Of course not. That, however, is not the point. We are dealing with a question of wasted effort. Since you will never be a judge or a commander, you have no need for such knowledge."

"I am sure it will enhance my teaching, although that in itself is not critical. Women are not commanded to study Torah but they are permitted to do so and receive reward. If they do study, they should do it well and not have superficial limitations placed upon them."

"I am willing to accept your position as far as Torah text and commentary are concerned. There are many judges, however, who are opposed to letting women become privy to the inner workings of judicial law. I am very much afraid that there will come a time when whole sections of Hebrew Law will be considered off-limits to women."

"I am afraid of that as well. But as long as there are no formal restrictions on the matter, you are still free to keep me posted on the latest judicial thinking."

"And, if I decline?"

Machla responded with a cool smile and a knowing look. "You will then have the delightful experience of teaching Yafa."

"You are an incredible manipulator, Machla, the likes of which I have never seen. I can only commit myself to teach you new text and commentary, nothing more, on condition that you take care of Yafa."

"I accept. It will only be a matter of time before you need another favor and I will bargain for the rest." Machla smiled with anticipation.

Again, at Machla's request, the first session of the training program was opened with a special assembly. All members of the education committee were on hand and Caleb was invited to bestow a special blessing upon the undertaking.

Once the training started, it became obvious that not all the candidates were suitable. For various reasons, both Machla and Elchanan lost students. Some couldn't keep up with the work and some wouldn't or couldn't attend regularly. After a month, Machla retained sixteen women out of her twenty and Elchanan was left with fourteen. The opening classes began with a review of the revelation of the Torah and the ten commandments. That was an event with which all the members of the classes could identify because they had participated in it. From there, the instructors proceeded to a lengthy discussion of the duties of a Hebrew and the purposes of each commandment. It wasn't until the third month that the students learned about the early history of the Hebrew people. The women listened intently and even chose to ask questions or offer opinions.

Teaching about Torah rather than teaching the Torah itself was a new experience for Machla. It took her away from the actual text and made her focus on the underlying meanings. She regretted that her students would not be inspired by the classic prose and poetry of the Torah but she had no choice. The survey was a critical element in the training plan. It was much easier for Elchanan to adjust to the method because he had never stressed literalism in Torah studies. To him, the thought was more important than the word and he stressed finding the reasons for commandments rather than memorizing the details. The different approaches to Torah study of Machla and Elchanan persisted for many generations after the Torah was revealed and long after the earlier Torah teachers left the scene.

Both sections of the class progressed nicely and Elchanan was soon able to focus on the second part of the educational plan, student recruitment. For the next twelve weeks, Elchanan and Machla interviewed an average of eight students a day. Only students with obvious emotional or mental problems were rejected. No attempt was made to classify students by academic potential. Rather it was decided to inform students that class assignments were flexible. Brighter students would be moved to special classes as would slower ones. Since all teachers would be teaching the same lessons, such liberties could be taken.

Machla continued teaching her regular class but now there were members of both adult classes observing each day. Machla explained to her students that their presence was necessary. She asked them to ignore the visitors and go about their business.

As the days lengthened, Machla was able to complete her work long before sundown. This freed Elchanan from escorting her home and left Machla saddened. She longed to be with him and talk to him on the way. The depth of her feelings surprised Machla, and revealed to her the power with which love rules over individuals. Elchanan, who was unusually burdened with his extra class and the process of student selection, did not feel the absence as keenly. Batya, of course, was relieved of a good deal of her anxieties.

As opening day approached, the trainees were given actual lesson plans and opportunities to teach a class of volunteers. Some of the teachers were understandably nervous and made glaring errors. Machla made sure that they did not become discouraged and explained that their problems were common to all inexperienced teachers. Where women needed extra help she met with them before and after class.

Only twenty-seven of the original teachers completed the training program and some 350 students were enrolled. The council was kept informed about the developments by monthly reports from Elchanan. Machla insisted upon presenting the entire graduating class to the council and having members of the teachers' families on hand for the ceremonies. She was far more sensitive to questions of status and morale than Elchanan and her insights proved correct. Some of the women had never had any public recognition in their lives and they were thrilled by the attention they were receiving. Machla gave them valuable advice on dress and appearance and raised their self esteem. She urged them to regard themselves as professionals and act accordingly.

The ceremony was held out of doors in the late afternoon after the heat of the day had eased somewhat. Members of the council, heads of families and judges of the tribal court were present. Speakers stressed the role of women in the family and the importance of enabling women to imbue children with the spirit of the Torah. Each teacher rose in her place as her name was called by Elchanan.

Machla granted her regular class a one-week vacation when school was about to open. She recruited volunteers among the commanders to help in the initial phases and she and Elchanan concentrated on problem areas. Opening a large school entails confusion and disorder but the organizers were well prepared and classes got underway without incident. Within a week, Elchanan was able to report that twenty-five classes of fourteen students each were meeting. Two teachers were kept for substitution and individual case work. The council was overwhelmed by the success of the project and commanders reported great happiness among their constituents.

In late fall, Elchanan resumed walking Machla home on a daily basis. She did ask Elchanan to make it known at the council that he was escorting her only for her safety. In fact, she let Elchanan send someone else along with her on several occasions to prove the point. The families got used to seeing her on the way and paid less attention.

When he did walk with her, Elchanan spoke very freely. He also let Machla reveal her full life story including many details that he hadn't known before. She told him of the tents she cleaned for Barak to learn Torah and how she kept her sisters up to date. By telling him, she revealed Barak as her patron. Elchanan did not know Barak well, but he had met him when both were commanders and he remembered that Barak was held in high esteem. After a while, Machla told him about her cousin, Eliav, and how he was waiting for her to relent and accept his proposal. She explained why marriage would weaken her claim to land in Canaan, and why she was therefore deferring it until the matter was resolved.

Elchanan, in turn, shared his life experiences with her. He spoke of his growing up in a wealthy home and having the best of tutors. By the age of twenty-three he was already a commander of 100 and two years later he was made a commander of 1,000 and won a seat on the tribal council. As a council member he was popular and was appointed in charge of higher Torah education for the tribe. At twenty-seven, he was named an alternate judge and legal advisor to the council. As such, he was the youngest man to ever hold a judicial title in the tribe of Judah. The promotion forced him to relinquish his seat on the council, but he was allowed to retain his educational position and serve the council as legal advisor.

"What are your ultimate goals in life?" Machla asked. Her face assumed a thoughtful position as she watched Elchanan ponder his answer. Although his ambitions were clear, he had never had the need to express them verbally.

"There are two positions for me to seek — a regular judge on the High Court, or chief judge of the tribal court. Caleb asked me if I wanted him to recommend me to Moses for a position on the High Court and I declined the offer."

"Why is that?"

"A judge on the High Court is removed from his tribal surroundings. Most of the time, the High Court deals with theoretical issues and not the needs of common people. I am not yet ready to withdraw from the world."

"What are the prospects of becoming chief judge of Judah?"

"Not promising at all. Judah has six representatives on the High Court and many of them are elderly. Vacancies arise there on a frequent basis. At the tribal court, however, the chief judge is young and effective. I am sure that I will be considered among others for the position when it arises but, for now, I will have to bide my time. What is your goal, Machla?"

"I look forward to tilling the soil of Canaan, milking cows and tending sheep. My role models in life are Abraham and Isaac, not Moses and Aaron." As usual, Elchanan was impressed by the strength of her convictions with regard to the Land of Canaan. Machla enjoyed such a high status in her tribe that she could easily avoid any manual labor for the remainder of her life. Nevertheless, she felt it would be wrong to exploit her profound knowledge of Torah.

On other occasions, Elchanan spoke of his family. He was married at the age of twenty-two to Batya, who was nineteen. Batya did not conceive easily and it was almost three years into the marriage before Dina was born. The first son was born two years later but then there was a four year lapse before the next son was born. Avi was born two years later and no other child thereafter.

"I know what you are thinking, Machla, but it is not the case. At the outset of marriage I was very ardent but Batya did not conceive. The same held true between the second and third child. Only lately, under the stress of serving as judge and educational director, has my attention been diverted to other things." The statement surprised Machla because she sensed that Elchanan regarded her with considerable passion. Since she wasn't the type to hesitate about asking personal questions, she probed further. "You no longer experience strong desire?"

"I was concerned about it until I met you, Machla. You have rekindled my ardor." Machla turned away to hide her deep blush.

When she regained her composure after his expression of intimate feelings, Machla whispered. "I hope that Batya is the beneficiary of your renewed vigor."

Elchanan was not too convinced by her sudden concern for Batya. "It probably works to some degree," he said nonchalantly. "Feelings in such matters, however, are not always transferable."

"Well, I am glad that you are thinking of me as a woman, rather than as an employee."

"I have done so from the first day, but now the feelings are growing stronger."

"That makes two of us who are letting physical attraction get in the way of an intellectual relationship."

"I, at least, have another outlet."

"I do the best I can." Machla said with resignation.

Several weeks later, when Machla's family was gathered at the Sabbath meal, Noah rose to make an announcement.

"I regret to inform the family that Machla has been stricken with a severe ailment."

"What are the symptoms, nurse Noah?" asked Milka, who had rehearsed the act with Noah before dinner.

"Among the symptoms are daydreaming, absentmindedness, poor appetite and excessive use of the looking glass."

"Is it a serious disease?"

"Very serious," Noah voiced with mock concern.

Achla who had not yet caught on started to worry. "Is Machla really sick?"

"Yes, indeed,"

"What is her illness called?" asked the mother.

"Love," said Noah. "Machla is lovesick."

"Is there any known cure, nurse Noah?" said Milka, getting back into the act.

"Yes," said Noah, "the cure is called marriage. Within a number of years it wipes out all traces of lovesickness."

Machla controlled her laughter. "I love only the Torah, my mother, the Land of Canaan, my middle sisters and, on occasion, Noah."

"The symptoms previously enumerated arise only in cases of romantic love. It is obvious that the patient is withholding vital information from the nurse."

"So be it. There is absolutely no reason why I do not have the right to make a fool of myself. My sisters have frequently done so over the years and, may I point out, they never told me with whom they were involved."

That terminated the discussion, except that Noah reiterated that all domestic duties remain in force regardless of the emotional state of the sister. This was a line that Machla had used very often and she had no choice but to accept her own rules.

Toward the end of the year, the weather turned cooler and windstorms were frequent. On one particular night, wind velocity was extremely strong, overturning tents and leaving personal possessions strewn about. Elchanan suggested to Machla that she sleep over in Judah but Machla was afraid that her family would worry too much. So they set out and found the going rather difficult. When they arrived at the border of Menashe, Elchanan insisted on taking Machla all the way home. Machla agreed as long as he understood that he would leave when he came within fifty cubits of her tent area.

The arrangement didn't work because her sisters were watching for her at the head of the path leading to the tribal border. They were worried about the winds and planning to help her home. As the pair arrived, Noah spotted them first and took a quick look at Elchanan. She had a trained eye in such matters and, even in a windstorm, she could see a remarkably handsome man. She signaled to her sisters.

"Quick, girls," she cried aloud, "take a look at the beautiful stag that Machla brought home with her."

Retribution was quick and savage. Machla edged close to Noah and, in a hardly noticeable move, under her robe, delivered a quick vicious kick to Noah's shin. Noah yelped in pain.

"Your Honor, Judge Elchanan," Machla said, "I would like to present my sisters." As she introduced her sisters one by one, Elchanan had a chance to note that they were all tall and dark, with softer features than Machla. Each one would have stood out in any circle of women. Elchanan was impressed by their bearing and had never seen such an imposing group of women in one family. Noah, of course, needed no introduction. Hers was a heavenly beauty for which there was no parallel in his experience. It took a major effort to keep from staring at her.

The truth was beginning to dawn on Noah about Machla and Elchanan. After the pain in her leg subsided, she displayed her winning personality. "Your Honor," she said sweetly, "I am so sorry I didn't recognize you. Machla led us to think that you were old, gray and feeble."

Machla aimed another kick in Noah's direction but this time Noah was too fast for her. She danced agilely out of harm's way. Sadly she realized that this was no stag that had arrived but a lion cub. Machla was the mother lioness and she was going to make absolutely certain that no predators came anywhere close to her little one.

"That is perfectly all right, Noah," Elchanan said graciously, "Your description of me may have been a little less than true. But all the descriptions I've heard of you don't even begin to do you justice."

"Thank you, Your Honor, that is very kind of you. May I call you Elchanan?" Noah smiled innocently as Machla glared at her.

Machla concluded the introductions and walked with Elchanan to the tent area to present her mother. Elchanan perceived her as a graceful and composed woman with fine features. Achla was pleased to see him and thanked him profusely for walking Machla home.

"You have a long walk back," she said. "Why don't you rest here for a few minutes and we will prepare some refreshments." They cleared a small sheltered area and Elchanan sat down with the family. They served him a warm soup with pieces of manna.

"Has Machla told you of the wonderful work that she is doing in our tribe?" he asked Achla.

"She has given us some idea. But, as you know, she is extremely modest and doesn't boast of her accomplishments." Machla had, in fact, told the family very little about the school for girls and the massive teacher-training program. Elchanan gave them a much more detailed picture of what Machla had succeeded in doing in the space of a year and a half. He also dwelt at great length on Machla's knowledge of the Torah and her keen sense of law.

"All of my daughters are learned in the Torah," Achla said with pride, "and all of them yearn for the Land of Canaan as did their father, Zelaphchad, of blessed memory."

"I don't have time to test them but I take your word for it. As for their problem of inheritance in Canaan, I am aware of the situation. I don't know if I can succeed in resolving the problem, but I give you my word that I will not rest until the matter is considered in the highest places."

Machla was jolted by the statement. Elchanan had never said anything to her about getting personally involved in the case. She realized the implications at once. Through Caleb, Elchanan could get the matter to the attention of Moses and that was truly the highest place.

"That would be wonderful," Achla said. "It would resolve a problem that I have with my daughters that they won't allow me to talk about."

"I am aware of that problem, too, but I wouldn't worry about it if I were you." He then turned to the sisters and asked, "Could we interest any of you in working in Judah?"

"Do you have any brothers?" Noah asked.

"None that would be worthy of your favor."

"That's too bad. I can only speak for myself in the matter and the answer is 'no'. There are sufficient opportunities for service in our own tribe to keep us busy."

Elchanan thanked the family for the hospitality and headed home. After he left, Noah was the first to deliver the verdict. "For a man like that, Machla, you have my blessings to make a fool of yourself. But I think you are overly protective of him. My shin will hurt for a week. Do you really think that I or any of your dear sisters would try to steal him away from you?"

"Yes," said Machla, "I am very insecure about it. You have some natural advantages and you can twist men around you fingers. He is the first man who makes my heart throb and I worry about losing him."

"What about his wife? What sort of a hold does she have on him?"

"She is a fine woman, but not learned and not especially attractive. She is not happy about Elchanan and me, but she seems resigned to it."

"Do you think he can do anything about our court case?" Milka asked.

"If anyone can, he is the man."

Machla mentioned the matter to Elchanan the following evening on the way home. "You never told me that you were interested in helping us with our cause."

"I wasn't planning to say anything about it last night either, but when I saw how troubled your mother was about the problem, I felt the need to offer some encouragement. I have in fact made a preliminary study of the matter and have had discussions with experts on the court. When I am ready, I will seek an interview with our master, Moses, and speak to him about the case."

"Did you find anything significant?"

"To tell the truth, I have not found anything that could be considered encouraging. It looks like an extremely difficult situation to resolve.

Nevertheless, if your family was good at making bricks without straw, my family is good at making laws without precedents. There is always hope."

"Thank you, Elchanan, our family would greatly appreciate your help. By the way, my mother and sisters think that you are an attractive and scholarly man."

"Speaking of last night, how is Noah? Was she able to walk this morning?"

"You noticed me nudge her?"

"Hardly a nudge. You just about broke her leg. I begin to feel that her defense at the council may have had some merit. I am quite thankful that I am protected from you by the Torah."[6]

"She has to be put her in place sometimes. I felt that she was disrespectful to a judge of the children of Israel."

"She was just joking, Machla. I enjoyed the compliment and didn't feel insulted. You have to lighten up a little. You can't take everything so seriously."

"What would you do to me if I called you a beautiful stag?"

"I would accuse you of insubordination, bring you up on charges and bar you from the tribe forever."

"Why should we not be equal in the eyes of the judge?"

"You should be, but sometimes I am just a little partial to pretty women."

Machla grabbed a manna cake from her bag and threw it at him. She missed by a wide margin, but she made her point. Even Elchanan was not allowed to trifle with her.

"Watch your temper, Machla. We are only in the courtship phase and you act as if we are already married."

"If we were married, I wouldn't have missed."

Elchanan was beginning to realize how much he meant to her and how she would protect his honor if it were ever threatened. She was not a light-hearted woman at all. Rather she was a God-fearing over-achiever, who took life very seriously.

"I'm sorry, Machla. Feel free to call me handsome any time you wish."

"That's better, my beautiful prince. Thank you for walking me home."

In Judah, time passed quickly. Spring followed winter and then it was summer. Machla felt alive as the weather warmed up and her spirits were high. The teacher-training program and all student classes continued without faltering. The teachers were gaining self-confidence and the level of instruction was improving daily. Their students had already reached the story of the ten commandments and examinations revealed a high level of retention. At the start of the summer, Elchanan asked Machla what would happen to her original class during the following year.

"I take it you are concerned with Dina," she stated.

"That is true. I cannot begin to tell you how much you have done for her. You have made me very proud of my daughter. What is even more gratifying is her desire to continue learning."

"Why can't you teach her?"

"Parents find it hard to instruct their own children. Dina has never let me teach her much of anything."

"It would not be fair to continue the present class for a third year. The girls all have a good foundation and it is time to give others a chance to obtain advanced knowledge. Furthermore, even if they were to advance, there is nothing that they can do with their knowledge except teach in the school. For that, they have enough background now, much more than the teachers we trained to teach."

"As a matter of fact, there is a special opportunity for them. I envision my daughter as a teacher of teachers as you and I are."

"You have weakened your case with that goal, for there are only three girls in the class who can ever attain that level. In addition to Dina, there are just Malka and Aviva who have the desire and capacity for it. I do not think that I can commit myself to a class of only three students."

"What other students would you teach? All girls who wish to learn may enter the regular school."

"That school gives only an introduction. It is not Torah in intensity and depth. My plan for next year is as follows. We have six sections in the school for the brighter students. From each section we can take the two best students and put them in my class for highly intensive study."

"That is a very sound idea but is still leaves us with our girls who have no class."

"I have a solution."

"Your solutions come with a price that I may not be willing to pay," Elchanan said cautiously but with some anticipation.

"In which case you are free to solve the problem yourself."

"Very well, then, go ahead and make your proposal. You never leave me any choice."

"If the girls will walk to Menashe three times a week, I will arrange for one of my sisters to teach them."

"Noah?"

"Possibly."

Elchanan, who was well aware of Machla's insecurity when it came to Noah, could not resist having a little fun at her expense. "Will she accept a middle-aged man in her class?"

"Be serious, Elchanan. You are letting your lusty imagination run wild."

"There is nothing wrong with dreaming. Tell me your price for this accommodation."

"All court decisions that affect the understanding of verses in the Torah."

"All of them?"

"All of them, bar none."

"You won't let anyone know your source?"

"I give you my word."

"I need a confirmation that you can convince a sister."

"You will get it if your agree to the terms."

"I agree."

Machla called a family meeting when she reached home and explained the arrangement with Elchanan. Her sisters were enthusiastic about the learning, but not one of them volunteered to teach.

"I would be very embarrassed, if I had to return to Elchanan empty handed," she pleaded with them. "Is there any inducement I can offer?"

"How about letting me teach in Judah?" said Noah.

"Never."

"How about my manna collecting?" Each girl went out on Friday because of the double collection and two other mornings during the week.

"That will mean going out five times a week for me. That's just too much."

"You can take my Fridays and one other day." Noah hated to collect the manna because it meant getting up early and being presentably dressed. She never appeared in public unless she was at her best, so she was constantly trading with her sisters to avoid the task.

"Is that your best offer?"

"Final offer."

"I will think of you kindly, Noah, when my back hurts and my body aches from all that stooping."

"The exertion will keep you in shape."

The deal was struck with Noah and Machla reported to Elchanan. "Remember," she said, "No parent-teacher conferences."

"How will I know of my daughter's progress?"

"You are free to ask your daughter."

"What if there are special problems?"

"I will be glad to convey messages."

"Now that you have everything you want," Elchanan asked Machla, "what will you ask from me the next time I need a favor?"

Machla didn't hesitate for a moment. "The next request will be that you actually speak to our master, Moses, on behalf of the daughters of Zelaphchad."

"I have made some progress in that area and I will have a definitive answer in two weeks. Meanwhile I am thinking of a favor that you will be able to do for me in a few weeks." It was only much later that it dawned upon Machla that Elchanan may have been thinking in romantic terms.

When he came home that night, Elchanan told Dina and Batya that he had made an arrangement for Dina and two other girls to continue their studies in the fall.

"Will Machla still be teaching us?" Dina asked.

"I thought you were very happy with her." Elchanan said in turn.

"She is a good teacher but very strict. She works us ten times harder than the girls in the general classes."

"The harder you work, the more you learn," said Batya, without the slightest sympathy, "I wish I had had a chance to learn as much as you."

"You are not a child anymore, Dina," said Elchanan with some anger, "and no one will force you to study further. If you wish to terminate your education, as others in the class will do, it is up to you."

"It most certainly is not up to her," said Batya vehemently. "Dina, if your father makes arrangements for a class, you will attend it."

Dina sensed a fight brewing and decided to play it safe. "I will attend of my own accord. All I asked, was if Machla will be teaching."

"Machla will not be teaching your class. Whoever we get to teach you may not be as strict as Machla but she will be instructed to teach you just as intensively. The girls in the general school are given a simplified program and they should not serve as your role models. You should strive to know as much as Machla."

"You don't even know as much as she does," Dina retorted, and earned herself a well-deserved slap from her mother. Elchanan had never seen Batya act as aggressively as she did that night. Both women in his life, it now seemed, were competing to protect his honor. He decided that it would be wiser to wait before revealing that Noah was going to teach Dina and the others.

When Machla arrived home that night, there was sad news awaiting her. Barak, her commander, had passed away. The funeral was scheduled for the following morning.

The five sisters cut their garments in an act of mourning required when one's teacher passes away. They followed Barak's body to its final resting place and vent their sorrow together with thousands of families whose lives had been touched by this saintly man. As a group, the sisters visited the widow and children and did what they could to offer them sympathy and comfort.[7]

CHAPTER

TEN

Two weeks later, Elchanan reported to Machla that the family's case was making good progress. "Caleb spoke to Moses about letting me present the subject and Moses gave his consent."

"That's wonderful, Elchanan. Do you have any idea how soon it will come to pass?"

"Our master, Moses, agreed to set aside a night during the second week after the holidays in the fall for this purpose. He has no time for such involved cases until after the festivals are concluded."

Machla's heart started beating rapidly, and she was frightened as she prepared to ask the next question. She was now aware that the favor Elchanan was seeking of her was of a personal nature, one that would affect their relationship. "Have you decided on the favor that I must grant you in return for your efforts?"

Elchanan thought for a minute. "I have. It is rather delicate, though, so I would prefer to deal with it at a more appropriate time."

Machla was vastly relieved as the tense moment passed and that a major problem for her had been deferred. The matter would come up again, for sure, but at least she would have more time to prepare a response.

The summer passed quickly. The general school was closed for vacation and Machla was not teaching. This was her first separation from Elchanan for an extended period and she missed him. She spent more time with her mother and sisters and she worked at the health center for a few days each week, but nothing could distract her from her loneliness.

Early one morning, Noah finally decided to intervene. "Machla, you are not helping anyone around here. Your heart is in Judah and nothing else seems to matter."

"I guess not. What do you suggest?"

"How about a family picnic?"

"Where would it be?"

"In Judah, of course. None of us have seen your school or met any of your teachers."

"The school is on vacation now. You will only be able to see empty tents."

"I have a better idea. I have to meet the students that I will be teaching for you in the fall. How about the two of us going down to see them?"

"Can I trust you not to try anything funny?"

"Yes."

"You won't flirt with Elchanan?"

"Somehow I feel that it is too late for that. I cannot help being charming but I sense that you have a secure hold over him. You have nothing to worry about."

Machla took a long look at Noah and was not at all reassured. Noah was dressed beautifully and looked like a princess. Her eyes shone and her innocent smile was even more dazzling than usual. "If I were not bored to death here, I would never trust you. Going myself would be too obvious, but taking you on a tour seems legitimate enough. You will show Elchanan proper respect?"

Noah cast her eyes low and faked a look of the sheerest humility. "Your Honor, your humble servant Noah is grateful that you have allowed her to walk on the same sand that you have tread upon. How is that for an opener?"

"Haughty and presumptuous. A little more humility."

Noah tried again. "Your esteemed Honor, your worthless servant, Noah, deems it a high privilege to walk on the same sand your worthy personage has tread upon."

"Much better. I am happy that you have finally realized Elchanan's high status in his tribe. Let's get started."

Machla, who was in excellent physical shape, had no trouble with the long walk. Noah found it much harder, but was encouraged by the admiring glances from men along the way. When they arrived at Judah, Machla pointed out Elchanan's tent. "I will stay outside," Machla said. "Go in and ask for Dina. Do you have a nickname?"

"Some of my friends call me 'Dodi.'"

"Good, use that. We are playing with fire and I don't want to get burned."

"What got into you, Machla? You never fool around and today you are a real devil."

"Elchanan thinks I'm too serious and it's causing him some doubts about me. The time has come to have a little fun, to prove to him that I am human."

Noah went over to the tent and asked for Dina. Batya took one look at Noah and sensed trouble.

"Who are you and why are you looking for my daughter?"

"Oh, I am Dodi. Elchanan Ben Uriah has appointed me to teach his daughter and two other girls. I came to meet my students."

Batya turned ashen. "Where does Elchanan find women like you? Are you sure you are a teacher? You look like something else to me."

"I beg your pardon. I trust your daughter is not as ill-mannered as you." Noah was now acting up a storm.

"I am sorry, Dodi. The last teacher he engaged — a woman by the name of Machla — stole his heart away from me. She is not even half as pretty as you."

"Are you talking about Machla, the daughter of Zelaphchad, from the tribe of Menashe? I have heard of her. She is very saintly and the most learned woman among the children of Israel. She certainly wouldn't steal a man's affections away from his wife unless, of course, his wife did not treat him properly."

"I treat him well enough. It's just that he lets pretty women turn his head."

"Most men do. But, if he is interested in Machla, I will not dare enter the picture. Two women are more than enough for a man. I will admit, though, he is a handsome fellow. Tall and dark, the type of a man a woman could really love." Noah rolled her eyes and appeared to be in a trance.

Batya thought that her behavior was somewhat strange, but she didn't have the nerve to make a scene. "Dina," she called to her daughter, "you have a visitor." Dina came out of her tent.

"This is your new teacher, Dodi."

Dina took one look and realized it could only be Noah. Since her mother didn't yet know who it was, she decided not to reveal the identity of the stranger.

"Mother," she said, "I am so happy for you. Your problem with Machla is solved. Daddy will take a look at this new teacher and forget all about Machla."

Noah burst out laughing. "I am not sure you are helping your mother by making such comments. In any event, I came here to determine your Torah level and see whether you can work harder than you have in the past."

"Thanks. That is just what I needed."

Noah gave Dina a short examination and Batya sensed that her daughter was doing well.

"I must tell you, Batya, that your daughter is well prepared. In at least one area you have reason to be thankful to Machla."

Noah asked Dina to take her to see Malka and Aviva. When Machla saw Noah leaving with Dina she knew that she had enough time to walk to her tent near the Tribal Center. One of the men working there told her that Elchanan was in court filling in for a judge and would probably be there all day. Machla waited for Noah to join her at the Tribal Center and Noah came with the three girls tagging behind her.

"Girls," she asked them, "will you be as nice to your new teacher as you were to me?"

"Of course we will," Malka said. "She promised us that she will teach us how to look pretty."

"I see," said Machla. "Let us show Dodi around."

"She's not Dodi," Malka said. "She's Noah and she is almost as smart as you."

"Did she say that or is it your own conclusion?"

"I asked her some very difficult questions and she knew all the answers."

"She came to examine you. You weren't supposed to test her. Did you know all the answers?"

"They all did very well," Noah said. After touring the Center, she sent the girls back to their tents.

"Girls, I will see you in Menashe in two weeks," she reminded them.

The sisters decided not to wait for Elchanan and started walking home. On the way, Machla asked Noah to evaluate her students.

"Malka is a once in a lifetime discovery. What a pity it is that such minds go to waste. If she were a man, she would surely reach the High Court. Aviva is the most motivated but she doesn't have the capacity of the others. Dina is the most complex situation. She is smart but lacks ambition and desire to work. She certainly does not take after her father in that respect."

"Noah, you judge people quickly and with remarkable accuracy. What do you think about Batya?"

"It is a real pity there. She is a very good woman. She loves Elchanan but she takes certain things for granted and that is costing her dearly."

"What do you mean?"

"Well, she was overmatched when she entered the marriage and hasn't improved any since. Meanwhile, Elchanan is advancing rapidly and leaving her far behind. Somehow she thinks that it is enough for a woman to prepare meals and bear children to keep a marriage going. It would be sufficient if men were limited to one wife and had no other choice. Our laws, however, allow men to take extra wives. A man like Elchanan, who can easily support two women, is free to seek the very best available."

"Do you think the Torah should limit men to one wife?"

"If I were married, I might feel that way. Right now the law is working to my advantage."

Back in Judah, Elchanan was in court until sundown. The case was then adjourned and carried over to the next day. He had a lot of work to take care of before going home. When he reached the tent it was late and the children were already asleep. Batya greeted him warmly in one of her better dresses and prepared a very fine dinner. Elchanan sensed that there was something brewing and braced himself for the storm.

"Well," she said, "I see you have gone and done it again."

"Done what, my dear?"

"Don't play dumb with me. We had a visitor today."

"Who was that?"

"Dodi."

"Dodi?"

"Yes, Dodi. You know. Dina's new teacher."

Elchanan was thinking quickly. Noah must have come by and used an alias or a nickname.

"Oh, Dodi, of course. Did she interview Dina?"

"Yes, she did, and I gathered that Dina did very well."

"Does Dodi appear capable to you?"

"It is not her capabilities that I am complaining about. It is her appearance in general."

"Why? Is there anything wrong with her appearance? You understand that I don't examine such things too closely."

"For a man who doesn't look closely at women, you have the remarkable ability of finding the most attractive, single women I have ever seen. This time you really outdid yourself. Your Dodi can make a man's head spin."

"I am glad you appreciate my taste, dear. That explains why I married you."

"I admire your taste but I don't appreciate it one bit. Listen, Elchanan, you are a judge and you aspire to be chief judge. You can't continue to seek out such attractive women."

"I never chase after women. Somehow they just seem to want to work for me."

"Very funny. If you get involved with this Dodi, you will wind up with three wives."

"Nothing wrong with that. Our ancestor, Jacob, had four and they bore him the twelve tribes of Israel." Elchanan didn't want to tell Batya that Dodi was Machla's sister and that under Torah Law a man was not permitted to be married to two sisters coevally.[1]

"Elchanan, I cannot understand why you have to seek women elsewhere when all that you need of women is available free, in your own tent, as often as you may want it."

Elchanan was smart enough not to say anything about quality as opposed to quantity.

"I am very happy to hear those thoughts. That, I assume, is the reason for the dress and the fine dinner."

"Yes. It is too late to do anything about Machla, but I am trying to keep you from Dodi."

"Your efforts, I assure you, will be entirely successful." Elchanan began to think about the event and the fuller picture emerged. Noah would not have come to Judah by herself without Machla's participation. In fact, he suspected that Machla was with Noah in Judah, although Noah visited his tent alone. He wondered if Machla was capable of such deviltry when she was so straight and severe in all aspects of life.

It was this heaviness that was the only remaining stumbling block in his relationship with Machla. He was afraid that if he married Machla, all joy and humor would disappear from his life. He would have to account to her for every minute that was not spent in learning or teaching the Torah. The fact that Machla could engage in a prank, even at his expense, was an encouraging sign.

In the morning, he took Dina aside and asked her about the events of the previous day. Dina said that she was able to recognize Noah from descriptions given by Machla in class but she was afraid to tell her mother.

"Was Machla in Judah yesterday?"

"I saw her at the Tribal Center and she and Noah walked home together."

"Where did Noah get this Dodi stuff?"

"Dodi means 'my beloved' in Hebrew. Noah claims that her friends call her that."

"Did you make a good impression on your new teacher?"

"I answered almost all of her questions but I think she liked Malka more."

"I don't think you convey as much eagerness and enthusiasm as the other girls. If you plan to become a teacher when you grow up, you should know that knowledge alone is not enough to make a good teacher. You have to show your students that you love the subject.

"Maybe Noah will help me. I am put off by Machla because she is so totally obsessed with the subject that nothing else has meaning for her. Noah knows the Torah, too, but she is not reclusive and she enjoys life."

"Machla may not choose to reveal all facets of her personality to her students. I have reason to believe that she has some lighter moments."

Dina found that somewhat hard to believe. While she had a chance to talk to her father, she used the opportunity to ask him the question that was uppermost in her mind. "I know how you feel about Machla. When are you going to marry her?"

"For my part I would be ready immediately after the holidays. She, however, hasn't the slightest intention of getting married."

Dina had mixed feelings on the matter so didn't pursue the subject. She was very loyal to her mother and felt sad about her plight. On the other hand, she adored her father and didn't want to stand in the way of his happiness. After a moment of reflection, she asked, "Should I let mother know who Dodi really is?"

"We will have to do so sooner or later so you may tell her at any time. I have to go to court now and I will see you tonight." A short time later, Dina spoke to her mother.

"Mother, do you know who Dodi is really?"

"Other than being your new teacher, no."

"She really is Noah, Machla's youngest sister."

"Are you certain?"

"Absolutely. That gives you one less thing to worry about."

"Why is that?"

"Under Torah Law, Daddy is not permitted to be married to two sisters at the same time."

"Are you sure? I heard something about it, but did not know if it applies in all cases."

"It's the law. I learned it in Machla's class and she never makes any mistakes."

"He may still marry one of the two?"

"Yes he can and yes he would. It will not be Noah, though."

"Then he is planning to marry Machla?"

"He will certainly ask her to marry him. It is my impression, however, that nothing will happen until Machla gets her inheritance in the Land of Canaan."

"From what you have studied, do you think there is a chance for her to win her case?"

"None whatsoever. It appears to be a totally lost cause. By the way, Noah will not be teaching us in Judah. We have to walk to Menashe three times a week."

"Why is that?"

"Noah lives by the principle that she never does any work when she can get others to do it for her."

"I hope you never learn such things from her."

"Why not, mother. It's the most useful art I can ever hope to acquire." Dina ran off in a hurry before her mother could react.

Two weeks later, the three girls walked to Menashe and began to study with Noah. It was a completely different experience from anything they had been subject to before. Noah walked with her students and played with them. She never made them memorize or recite verses. She was happy to discuss everything with them, even if it had no connection with what the class was studying at the time. She paid attention to their speech and dress and gave them basic training in manners.

Malka missed some of the intellectual challenges, but welcomed the changes in her personality. Dina and Aviva blossomed under Noah's tutelage and became so refined that their parents were amazed at the transition.

"It is unbelievable what this woman has done for Dina," Elchanan said to Batya. "I can hardly recognize her."

Batya agreed in full. "She talks respectfully and even helps me when she can tear herself away from the mirror. It will not be long before we hear from the matchmakers."

"I already have," said Elchanan.

"What did you tell them?"

"I told them to work on the old maids and not play with children. The problem is that some people mistake her for a woman of eighteen." The cause of the error was not hard to grasp. Dina now dressed with great care and carried herself with poise. She was tall and fully developed. Noah had shown her how to stand straight and walk gracefully.

"How come Noah doesn't teach in Judah and the girls now have to walk to Menashe?" Batya wanted to know.

"Malka asked her that and Noah said that if she were in Judah, Machla would force her to stick to the curriculum. In Menashe she is free to teach as she wishes."

"What is the real reason?"

"I suspect that Machla is afraid that Noah would steal me away from her."

"It would serve that husband-stealer right."

A few days later school resumed in Judah and Machla came back in high spirits. She enjoyed her work and the vacation had been hard on her.

"I am happy to have you back, Machla," said Elchanan as he welcomed her. "I missed you very much." Elchanan examined her with loving eyes. He noticed that she hadn't changed much in appearance, but there was a look of serenity on her face reflecting great inner happiness.

"I missed you, too, Elchanan."

"How come you sent Noah down to see Batya under an assumed name?"

"You had given me the impression that you enjoyed light-hearted women," Machla said, with a broad smile.

"I do. I told you that many times. What I forgot to add is that I enjoy it as long as the fun is at other people's expense, not mine."

"It's good you told me. I was just cooking up another prank."

"Please, no more. I am happy with you the way you are. It took me three whole weeks to placate Batya after your little joke."

"All right, I'll be serious for a change. Did any problems arise during the vacation?"

"We lost a few teachers. One is pregnant and two have an illness in the family."

"Did we lose any students?"

"Not that I know of. What do you suggest we do?"

"In the short run, we can increase class sizes by two. The teachers are more experienced now and the extra load won't hurt them. If we lose additional teachers we will be in trouble. Maybe we ought to do something about it now?"

"Like what?"

"Now that you have shown the way, I think you can get a commander to teach the background material to a group of ten women. After the summary course, we will teach the newcomers the lesson plans."

Elchanan reported the situation to the council. Much to his surprise, a commander — whose wife was one of the teachers — volunteered. His name was Aryeh and he was held in very high esteem on the council. He told the council that his wife's position had given her a new lease on life. She now had a better understanding of his work. Given a sense of purpose, she stopped complaining about housework and assorted aches and pains. "If I can make another ten couples happier by training the wives to teach, it will be well worth my time."

The replacement teachers were easily recruited. Under the guidance of Machla and Elchanan, Aryeh began to teach them. Machla's special students were selected and she began their instruction. Having excelled in their first year of studies, they did not find Machla's class as difficult as they had feared. They did have to start the Torah over again, but were able to do so on a level in keeping with their potential.

On the first day of school after the fall holidays, Elchanan resumed walking Machla home. He told her that his appointment with Moses was set for the following Monday and that he would send someone to escort her home that evening.

"Have you decided upon the favor that I must grant for your efforts?"

It was a cool starlit evening with a slight breeze. Machla sensed that Elchanan was somewhat nervous. "I have," he replied.

"May I know what it is?"

"It has nothing to do with work."

Alarm bells started ringing in Machla's head when she heard those words. She sensed that the man she loved so much was going to propose to her.

"Sit down on the ledge here," he said to Machla. "I want to talk about us. The favor I ask reflects the fact that I am deeply in love with you and want to marry you."

"Thank goodness. For a moment I was afraid that you would ask for something important."

"It is important."

"Weren't you the light-hearted one. I don't know if I can marry someone who is so serious about life."

"I am only serious about you, dear."

"In that case, I will give you my answer." Machla spoke carefully, weighing each word. "I have no further reservations about you personally and I am willing to accept you as my husband, even though you come with a dowry of a wife and four children. You are a first-rate scholar, a distinguished leader among the children of Israel. What is more, you are a handsome man and I am very attracted to you. I long to be yours and to be held in your arms. I want you to possess me body and soul.

"My problem remains an external one. I will not get married to anyone as long as my claim to land in Canaan remains unresolved. If, by any miracle, your appeal to Moses results in our getting the land, I will marry you right away. It will disappoint Eliav and Batya but I am not in love with Eliav and your love for Batya is apparently not sufficient to deter you from proposing to another woman. Even though my commitment is conditional upon your success, I feel it is a sufficient reason to warrant your intercession with Moses.

"I will add this to it, without a formal Torah vow. I know that the likelihood of a definitive answer from Moses is remote and the case will have to go court. If you get the case to court, I will accept your proposal regardless of the outcome. If we win, I will have achieved my goal and removed all impediments to marriage. If we lose, the cause will become so hopeless that there will be no reason to wait. Win or lose then, we will get married."

"It is not the answer I was hoping for," Elchanan replied sadly, "but since there is a slight chance of success, I will not cancel my visit with Moses. I only ask this of you. If Moses says that it is absolutely hopeless, I would want you to give up the cause and not delay our marriage."

"I can't commit myself to that in advance. I can only say that if that is the outcome of your visit, I will sit down with my sisters and reconsider the entire matter."

"That is a little better." The pair resumed their walking to Menashe. Upon reaching home, Machla retired to her tent with her mind in turmoil. When Noah saw that Machla didn't come out of the tent, she went in to check on her.

"Something big must have happened to leave you in such a daze. Is it good news or bad?"

"It is up to the Lord. I cannot tell."

"If it concerns us all, you may as well tell me."

"The first part concerns all of us. Elchanan is presenting our case to Moses next Monday night."

"Tell me about the proposal as well."

Machla was surprised at Noah's perceptiveness. She told her everything and held nothing back.

"I am not going to dust off my list of suitors, yet," said Noah, "but I will get myself some new cosmetics just in case."

The following Monday night, Elchanan walked to the Tent of Meeting and was ushered in. This tent was not the main Tabernacle of the Hebrew people. It was situated outside the camp border and served as the residence and office of Moses. Joshua, the devoted disciple of Moses, worked here and supervised activities at the tent. The men in the tent were already in place when Elchanan entered. Seated at the head of the table was Moses, his face covered by a thin veil. Since his descent from Mount Sinai, the face of Moses radiated light so brightly that men were afraid to look at him. From then on, he covered his face with a veil when speaking with people privately. The veil was removed only when Moses communicated with the Lord or when he conveyed the words of the Torah to the children of Israel at large public assemblies.[3]

Across the table from Elchanan to the left of Moses, sat Aaron and his son, Elazar. Aaron's other son, Itamar, who usually was present at such meetings, was on duty at the Tabernacle and could not attend. Opposite Moses, at the foot of the table, sat Joshua. Caleb was sitting on the near side of the table facing Aaron. Elchanan was guided to the chair next to Caleb. Caleb was on his left and Elazar was sitting directly across the table. Joshua was to his right. Elchanan had previously attended meetings of judges and commanders who were addressed by Moses and he was sure that Moses had heard of him. Never had he been so honored as to sit in the presence of the great leaders and prophets of Israel.[4]

"Your Excellency," said Caleb, "it is my privilege to present to you and to the others present tonight, Elchanan ben Uriah. Elchanan, a former commander of 1,000, is now the judicial advisor of the council of the tribe of Judah, an alternate judge of the tribal court and director of religious education for the tribe.

"In the latter capacity, I may point out, in addition to all the Torah schools for men in the tribe, Judah has a school in which almost 400 young girls receive religious education. The tribe has expanded upon the efforts of Miriam in providing Torah education for the daughters of Israel. Your Excellency taught us when he organized the administration of the tribes of Israel, that small matters should be resolved at the local level, while matters of complexity should be brought to his personal attention. It is under that directive that I have asked for and received permission for Judge Elchanan to bring an urgent case to Your Excellency's attention."[5]

"I have heard of Elchanan," Moses replied to Caleb, "and the excellent work he is doing in Judah. I have also heard about the school for girls although I did not have an opportunity to examine it. I will ask you at a later time for a full report on that undertaking." Turning directly to Elchanan, he said, "You may present your case, my son."

Elchanan rose before the assembled elders. "Your Excellency and revered elders. The woman I represent is one person, but her plight is shared by thousands of women among the children of Israel."

When the elders heard that the problem was of national significance, their attentiveness increased. Elchanan continued.

"The woman is an employee of the tribal council of Judah and her name is Machla, the daughter of Zelaphchad."

"Did you say Zelaphchad? Zelaphchad of the tribe of Menashe?" asked Moses.

"Yes, Your Excellency."

"He was a dedicated and loyal man who met a tragic death."

Aaron added, "I went to console the family at the time. I understood that his widow, Achla, had four daughters and was with child when he died. Go on, Elchanan."

"About two years ago, Machla came to Judah in response to my notice seeking a teacher. She requested to teach men, but I could not permit it. There was no doubt about her qualifications. With the exception of Miriam, the prophetess, there is no woman in Israel who can compete with her in knowledge of the Torah. She could easily sit on the High Court and acquit herself with honor."

"He is not exaggerating at all," interjected Caleb.

"Since she was not allowed to teach men, I appointed her to teach women. In the space of two years, she was responsible for the training of many teachers and the schooling of close to four hundred girls. Machla is thirty-six years of age. Despite her wisdom and beauty, however, she is not married. That is at the heart of this problem.

"As the High Priest pointed out, Zelaphchad had four daughters before he died. The child who was born after his death was also a girl. The mother made determined efforts to remarry and even went so far as to petition the council to force Zelaphchad's brothers to take her as a Levirate wife. The council ruled against her because they felt that Levirate applies only where a woman has had no children at all. Once she has children, even if they are all girls, she is disqualified."

"They were correct," said Moses, "The formal Levirate laws which will be released in the future will confirm their position."

"Machla and her sisters inherited Zelaphchad's fierce love of the Land of Canaan. When Machla learned the Torah and found out that she and her sisters would not inherit their father's land in Canaan because they were women, she was desolate."

"How did they know that they would not inherit any land?" Joshua asked.

"They were so advised by Barak, the judge who recently passed away, their commander at the time. Barak ruled that in the absence of any explicit Torah law to the contrary, existing social traditions prevail. Such traditions do not allow women to inherit property.

"To fight for their cause, the five sisters undertook a covenant that none of them would get married until the law was changed."

A number of eyebrows were raised as Elchanan spoke these words. The elders had never heard a case so unique and complex.

Elchanan went on. "Since the sisters had many suitors who wanted to marry them, they were brought before the council on charges of conducting an illegal conspiracy and were censured by the council."

"That is an interesting verdict. I wonder how it came about," said Moses.

"That was my first involvement in the Zelaphchad case," answered Elchanan. "Machla was her own defense attorney and easily dealt with the charges on the grounds that women are not subject to the commandment of procreation. The tribe, however, had earlier sent some men to Judah to secure an opinion on the case. They were referred to me, because I serve as legal advisor to the council of Judah. I ruled that the conspiracy was not a plot to violate a specific commandment but a conspiracy to endanger the survival of our nation, similar to the conspiracy of Korach or the spies. In that case, it was the duty of the council to act in protection of the tribe and censure those whose actions might endanger its survival. After hearing my opinion, the council proceeded with the censure."[6]

"Your ruling was sound, even brilliant, Elchanan, but about twenty years ahead of its time. You anticipated the rights we hope to bestow upon the courts and the administrative bodies of our nation in the future. Why didn't Machla challenge your decision?"

"Either she was inexperienced as Gamliel, the president later said, or, as I prefer to believe, she accepted the inherent accuracy of the ruling."

"What happened next?" asked Moses.

"The sisters ceased their organized actions and protest marches. Acting solely as individuals, however, they still chose not to get married and none of them are married to this day. May I make it clear that I am not seeking to change all the inheritance laws and allow women to inherit property when there are sons in a family. That would be too drastic a change. What I am seeking is a ruling that daughters in families where there are no sons should inherit their father's property. As matters now stand, Zelaphchad's property will go to his brothers and his name will be forever forgotten among the children of Israel."

Moses went into deep concentration before he was ready to advise Elchanan. During that time, the elders at the table besieged Elchanan with incisive questions. Among the points they raised were: would the new law apply to women who did get married or only single ones; what was the rational basis for distinguishing between women who had brothers and those who did not; was there any other way of resolving the problem without changing the inheritance laws? The elders also wanted more details about Machla and her work. Elchanan was well prepared and he answered all the questions wisely in a clear, concise manner. Moses noted Elchanan's skill even though he was concentrating on his own conclusions. After the questions subsided, Moses spoke to Elchanan.

"My son, it is very noble on your part to seek to help this family and, with them, thousands of others. While your efforts are not hopeless, your path is strewn with difficulties.

"As you know, there are two ways in which laws are established for the children of Israel. One is by revelation of the Divine will and the other is by human judicial action. Frequently, when I hear a case, the Lord puts the answer in my mind and I can convey the answer immediately. Sometimes, as in the case of the second Passover, I refer the case to the Lord and he favors me with an answer. In this case, I have had no indication from heaven.[7] It is obvious that the Lord does not want to reveal his will to me at this time. It may mean that the Lord prefers that we resolve this case on earth and that He will abide by the will of human justice. This does not necessarily mean that He will not intervene at some time in the future. It only means that we must proceed on our own, unless and until we hear otherwise.

"The full set of laws relating to judicial authority will not be released until the year before the children of Israel enter the Promised Land. Under those laws, the courts will have the authority to enact social legislation as long as the laws they promulgate do not contradict that which is written in the Torah. Let me explain the difference between Torah Law and judicial law. The Torah laws are eternal and may never be changed. Judicial laws, even though they are written in the spirit of the Torah, are temporal. They can be revised or overruled by different judicial bodies in subsequent generations. The Torah will make it a positive commandment for all Israelites to abide by judicial laws passed by duly authorized courts. There will also be a prohibitive law providing for punishment of those who fail to abide by such rulings.[8]

"Without express authority to enact social legislation, the court will not even consider your case at this time. There is another important factor too. Even if the court decided to hear your case, they would defeat it by an overwhelming margin. The court is comprised of judges who were slaves in Egypt. They are inherently conservative and will shy away from bold legislation. In the forthcoming years, many of the judges will be replaced by younger and courageous men such as yourself, who will be more inclined to enact rules for the welfare of the people.

"This is now my official advice to you, my son. Bring the case at once to the tribal court of Menashe and secure a court ruling that allows you to pass the case up to the highest court. I believe that you and Machla working together will succeed in getting one. Without such a ruling, the High Court is not allowed to consider the case. Once you get the order, I give you my solemn word that if you ask to have the case heard at any time after judicial authority to enact social legislation is in place, I will instruct the High Court to hear the case immediately. Of course, if the Lord chooses to reveal His decision in the matter before then, you will not have to resort to human courts."

Elchanan felt pleased that he had made substantial progress in that he had won a guarantee from Moses that the case would be heard at the High Court. That meant that someday he would be free to marry Machla. Eight years, however was a long time to wait.

Caleb sensed his agony and spoke up for him. "If it please Your Excellency, there is an aspect to this case that Elchanan has not brought up because of his humility, but it does cause him great pain. It happens that Elchanan is deeply in love with Machla and his soul is tied to hers. He has proposed to Machla and she is waiting for resolution of the case before she accepts. She feels, with justice, that if the court knows she is married to a well-to-do man, the judges will not be sympathetic to her cause. Eight years is a long time to wait for a man so deeply in love."

Moses reflected for a moment and said to Elchanan. "You are married now, my son?"

"Yes, Your Excellency."

"You have fulfilled the first commandment to be fruitful and multiply?"

"I have one daughter and three sons."

"I understand that your love for Machla is based on her spirit and knowledge and not on carnal desire."

"While I am not an angel, I am certain that the love is primarily spiritual. Machla has a sister, Noah, who is far prettier than she, but I have no desire for her. I wish to marry Machla so that I will be sure of always having her close to me so that I can communicate with her. In her company I experience a fulfillment I never knew before."

"In that case, my son, your problem is not that urgent. You can have this woman as a friend and companion and rejoice in her wisdom. If she loves you and knows that someday her case will be resolved in court, she will wait for you.

"Let me further add, Elchanan, that as attorney for the Zelaphchad family, you must represent them in a manner that is consistent with their interests, not yours. If you present the case prematurely and lose it, you will have committed a severe breach of trust."

On that note the session ended and Elchanan left the Tent of Meeting. On a personal basis the results were not quite satisfactory but Machla's case had advanced.

At work the next day, Elchanan told Machla that it was only fair to relate the opinion of Moses to the entire family and he asked her to wait until he walked her home. Machla was content to do so because she knew that Elchanan would not convene the entire family unless there were important developments.

As they approached the tent area in Menashe that night, Noah saw them coming and cried, "Your Honor. Your humble servants in the tribe of Menashe are greatly privileged to be able to stand in your worthy presence."

"You have repented your past arrogance, Noah?"

"Indeed, I have. Machla, in her wisdom, has shown me the error of my haughty ways."

"Somehow, I don't believe you have changed one bit but miracles do happen and one cannot be sure."

Dinner was set and Elchanan spoke to the family at length. Having a distinguished man at their table was in itself a privilege for the family and they were attentive to every word. The judge related the words of Moses verbatim except for the passages relating to him and Machla.

Elchanan then concluded, "I am willing to help represent the family in the tribal court of Menashe as Moses directed."

"I would like to represent the family too," Noah said.

"Never," all the sisters screamed.

Milka put it best. "If you represent us you will probably ask for a ruling that only the youngest sister may appeal to the High Court."

"You think I would put my own selfish interests ahead of those of my dear sisters?"

She was greeted by a loud, resounding "yes" from all those present.

"It is not really a matter of trust, Noah," Elchanan said. "It is simply that Moses specifically recommended that Machla and I present the case to the tribal court."

Each night Machla and Elchanan worked on the presentation as they walked home. She was amazed at the amount of preparation he made for a case that seemed assured of victory.

"One lesson I learned," he explained, "is that more cases are lost because of overconfidence than from any other cause."

The first step to be taken was to secure a resolution from the tribal council of Menashe in support of the Zelaphchad case. The council had promised that it would do this in the event that the family brought the case to court. Enough members of the council remembered the original resolution and the request was granted. The council then appointed a senior commander to appear in the tribal court when the case was being heard to convey the support of the council for the daughters of Zelaphchad.

The case was presented to the court a month later. All the sisters were on hand as was their mother. Eliav was there, too, more out of curiosity than opposition. He wondered about Elchanan but Noah told him that she and Machla merely worked for Elchanan as teachers and that he had volunteered to help with the case. She also mentioned that he was married and had four children.

The case was heard early in the morning. The twenty-three judges were all present and sat in a semicircle. Both Elchanan and Machla made masterful presentations. Elchanan was a courtroom veteran and his presentation was polished and perfect. Machla's presentation was a revelation. Under Elchanan's tutelage, she had mastered the art of conducting herself in the courtroom. She addressed the court with such poise and confidence, that even Noah had to admit that she could not have done better herself.

Elchanan revealed to the court for the first time that future Torah rules would allow the High Court to legislate social laws. It was through this channel that the daughters of Zelaphchad would seek to resolve their case. He pleaded with the judges not to deny these saintly women their day in court and to issue the pass-up ruling.

With only one negative vote, the court granted the petitioners the right to proceed to the High Court with their case. The family rejoiced in the victory even though it was mostly symbolic. For her part, Noah cornered the judge who cast the negative vote and asked him why. He told her that he had actually done her a favor. "In capital cases," he said, "if all twenty-three judges vote to condemn a murderer, the case is dismissed. It is inconceivable that not one judge out of a whole court could find some way to exonerate the defendant. It is taken as a sign that the judges were swayed by outside factors and did not thoroughly deliberate the case.[9]

"Similarly," he continued, "if historians review the current case and find that all twenty-three judges voted to grant the petition, they may suspect that the court did not sufficiently deliberate the case. As long as at least one negative vote was cast, it means that some members of the court considered the question thoroughly."

"But can there be any reason why we shouldn't be allowed to present our case to the High Court?" Noah persisted.

"I sincerely feel that social legislation should not be sought by individuals who stand to gain personally from the new laws. There is an incongruity when individuals claim to represent an entire class when they are only campaigning for themselves. Cases on behalf of groups should be brought by the tribe itself, or by some organization acting in behalf of all people in the same situation."

"But the tribe did endorse our cause."

"I am aware of that. I feel, however, that the tribe itself should present the petition. If you do get to the High Court it may be to your benefit to have members of at least several tribes join you in the petition."

Noah related the opinion to Elchanan who felt it had some merit. "Perhaps when we go to the High Court we should allow the judges to hear from other persons who stand to be helped by the new laws."

After the case was over, Machla and Elchanan went back to talking about things other than the court case. It was then that Elchanan told her of what Moses said to him about his personal problem.

"In the light of what Moses said, I am proposing to you again but this time on a spiritual basis. We will be one soul but not one flesh."

"I don't think that would violate my resolution," said Machla. "In a marriage of the minds you will not be obligated to support me and the court would not place any monetary value on it."

"You are not asking for any money or support?"

"You have already given me many things that are worth far more than money."

"Like what?"

"You have taught me Torah and Hebrew Law. You have given me the opportunity to teach Torah to the daughters of Israel. You have given me hope that I will inherit land in Canaan. You have made me feel wanted as a woman. You have raised my self-esteem. For all these things I love you and accept your proposal for an intellectual marriage."

"I wonder how we can solemnize such a marriage," Elchanan asked half seriously.

"I will embroider a cloth for you showing the wild ox of Menashe grazing side by side with the Lion of Judah."

"I can't think of a better idea."

The symbolic marriage flourished for more than seven years, the happiest years in Machla's life. Elchanan, too, was content with his lot. Batya was happy that Elchanan did not bring Machla into their household but she knew to whom Elchanan's heart belonged and she grieved over it.

Noah taught her three students for two years and then picked up another group of five from Machla's second class. More than 3,000 girls went through the school in Judah and, by the ninth year of Machla's work, the schools had reached a point where there were sixty trained teachers instructing over 800 students. One of Machla's proudest moments came when Malka, at the age of twenty, was appointed in charge of all Torah education for women in the tribe of Judah.

One other event of interest occurred seven years after Machla first arrived in Judah. Batya's son, Avi, was now eleven and attended Torah classes regularly. Batya, with time heavy on her hands, applied to enter the teacher-training program.

"I have no reason to reject her application," said Machla, "and the commander will be afraid to do so because she is your wife. That leaves only you who can turn her down."

"I have numerous reasons to turn it down and some are very valid but I cannot do so."

"Why is that?"

"My dear wife has given me the clear impression that if I dare do such a thing, I will be confronted with two intellectual marriages instead of one and my mind isn't big enough for two."

"I see. Who will be her instructor?"

"Count me out. I will not be able to teach the class if my wife is in it."

"She certainly won't be happy in my class."

"Well, we will assign her to Aryeh, although she will have to observe your class on occasion."

Batya was accepted and performed very well. She watched Machla teach and began to understand why Machla was so highly regarded. In time, Batya was given a regular class and enjoyed teaching very much.

The eighth year of Machla's special relationship with Elchanan coincided with the fortieth year of wandering in the desert by the tribes of Israel. The entire generation of those who had left Egypt over the age of twenty were gone. The new generation was physically and mentally ready to enter the Land of Canaan. Moses was releasing the last parts of the last book of the Torah in preparation for writing the entire book.

A few days after Passover in the fortieth year, Elchanan was waiting for Machla before the start of class. He was in a high state of excitement and his face was flushed. He could hardly wait to blurt out the news.

"I was at a meeting of the High Court with the judges of Judah, Issachar and Zebulun. At the meeting, Moses explained how Torah Law would be dynamically maintained in the Land of Canaan. The courts are now empowered to make laws for the good of the community, to enhance the study of Torah, and to protect the basic laws of the Torah itself. Each Hebrew person is required to respect the laws of the duly appointed courts."

"They have the rights to alter inheritance laws?"

"I specifically asked Moses that question and he said they could do so as long as they did not usurp the written Torah Law."

"It means that we will be going to court soon?"

"Certainly within the next six months. But it means far more than that."

"What else?"

"I am preparing a bill of divorce to end our intellectual marriage, and enter into a real one."

"How do you solemnize a divorce decree for an intellectual marriage?"

"Remember the cloth you gave me with the ox and the lion grazing peacefully?"

"Yes, I do."

"Well the cloth is now with the embroiderers. They have been instructed to prepare a new cloth, more in keeping with our changing situation. The ox is departing from the scene and a lioness is replacing her. They will still be grazing, but their appearance will be somewhat more amorous."

The symbolism was not lost on Machla. Hard though it would be to part with her native tribe, Elchanan was telling her that her future was with lions of Judah. She reflected that Abraham must also have felt a few pangs upon leaving the city of the birth when obeying God's command to go forth to the Land of Canaan. Nevertheless, the patriarch went willingly, because that was the path of destiny. The warmth of Menashe would have to yield to the intellect of the Judean scholars.[10]

Machla brushed away her tears of joy.

CHAPTER

ELEVEN

"THE TRIBES OF REUBEN AND GAD HAD MUCH CATTLE"

A few weeks later, when Elchanan was walking Machla back to Menashe, he informed her that the time for the Zelaphchad trial was nearing, and they should start preparing for it.

"When do you think we will go to trial?" she asked.

"Definitely before the end of the summer. Possibly in the fifth month, but no later than the sixth. As soon as the section on Levirate marriages is released, I will schedule a date."

Machla had already indicated that she would not resume teaching in Judah after the school recess. She wanted to have more time to prepare for the court trial, for her subsequent marriage, and for entry into Canaan. There were plenty of graduates of her first class who could take over teaching and Malka would assume her administrative work. Elchanan agreed but insisted that she visit Judah at least twice a week to assist Malka during the transitional period.

As soon as the school recess started, Elchanan came to Menashe daily to discuss the court action and to train the sisters in their parts. Tension ran high in the family with the knowledge that its pattern of life would change in a few weeks, pending a verdict in the High Court. Elchanan did his best to calm the sisters and soothe their nerves. The Levirate laws were released in the last week of the fourth month and Elchanan showed them to Machla. They formally stated:

"If brothers dwell together, and one of them dies and has

no son, the widow of the deceased shall not be free to marry a stranger. The brother shall take her in Levirate marriage. The first born child of this union shall bear the name of the deceased brother and that name shall not be erased from the children of Israel."[1]

"I can't believe what I am hearing," said Machla. "It specifically says that if a man dies without a son, the brothers-in-law are required to marry his widow. That means that Shafat or Azriel would have been required to marry my mother."

"It means no such thing," said Elchanan. "I checked the point several times with Moses and he made a statement to our judges on this question. As used in the verse, the term 'son' does not mean a male child but any child, male or female. Moses added that when a man had a son or daughter who died before him, however, his widow is eligible for Levirate."[2]

"But then that means," Machla argued, "that in respect to this law, women are fully equal to men and, if so, they should be fully equal in laws of inheritance."

"That is precisely the point," Elchanan answered, "We now have a strong precedent of sexual equality in family law. No one will be able to rise and say that women are never equal to men. We shall stress that point constantly in our case, even though it is no guarantee of victory. There are still many areas where women are not considered the equals of men."

"Isn't that mostly in ritual law?"

"Yes, but it occurs in civil law as well. A woman may not be a king or a judge or a commander and some will say that it is because the Torah felt that they didn't have the capacity to assume responsibility. Managing property is not an easy matter and these people will repeat the same sentiments about such tasks."

"Well, what is the reason for restricting women from leadership positions? Do you yourself feel that we are inferior to men?"

Elchanan exercised caution in answering such a sensitive question. "After working with you for ten years, if I ever felt that way, I certainly do not feel that way anymore. My personal feeling is that the restriction has nothing to do with ability. I am convinced that the Torah keeps women away from political and religious responsibilities because it doesn't want any conflict with their domestic roles. A president or commander of 1,000 is on call day and night. If she were giving birth or caring for sick children at the time of an emergency, it would be a problem. It is clear that the Torah considers a woman's family responsibility as primary.

"In social discrimination against women, as opposed to Torah laws, there may be other factors involved. In some cases, there may be concern that dictates of modesty may prevent women from doing certain work. In other cases there may be fears that an attractive woman such as you, might distract people from the business at hand. Whatever the reason, there is unequal treatment of women in society and it may possibly hurt your cause. In your case, we will have to present you and your sisters as strong, capable women."

"Poor Noah, she treasures her femininity."

"She will have to de-emphasize it for one day."

"Now that the Levirate laws have been released, when are you going to ask for a date in court ?"

"I already have. Tomorrow is the New Moon, the first day of the fifth month. I should get an answer by the beginning of next week."

Elchanan did get an answer, but it was in the form of a delay. It seemed that Aaron, the high priest and brother of Moses, was called to his eternal reward on the first day of the month. He, Moses and Elazar had ascended the Mountain of Hor. There, Aaron's priestly garments were removed and transferred to his son. Aaron then closed his eyes on his deathbed and his soul departed. When Moses descended with Elazar, who was wearing the priestly robes, the children of Israel knew that Aaron had passed on, and that Elazar had succeeded him in the high priestly office.[3]

The children of Israel wept for their departed leader. Except for his role in the incident of the golden calf, Aaron had been a man of outstanding piety and dedication. He loved his people and was particularly warm-hearted.[4] He had settled many disputes among the Hebrews and played an important role in helping families with domestic problems. He carried out his priestly duties perfectly for close to forty years. Humans are mortal, however, and not even someone of Aaron's stature could escape the fate of all men.

Upon his death, the Hebrew people went into deep mourning for thirty days.

All public functions came to a halt and the courts did not meet. The Zelaphchad case was postponed and no new date was set. Elchanan advised Machla of the delay and she took it philosophically. "After waiting twenty years, I guess another month won't hurt."

Things, however, were not as simple as they seemed. Elchanan had the sad duty of informing Machla that the delay would be far more substantial. "Even if everything were in order, a hearing for such a case would probably not be granted during the sixth month, the time before the holidays. Unfortunately, things are not at all well with our people. I just heard that the King of Arad staged a raid upon our camp and took captives. He chose this time to attack because he apparently felt that without the presence of Aaron, our people would lose their Divine protection.[5] What is more, Caleb told me that if the army is mobilized to fight the Canaanites, they will not be demobilized before they wage a full war against Sihon, King of the Amorites, and Og, the giant King of Bashan. I have no doubt that with the Lord's blessings we will be victorious. But I can foresee that we will be at war for the entire month before the holidays and for two or three weeks after the holidays. There will be no regular court cases during wartime. I would say that the best you can hope for is a date at the end of the eighth month or the beginning of the ninth."[6]

When the sisters heard the news from Machla, their spirits were depressed. Like all other Hebrews, they were mourning for Aaron. They also understood that the welfare of the nation was more important than their personal problems. In a war, Moses would be concerned with the survival of the children of Israel and could not be involved in domestic matters.

Aside from the delay in the trial date, the sisters were affected in another way. As part of his duties, Aaron often presided over the High Court. Now that he was departed, Elazar would be in his chair and would be conducting the Zelaphchad case.[7]

"Will that hurt us in any way?" Machla asked Elchanan.

"It is hard to say for sure," he answered, "but I don't think so. Aaron was a very warm-hearted person and loved people. Elazar may be a little more aloof, but he is a younger man and might be more amenable to social change."

Elchanan's information turned out to be quite accurate. The children of Israel defeated the Canaanites and Amorites before the holidays and the kingdom of Og after the holidays. They then moved to the plains of Moab where they were beset by another problem. Men of certain tribes began to fraternize with the daughters of Moab and committed immoral and idolatrous acts. The Lord was very angry with the sinners and imposed a severe plague upon them.[8] The children of Israel also waged war against the Midianites for their acts against the Hebrew people.[9] After the wars and the plague, Moses, at God's behest, ordered a new census of the nation. The enumeration served to determine losses in the tragic events and to establish a data base for the division of the land of Canaan among the Hebrew tribes.[10]

The census results pleased the children of Israel and the tribe of Menashe. For the daughters of Zelaphchad, though, they brought a mixed blessing. They did bestow prominence upon the family, but they also caused internal friction among the sisters.

After the holidays, Machla didn't teach in Judah but she visited often to help Malka administer the educational program. When she worked late, Elchanan would walk her home. On one such night, he revealed to her that he had finally been able to get a court date for the Zelaphchad case. It was now scheduled on the court calendar for Monday morning, the tenth day of the ninth month. When Machla bid farewell to Elchanan at the Menashe border, she hurried home to tell her family the good news. A critical point had been passed in the struggle of the daughters of Zelaphchad to win their inheritance. Machla pictured the barren desert giving way to verdant fields and the sheep running wild in the pastures of Canaan. Her reverie was broken by the sight of Milka waiting for her at the head of the path as she approached the tent area. There was no reason for Milka to be there, so Machla assumed that something was very wrong.

"Is everything all right? Is anyone sick?" she asked.

"We are in real trouble," Milka answered, "terrible trouble. We need help badly."

Machla felt an overwhelming anxiety. The family had seemed fine in the morning when she left them. If a sad event had occurred, the family would usually sit quietly around the tents waiting for her. Milka's attempt to prepare her before reaching the tents was an indication that something out of the ordinary had taken place.

As she approached the tents, she heard sounds of hysterical crying and the sound of wailing. She knew that the wailing was her mother's, as she recognized the traditional elegiac moaning. The crying sounded very much like Tirza's, but she couldn't be sure.

"Oh, my Lord! Did anyone pass away?" she cried.

"No, but there was a violent fight between Tirza and Noah. Noah ran away and Tirza is hysterical."

"Noah hasn't done that for some twenty years. Why did she have to run?"

"Tirza was coming after her with the sand broom and was about to beat her with it. She was in such a rage that Hogla and I could barely hold her while Noah ran away."

Machla first ran to her mother who sat with reddened eyes and disheveled hair, clasping her hands in grief. Achla was wailing, "Is this the Torah my daughters learned; to fight with each other and hate each other, to have all the families run out of their tents to see what is happening? Woe is me that I should live to see the daughters of Zelaphchad carry on this way. Why does the Lord afflict me so?"

Machla tried to calm her mother but she was inconsolable. She then attempted to hear what Tirza was screaming. All she could make out was "...my birthright. She stole my birthright. That ungrateful wretch stole my birthright..." Machla told Hogla to stay close to Tirza and see that she didn't harm herself.

"Milka," she called, "tell me as quickly as possible what happened. What is this about a birthright?"

"It happened this afternoon. Chemlon, the new legal advisor to the council, came by on his way to the Tent of Meeting where a special briefing is being given."

"I know about that," Machla said. "Elchanan's group was there for the morning session."

"Chemlon said that earlier in the morning one of the judges had asked him about a section in the Torah relating to the recent census of all the tribes. You know that the census is being included in the Torah in the same way as the first census, which was taken when the children of Israel left Egypt."

"That shouldn't be any problem. Menashe must have done very well."

"That's not the trouble. Menashe was listed as having 52,000 families.

During our stay in the desert, Menashe jumped from being the second smallest tribe to one of the largest. The trouble derives from the fact that we, the daughters of Zelaphchad, are individually listed by name in the Torah under the tribe of Menashe."[11]

"That absolutely cannot be true," Machla protested. "In most tribes only the first generation families are listed. In relatively few cases, the first-born family of the second generation is also included. We are the fifth generation from the tribal founder, Menashe. Our grandfather, Chefer, was the sixth child to Gilead, grandson of the founder. There is no way that we could be listed in the Torah."

"You are wrong, Machla," Milka answered. Whether you are ready to believe it or not, our names are there. I memorized the passage that the judge recited and it reads:

> 'And Zelaphchad, the son of Chefer, did not have any sons but only daughters and the names of the daughters of Zelaphchad are Machla, and Noah, Hogla, Milka and Tirza.'"[12]

"Why are you reading our names out of order?" Machla said angrily. "I've told you many times that verses in the Torah must be recited exactly as they are written."

"That's what makes this problem so awful. I did recite the verse correctly. It is in the Torah itself that the names are out of chronological order."

"Oh, my heavens! How can that be?"

"That is the question that was put to Chemlon. The judge remembered from years ago that you were the oldest sister and Noah the youngest. So he asked Chemlon to find out the correct order of all the sisters and check at the Tent of Meeting why the revealed order was in error. I gave him the correct order on a little slate and he took it with him."

"I do hope there was some mistake in the transmission to the judges. The Torah itself is the word of God. Moses writes it as it is revealed to him and there can be no mistakes there."

"Tirza won't believe that and, what is more, she is convinced that Noah was responsible for the switch. You understand that Noah's name was not just inserted after yours and all the other names pushed back. What happened is that

Tirza's name, which should have been second, was exchanged with Noah's name, that should have come fifth. All other names are in the correct order. That's what threw Tirza into a rage. If Noah had to be elevated ahead of her for any reason, Tirza could have lived with being third. Now Tirza's name is last on the list and she is so humiliated, she wants to die."

"When is Chemlon coming back?"

"He said that he will be here later this evening."

"What happened between Tirza and Noah?"

"Tirza accused Noah of deception and Noah claimed she had nothing at all to do with it. What emerged during the fight was that Noah did talk to the council secretary on the subject. It seems that the census was conducted by Elazar, the priest, who asked each secretary to verify the count of the tribal families and submit the results to him. In the case of Menashe, he asked the secretary to list the sons of Gilead and the daughters of Zelaphchad. He met Noah last week and asked her for all the names. Noah swears that she said to him, 'You know there is me and Machla. The other sisters are Tirza, Hogla and Milka.' She claims the secretary knew full well that she is the youngest. Even if he were misled by her words and put her second, he definitely had the right order of the rest of us.

"At that point, Tirza flew into a hysterical rage and started screaming at the top of her lungs. 'You thief. I told you it was your fault. You stole my birthright.' She grabbed the broom and went after Noah. All the neighbors heard the screaming and ran out to see what the commotion was all about."

"That is absurd." Machla said. "Tirza is the nicest and meekest person you can ever hope to meet. She lends Noah her clothes and cleans up Noah's half of our tent. She even gathers the manna when Noah oversleeps."

"And don't forget she runs every day to gather food for the lepers who are isolated outside the camp. Some of them would starve if it were not for her. Do you think you could talk to her?"

"I'll try." Machla walked over to where Tirza was sitting, crying her eyes out. She was so distraught that she wasn't even aware that Machla had returned home. Machla sat down next to Tirza and put an arm around her.

"Try to calm yourself, Tirza, and talk to me. Your crying is upsetting mother, and I am afraid for her well-being."

Tirza fought to regain her self-control. "After all that I've done for her, Machla, how could that worm do this to me? Here we have attained a distinction that few other men or women have achieved. Our names appear in the Torah and for thousands of years people will read about the daughters of Zelaphchad. But I won't even be able to teach it to my own children. They will ask me why my name was put at the bottom. Did I ever sin against my sister? Did I ever harm anyone?"

"Wait a minute, Tirza. Before you try to beat anyone or hurt them, you have to be sure of what you are doing. First of all, a mistake may have been made. We are not absolutely sure that we have the final Torah text. Even if it is the correct Torah text, it is at least theoretically possible that a correction may be made. We may also get our names again in the Torah after the court trial and we will then try to get it right. Whatever the case, I don't believe that Noah is at fault. She may be lazy and thoughtless but I don't consider her a thief. I don't think that the information she gave the clerk was the source of what is in the Torah."

"Well, I do consider her a thief. Now I know how Esau must have felt when Jacob came to Isaac, in disguise as his older brother, and stole the blessing from him. You know that I am the second daughter in this family and that is where my name should appear on the list. I am only surprised that she didn't try to put herself ahead of you, Machla."[13]

Machla persisted in her efforts to calm Tirza. "I am trying to convince you that Noah is not at fault. If the names are indeed out of order in the Torah, then it must be God's will to have them written that way."

"I can't believe that the Lord would elevate a spoiled, selfish woman ahead of Hogla or Milka, or even me for that matter."

"If He did, then we have no choice but to accept the heavenly judgment."

Machla asked Hogla to remain with Tirza while she talked with her mother. Carefully she explained the story in a way that her mother understood that the matter was not trivial. "Be proud, mother, that your daughters are the only younger people mentioned in the Torah for this census. It is regrettable that an error was made in the listing and our names do not appear the order of our birth. Maybe we can straighten it out or maybe we will have to live with it. Tirza is badly hurt by it all and she is the kindest of your daughters. She has never behaved this way in the past and I don't think she will ever embarrass you again."

The firm voice of Machla calmed her mother to some degree. With her sister's crying less audible, Machla ate her dinner and told the family what the sessions with the legal advisors were all about. She explained that the courts now had the power to enact laws about inheritance and that the Zelaphchad case would be brought up in the near future. In the prevailing gloom, the good news did not have the impact it normally would have.

"How far does the secretary live from here?" Machla asked.

"His tent is very near to the Tribal Center," said Milka. "I see his wife when I go to work."

"I am sure he is home now. Milka, take Hogla and walk over there. Ask him to tell you exactly the order he used in submitting our names to Elazar the priest."

The two girls left on their mission. In that space of time Chemlon arrived and asked to talk to Machla.

"You are aware of the situation with the Torah listing?"

"Yes, and it is a very difficult situation for Tirza."

"I am very much grieved that I cannot rectify the situation. I spoke to Joshua about it and he checked the scroll in the handwriting of Moses. When Moses asked him what he was looking for, Joshua told Moses of the departure from chronological order. Moses answered, 'I was aware of the right order because I had heard from Judge Elchanan that Noah was the youngest daughter. When the Lord sensed my hesitation in writing the verse, He instructed me to write as told. Joshua was not able to determine why a complete exchange was made between Noah and Tirza when it would have been simpler to insert Noah's name and move everyone down a notch."

"How can I explain such a thing to Tirza?"

"I did not ask you to. I spoke to you out of courtesy because you are the oldest sister. Since I was assigned to investigate the matter, it is my responsibility to report to the family and explain the situation to Tirza, unpleasant though it may be."

"You are certainly welcome to try. I think Tirza is sufficiently calmed down to listen. I did send Hogla and Milka to check with the tribal secretary whether Noah had in any way caused him to send in erroneous data."

"It wasn't necessary, because the Torah is Divinely dictated and human submissions are of no consideration. But, if it will make you feel better, I checked the tribal reports and I found that our secretary had submitted the names in the correct order. Let me talk to Tirza privately and keep the other sisters away while I do so."

Machla admired this new advisor greatly. He was a man willing to fulfill his responsibilities and he had a lot of confidence. His bearing and his appearance were very impressive. All members of the tribe were, of course, related. Chemlon, though, was closer to the family than others, because his grandfather and Achla's father were brothers. There was, in fact, a strong family resemblance between him and the Zelaphchads. He called Tirza over to a more private place and spent the better part of two hours trying to help her accept the situation.

"You are a girl with great Torah knowledge," he began, "and you believe that every word is sacred. You must believe that no human is responsible for the way the names were listed, including Noah. I personally saw the report of the tribal secretary and he had submitted the names correctly.

"You know that on several occasions the Torah lists the names of tribes out of chronological order. Jacob blessed Ephraim ahead of Menashe and Zebulun ahead of Issachar.[14,15] When the tribal presidents brought their gifts to the Tabernacle, they did not follow the birth order of the tribes. We can only guess at what standard the Lord uses in rating people. He rarely explains His reasons because He wishes to spare the feelings of the demoted ones.[16]

"What really counts is the fact that you were listed at some point in the Torah. It doesn't necessarily matter who is listed first or last. When our tribal father, Joseph, tried to correct Jacob's reversal of the birth order, Jacob told Joseph that Menashe would be great but Ephraim would be greater. Still, in the last forty years, Menashe has almost doubled in size while Ephraim has lost population. Perhaps a lower listing may be intended to motivate the weaker party to improve.

"One thing you must realize, though. Someone has to be first and someone has to be second. Naturally, the one listed second will feel badly. Cain felt remorse and his face fell when his younger brother Abel offered a more acceptable sacrifice to the Almighty than he did. The Lord told Cain to improve but, rather than do the correct thing, Cain rose up and slew his brother.[17] I understand that you raised a sand broom to beat Noah and that was very wrong. You judged her guilty when she was innocent and you were ready to take the law into your own hands."

"I am sorry, Your Honor, I lost my head. Noah has provoked me hundreds of times over the years, and I never even raised my voice to her."

"If it is of any comfort to you, it is my feeling that you were rated only against Noah and not your other sisters. I suspect that the Lord did not wish to move your other sisters from their rightful places. As it now stands, three sisters are in the order of birth and only two are not. If you were inserted after Noah and the others also moved down one notch, only one sister out of five would have been in her rightful place."

"That already makes me feel better. I concede that Noah knows more Torah than I do but, Your Honor, tell me which is more important, knowledge or good deeds. I rise early to serve my God, as Abraham did, and I make a supreme effort to love my neighbors. I waste no time in idle chatter and I do not indulge in games or pranks. God has the right to play favorites, but I have a right to feel that I have been unfairly judged."[18]

Chemlon took a moment to organize his reply to such a complex issue. "Both knowledge and good deeds are important," he said, "and they go hand in hand. You have already conceded the knowledge so we have to consider the deeds. On the surface, it appears that you are far ahead, but numbers are not critical here. Each deed is rewarded by the Almighty based on the circumstances of the event and the nature of the person involved. When Moses committed a small infraction, he was judged very harshly because a man on his level should be perfect. Lesser men could commit the same sin and not even be punished.

"You may have once committed a slight sin but, since your character is so pure, you were judged very harshly. Noah, on the other hand, who is not as eager to do good deeds, may have on one occasion done something lofty that for you would have been routine and trivial. For that deed she may have earned a monumental reward while in your case it would have hardly been noticed."

"I am beginning to understand a little, but the bitterness is hard to overcome."

"You must not hate your brother in your heart, the Torah teaches us. Our wise men have also taught us that you must accept Divine judgment with grace."[19]

"What do you want me to do, Your Honor?"

"Do you know where Noah is hiding?"

"Milka knows. We can ask her."

"Let us do that."

They called Milka and asked her about Noah. Milka replied, "On my way to the tribal secretary I saw Noah who was still crying. She begged me to tell Tirza that she swears she is not responsible for the order in which we were listed in the Torah." Milka then described the location.

Chemlon asked Tirza to walk with him to see Noah. Much to the surprise of the sisters, she agreed to go. When they left, Machla could not help but marvel. "That man has the talent of Aaron, the high priest." Aaron had built a reputation of settling domestic and neighborly disputes in a way that no one else could.

Noah had more or less expected Machla to come out and serve as intermediary. She was very much surprised to see Chemlon leading Tirza. "Your Honor," she said, "as God is my witness, I had no intention of usurping Tirza's rightful place. I am convinced that the conversation I had with the secretary had no bearing on the Torah listing."

"I now believe you, Noah," Tirza said. "I am sorry that I lost my temper and threatened you with harm. It won't happen again."

"In my opinion you really belong after Machla," Noah conceded.

"I thought so to, but the Lord has deemed otherwise. I am happy that I didn't harm you because I would have had to bear the mark of Cain all my life."[20]

Hand in hand the sisters walked back to their tent. Neighbors who had heard the commotion earlier, were happy to see them together in their usual amicable manner. Chemlon, who was experienced in such matters, felt that it would be best for him to stay close at hand. He did not leave them until they were safely back in the tent area. Achla, who rejoiced at seeing her two daughters hand in hand, thanked Chemlon profusely. "May God reward you for what you have done."

Tirza walked Chemlon back to the path. "I am sorry for wasting so much of your time, Your Honor."

"Think nothing of it," he said. "This is one of the duties that my position entails. If you have any more problems, please feel free to call on me at the Tribal Center." As it happened, Tirza and the entire family had many occasions to see Chemlon during the next month as a bitter internal struggle rocked the tribe of Menashe.

It started after the war between the children of Israel and the Kingdoms of Og and Sihon. Those kings ruled over vast areas on the east side of the Jordan and their land was especially suited for cattle. The tribes of Reuben and Gad were the chief cattle-raisers among the children of Israel and they coveted the captured land. In fact, they were willing to forego their share of the Land of Canaan, west of the Jordan, in order to occupy the east side of the river.[21]

When the two tribes first made the request, Moses was very upset. He accused them of trying to evade the responsibility of sharing in the conquest of Canaan and of undermining the determination of the children of Israel to inherit the Promised Land. After a period of negotiation, however, an understanding was reached. In broad terms, the two tribes would join the rest of the nation in fighting for the Land of Canaan. The men of the tribes would defer their return to their land in Trans-Jordan until all the other tribes were settled in Canaan. While the settlement was satisfactory, Moses was still concerned about the spiritual problems confronting the two tribes. Living apart from the rest of the tribes of Israel, their religious observance could deteriorate. Moses therefore issued a call for all or part of some more spiritual tribe to join Reuben and Gad and strengthen their religious life.[22]

The tribe of Menashe was a strong choice for this assignment because they were blessed with herds of sheep and cattle and were also very observant. They were the first tribe invited by Reuben and Gad to join in the Trans-Jordan venture. The cattle owners of Menashe were inclined to accept the invitation but they could not do so as individuals without authorization from the tribal leadership. Instead they undertook to compel the entire tribe of Menashe to join with the tribes of Reuben and Gad and they prepared a motion to that effect for consideration by the tribal council. While the owners were not that numerous by themselves, they provided employment for thousands of men who depended on shepherding work for a livelihood. When their intentions became known, the factions who wanted the entire tribe to live in the Land of Canaan proper, prepared a counter resolution that would force the entire tribe of Menashe to settle in Canaan. By sheer chance, the latter motion reached the tribal secretary first. Chemlon ruled that the motions would have to be considered in the order that they had been received. Due to the importance of the issue, a special meeting of the council would have to be held after all members of the tribe were notified. Haniel, the new tribal president after Gamliel, set a date for the meeting and asked the commanders to spread the word. When the daughters of Zelaphchad received the news, there was great consternation.

"We waged a twenty-year struggle to get our land in Canaan and now they want us to live in Trans-Jordan." Machla said in disgust.

"Will the new area become part of the Land of Canaan?" Milka wanted to know.

"It may, in a legal sense. If not acquired as an historical inheritance, it will certainly be considered as Hebrew land by conquest. I would venture to say that all the laws of the land, as required by the Torah, would apply there inherently or by order of the courts. The important question is whether the area would be part of the Hebrew nation in a religious sense. It will be far removed from all of the spiritual and cultural activity of our people in Canaan. Living in such isolation, the tribes will surely stray from the teachings of the Torah."

"Is there anything we can do about it?" Milka asked.

"It does not look promising at all. The motion to force the entire tribe into Canaan will never succeed. There simply is not a majority of people in our tribe who would impose the Land of Canaan upon those who prefer to live elsewhere and have good reason to do so. Our only hope is to defeat the motion compelling all of us to go to Jordan."

Noah immediately objected. "If both motions lose, then each family would be free to do as it wishes. That would split the tribe of Menashe in two."

"Given a choice between a unified tribe with all families living in Trans-Jordan, or a split tribe with half living in Canaan and half across the river, I, for one, would prefer the latter," said Machla. Machla's position was shared not only by the sisters but by the cousins, nephews and nieces of the Chefer families.

"We must get organized and campaign for our beliefs," said Noah. "There are less than two weeks left until the meeting, so we will have to work fast. Since there are now fifty-two commanders, each of us has to visit at least one commander a day and plead our case." Names were given out and the sisters started canvassing. Two days before the meeting, the sisters concluded that more than half of the commanders would vote for Trans-Jordan.

"Did anyone speak to Haniel?" Machla inquired.

"What for? The president doesn't vote," said Noah.

"He does in case of a tie. With him on our side, we would have one vote less to change. Noah, I want you and Milka to see him. The rest of us will go see the weakest supporters of the Jordan move and work on them. Is there anyone in the tribe who can help us?"

"Chemlon is a strong believer in Canaan proper," Tirza volunteered, "but as legal advisor he can't take sides openly. He offered to help me prepare a speech, if I were willing to make one at the council meeting."

"Well, what do you know," said Noah. "Tirza is campaigning for something other than our cause."

Tirza was blushing fiercely. "Weren't we supposed to be good friends now, Noah?"

"Of course."

"Then stay out of my personal affairs."

"You aren't going to run for the broom again, I hope?

"No. Chemlon has been instructing me in matters of self-control and tolerance."

The sisters said no more, but they understood the significance of the brief exchange.

"Are you willing to make a speech at the council?" Machla asked Tirza.

"If you are willing to forego the honor, Machla. I am next in line, at least by my estimation."

"I yield my rights and Noah will voice no objection."

"Wait a minute," said Noah, in exasperation. "You didn't even ask me!"

"Tirza is speaking in *my* place the day after tomorrow," Machla said. "If you have any objections, Noah, I will entertain them next week."

"Thanks a lot."

The council meeting at Menashe drew many distinguished visitors. The legal advisors to the councils of Reuben and Gad were there, hoping that Menashe would join with their tribes. A bloc of three tribes would make it that much easier for the groups who wanted their land in Trans-Jordan, to deal with Moses. Elchanan was there in his official capacity, as were officials from other tribes. Their concern was the impact that such a defection would have on the conquest of Canaan. No one knew for sure as yet whether the tribes going to Jordan would help their brothers fight for Canaan.

With the growth of the council, the council tent had been enlarged and now there was room for the dignitaries to be seated inside. Tirza was also inside the tent as a scheduled speaker, but the other sisters had to find seats outside. Fortunately, the tent flaps were open and they were able to locate places in the first row.

Haniel opened the meeting and read the two resolutions that were before the council. Confident of a majority, the anti-Canaan faction did not even put up a speaker for the first resolution. Machla's cousin, Meir, did speak on behalf of the motion and surprised the audience with his learning and erudition. He was clearly an outstanding scholar. Now that his only son was grown, he spent all of his time studying Torah. He spoke of the sanctity of the Land of Canaan and the value of a unified tribe. "To preserve unity," he said, "the tribe as a whole must go either to Jordan or Canaan. It is my belief that unity should go with holiness and that if half the tribe has to concede its point of view, those who are motivated by material considerations should yield to those who are moved by the spirit."

Apparently, his words had a strong effect on the commanders, because the vote on the first resolution was closer than anticipated. Twenty-four commanders voted to force the entire tribe to settle in Canaan, but they were outvoted by twenty-eight who raised their hands against the motion.

Haniel rose to explain the second resolution. "If this resolution carries, the entire tribe will have to live in Trans-Jordan. If it is defeated, the tribe will take no action compelling its members to go anywhere. Those families that wish to settle in Jordan will be free to do so. Those who prefer the Land of Canaan, will receive their land there."

Alarmed by the closeness of the first vote, the pro Jordan group sent up three speakers. The first was a representative of Reuben, who spoke of the need to recruit as many residents for Trans-Jordan as possible. "Menashe now has 52,000 families," he said. "If the tribe splits, we estimate that at least 25,000 or so families will stay in Canaan. Those families are needed in Trans-Jordan because they will make our tribes stronger and also add a spiritual element. They will help us preserve our Torah way of life, and this is what our revered leader, Moses, had in mind when he sought another tribe to join with us."

The second witness in favor of the resolution was the legal advisor to the tribe of Issachar, an expert on tribal administration. After establishing his credentials, he surprised the audience by saying that his personal position was that all tribes should settle in the Land of Canaan. "If, however," he explained, "it is obvious that a clear majority of a tribe wishes to settle elsewhere, then the minority should concede and not split the tribe in two. Menashe has labored for forty years to become one of the leading and most powerful tribes of Israel. What a tragedy it would be if a split would nullify all the progress and leave just two weak tribal sections struggling to survive."

The final witness for the resolution was the commander who had undertaken to lead the faction fighting for Trans-Jordan. "It is true," he said, "that our efforts are motivated by economic considerations. Families must be concerned with their livelihood, for without bread there can be no religious life.[23] Nevertheless we are concerned with the spiritual question as well. We have negotiated with Reuben and Gad that if we go in with them, Menashe will be allowed to settle in the Bashan close to the Jordan. That way we will be closer to the holy cities of Canaan than some of the tribes along the Great Sea or tribes in the north of Canaan."

It was apparent that all of the speakers were reacting to Meir's claim that the spiritual element should take priority. When they completed their presentation, the chairman announced that Tirza, the daughter of Zelaphchad, would speak against the resolution. There was some surprise among the spectators that it wasn't Machla or Noah, but Tirza had a good reputation in the tribe for acts of kindness, and they were quite eager to hear what she had to say.

Before she got up to speak, however, the commander of the Jordan group objected to her speaking and sought to disqualify her. "I object to Tirza speaking in this case," he said, "because she and her sisters will not be landholders in the tribe of Menashe and may in fact leave the tribe to marry outsiders. She has no real interest in the outcome of this debate. While it is true that our side had speakers from outside the tribe, it was only after we had established their expertise or relevance to the case, that we called upon them to testify. Tirza has no special expertise in these matters."

Elchanan could barely contain his anger at this attempt to prevent testimony, but he had no way of intervening. Fortunately, he did not have to because Chemlon was asked to rule on the point in question. The legal advisor lost no time in delivering his advice. He commanded great respect in the tribe and people listened to him attentively.

"The objection of the commander has no basis in fact or logic. The statement that the daughters of Zelaphchad will not inherit their father's property is only an assumption. Their case is still pending and will shortly be heard at the High Court. Even if they lose their case, the council of Menashe is on record that it will reward them in such an event with a parcel of public land in return for services rendered to the tribe. Thus, they qualify as landholders.

"The logic used by the commander is also at fault. This is a major issue with which we are confronted and the outcome will affect every last person of the children of Israel. That includes both the tribes going to Trans-Jordan and those going to Canaan. I would rule that any Hebrew who wanted to speak in this case should be entitled to do so.

"There is one further aspect to be considered. Since the spiritual and religious aspects of the case were mentioned and are relevant to it, the expertise of the witness can be established. The daughters of Zelaphchad are well-versed in the Torah and are the only living members of the tribe, whose names are specifically mentioned in the latest census that is recorded in the Torah. It would thus be absurd to deny the courtesy of saying a few words to a woman whose worth is recognized by the Torah itself."

On the basis of the ruling, Haniel quieted the audience and told Tirza to go ahead. Tirza was nervous at first because she lacked the speaking experience of her older sister. After a while, though, she spoke smoothly and it was evident that she had been beautifully coached in both contents and delivery. Most important were the emotions that were projected with her words. She spoke with such feeling that the audience was spellbound.

"The Land of Canaan," she said, "is the eternal inheritance of the Hebrew people. It was here that our father, Abraham, taught the belief in one God, that Isaac dug wells and that Jacob dreamt of a ladder extending to the stars. It was here that our tribal father, Joseph, wore his coat of many colors. All of these great events in our history occurred within the borders of Canaan as they are described in the Torah.[24] Those borders do not include the captured lands on the east side of the Jordan. I am not saying that the new land is not the property of our nation. It does indeed belong to us but only by conquest. It is land which we have to sanctify by ourselves rather than land that is inherently holy."

Tirza paused to catch her breath. She could still feel her heart beating but her confidence was restored. Her voice carried far and radiated power. She continued dramatically in a style reminiscent of Machla at her best. "In the hundreds of years of our exile and bondage, we dreamt of returning to the original Canaan. This dream kept us alive and sustained us. Our parents and grandparents were not privileged to see the fulfillment of the dream, for they died in Egypt and in the desert. Only our generation will be privileged to enjoy the Divine favor of inheriting the Promised Land. I cannot fathom the mentality of those who are offered a land of milk and honey, by the mercy of God, and reject it. Even if I could somehow come to understand what drives these families, I will never understand how they would force faithful people to abandon their love for Canaan and voluntarily live in exile. Despite all statements made today, the fact remains that Trans-Jordan is not Canaan.

"My sisters and I have a God-given right to live in Canaan. Our father and uncle, of blessed memory, lost their lives fighting for Canaan. We ourselves have given over twenty years of our lives fighting for our inheritance in the Promised Land. Would it not be tragic if we were to win our struggle in the High Court, and then find out that our tribe is forcing us to take that inheritance in what is not Canaan at all? I am aware that Moses, our teacher, called for additional families to move to Jordan and I admit that in the short term we could help these tribes in a spiritual sense. Even with our help, however, these tribes will not survive in the long run. The isolation is too great and the spiritual level of the tribes insufficient. The Torah does not require anyone to give up his own life to save the life of someone else.

"Members of the council, I plead with you to have mercy on the children of your tribe to whom the word of God is precious. Let those who place sheep ahead of Torah stay in Jordan, but let those who will kiss the soil of the Holy Land when they enter Canaan, attain their life's ambition. Yes, I believe in following the majority, but the Torah has instructed us 'Thou shalt not abide by the majority in the pursuit of evil.' There are none in this gathering who have worked harder for the tribe of Menashe than my family. We have served the tribe loyally for more than twenty years. Would the tribe see fit to repay our loyalty by barring us from our destiny? Members of the council, let us not stain the good name of our tribe by promulgating this evil decree. May the Lord reward those who follow His will and love the good land that He has given us."

There was a hushed silence when Tirza finished and then a long burst of applause from those outside. Her words almost carried the day. Two commanders who had voted against the first resolution changed their position and voted against the second resolution as well. Their action resulted in a tie vote of twenty-six to twenty-six. The vote held after several recounts so Haniel, the president, rose to resolve the tie.

"This is the hardest decision that I will have to make in my life," he said. "If I decide in favor of the resolution, I will deny to more than 25,000 families the right to live in Canaan proper. If I decide against it, the tribe will split into two parts. I will thus reduce the status of Menashe to that of a weak tribe and undo forty years of growth and progress. In such a case, a president has to follow his conscience and act according to his beliefs and his understanding of the Torah.

"My conscience allows me to choose only the Land of Canaan. To the best of my ability, I will represent those who wish to live in Trans-Jordan in their negotiations. But I will not cast my lot with them. God willing, I and my children will live in Canaan. My name may not have been mentioned in the Torah in connection with the tribal census, but it does appear in the Torah in a paragraph ending with the verse 'These are they whom the Lord commanded to divide the inherited land to the children of Israel in the Land of Canaan.' This was my charge when I was appointed president of the tribe and I must be loyal to my assignment. It is my intention to cast my vote against the resolution."

The supporters of Canaan gave the speaker a thunderous ovation. The president did not say that it was Noah who cited the verse to him during her visit a day earlier. As the president completed his statement, a commander rose and requested the floor. The president recognized the commander who wanted to know if it were possible to change a previous vote. The president turned to Chemlon for a ruling. Chemlon reflected for a minute and said. "If a motion were passed and officially recorded, it would be necessary to vote first on a reconsideration of the question. In this case, however, we have not reached that point. The presidential vote has not yet been formally cast. Thus far, president Haniel has only revealed his intentions. A vote may still be changed." Chemlon knew that the commander had earlier voted for the resolution and any change would be in favor of Canaan. He did not, however, let that knowledge affect his decision.

The commander who requested the floor said, "I wish to relieve His Excellency from his heavy burden. I am recalling my vote for the resolution and voting against. Given the president's intentions, it will in no way change the outcome of the debate, but it will look better for posterity if the issue is decided by a clear majority rather than a presidential tie-breaking vote. Furthermore, if there is disunity in the tribe as a result of the motion, I do not want the president to bear the blame alone."

"That is very considerate of you," Haniel said. "If you change your vote, I will not be called upon to cast mine. If there is no further business, this meeting stands adjourned."

The sisters hugged and kissed Tirza for her splendid presentation. Even Noah conceded that she could not have done much better herself. Scores of well-wishers expressed their appreciation and complimented her on her work. Elchanan was lavish in his praise. "If you keep up such good work," he said, "the Torah will someday put you back in your rightful place among the daughters of Zelaphchad." Chemlon also praised her and she whispered quietly to him, "I could never have done it without your help and guidance." A radiance spread over Tirza's countenance and she felt deep happiness with her accomplishment.

The fears of the president with regard to tribal unity were not confirmed by reality. The number of Menashe families who ultimately settled on the eastside of the Jordan, was far less than anticipated. The families of Machir and Gilead and their brothers joined with Reuben and Gad. But the families arising from the six children of Gilead, which included Chefer, chose Canaan. Those in Canaan were sufficient in number and strength to keep the tribe viable.

The time of the Zelaphchad trial was rapidly approaching. On Sunday, the ninth day of the ninth month, the daughters of Zelaphchad and their mother rose early and walked to the bier of Joseph. There, each of the sisters knelt and prayed for the blessings of heaven when they stood before the elders of Israel at the bar of justice. Life and death hovered in the balance and generated a river of tears. Achla, too, prayed for her daughters, asking Joseph to plead with the Lord to send her five worthy sons-in-law as soon as possible.

CHAPTER

TWELVE

*"GIVE US LAND AMONG OUR
FATHER'S BROTHERS"*

As dawn broke over the fields of Moab on Monday morning, the daughters of Zelaphchad awoke early from a restless sleep. This was the most critical day in their lives and their anxiety was overwhelming. The clothes to be worn on this occasion, long, elegant and luxurious, had been set aside for months. Every last item of apparel had been meticulously planned and diligently produced. Machla was in charge of putting Noah together so that there would be no last minute frenzy. Actually, Noah got out of bed without any prodding and required little assistance.

The sisters planned to walk slowly with their mother to the Tabernacle, allowing plenty of time for quiet reflection on the way. Their plans went awry because they underestimated the overwhelming public support they would receive from their tribe and family. By the time they finished breakfast, massive crowds had gathered on the path outside the tent area as far as the eye could see. Chemlon had announced the trial date at the council meeting a week earlier. Upon hearing the news, the council passed a resolution urging all members of the tribe to rally behind the daughters of Zelaphchad in their great moment.

The commanders spread the word and the members of the tribe responded in force. All former students of Achla's classes were there, as well as those who had ever been helped by the health service. Also on hand were many members of the Chefer clan. What the tribal leaders had in mind was a triumphant procession to the main camp.

"They're crazy," said Noah. "How can they celebrate our victory before our case has even been heard? Perhaps we can sneak out through Ephraim and get there by ourselves."

"These people have come to honor us," said Machla. "We cannot show disrespect to our kin and families. In any event, the presence of thousands of supporters will undoubtedly help our cause. I'll go out and speak to Haniel." Machla found him at the top of the path and greeted him with a warm smile. A wave of cheering erupted as people saw her.

"Good morning, Machla," Haniel said. "The members of your tribe are here to escort you to the High Court. Are your sisters ready? We will walk behind you all the way."

"I am deeply honored," Machla said, "but we cannot let the judges and commanders walk behind us. Nor will we walk ahead of the tribal flags. This has to be done properly. The flag bearers will go first and then the judges. They will be followed by His Excellency and the commanders. At that point we will join the procession."

"This is your special day and we will respect your wishes," he answered. "I will organize the tribal leaders while you get your mother and sisters."

Machla gathered her family and they stood in respect as a special honor guard of flag bearers marched by with the tribal banners. Each banner carried a caricature of a wild ox in blue on a field of white. The tribal leadership, comprising twenty-five judges and alternates, fifty-two commanders, the president and the administrators, walked behind the flags. At that point, the Zelaphchad family joined in, marching in two rows. Achla was in the first row flanked by Machla and Tirza. Noah was in the second row flanked by Hogla and Milka. The order of the second row was in part determined by Machla's desire to limit any theatrics that Noah might undertake in response to the crowd.

The commanders of 100 and of fifty followed the sisters. Behind them came the other families of the tribe. Well over 10,000 members of Menashe marched. All along the way, they were cheered by thousands of others. As the procession from Menashe was crossing the Levitical border from the east, an even larger procession from the tribe of Judah was crossing from the west. All current and former students of Machla's school and their teachers were present. Elchanan felt that attending a case before the High Court was a greater learning experience than anything taking place in a classroom so, without hesitation, he canceled school for the day. All students over the age of twelve were allowed to attend. Some 5,000 students, their teachers and their parents were on hand to watch history in the making.

Elchanan was hoping that in addition to seeing the High Court in action, the students might witness some manifestation of revelation. If Moses received prophecy during the trial, the students would gain valuable insight into how the Torah was written to reflect the will of God.

The tribes of Menashe and Judah and visitors from the other tribes filled every vacant spot in the Levitical area. Not since the return of the spies, thirty-nine years earlier, had there been such a large gathering of the children of Israel. Teams of officers were stationed to relay the trial proceedings verbatim from the court area to members of the crowd standing further out. At precisely nine, Elazar, the high priest, opened the hearing. A hush of eager anticipation came over the vast crowd as Elazar expressed his introductory remarks.[1]

"On this day, the High Court will hear a petition from the daughters of Zelaphchad: Machla, Noah, Hogla, Milka, and Tirza. The petition requests the court to enact legislation that will enable the daughters of a man who had no sons, to inherit their father's property in the Land of Canaan. Since no provision for such cases appears in the Torah, the petitioners are requesting this court to enact such laws under rights recently assigned to us by the Torah in the area of social legislation.

"Proper documentation has been submitted by the petitioners proving that they have exhausted all possibilities of securing such enactments in the lower courts and are thus entitled to seek relief for their problem before this court.

"Procedures of the High Court require the petitioners to introduce themselves to the court and to read a very brief statement of the arguments they wish to present." He glanced at the daughters of Zelaphchad, who were standing in the first row. Benches had been provided only for tribal presidents and attorneys representing the court and the plaintiffs. A chair was also made available to Achla.

Elazar continued. "After the opening statement by the petitioners, they may elaborate on each argument by presenting explanations, documents or supporting witnesses. Witnesses summoned by the petitioners shall be presented by their attorney. The attorney for the High Court may examine them, if he feels the need to do so. Members of the nation as a whole who wish to testify will be presented by the court attorney. The petitioner's attorney has the right to question them. After the conclusion of all testimony, the court will debate the case and vote either to grant or to reject the petition."

Elchanan was an expert on High Court procedures. He often audited cases there after they were sent up by the lower courts. The Judean court frequently assigned alternate judges to such tasks because they could not spare a sitting judge for the work. After hearing the High Court judgments, Elchanan would report back to Judah so that the tribal court would be informed of the latest precedents.

Elchanan's plan of action was to present the sisters in reverse chronological order. Noah would introduce the sisters and she would be followed by Milka, who would defend the character of Zelaphchad. Elchanan knew that the court would not help the children of anyone who was guilty of a conspiracy against Moses or worshipping the golden calf. He felt relieved by the knowledge that Zelaphchad's sin was not of this nature.[2]

Hogla would then testify as to the status of the family and invoke the argument of the Levirate law. Tirza would argue against wiping out the name of Zelaphchad from the records of the children of Israel. The last speaker would be Machla, who would present the request to the court for property in Canaan.

Elchanan's strategy was clear. He anticipated that most of the questions would be directed to the last two speakers and he wanted the most gifted sisters to respond. Noah was much sharper than Tirza, but Elchanan was afraid that she was too aggressive. If asked a hostile question, she might counter with an equally hostile reply.

All eyes focused on Noah as she stepped a few paces forward from the row in which she stood with her four sisters and addressed Moses and Elazar, who were seated to the right of the rows of judges.

"Revered Prophet of the Lord, Moses, our teacher; His Grace, the High Priest, Elazar, presiding judge; honorable associate judges of the High Court of the Children of Israel. We who stand before the court are the five daughters of Zelaphchad, the son of Chefer, the son of Gilead, the son of Machir, the son of the founder of our tribe, Menashe. Our names in order of birth are Machla, Tirza, Hogla, Milka and myself, Noah. Our mother Achlama — she should live and be well — is seated in the audience. We have no children and none of us is married. We have chosen as counsel for our case, his honor, Elchanan ben Uriah, alternate judge and legal advisor to the tribal council of Judah. He will be assisted by his honor, Chemlon ben Shalem, alternate judge and legal advisor to the tribal council of Menashe. Each of the daughters of Zelaphchad will read a verse of our opening statement."

In a clear, resounding voice, Noah began:

> "OUR FATHER, ZELAPHCHAD, DIED IN THE DESERT....."

Milka stepped up and continued:

> "OUR FATHER WAS NOT IN THE CONGREGATION OF THOSE WHO REBELLED AGAINST THE LORD IN THE CONSPIRACY OF KORACH..."

Hogla added:

> "HE DIED BECAUSE OF HIS OWN SIN AND HE HAD NO SONS"

Tirza advanced and said:

> "WHY SHOULD OUR FATHER'S NAME BE ERASED FROM HIS FAMILY BECAUSE HE HAD NO SON?...."

Machla moved up and ended the outline with,

> "GIVE US OUR LAND AMONGST OUR FATHER'S BROTHERS."

When the daughters completed the summary, the four older sisters returned to their original positions. Noah walked from her location to a more central position to elaborate upon the outline. She surveyed the ranks of the judges and paused for dramatic effect. Noah usually spoke in a soft voice but now she raised it, in order to be clearly heard. Elchanan had practiced with her many times and cautioned her repeatedly against any departures from the prepared texts.

"Modesty prevents me from describing the full nature of our character and accomplishments to the court, but we feel the court should know about us and I will present two character witnesses shortly. Before I call them, however, I wish to say for the record that we are the only persons of the fifth generation from the sons of Jacob, either men or women, whose names the Almighty saw fit to mention individually in the last census of the tribes as it appears in the Torah.

"My first witness is His Excellency, the distinguished president of the tribe of Judah, Caleb, the son of Yefuneh." Elchanan escorted Caleb to a chair in front of the judges but Caleb preferred to stand. The president was a revered figure among the Hebrews for almost four decades. Out of respect to him, the judges rose from their places and honored both his age and his important contribution to Hebrew history. Elchanan took over the examination of the witness.

"Your Excellency, how long have you know the petitioner's family?"

"I knew Chefer and his son, Zelaphchad, in the land of Egypt. They were among the most righteous members of the children of Israel. I remember the day when Zelaphchad appeared before Pharaoh when that evil king sought to place a wedge between Moses and the Hebrew officers. Despite Pharaoh's prodding, Zelaphchad refused to turn against Moses. For that act he won the personal praise of our revered prophet."

"Do you know any of the daughters of Zelaphchad?"

"I know Machla very well and have met Noah. As president of the tribe of Judah, I was concerned about the religious education of the daughters of our tribe. Ten years ago, Machla came to the tribe and volunteered to teach our children. Let me say that other than my wife, Miriam, of blessed memory, no woman among the children of Israel knew more Torah than this daughter of Zelaphchad. She started with a group of eight girls of Judah and then trained our teachers and built our schools. Thousands of daughters of our tribe, who stand today in the congregation outside the court, received their Torah education as a result of her efforts.[3]

"I personally examined her classes and found her students so knowledgeable that I cried tears of joy. I might add that one of her original students, who was further trained by Noah, has been chosen to fill the position of Director of Torah Education for Women in our tribe."

"Thank you, Your Excellency, I have no further questions."

The attorney for the court did not intend to question Caleb, so Noah returned to her position and said, "I now have the honor of calling the next witness, His Excellency, Haniel ben Ephod, President of the tribe of Menashe."

"Your Excellency," Elchanan asked, "how long have you known the Zelaphchad family?"

"For at least thirty-five years."

"Are you a close relative of the family?"

"No."

"Can you tell us in what connection you know the family."

"Before I became president, I was a commander of 1,000 and I sat on the tribal council for more than twenty years. One of my duties at the council was to supervise activities at the Tribal Center. Achla, the widow of Zelaphchad, has maintained a sewing class for twenty years at the Center. For almost the same length of time, her daughters have maintained the tribal health service which they organized. Over the years, they have trained hundreds of women in this work."

"What does the service do?"

"It provides health care for young children and the elderly as well as assistance to pregnant women. As the last census revealed, the tribe of Menashe has the highest population growth of all the tribes. To an important degree, this reflects the excellent health care that our tribe provides."

"During the last decades, has Your Excellency or the tribal council received any complaints about the personal or religious behavior of the daughters of Zelaphchad?"

"We have received nothing but praise, particularly for Tirza who has organized a food service for the lepers outside the camp in addition to her other work."

"Would you have been willing to accept any of the sisters as your own daughter-in-law?"

"My son was an ardent admirer of Noah. Often we prayed that she would accept his proposal, but it did not come to pass." There was an audible murmur from the audience.

"No further questions, Your Excellency."

The court attorney, however, did have some. "This may not bear on the case directly, but I think the court would enjoy hearing your opinion on a matter that was raised here earlier. How is it that the daughters of Zelaphchad introduced a life-saving innovation in the tribe of Menashe and none of the other tribes adopted it?"

Haniel paused to reflect on his response to this sensitive question. "Of course, I could say that no other tribe is privileged to have the daughters of Zelaphchad, but that would not tell the whole story. The answer is very controversial and will distract from the conduct of this trial, if we pursue it at this time. Suffice it to say that we have a very high degree of tribalism among the children of Israel and sometimes we forget that we are one nation."

"Your point is well taken and I will not pursue this line of questioning. Given the strong support of the daughters of Zelaphchad and the gratitude for their deeds, has the tribe of Menashe itself done anything to resolve their inheritance problem?"

"We have, Your Honor. The council has committed itself, if this action fails, to giving the daughters of Zelaphchad public tribal land in Canaan. The aim of this case, however, is not limited to helping just one family. It concerns all women in a similar situation. In Menashe alone there are many hundreds of families composed of only daughters. All the other tribes have the same situation, to a greater or lesser degree."

"I have concluded my questions, Your Excellency, but one of the judges has a question for the first petitioner."

Noah returned to the central area and the judge rose to ask. "You mentioned, Noah, that you and your sisters are not married. It has already been shown that you had at least one proposal of marriage. I am not the world's greatest expert on beauty and talent, but it should be fairly obvious to anyone with eyes in his head that, given the piety, wisdom and attractiveness of the daughters of Zelaphchad, marriages could have easily been entered into by all of them. I therefore must ask you if you and your sisters are against the sacred institution of marriage. Secondly, if you were married to a landholder in Canaan, would you then have any need to petition this court?"

Elchanan had not foreseen such a question to Noah, but he hoped for the best. "Your Honor," Noah said, "I will answer your second question first. In the course of this action you will not hear anything to indicate that we are entering this petition because we personally fear destitution or poverty if we have no land in Canaan. Our situation, as you have heard, is secured by tribal concern for our welfare. We argue our position as a matter of principle. We sincerely believe that women should not be disinherited and that men, who have no sons, should not have their memory blotted out of Hebrew history. As far as others are concerned, however, the question of poverty is a very serious one and marriage is not always the answer. Some women may not find mates and others may become divorced and widowed. The women, for whom we plead, have no brothers to give them moral or financial support should the need arise.

"With regard to your first question, I can only speak for myself and not for my sisters. I have nothing against the institution of marriage. I had the highest regard for those men who did propose to me and I weighed each of more than a hundred proposals very carefully. I turned these proposals away and deferred marriage because those who wanted to marry me did not share my dream of owning land in Canaan and would not have supported me in my struggle. Marriage would have meant abandonment of my efforts to win my inheritance. The Holy Land has been the goal of our people since the days of Abraham, when God promised the land to him and his progeny." With the audience hanging on every word, Noah spoke deliberately. "Taking any action that would cost me the chance to possess the soil of Canaan, was utterly unthinkable. My tribe descended from Joseph who loved the Holy Land, and I am a daughter of Zelaphchad, who died fighting for Canaan."[4]

With her testimony concluded, Noah stepped back into the row of sisters and Milka came forward.

"Honored judges, I will prove that our father, Zelaphchad, was innocent of any sins that could have resulted in his forfeiting his claims to the Promised Land. I now call upon my revered mother, Achla, to testify."

Elchanan asked Achla, "Do you remember your husband's reaction when he heard about the golden calf?"

"I do, indeed. He said that he could not understand how people who had heard the word of the Lord seven weeks earlier would turn to idolatry. He feared that the wrath of God would come down upon the sinners and he strictly forbade all members of the family to go anywhere near the golden calf."

"Did you know Korach?"

"I did. He once came to Zelaphchad to enlist him in his conspiracy and my husband chased him away. For all of Korach's money, Zelaphchad hated him with a passion. He could not comprehend how anyone could find fault with the man who brought us forth from bondage and performed so many miracles."

"Did Zelaphchad ever complain about the difficult conditions in the desert?"

"Never. He much preferred them over Egypt where, as a crew master, he regularly suffered savage beatings."

"No more questions."

The attorney for the court asked Achla. "Do you agree with your daughters' campaign and how do you make peace with the fact that these lovely daughters have not presented you with a single grandchild to hold in your arms?"

The daughters expected the mother to repeat her conviction that the girls were mad to do what they were doing. Instead, Achla surprised them.

"Of course I would like to see them settled but I have no complaints against them. They have made me prouder than any mother in Israel with their knowledge, their good deeds and their dedication to Canaan. They promised me to get married immediately after this case, whether they win or lose. I believe them. I have faith that I will live to hold their children in my arms. Dare I complain when more than 25,000 people come out to support their cause and my daughters' names will appear at least twice in the Torah?"

Milka returned to the row and Hogla stepped forward.

"It is true that our father Zelaphchad died because of a sin. But, even in his sin, he showed greatness and love for the Land of Canaan. The next witness is Yerachmiel, the son of Ophir, of the tribe of Menashe."

Yerachmiel was a man of fifty-eight years who had been close to the family throught the forty years in the desert. His hair was turning gray, but he retained a youthful appearance. Elchanan spoke to him gently.

"How old were you when Zelaphchad died?"

"I was eighteen, Your Honor."

"Were you with him at the time?"

"I was with him when he was wounded and with him later when he died."

"You participated in the war against the Canaanites?"

"I did."

"Did Zelaphchad encourage you to take part in it?"

"No, Your Honor, he told me not to go."

"Why was that?"

"He told me that I was only eighteen and not doomed to die in the desert. If I went to war, I might be killed. If I didn't, I would at least reach Canaan in my old age."

"You chose not to heed his advice?"

"Your Honor, Zelaphchad was my foreman in Egypt. He protected me from the cruel Egyptian taskmasters. I would have followed him anywhere. Zelaphchad felt that someone had to remove the stain cast upon our national reputation by the spies and by the cowardice of those who wanted to return to Egypt. He reasoned that if he were to die in the desert anyway, he would rather die fighting for the Land of Canaan."

"Was he suicidal?"

"No, not at all. He felt that if the Lord saw that there were people who were ready to fight for Canaan, He would be merciful and grant them victory."

"What happened during the battle?"

"I was with the larger group that ascended to the top of the mountain. Zelaphchad, his brother, Ram, and a few others, were stationed behind us to protect our avenue of retreat. The Amalekites, who were waiting in ambush in the middle of the mountain, tried to cut off the road and encircle us. Zelaphchad sounded the retreat signal and fought to hold back the Amalekites. My group ran back down the road and passed Zelaphchad. I saw Ram, already dead, and Zelaphchad still fighting despite heavy injuries. I wanted to stay with him but he waved me away. As a young man, I was able to run fast and escape, but I do owe my life to Zelaphchad."

"What happened after Zelaphchad died?"

"I remember that Aaron, the high priest, came to console Chefer on the loss of his sons and Achla on the loss of her husband. He said that Moses couldn't come because Zelaphchad had not obeyed the Lord's will, but he did ask Aaron to convey his condolences to Chefer and his surviving sons."

The testimony had a profound effect on the audience because very few of them had heard the story before. The court attorney asked Yerachmiel. "Were you there when Moses asked the group not to attack?"

"I was, Your Honor."

"What did Zelaphchad say?"

"He told Moses that he was doomed one way or another, and he preferred to die fighting the Canaanites if death was unavoidable."

There were no further questions addressed to Yerachmiel, so Hogla moved to introduce the next witness. He was Ariel ben Abba, the chief judge of the tribe of Asher. While Asher was not one of the more important tribes of Israel, Ariel had acquired great prominence among the Hebrew jurists for his wisdom.

Elchanan established the credentials of the witness and then asked him, "Given your knowledge of the Torah, would the court violate the letter or spirit of any Torah law by allowing daughters of a man who died without sons, to inherit his property?"

"I know of no such law. It is my feeling that our nation adopted this attitude in imitation of non-Hebrew nations who regarded their women as so much cattle."

"Is there any place in Torah family law where females are regarded as equal to males?" Elchanan had not discussed the case with the judge but he was confident that a man of such great learning would know the correct answer.

"In the case of the Levirate marriage laws, the Torah denies the rights of Levirate to a woman who has had children, even if the children are female. Although the Torah uses the word 'son' in the text, we understand that there is no difference, under the law, whether the mother bore a son or a daughter. For the purposes of the Levirate law then, girls are equated with boys."[5]

Elchanan didn't know of other similar cases, but he ventured that the judge might know of some and he asked him, "Are there any other cases in the Torah where such equality prevails?"

The judge replied hesitantly. "The laws have not yet been released but the Torah will ordain a national assembly in Canaan every seventh year to hear readings from the Torah. On that occasion women will be equally bound to attend."

The revelation came as a surprise to everyone because it was generally known that Torah studies for women were optional rather than obligatory.

"One last question if I may," said Elchanan. "Do you feel that if a woman is allowed to inherit property, it will in any way undermine her moral values or endanger Hebrew family standards?"

"Not at all. If anything, it will enhance them. When a woman has a good self-image, she will avoid behavior that could endanger her reputation. Being a landholder in the Promised Land would certainly make her a more responsible person."

"Thank you, Your Honor."

The court attorney had no intentions of asking the judge any questions. Although the Chief Judge was obviously very learned, he was still a tribal judge. It was not in keeping with protocol for High Court members to learn anything from local judges. "I myself have no questions," he said, "but I do have a distinguished personality here who wishes to say a few words at this point. The petitioners may reject his request to appear at this time or they may waive their right and let him testify now. If there is such an objection, the witness will have to wait until later."

Elchanan quickly agreed to hearing the witness. He wanted the case to go for decision immediately after Machla's testimony. The testimony of hostile witnesses after Machla, could undo much of his carefully planned work. "We have no objections, Your Honor."

"I wish to present Armon ben Karni, distinguished senior commander of the tribe of Dan." Elchanan had heard of Armon, but did not know him personally. The commander had a very somber appearance. Short and heavy-set, he conveyed a harsh view of life.

The attorney started in a cautious manner. "Commander Armon, would you tell the court why you have requested to testify at this time?"

"I have chosen this point because I am upset with the testimony of the Chief Judge of Asher. Mind you, I do not question his scholarship. But I must say that critical social issues should not be decided on pure theory. Torah scholars are removed from the everyday world and its problems. I speak as senior commander of one of the larger tribes and I come from the world of real life.

"I am of the opinion that if this petition is granted it would have a devastating effect on the economic and family lives of the children of Israel. You can always put up a Machla or a Noah to influence the court. But these are exceptional women who might be able to manage property. The ordinary women of Israel, especially those who grow up in homes without fathers and brothers, are simple-minded illiterates. There is no way that they could handle complex agricultural matters. They should stick to their cooking and sewing and let men manage the business." Undoubtedly, there were people in the audience who shared the speaker's point of view, but very few would have ventured to express such thoughts openly.

Armon continued in his strident voice. "Furthermore, women who own property will resist the authority of their husbands and that will lead to domestic instability. It may also lead to immorality. Can you imagine women in the marketplaces and meeting halls? I say that this petition is not only nonsense but dangerous. We must protect our traditional values and not experiment with wild social schemes."

The court attorney sensed that such a bigot was a liability and did not want to prolong his appearance. He immediately turned the witness over to the petitioner's counsel. Elchanan, who had dealt with such people before, knew how to handle them.

"Commander," he said, "I am willing to concede that there are simple-minded women in the tribe of Dan. Since you are a senior member of the Danite council which is in charge of religious education, what have you done to teach the women of Dan and alleviate their ignorance?"

"Your Honor, we have a Torah Education program for men that compares favorably with that of the other tribes. We and many other tribes, including even Zelaphchad's tribe of Menashe, do not believe in Torah studies for women. We feel they should get their domestic and moral training at home and then be turned over to the supervision of husbands."

"Don't you feel it is unfair to deny women education and then classify them as 'simple-minded?' To me it is like the farmer who doesn't feed his animals and then complains that they are thin."

"I will not debate with you whether this simple-mindedness is due to the lack of teaching or stems from biological inferiority. There are many people who feel that ordinary women are not capable of Torah study and I am sure that you are extremely selective when you admit female students to your schools. We feel that it is wrong to teach women Torah because they will abuse the knowledge. If they have any questions, they should ask their fathers or husbands."

"Then you see the education of women and their managing property as a threat to tribal morality?"

"I do indeed."

"Commander, have you ever walked along the outer borders of the tribe of Dan late at night?"[6]

"It is not my practice to do so."

"Are you aware of what goes on at those borders?"

The witness was feeling a little uncomfortable. "I have no idea as to what you are alluding."

"Would you prefer to have me call a few witnesses to refresh your memory?" A sense of excitement surged through the audience. In a civil petition, it was rarely expected to run into a direct confrontation between a witness and an attorney. Nor was it expected that an attorney would seek to subject a distinguished witness to an aggressive attack. Armon's discomfort was now at a stage of panic. He knew full well that Elchanan would not relent and he certainly could not deny the sordid situation on the outskirts of the tribe of Dan.

"That won't be necessary," he said. "We have a little problem there, but I don't see how it bears on the case."

"I would suggest, commander, that it would be best to put your own house in order by teaching the daughters of Dan the moral laws of the Torah and worrying less about the effect of property ownership on the virtue of pious women who love the Land of Canaan."

After the commander left the witness area, the court attorney asked Elchanan if he would take another witness. Elchanan agreed. The attorney asked a short pale man in his middle forties to come forward. The man was nervous and seemed a little hesitant.

"What is your name?" the attorney asked.

"My name is Abraham, the son of Kalman, of the tribe of Zebulun."

"Why have you asked to testify?"

"Because I am afraid of what may happen in the case today."

"Why is that?"

"The daughters of Zelaphchad who have brought this case today are beautiful women. They are educated in Torah, they speak eloquently and are dressed elegantly. They certainly can get married to the richest and noblest men. I am afraid that the court may feel that such women need no special legislation and will fare just as well without it.

"I want the court to know that the petitioners speak for thousands of women who are not as privileged or gifted. I want the court to know that they speak for me, a poor man from the tribe of Zebulun. In the course of bearing our fourth daughter, my wife encountered difficulties and died. While my daughter survived, she is less than perfect. I love my daughter and raise her with my other children to the best of my ability. It is hard for me to remarry, not just because I am poor, but because I cannot find a woman who is ready to give such a child the special care and attention she needs. Likewise, there will be great difficulty in finding a husband for my daughter. I have no sons whom I may instruct to take care of my special daughter when I die. What is more, I cannot leave my daughter any property because my brothers, or their heirs, will claim it all." The witness had now gained more confidence, and his voice became stronger as he continued.

"If the Zelaphchad petition is granted, then at least my daughter will have some resources. In return for managing her property, some family may offer to take care of her. I, too, petitioned my tribal council but they could do nothing to allay my fears. Common people can do no more than that. I thank God for the daughters of Zelaphchad who persevered long enough to get the attention of the High Court, to secure the finest counsel, to rally 25,000 people to their cause, and to present their case so well. May God bless them and help all those who depend on them for victory."

There were no further witnesses so Hogla stepped back and Tirza came forward. "I do not intend to call witnesses but I wish to explain why the name Zelaphchad should not be dropped from Hebrew history.

"As has been adequately demonstrated this morning, Zelaphchad was a brave and honorable man whose life was cut short before he could have a son. If he had had a son, the name Zelaphchad would be perpetuated on four parcels of land in Israel. It is well known that all those who left the Land of Egypt were entitled to inherit land in Israel. Both Zelaphchad and his father, Chefer, were in this category. In addition to his own parcel, Zelaphchad was entitled to a double share in the property of Chefer, because he was the first born son. The final parcel due to Zelaphchad came from the property of Ram, who had left the land of Egypt, and predeceased Zelaphchad, while still childless.[7]

"What will happen now? This property will go to his brothers' children, our cousins. There will be no soil in Canaan recalling the name of a man who labored with his brothers in Egypt. There will be no soil in the Holy Land recalling the name of a man who fought and died to conquer Canaan. There will be no soil in Canaan recalling the name of a man who is mentioned by name in the Torah. Judges of the court, I plead with you not to allow this to happen."

Machla then took her position in front of the court. She was in absolute command of her presentation. Every word had been repeated in her mind thousands of times. She wasn't nervous or afraid, though she was fully cognizant of the awesome precedent she was setting. Never before had Hebrew women initiated or presented a petition at the High Court. Win or lose, she was making history.

A victory, of course, would be even more historic. She knew of no society anywhere in the world that allowed women to own property. Even if only a relatively small number of women were granted such privilege, it would forever change the status of women in the Hebrew society. In time, the standing of women would improve further and such advances could set a pattern for non-Hebrew nations, as well. She turned to the court and, with all the strength she could muster, made her case. Machla cut a magnificent figure as she spoke to the judges. She was the tallest of the daughters and her features had been inherited from Zelaphchad. Her voice was deep and carried a long way.

"Honored judges. I have waited patiently for this moment for twenty-five years. Not once did I waver in my faith that the Lord would respond to my pleas and that justice would be done.

"My father, Zelaphchad, died when I was five-years old leaving me and my three other sisters as orphans. The fifth sister, Noah, was born six months after the death of my father." Here Machla recounted vividly the despair and suffering of her mother, Achla. "My dear mother tried valiantly to remarry. She was mainly seeking a Levirate marriage because the birth of a son in such a union would perpetuate the name of Zelaphchad under Torah Law. She would have accepted any husband, however, since she needed help in raising and educating her daughters. Unfortunately, she was not successful in finding a partner in either a Levirate marriage or a regular one. Her five daughters were a liability to her in both cases. Potential husbands did not want the responsibility of such a large family of young girls. Levirate candidates claimed that the existence of female children exempted them from the Levirate laws. In that regard, women are considered equal to men."

Machla felt that it was important to explain to the judges how she had become so well-versed in the Torah. While they had heard from witnesses about the scope of her erudition, they did not know how she had acquired her knowledge. She wanted them to understand that the treatment of women was unequal to that of men, and that they were not respected for intellectual capabilites.

"I heard my first verse of the Torah at thirteen when I was hiding behind a tent where my cousins were being tutored. The very first words I heard told how the Lord instructed Abraham to go the Land of Canaan where God would make him a great nation.[8] Thus was kindled my love of Torah and my love of Canaan. I continued learning behind the tent for two more years. I then spent another five years cleaning the tents of my commander in order to overhear more words of Torah. As soon as I learned a verse in the Torah, I committed it to memory and taught it to my sisters. I have never ceased studying Torah and teaching the word of God to others.

"From the Torah, I learned the importance of ethical and moral behavior. From the Torah, I learned that it was the destiny of the children of Israel to build in Canaan a perfect society, in which high moral codes and economic justice would prevail. My sisters were thrilled when they heard me teach the laws for helping the poor and the weak, the orphans, the widows and the strangers. Can you imagine the pain we felt when we learned that our father's property in Canaan would not be passed to us because we were women?" Here Machla's voice took on a melodic quality as she intoned a litany of discrimination against women.[9]

"Can you imagine what it means to be told: 'You as women will not be able to raise sheep and sacrifice the first born of the flock. You as women will not be able to leave the corners of fields to the poor. You as women will not bring the fruits of the land to the holy city and make a declaration of thanksgiving to the Lord for redemption from bondage and deliverance to a Land of milk and honey.'

"I will not hide the fact from the honored judges that, in theory, we believe that all women should have the right to inherit property in the Land of Canaan. At some point in the distant future that, too, may come to pass. For the moment, we have to be practical as to what can be granted by the courts without causing major social upheaval. We have, therefore, limited our request to women whose fathers have never had any sons at all. In such cases, the need for legal relief is most acute because, in the absence of brothers, the father's name will be erased from the national history, and such women will have no one to turn to in the event of poverty and destitution.

"I speak for all of my sisters when I say that we are not opposed to marriage. A woman is not complete without a husband for she was created to bear and raise children. But for each social and historical advance of a nation, there must be sacrifice. My father gave his life to remove the stain of the spies from the people of Israel. We have given most of our fruitful years to secure for certain women a share of the Promised Land.

"Do not cry for us. We were motivated by a cause that is supreme for the children of Israel. Without a land our people will be doomed. Even if we have a land, it will require the maximum sacrifice to build it, to defend it and to support it. My sisters and I pledge in front of this court and the congregation gathered here that, if we are entrusted with the sacred soil of Canaan, we will guard it with our lives. We will till the soil in peacetime and defend it with our lives and sacred honor in times of war.

"To the men and women who have supported us in our cause, I say that your faith in us will not be misplaced. To the many thousands who have come out in our behalf, I say, 'Be proud that you have seen Torah in action. You have witnessed the High Court of Israel listening to the pleas of ordinary citizens.'

"To the honored judges of the court, I say, 'this is an historic moment. You will sanctify the name of God and enhance the love of the children of Israel for the Land of Canaan by extending the right to hold land to those women who crave it. Have mercy on the daughters of Israel who plead with you to give them their inheritance in the Land of their fathers.'"

Machla couldn't control her emotions as she cited the verses of the Torah. Tears flowed down her cheeks, but her voice remained strong and powerful.[10]

"FOR THE LORD THY GOD BRINGS THEE INTO A GOOD LAND;

A LAND OF WATERCOURSES, OF FOUNTAINS AND DEPTHS
THAT SPRING OUT OF VALLEYS AND HILLS;

A LAND OF WHEAT AND BARLEY, AND VINES, AND FIG
TREES AND POMEGRANATES;

A LAND OF OLIVE OIL AND HONEY; A LAND IN WHICH
THOU SHALT EAT BREAD WITHOUT SCARCENESS, THOU
SHALT NOT LACK ANYTHING IN IT;

A LAND WHOSE STONES WILL YIELD IRON AND OUT OF
WHOSE HILLS THOU MAYEST DIG BRASS. THOU SHALT EAT
FROM THE LAND AND BE SATISFIED, AND BLESS THE LORD
THY GOD FOR THE GOOD LAND WHICH HE HAS GIVEN
THEE.'

May God bless you all."

Machla's presentation was so awesome that even the judges remained in stunned silence as the echoes of her ringing voice faded away. The spectators were the first to recover and broke the stillness with a massive eruption of cheers and applause. When the sound subsided and the case was about to go to the court for a decision, Moses rose to make a dramatic announcement.

"This case has no precedent for complexity and the issues involved are of supreme importance. I must confess that I cannot resolve this matter on my own and the will of the Lord has not yet been revealed to me. I therefore beseech the court to pause for several minutes while I pray to the Lord for special guidance as to how to proceed."

Elazar quickly announced that there would be a short recess and expressed the hope that the Divine word would be forthcoming. "If the will of the Lord is not revealed, the court will commence deliberations and vote on the petition."

Elchanan sought out Machla during the break. "I have never heard a more beautiful speech. I feel that if we win, it will be because of your words."

"Everyone did very well today," she said, blushing with her typical modesty. "What are our chances now?"

"It is hard to say, because I think it will be very close. The court votes in a peculiar way. The lowest-ranked judges cast their votes first. If one of the higher-ranked judges voted first, the younger ones would never vote against him. Our strongest support is among the newer judges, who are more receptive to change.

It means that we have to accumulate a large lead among the younger judges to offset the negative votes that we can expect from the older ones."[11]

"I am more optimistic. I have a feeling that we will win, but I will abide by the decision of the High Court of the children of Israel in any event."

"Machla there is something I want to talk to you about."

"I think I know what is on your mind."

"Do you agree that I have fulfilled my part of our agreement to get you your day in court?"

"I do."

"Do you feel I presented the case to the best of my ability?"

"Yes, Elchanan."

"Do you remember that you said you would marry me after the trial whether you won or lost?"

"I do have some vague recollection of that, but it was so long ago. I hope you are still interested in marrying me?"

"Of course I am, Machla. I will allow you a week for the ritual purification and other preparations for marriage."

"I am ahead of you, as usual. I examined myself last Tuesday night before sundown and there was no sign of menstrual blood. I started to count my seven clean days on Wednesday." In those days, seven clean days were not required before immersion in the Mikva. Nevertheless, many women already imposed this requirement upon themselves, because they could not be sure that their bleeding was menstrual, and not that of a "Zavah," which did require a period of clean days. "Tomorrow, at sundown, I will purify myself, and Wednesday afternoon we will get married."

"You are not planning a big wedding, I hope?"

"I don't see why we shouldn't invite everyone who came out to support our cause today."

"One member of the audience is my wife, Batya. The other 25,000 are equally unnecessary. If you wish to abide by the most recently released marriage regulations, a pair of witnesses and a total of ten men in attendance is quite sufficient."

"I was only having fun, Elchanan. As long as the marriage is legal, the rest is inconsequential to me."

Tirza meanwhile was talking to Chemlon, who was lavish with his praise. "You are becoming quite a public speaker," he said. "You would be a wonderful asset to an aspiring legal advisor."

"You are offering me a position?"

"Something more than that."

Tirza started blushing, but didn't speak.

"I was thinking perhaps of marriage."

"Aren't you a married man and the father of three children?"

"The children are grown and marriages are being arranged for them. I have room in my heart to love another wife and I can think of no one better than you."

"You know that I am prone to violence."

"As long as you don't try any on me, I can live with it."

"I am honored, Chemlon. I certainly will not make you wait too long before I advise you of my decision. I cannot do anything, though, before Machla reveals her intentions. The only comforting thing I can tell you, is that the daughters of Zelaphchad will get married in order of birth rather than in the way they are listed in the Torah."

Suddenly everyone's attention was drawn to the area of the court. Moses had been praying silently to the Lord, pleading for revelation on the case. Cries of excitement rose from the audience as they noticed the cloud of glory starting to move. Rapidly, the cloud descended lower upon the Tent of Meeting, signifying that a revelation to Moses was impending. The judges began to move out of their seats and distance themselves from the area. The last thing people could see was Moses lowering the flaps of the tent to commune privately with the Lord.

Word spread quickly through the crowd that the revelation would preempt the court vote. Many people felt better about the situation because with Divine revelation there was no room for error.

Elchanan gathered the Zelaphchad family around him and said. "The appearance of the Lord on the scene is the most favorable development that we could have."

"Why is that?" Noah asked. "The Lord could say no as well as yes."

"It is a little complicated but I feel that my logic is correct. Everything that the Lord reveals to Moses goes into the Torah. To this day, nothing has appeared in the Torah regarding the laws of inheritance for woman. To me, that is a sign that the Lord was satisfied with the status quo and didn't feel the need to change it. If the court was going to vote against us, the Lord would not have to come down. He would leave the decision to the court because it would be upholding the status quo which was acceptable to Him these many years. The only possible reason for revelation is the fact that the Lord senses that the court is going to vote for the petition. In such circumstances, He prefers that the new laws become an integral part of the Torah. He does not want people to consider them as laws of human origin for that would encourage attempts to overrule them in the future."

"Why can't God come down to reveal that he is against the court and prevent it from acting in our favor?" Machla asked.

"There are several reasons. It is not the pattern of the Lord to overrule the highest human courts. Secondly, I don't think He would have let things come this far. He could easily have advised Moses not to encourage the daughters of Zelaphchad in their efforts because it would do no good. Would anyone care to hear my own theory as to why the Lord did not reveal His will earlier?"

"Yes," they all said.

"The elders of Israel ask why is it that our matriarchs Sarah, Rivka, Rachel and Leah, were all barren for long periods of time. The answer given is that the Lord enjoyed listening to their prayers. Do you know why the Lord did not intervene in the Zelaphchad case before this time? I feel it is because he wanted to hear the prayers of Machla, Tirza, Hogla, Milka and Noah as they stood before the High Court and the assembled Congregation of Israel."[12]

As Elchanan was finishing his explanation, the judges started filing back into the court area. An eerie silence descended over the massive gathering as Moses rose to reveal the will of God with regard to the daughters of Zelaphchad.

Part 3

THE SECOND TRIAL

CHAPTER

THIRTEEN

"Thus hath the Lord spoken to me," said Moses. "The daughters of Zelaphchad speak correctly. They are to be given land amongst their father's brothers and permitted to inherit their father's property in Canaan.[1]

"These shall now be the new laws of inheritance for the children of Israel:

> "If a man dies and has no son, his property shall go to his daughter. If he has no children at all, his property goes to his brothers. If he has no brothers, the property goes to his sisters. If he has no sisters, his land goes to his uncles. If there are no uncles, the land goes to his aunts. If there are no aunts and uncles it goes to the next nearest of kin.
>
> "The new principle of law established today is that if there are no men on a given level of family relationship, the women on that level receive the inheritance prior to any men on a more distant level of kinship."

Moses then added: "The daughters of Zelaphchad have done this nation a great service by helping to expand the laws of the Torah. The outline of their claim will be included in the Torah together with the new laws. This section of the Torah shall be known, in all future generations, as their section of the Torah."

Pandemonium broke out among the spectators and cheering erupted throughout the Levitical area. Elazar adjourned the court but not even the judges could hear what he was saying. Machla and her sisters were crying with joy and even Achla could not restrain her tears. Haniel came forward to congratulate the sisters accompanied by the honor guard to escort the family back to Menashe. All along the way, people sang and danced and it wasn't until mid-afternoon that the family returned to their tents.

"What are you going to do now with your newly-won fame?" Noah asked her mother.

"I am going to sew five wedding dresses," Achla answered without hesitation.

The family couldn't talk much more because a steady stream of friends and neighbors came by to congratulate the sisters on their victory. When the last of well-wishers drifted away and quiet was restored, Tirza asked Machla, "Where's Elchanan?"

"He had to walk Batya back home."

"Where's Chemlon?" Machla asked in turn.

"He walked back with Haniel. I think they had some legal matters to attend to. He asked me to meet him at the Tribal Center at six."

On their way back from the court, Haniel explained the matter to Chemlon. "I have a request from a group representing all six heads of families of the children of Gilead. At tomorrow's council meeting they want the council to ask the tribal court to grant a pass-up ruling to take a case to the High Court."

"What sort of a case?"

"The families, who represent a majority of Menashe, want the court to rule that all women who inherit property under the new Zelaphchad law be restricted to marriages within the tribe."

"On what grounds can they regulate marriages? If we are not dealing with priestly families, and no ineligible persons are involved, marriages cannot be restricted."

"They claim that marriages with men from other tribes would cause the property that these women inherit under the Zelaphchad rule to accrue, in time, to the husband's tribe."

Chemlon mentally reviewed the relevant Torah laws regarding property and the Jubilee years. "It is a complicated issue, but there may be some basis to their claim. But why should it bother anyone if we are all supposed to be part of one nation?"

"As a younger man, Chemlon, you think a little differently than tribal presidents who are more mature than you. As I said at the trial today, tribalism is still very strong among the children of Israel. Can you expect tribes to give up land one to the other when they don't even share constructive ideas amongst themselves?"

The tribal tents of Menashe were coming into view as Chemlon was beginning to grasp the magnitude of the developments. "Who organized this action?" he asked.

"It's Meir, the son of Azriel, the head of the Chefer family."

"I might have known. You realize, of course, that the last thing he has in mind is tribal territory."

"What then is the issue?" Haniel asked in surprise.

"He wishes to prevent Machla from marrying Elchanan ben Uriah of Judah."

The news came as a shock to Haniel. "I didn't know that they were planning to get married. Now I see why Meir is so involved. He wants Machla for his cousin, Eliav. I remember that twenty years ago, Eliav's father was willing to give Machla quite a dowry if she would marry his son. As far as I know, Eliav is still single."

"Why can't Meir's group go directly to the tribal court and get them to issue the pass-up ruling?"

"The tribal court doesn't handle cases unless they are referred by the council or by commanders of 1,000. Regular civil cases that are sent up by commanders usually have to wait from between ten days to two weeks for a court date. If the council certifies a case, it is handled at a special session of the court on the next day."

"I certainly will not assist Meir in this unholy business."

"We still have to meet with the group. They represent the majority of the tribe of which I am president."

"We can meet with them but I will object to their getting an endorsement from the council."

"Just be sure you are on solid legal ground. Meir has become an expert in Torah. You heard him in the Reuben and Gad case."

"He may know the Torah, but I am willing to wager that he has engaged the best legal advisors that can be found in the nation."

They walked to the Tribal Center where Meir and the other family heads were waiting for them. When they were all gathered in the council tent, Haniel officially opened the meeting from the president's chair.

"Gentlemen, what can we do for you this evening?"

Meir rose to face Haniel. "Your Excellency, we are asking the council to pass a motion at its meeting tomorrow, requesting the tribal court to grant us the right to bring a case to the High Court as early as possible."

Haniel asked Meir to outline the motion which Meir did at length. When he finished, Haniel turned to Chemlon and asked him for a ruling.

"Your Excellency," Chemlon responded, "the answer is absolutely not."

Meir was distraught and angry for he hadn't expected any problems at the local level. "Why is that, may I ask?"

"Meir, did you hear the testimony of the president at the Zelaphchad trial when he announced that hundreds of families in Menashe would be affected by the issue at stake? We could easily be talking about more than 1,000 women in our tribe. Do you expect the council to act on a motion, which may deprive so many women of their rights, without as much as a public notice? These women have every right to be heard on such an issue."[2]

"What difference does it make what happens at the council? The women can present their case at the High Court."

"Listen, Meir. The council of the tribe of Menashe may issue three or four requests a year for High Court pass-ups. In all the years that I have been part of the council, we have never issued such requests without public notice and much testimony. The tribal court itself will not take a case from a commander of 1,000 either, unless the certifying commander proves that he has informed all interested parties. The fastest you can get tribal court consideration for your case is at least a week. It is also possible, I should warn you, that either the council or the court can reject your action if they deem it frivolous."

"I hate to say this, Chemlon, but I think that you are putting some other considerations ahead of important interests of the tribe of Menashe."

Chemlon did not lose his temper in the face of the accusation but he didn't let it pass without a rejoinder. "You are the last one with a right to say such a thing, Meir. Everyone in this room knows that what is driving you to this obscene haste is the unrequited love of your cousin, Eliav, rather than the welfare of the tribe. You are entitled to your concerns, but not at the expense of judicial propriety."

Meir was livid with anger as the blood drained from his face. "I sought this pass-up to avoid any problems later, but I have been advised by the best Torah counsel available that we can go to the High Court directly without wasting time in Menashe."

"Then I would suggest you do exactly that. Going through Menashe will not only cost you time, but it may cost you the opportunity to ever get to the High Court."

The president and the other family heads left the meeting but Meir stayed to argue further with the legal advisor. "I don't know what your interest is, Chemlon, but your remark about me at the meeting was entirely uncalled for."

"Although it was you who first suggested ulterior motives, I should not have spelled it out so sharply. I am sorry for that. I do admire Eliav for his persistence, but you must admit that he is chasing rainbows. Machla has high regard for Eliav, too, but that is not love. I sense that her affections are directed elsewhere."

"I won't hide the truth from you in private. Saving a life is the highest priority of the Torah. I am afraid that if Machla marries someone else, Eliav will suffer a physical or mental breakdown."

"It is a tragic case, Meir, but, if you add up the cases in all twelve tribes of Israel, you are denying the rights of well over 10,000 women to save one man. Given your highly proficient counsel maybe you could come up with a better alternative. Not only is your present course unfair, but it has a good chance of failing. There are very few attorneys who can beat Elchanan ben Uriah in such a case, and the daughters of Zelaphchad are at the height of their popularity."

"I have been trying to find a solution for twenty years and this is the only approach that has any chance of success. It is simple, it is clear and it has the support of all the presidents of the tribes."

When Chemlon grasped the full scope of Meir's action, he instinctively guessed the truth. "There is only one person in the entire nation who could have engineered such a plan. I take it that you have secured the assistance of Carmiel, the sage of Naphtali."

"You will find out in due time who is helping us," Meir said and walked off.

Chemlon waited another few minutes for Tirza to arrive. When she came along he sat down with her and informed her of the latest developments. "Do you want to help Machla?" he asked.

"Very much."

"Someone has to get word to Elchanan and inform him of the situation. He must try to prevent the opposition from getting a date at the High Court."

Tirza was very worried that Chemlon might endanger his position by getting involved. "If I do that, Meir will know that you advised Elchanan. If word gets out, you will be in very serious trouble."

"Let's not worry about it. Nothing will happen to me if we do this carefully. Elchanan has to wait until Meir submits his application to the clerk tomorrow and leaves the High Court area. I suspect that Meir will be there as soon as the court opens. The clerk only takes the information and has to get an approval from the senior judge. It should take a couple of days before Meir gets an answer. Elchanan can get there at ten in the morning and raise an objection with the clerk."

"How will I find my way in Judah? I can't take Machla because she has to go to the Mikva tomorrow, and I don't want to upset her. She also believes in the custom that a bride should not see her groom during the final days before the wedding. I could find my way to Elchanan's tent but Batya will be there. Rest assured, she will not be helpful to Machla."

"That is what I like about you Tirza. You are all innocence with no political skills at all. Take your new friend, Noah, with you. She will know how to get word to Elchanan."

Tirza ran home and told Noah what was happening. After dinner, Noah said she was taking Tirza for a walk to celebrate the family victory. She suggested that Hogla and Milka do likewise to allow Achla to give Machla instruction in anticipation of her marriage.

"I thought I knew the facts of life," protested Machla.

"Mother has some insights that might do you some good. After she finishes, go to sleep early and sleep late tomorrow. Tirza will gather the manna for you in the morning." She and Tirza then went off to Judah.

"I don't remember volunteering," Tirza said, "but you won't get up in time, so I guess I will have to do it. How are we going to reach Elchanan in Judah?"

"It's not too hard. We get Malka to call on Elchanan. She will tell him that he has important visitors from another tribe waiting to see him at the Tribal Center about matters that were raised at today's trial."

When they got to Malka's tent, Noah had little difficulty enlisting Malka, who would do anything to help Machla. "Tell Elchanan that there are urgent matters that came up today while he was away and that you want to talk to him about them at the Tribal Center. If he suggests that it can be done at home, tell him that two very distinguished visitors from another tribe are waiting to see him."

Malka went to Elchanan's tent while the sisters walked to the Center. Elchanan agreed to go to the Tribal Center and was gravely concerned when he saw Tirza and Noah waiting for him. He realized that Machla would not be inclined to see him before the wedding and she would have to send her sisters to communicate with him. He listened to Tirza with growing astonishment.

"Does Machla know anything about this?"

"I don't believe so," Tirza said. "We didn't want to upset her at such a time."

"Tell Chemlon I will do what I can. If you have to reach me, leave word at my friend's tent." He gave them the name and location of a friend who studied with him and whose presence wouldn't alarm Batya.

Batya was in a good mood when Elchanan returned home. She was still dressed in her best outfit, the one she had worn at the Zelaphchad hearing. It was a well-fitting white robe that contrasted well with her dark complexion. "You were wonderful today, Elchanan. I was so proud of your performance that I could hardly contain myself."

"You inspire me, my dear."

With a slight trace of bitterness in her voice, she replied, "Unfortunately, I am not your only source of inspiration. How long will I be your one and only wife?"

"In a romantic sense, forever. A man never forgets his first love. In a legal sense, just a couple of days. Machla is going to the Mikva tomorrow night."

"She certainly is not wasting any time," Batya said with resignation.

The next morning, Elchanan was at the Tent of Meeting at ten. He spoke at length to the clerk of the court, a man whom he knew well. "You accepted Meir's application for a court date without a pass-up document?"

"Yes, I did. I asked Meir for it and he said it was not necessary. I do not have the authority myself to reject a request for a court date, but I warned Meir that the senior judge might reject the application on those grounds. Meir didn't seem worried. He said that he would have the endorsement of all twelve tribal presidents, a fact that gives the case emergency status. Secondly, he said, the case derives logically out of the Zelaphchad case which was legally scheduled."

"He's getting some good counsel. Did he name the attorney who will present his case?"

"He listed Carmiel, the sage. Carmiel is one who virtually never loses a trial."

Elchanan groaned. "You don't have to tell me that. Believe me, I have watched him in action many times."

"There is something I do have to tell you, though. Meir requested an appointment for Carmiel with the senior judge tomorrow at nine in the morning."

"What on earth for?"

"As I understand it, he is seeking a court order enjoining any of the daughters of Zelaphchad from getting married until after the trial."

Elchanan felt as if he had been hit by a load of bricks. "He's crazy. There has never been such a document issued by a court in advance of a trial."

"There may be one tomorrow. I can arrange an eight o'clock appointment for you with the chief judge tomorrow morning and you can plead with him."

Elchanan accepted the offer and asked only one more question. "If they get a court date, when will it be?"

"The earliest they can hope for is a week from next Monday," the clerk answered.

Elchanan headed home in a daze. A court injunction prior to a case was something he had never heard of. He could see a function for it in a civil case where a defendant had to be prevented from disposing of contested assets, but it had no place in religious matters. Until the court ruled on a Torah case, everyone was free to behave in accordance with the pre-existing status quo. He was afraid, however, that Carmiel would come up with some precedent or convincing argument.

Back in Menashe, Machla was making arrangements for the wedding.[3] She didn't want to make it in the tent area because Eliav would be hurt. She arranged for a pair of witnesses and eight other men to be present at a modest ceremony at the Tribal Center. Only her mother and sisters would be invited.

After that was taken care of, she returned to the tent to prepare for immersion. Achla trimmed her nails and combed her hair. "I saw Batya with Elchanan yesterday and you have nothing to worry about, Machla. You are so much prettier than she is."

"Probably so, but looks are not everything. Batya gets along with Elchanan very well. She is very submissive while I am aggressive and competitive."

"I think Noah was right. There are some facts of life that you have to be taught." For the next hour, Achla patiently explained to Machla what a woman had to do to keep a man happy.

After all the preliminary washing and preparations were over, Noah and Achla took Machla to the Mikva. The area was screened off for privacy and volunteer attendants were present. Brides were allowed to immerse before sundown which meant they would get into the water while it was warm from solar heat. The immersion pool was linked to a second pool that derived its waters from a well. A plug between the basins was removed only before the actual immersion so that the water in the immersion pool would not be cooled too rapidly from the well water.

Before Machla disrobed, she asked for time to recite a personal prayer.

> "O Lord, in keeping with the sacred laws of the Torah, I am about to purify myself in the waters of the holy Mikva, for the purpose of marriage. I pray Thee, bless my marriage to Elchanan ben Uriah. May I be worthy to be the wife of this great scholar and devoted servant of Thy will. May I be respectful to him and serve his needs.
>
> "May our love be undying and may our marriage be based on a total meeting of mind and body. May I satisfy his spiritual and physical needs to the fullest extent. May I inspire him to rise to great heights in the study of Torah and may he judge the children of Judah wisely.
>
> "May I follow in the footsteps of Sarah, Rivka, Rachel

and Leah, who built the House of Israel, and of Asenath, the wife of Joseph, the father of our tribe.

"Protect me from temptation and evil thoughts. May I live in peace with my husband's first wife and not hurt her in any way.

"Protect Eliav, and grant him happiness with some other woman.

"May my union with Elchanan be blessed with a son, who will bear the name of my sainted father, Zelaphchad. May my son grow up to fear God, learn Torah and perform good deeds.

"Bless my dear mother with long life and good health. Bless my sisters with life and health and may they find suitable husbands. Bless the children of Israel and crown their efforts to conquer the Land of Canaan with victory. Last, but not least, I thank thee O Lord for giving me a share of the Holy Land. Amen."

Machla could not remember ever being happier. This was going to be the beginning of the most important phase in her life.

With her prayers concluded, she undressed and entered the pool. She emerged feeling pure and exalted. Noah and Achla helped her get dressed. Suddenly, Noah said, "Oh, no, look who is here tonight."

There was cousin Bracha, Eliav's sister, waiting her turn to enter the pool and eyeing Machla and Noah very strangely. "So the spinster is finally getting married," she said, and walked away.

"She is not going to lose any time telling Eliav," Noah said in resignation.

Machla was even more disturbed than Noah, but she was much better at controlling her emotions. She retained her composure, and they all walked home. Machla lay down in her tent for a well-deserved rest.

At about ten at night, Noah came into the tent. "Machla, you have a visitor. It's Elchanan and he looks terrible. Something bad must have happened."

"He is not supposed to see me now."

"I know that, but he wouldn't have come unless it were urgent. You'll have to get up and see what brings him here at this time of night."

Machla arose and greeted Elchanan. He didn't say much but took her for a walk to a private area at the border of Menashe, where they often sat before Elchanan left her to return to Judah.

"What is the matter, Elchanan, you look awful."

Without saying anything, Elchanan opened his robe and draped part of it around Machla's shoulders. In so doing, there was some physical contact but Machla did not object because she was in a state of purity. What alarmed her was the significance of the act. It meant that Elchanan was asking her to get married in a way that was not in keeping with the latest Torah requirements, although acceptable in earlier periods of Hebrew history.

"Machla, I want to get married this evening. I want to get married as your parents did and as my parents did and as virtually all the children of Israel still do."

Machla quickly removed Elchanan's robe from her shoulders. "I am flattered by your proposal, Elchanan, but you know very well that we cannot do what you have in mind. You waited ten years for me. You can certainly hold off for another few hours. The new laws of the Torah require you to betroth me with a signed document in the presence of two qualified witnesses. The wedding itself has to be a public ceremony attended by at least ten adult men."[4]

"Machla, those laws are only two months old and have not yet taken hold. If there is any punishment or censure it will be on me. The marriage, though, will be valid. We might even find witnesses tonight but the marriage must be consummated. Given the circumstances of our case, the court would not hesitate to annul a mere betrothal ritual that was not followed by living together."

Machla responded in alarm. "Elchanan you are a judge in Israel. If you indulge in this passion you will forfeit your position as judge and all hopes to be chief judge. Why are you doing this? It is not worth it."

Realizing he couldn't sway Machla, Elchanan sat down on a ledge, put his head in his hands and began to sob. Machla sat down next to him waiting for him to compose himself. When he calmed down to a degree, he told her what Meir was doing and how he had requested a court date.

"Don't worry," Machla said. "He won't get a date for a week and we are scheduled to get married tomorrow afternoon. They can't make us get divorced."

"We may not be allowed to get married tomorrow afternoon or ever, for that matter. Carmiel is filing for an injunction tomorrow to prohibit the daughters of Zelaphchad from getting married until the trial resolves the issue. He will certainly argue that betrothals are always made on the condition that they meet Torah and court approval. Therefore, any betrothals not in keeping with those standards should automatically be annulled. Unless we are fully married before the trial, we will have to win our case in court in order to ever become man and wife."[5]

"Oh, my God," Machla gasped. She had not fully anticipated the far-reaching consequences of Meir's actions.

"I love you enough, Machla, to give up the courts and the schools. The only possibility to secure our future together is to let me break the law and get married in fact."

"Elchanan, if a marriage is started in a way contrary to the will of the Lord, it will not be blessed. I would marry you even if you were not a judge, but I will not marry you if you are a sinner. I know that it is a new law and it is not a major sin to do it the old way. But God showered his favor on me yesterday, and I cannot repay His mercy with evil. Listen to me. The chief judge of the court may refuse to grant the injunction. You might win the trial. The verdict may only apply to future generations and not to us. I believe that you are as smart as Carmiel. Trust in God and you will win."

"You have great faith, Machla. I have an unerring instinct of knowing when I am not in favor with the Lord. The hand of God has gone up against me. I have a dreadful premonition of doom."

Elchanan walked Machla back to the top of the path and, head bowed, made his way to Judah. Noah was waiting up when Machla returned to their tent. "You don't have to tell me what happened," she said, "but perhaps I can help you if you do. Is the marriage still on?"

"I don't know. Our cousin Meir is trying to get a court order to prevent it."

"Maybe we should have scheduled the wedding for tonight."

"It was a dreadful mistake to delay it. The trial took so much out of me, though, that I didn't feel I could be ready in less than two days. Anyway, thanks for running to Judah last night."

Machla updated Noah on the latest developments in the case but didn't tell her all that all that transpired between her and Elchanan.

"Why did he come to see you tonight?" Noah asked.

"He didn't want me to be surprised in case Meir came to the Tribal Center waving a court order forbidding the marriage."

Totally exhausted, Machla went to bed and fell into a deep slumber. Her last thought before she fell asleep was that if she married Elchanan it would be exciting. His evil inclination was as powerful as his mind was brilliant. She would never forget the minute he draped his robe around her.

Elchanan came home and couldn't fall asleep for a long time. He did not wake up at dawn, as accustomed, and was unaware that Batya had slipped out of bed and quietly donned her robe. She hadn't expected Elchanan to come home, because when he told her that Machla was going to the Mikva that night, she had automatically assumed that the wedding would follow. When he did return, she knew there was still time.

Quickly Batya made her way to the border of Judah and crossed over to the Levitical area. She arrived at the Tabernacle as preparations for the morning offering were underway. There were no other women present as she stood in the women's section. She poured out her heart in prayer.

> "God of my fathers, Abraham, Isaac and Jacob. I come before Thee with my soul in distress and my heart broken. I love my husband Elchanan and at one time he loved me. Now another woman has stolen his heart and he is taking her to wife. I know of no way of preventing the situation so my only recourse is to come before Thee in prayer.
>
> "Let not my husband cast me aside and humiliate me. Let him not feel that because Machla is more attractive than I am, he does not have to visit with me. Let him not feel that because Machla is more learned, he does not have to converse with me. Let him not exploit the fact that he is my entire life and I am so dependent on him.
>
> "I wish Machla no harm. I would have been happier

had she never appeared on the scene but the reality is that she is here, that she helped further my husband's career, that he regards her highly and loves her very much. Let me not engage her in conflict and let me not fall into bitterness and despair. Let me not become a widow or divorcee in essence, if not in fact.

"I thank thee, O Lord, for being chosen originally by this great and learned scholar. I thank thee for my four children who are versed in Torah. I thank thee for the Torah I have learned. Reward a common person of simple faith. I trust in thee O Lord. *Hear O Israel, the Lord our God the Lord is one.*"

At the very moment that Batya was concluding her prayer, Eliav was praying at the coffin of Joseph. He had risen up early after a sleepless night. Bracha had told him the night before that Machla was at the Mikva, and he had heard some reports of a wedding being planned for the next afternoon at the Tribal Center. He was aware of Meir's efforts in his behalf but was of the opinion that they were too little and too late. He had seen Elchanan in action at the trial and he knew that he was a formidable opponent. He also knew that he was outclassed by Elchanan in his struggle for Machla's heart. The only recourse he had left was prayer and, at Joseph's bier, he prayed with fervor.

"O Joseph, righteous father of our tribe, one of your sons has come to thee in his hour of distress. Is it not commanded to us to seek the most suitable of women to be one's partner in life? For twenty-one years, I have waited for Machla to open her heart to me and accept me as her husband. Is it wrong to desire the most pious and learned women among the daughters of Israel for a wife? It is not for the pleasures of the flesh that I crave this woman. There were others available to me who were equally attractive.

"I wanted Machla because she would guide me to a holy and elevated life. In her presence, I would be inspired to serve God in a way that I, with my limited knowledge, could not hope to attain by myself. With her, I could raise children that would be a pride to the Lord, God of Israel.

"Now my long struggle is about to end in failure. I have no regrets for striving for the impossible. But I know that it is never too late to pray for miracles. Father Joseph, bring my request to the Lord. Even as darkness descends on my life, implore Him to look upon me with mercy and save me from the pit, as you yourself were saved."

Eliav could not continue because of his emotions. He stepped backward out of the tent and walked to the Tabernacle nearby. It was there that he met Batya and, despite her reddened eyes, he recognized her. During the trial someone had pointed her out to him as Elchanan's wife. After telling her who he was, he asked her, "Did you come here today for the same reason I did?"

"You might say so. You don't want to lose your beloved Machla and I don't want to lose my beloved Elchanan."

"If I am not worthy, maybe the Lord will answer your prayer."

"I feel exactly the same way."

Eliav spoke to her for another few minutes and then headed back to Menashe. She in turn went back to Judah and set out to gather the manna while Elchanan was still sleeping.

At about the time that Batya and Eliav were at prayer, Machla was stirring in her sleep. All of a sudden she was engulfed by an excruciating pain in her womb. She screamed so loud that Noah, who could sleep through anything, awoke with a start. Tirza, who was up, also heard the scream and came running. Machla was writhing in anguish and sweat poured down her brow. "O my Lord, help me," she cried. "Do not take my life on my wedding day."

The pain started to subside slowly and it was then that Machla felt the wetness between her legs. She prayed that it was not blood, but in her heart she knew that it was. She was hemorrhaging badly and going into shock. By now, Noah was wide awake and quickly assessed the situation. She motioned to Tirza and together they started working on Machla. Tirza instructed Noah to raise Machla's legs and lower her head. Noah also knew that she had to cover Machla and keep her body warm. Tirza tried to stem the bleeding by pressing her hands against critical parts of Machla's body. The other sisters came in to help and the four trained nurses gradually won control of the situation. Achla was praying for her daughter outside the tent when three of the sisters emerged.

"Machla will be all right, but you can cancel the wedding plans." Noah stayed with Machla inside the tent and kept the other sisters posted. She didn't allow Machla to move because she was afraid the blood would start flowing heavily again.

"That wasn't passion bleeding?" Machla asked, referring to menstrual periods brought on by strong emotions.

"Not at all," Noah answered. "Menstrual blood generally comes out slowly and isn't accompanied by the savage pain you experienced."

"What was it, then?"

"I don't know, I never saw anything like it. If I didn't know better, I would have said someone must have stabbed you with a knife. You were bleeding so rapidly, you just about went into shock."

"Now that you mention it, it actually felt as if I were struck by a lightning bolt. Thanks for your help. It's fortunate that I live with four nurses. What's the outlook for my recovery?"

"We are looking at about three days of bed rest. I hope that the bleeding will stop within five to seven days."

"Do you know what that means?"

"It means that you will be a 'Zavah', a women bleeding outside the time frame of her menstrual period. You may count your seven clean days only after the bleeding stops and you may not get married until the seven clean days are counted."[6]

"How do I get word to Elchanan?"

"If Tirza will watch you, I will talk to him. Give me one of those bloody cloths."

Elchanan was meeting with the senior judge at the time of Machla's troubles. He asked that the court date be withheld from Meir's group and that no injunction be granted. After listening to his arguments carefully, the judge answered.

"We no longer deny court dates in advance for public cases simply because a pass-up is not available. The opponents of the motion may, however, challenge the action in court on the grounds that all of the required preliminary procedures were not followed. The court then takes a vote whether to continue listening to the case. It has happened on some occasions that the court decided not to hear a petition for such a reason. But, if Meir does bring out twelve tribal presidents as part of the case, you can rest assured that the case will proceed."

"As far as the other question," the judge continued, "you can be certain that Carmiel will not get any injunctions from me. There is no precedent for such actions. If we started a pattern like that, people would bring frivolous cases not to win them but to get injunctions to disturb the lives of others."

Elchanan thanked the judge, feeling much relieved that his wedding could take place as scheduled. It was then that he saw Noah running towards him carrying a pouch in her hand. He took one look at Noah, disheveled and distraught and he knew that another disaster was in the offing.

"Let me sit down, Noah. I don't know if my heart can take another shock."

"It is bad, Elchanan, very bad. At dawn this morning, Machla suffered a severe hemorrhage from her womb. She went into shock and almost didn't make it." She pulled out the bloody cloth to show him.

"That surely is not passion blood. Is she better now?"

"She was somewhat improved when I left her, but she will need a lot of rest."

"Has she ever had anything like this before?"

"Never. Her periods come like clockwork and she has never been seriously ill in her life."

"What is the outlook?"

"She will be in bed for at least three days and bleed for six or seven. She will be a full Zavah. You are looking at thirteen to fourteen days before she can get married."

"That will be after the trial."

"You have to win the trial, Elchanan, to get Machla."

"Noah, I am not afraid of Meir, and I am willing to compete with Carmiel. But I have the feeling that I am fighting more than human opponents in this battle."

Elchanan headed home with the weight of the world resting on his shoulders. He spent the next two days working in a desultory fashion. With the school year only three weeks gone, there was a lot of work to be done, but Malka was doing her work in a spectacular manner and didn't need his help too often.

The educational program for men was well established from the earliest years in the desert and worked without much supervision. In the absence of any special problems, each commander of ten was responsible for the Torah training of the twenty to thirty boys in his charge. Each young boy received a very basic training and those who showed promise continued in intermediate schools. From the ranks of the intermediate schools were drawn the candidates for the higher Torah schools which were under Elchanan's supervision.

Friday night, after the Sabbath meal, Elchanan's children left the tent to congregate with friends. Avi was already past thirteen and very popular. Dina was twenty-one and had frequently spoken to her father about getting married. When they were alone, Batya spoke to Elchanan. Her heart was beating rapidly, and she was deeply frightened.

"Are we still a monogamous family?" she asked, bracing herself for the worst.

"Yes, my dear, that is our status at the moment."

"You are not practicing these new laws where you betroth a women with a document and then wait for an interval before consummation?"

"Once you have a betrothal, you are considered by the Torah as a married couple in virtually all respects. So, if a married man betroths another woman, his family is no longer considered monogamous."

"You mean we celebrated the end of our monogamy somewhat prematurely?"

"I am afraid so, Batya."

"Is it all over, or just some delay?"

"It is in the hands of God and the courts. Members of Machla's family have undertaken a court action that would prohibit her from marrying outside the tribe because then her newly acquired land in Canaan might revert to the tribe of Judah instead of Menashe."

"That is not very nice at all."

"It shouldn't bother you."

"I have no problem with Machla marrying a Judean. As long as it isn't you, of course," she added with a smile.

The remark gave Elchanan a chance to determine whether a lurking suspicion that had formed in his mind had any basis in truth. "Batya, I won't hurt you in any way, but tell me the truth. Did you place any curse or cast an evil spell on Machla?"

"Me?" she cried and went into a such a letter perfect imitation of Machla that even Elchanan had to laugh. "It says in our holy Torah that you shall love your neighbor as yourself and that you shall not hate your brother in your heart. Why would I cast a spell on a pious, God-fearing woman?" Elchanan was pleased at the way she now quoted the Torah, but he noted that she was evading the question.

"I am pleased with your knowledge of Torah, my dear, but just answer the question."

A look of fear crossed Batya's face.

"Tell me what you did," Elchanan insisted. "I said I won't harm you."

"I did not curse her or seek to hurt her. That would not be proper. I did go to the Tabernacle to offer a prayer."

"Do you remember your prayer?"

"Of course I do." Here Batya went into another imitation of Machla. "When we appear before a mortal king, we rehearse our words over and over again so that we should not stumble or stutter. How much more so is it important that we do not stumble or hesitate when we stand in prayer before the King of Kings."

"I see that you learned quite a bit from Machla."

"I heard that when I was observing her teaching a class. It is a pity that you never taught me Torah the way she knows it. Anyway, I memorized my prayer and I will recite it for you." She then repeated the prayer perfectly to him.

"Those words seem quite benign, I can't see how such a prayer could cause Machla any harm."

Batya paused for a moment and then started to cry.

"There's more to the story?" Elchanan asked.

"There is more," Batya confessed.

"What is it?"

"I was not alone in my prayer."

"You mean you had a Priest or Levite assist you?"

"No. I prayed alone but I was not alone in prayer."

"I don't quite understand what you mean."

"I mean that someone else was praying for the same thing at the same time."

"Our children?"

"Certainly not. It was Eliav, Machla's cousin. He said his prayers at the coffin of Joseph."

"How did he know that Machla had gone to the Mikva?"

"His sister Bracha happened to be at the Mikva that night for a regular visit. She hates Machla with a passion."

"I see. Did Eliav tell you his prayer?"

"No. But he didn't pray to harm her. He loves her more than you do, if that is possible." Batya was still anxious, but her fear had lessened when she realized that Elchanan had retained his self-control.

"What did Eliav say to you?"

"He indicated that it was possible that our combined prayers might achieve what his pleas alone failed to do in more than twenty years."

"They certainly did. They certainly did. What can I promise you, Batya, so that you will refrain from indulging in further prayer on this matter?"

Batya didn't hesitate. "Promise me Friday nights. If you do marry Machla, or anyone else, reserve the Sabbath night for me. You can do what you want on nights in middle of the week but keep the Sabbath night sacred for us."

"I agree. It is small price to pay for avoiding the dreadful power of your prayers combined with those of Eliav."

On the following Tuesday night, Elchanan visited with Machla. She was up and around but showed the strain of her recent episode. She was, of course, happy to see him, although her future was now uncertain. Before Elchanan spoke to Machla privately, he gathered the family around and said to them,

"I had the scribe of Judah prepare a papyrus giving the exact text of the Zelaphchad case as it appears in the Torah. He copied it verbatim from the scroll that Moses is writing. Elchanan then proceeded to read:

"THEN CAME THE DAUGHTERS OF ZELAPHCHAD, THE SON OF CHEFER, THE SON OF GILEAD, THE SON OF MACHIR, THE SON OF MENASHE, OF THE FAMILIES OF MENASHE THE SON OF JOSEPH, AND THESE ARE THE NAMES OF HIS DAUGHTERS: MACHLA, NOAH, AND HOGLA, AND MILKA,

AND TIRZA. AND THEY STOOD BEFORE MOSES AND BEFORE ELAZAR THE PRIEST, AND BEFORE THE PRINCES AND ALL THE CONGREGATION, BY THE DOOR OF THE TENT OF MEETING, SAYING, OUR FATHER DIED IN THE WILDERNESS, AND HE WAS NOT IN THE COMPANY OF THEM THAT GATHERED THEMSELVES TOGETHER AGAINST THE LORD IN THE COMPANY OF KORACH; BUT HE DIED IN HIS OWN SIN, AND HAD NO SONS. WHY SHOULD THE NAME OF OUR FATHER BE DONE AWAY FROM HIS FAMILY BECAUSE HE HAS NO SON? GIVE TO US A POSSESSION AMONG THE BRETHREN OF OUR FATHER. AND MOSES BROUGHT THEIR CASE BEFORE THE LORD.

AND THE LORD SPOKE TO MOSES SAYING, THE DAUGHTERS OF ZELAPHCHAD SPEAK RIGHT: THOU SHALT SURELY GIVE THEM A POSSESSION OF INHERITANCE AMONG THEIR FATHER'S BRETHREN; AND THOU SHALT CAUSE THE INHERITANCE OF THEIR FATHER TO PASS TO THEM. AND THOU SHALT SPEAK TO THE CHILDREN OF ISRAEL, SAYING, IF A MAN DIE, AND HAVE NO SON, THEN YOU SHALL CAUSE HIS INHERITANCE TO PASS TO HIS DAUGHTER. AND IF HE HAVE NO DAUGHTER, THEN YOU SHALL GIVE HIS INHERITANCE TO HIS BROTHERS. AND IF HE HAVE NO BROTHERS, THEN YOU SHALL GIVE HIS INHERITANCE TO HIS FATHER'S BROTHERS. AND IF HIS FATHER HAVE NO BROTHERS, THEN YOU SHALL GIVE HIS INHERITANCE TO HIS KINSMAN THAT IS NEXT TO HIM OF HIS FAMILY, AND HE SHALL POSSESS IT: AND IT SHALL BE TO THE CHILDREN OF ISRAEL A STATUTE OF JUDGMENT, AS THE LORD COMMANDED MOSES.[7]

"I am very happy," said Tirza, "but they still didn't list our names in the correct order."

"Run, Noah, Run!" They all screamed at once.

"I don't have to anymore. I hid the sand broom where Tirza will never find it."

When Elchanan had a chance to speak to Machla privately, he asked. "How are you feeling?"

"Much better, thank you. I get excellent care and Noah even gathers the manna for me. I have good news, too. The bleeding stopped yesterday and I was able to count my first clean day today. If nothing further happens, I will we able to go to the Mikva again Monday night and have a few days before my next regular period."

"The trial has been set for Monday."

"Speaking of the trial, Noah told me that you got the chief judge not to issue the injunction."

"The senior judge works with conventional laws. With him I have no great problem. With the 'Judge of all the Earth,' however, I do have some difficulties."

"What does that mean?"

"Simply this. If the court had issued an injunction, it would have affected the lives of more than 10,000 women, rich and poor, illiterate and learned alike, without distinction. When the Lord delivers an injunction, He hits the specific target at the exact time and the exact place."

"You think the Lord wanted to delay our marriage?"

"I have no doubt of it." He told her about the combined prayers of Eliav and Batya.

"We who run the human courts," he continued, "are enjoined not to favor the poor, but to treat equally everyone who comes before the court. In the heavenly courts, there is tremendous prejudice. The poor come ahead of the rich, the widows ahead of the married women, the orphans ahead of those who have parents and the common people ahead of those who have given their lives for Torah. The Batyas and Eliavs of this world have the ear of the Creator more than we do. When they pray they get answers."

"I prayed at the Mikva, Elchanan." She repeated her Mikva prayer to him. "Why didn't I get an answer?"

"That was a beautiful prayer and you did get an answer. The answer, however, was 'no.' Incidentally, I don't think that you should undertake to attend the trial. It may be too much of an emotional strain."

"Don't be silly Elchanan. I wouldn't miss your performance at the High Court for all the gold in Havila."

"You might see me lose a case for the first time."

"I may not welcome the outcome but, if I had to take anyone in this world to defend me, it would be you. Anyway, it matters not what you feel about my attending. This morning I received an order from the court to testify at the trial."

"Did I hear you right? You've been asked to testify?" Why would they want to have you as a witness?"

"Apparently they heard that a certain man has been making eyes at me for ten years and he is not from the tribe of Menashe."

They conversed for a while and then Elchanan returned to Judah. On the next day, he had an appointment with Caleb.

"Did His Excellency get an invitation to appear at the trial next Monday?"

"I did get one, and I plan to attend even though I think it is a dreadful motion."

"They are using the presence of the presidents of the tribes to bypass the usual court procedures."

"I am aware of that. Nevertheless, as part of my presidential duties, I must attend. We are talking of one tribe acquiring territory at the expense of another. Although the amount of land is small, it is a legitimate presidential concern. Nor is the matter as simple as it looks. If the shifting of territory worked out evenly, it would be trivial. But that is not the case. Judah is rich and populous. We draw more women to Judah from the other tribes than we lose to them. What the smaller tribes fear is that the larger tribes will get bigger and richer at their expense."

"In any nation there are rich cities and poor ones, wealthy areas and impoverished ones," Elchanan argued.

"Ah, but we are not yet a nation. We are a conglomeration of tribes, and there may be strong indications that the Lord wants it that way. You may defend the case brilliantly, Elchanan, but there will be nothing you can do if the Lord reveals himself in middle of the trial and rules against you."

The meeting with Caleb ended on that unhappy note. Elchanan didn't know whether Caleb was speculating or had some indication from Moses. He was determined not to be discouraged. Rather he would shift the emphasis of his defense. If he couldn't save all women from the marriage restriction, he would at least try to save the daughters of Zelaphchad.

Friday night he spoke to Batya and asked her not to attend the trial on Monday.

"Why, Elchanan, it gives me great pleasure to see you perform so brilliantly."

"You have never seen me lose a case, and I don't want you ever to see that."

"You cannot lose this one, Elchanan."

"Why is that?"

"Regardless of the outcome you will be a winner. Regardless of the outcome, one of the women who love you will celebrate a tremendous victory."

CHAPTER

FOURTEEN

*"THE SONS OF JOSEPH SPEAK WELL,
THEIR PETITION IS GRANTED"*

When Elchanan arrived at the High Court on Monday morning, the scene was far different than what it had been two weeks earlier. Most conspicuous by its absence was the audience. Carmiel had advised Meir to keep the case as quiet as possible so as not to attract a hostile crowd. About 100 or so spectators milled around the High Court tent, not many more than the number of sightseers who observed court sessions on a normal day. Despite the small crowd, Elchanan was filled with dread. However, he was pleasantly surprised when the senior judge opened the proceedings in place of Elazar, the High Priest.[1]

"I have a statement to read from Elazar, the Priest," the judge intoned. "He has written as follows: 'I do not wish to preside over this trial because I feel that vital steps necessary to bring this case to the attention of the court were omitted. This court is a judicial body, not a political one. It must not overrule its regular practices in deference to men in high office. In the event that the results of this case are recorded in the Torah, the revered prophet will have no reason to list my name in the description thereof.'

"In the absence of the High Priest, I now open this case. This morning, the court will consider a petition filed by the heads of the six families of Menashe. The petitioners seek to forbid marriages of women who have inherited property under the Zelaphchad rule, to men not native to the woman's tribe. The petitioners will introduce themselves and their counsel, recite a brief outline of their case, and then offer more elaborate arguments. Witnesses may thereafter be presented from any tribes of the children of Israel."

Meir stepped to the center of the platform facing the judges. Before he could start his presentation, however, Elchanan was on his feet. "Your Honor," he said, "we object to the continuation of this trial."

"In what capacity do you make your objection?"

"I am counsel for a group that is opposed to the petition."

"At this point you may only object on procedural grounds."

"I am fully aware of that. What I am objecting to is most certainly a procedural matter. The petitioners have not secured the documents that are necessary for this trial to take place. They have not presented proof that the motion in the petition was considered in the lower courts and that such bodies authorized referring the matter to the High Court. It is well established that the High Court entertains petitions only after the petitioners have exhausted all remedies of the lower courts. I believe that it is this very issue that has caused Elazar, the priest, to withdraw from the case."

The chief judge responded. "It is a valid question that you raise and it must be resolved before we can proceed. Does the petitioner wish to respond to this objection?"

Meir answered in a deliberate manner. "I am requesting that I at least be permitted to introduce the petitioners and the counsel before dealing with procedural matters." Meir made the request so that Carmiel, once introduced, would be eligible to respond to Elchanan's objection.

"If the attorney for the opposition has no objections to it, you may do so."

"No objections," Elchanan said.

"I am Meir, the son of Azriel, the son of Chefer. My father, of blessed memory, was the second son of Chefer. Since the first born son, Zelaphchad, is deceased and had no sons, I represent the family of Chefer in this matter. Joining me in this petition are the heads of the five other families descended from Gilead. As such, we represent a majority of the tribe of Menashe.

"As counsel for the petitioners we have Carmiel, the sage of the tribe of Naphtali. He will now deal with the point raised by counsel for the opposition."

Carmiel was a short man with a flowing white beard. Hunched over from years of study, he looked even shorter. His voice, however, was clear and mellow. He focused his eyes on the judges and spoke slowly.

"It is well known that cases between ordinary citizens must follow a standard procedure. We feel that this petition is not of that nature for three reasons. This petition arises from a case that was resolved by the High Court only two weeks ago. The results of the Zelaphchad case, if not immediately controlled, may have a devastating affect on the tribes of Israel. The latter case was properly presented to the court. I would like the honored judges to consider this case not as a new one but as a continuation, as it were, of the Zelaphchad case. Major change in the laws of Torah always brings up related issues that have to be resolved as part of the new legal structure.

"Secondly, even if that point is not sufficient, I would like to advise counsel for the opposition that matters between tribes must be resolved in the national court because there is no other place in which they can be adjudicated. The purpose of clearing matters in lower courts is to avoid overloading the High Court. Very often, the commanders and the lower courts can successfully resolve issues by themselves and it is wise to compel people to turn to them first. In cases between tribes, however, there is absolutely nothing the lower courts can do. Why then waste people's time in formalities and delay resolution of such major cases as the one before us?

"I further submit that this case is of an emergency nature, and we will offer testimony that if the matter is not resolved immediately, the tribe of Menashe will lose a substantial amount of property. Other tribes may lose property as well. I would like to point to the presence here today of all twelve tribal presidents as an indication of the great urgency of the matter."

In his reply, Elchanan stressed that the current case was not a derivative of the Zelaphchad case, but an entirely new one. Only an appeal of the original verdict could be supported by the legal steps of the primary case. He then showed that all cases, regardless of the parties involved, were required to proceed through the lower courts. True, the lower court could not resolve inter-tribal issues, but the lower court could bar a case from going any higher on the grounds that it was trivial and not worthy of High Court attention. He chided Carmiel for assuming that one could bypass legal procedures simply because he, Carmiel, could not understand the logic behind them.

He ridiculed the idea of emergency. There were only five women in all the tribes of Israel, specifically the five daughters of Zelaphchad, who withheld marriage pending the outcome of the Zelaphchad case. The rest were going about their business as usual. There would be no flood of marriages following the Zelaphchad case. In the week that it would take to submit the case properly, only one of the Zelaphchad women could get married. He cited the Torah precedent of Laban, to show that a family would not allow a second daughter to get married during the week following the first daughter's marriage.[2]

"The High Court," he summed up, "is being rushed into this major case improperly to prevent one woman of the children of Israel from marrying the man she loves. I think it is now even clearer why Elazar the priest wanted no part of this travesty of justice."

The arguments of Elchanan had an unusually heavy impact. Normally, motions to dismiss a case on procedural grounds were decided by a show of hands. Here the votes had to be counted. With the chief judge presiding in Elazar's absence, only sixty-nine judges were eligible to vote. After several recounts, Elchanan's protest lost by one vote, thirty-five to thirty-four.

Carmiel was quite shaken by the close vote. He realized that while he was a greater Torah scholar than Elchanan, the latter was a courtroom veteran and a magnificent orator. Carmiel sensed that he had a difficult road ahead of him.

Meir then proceeded with the case and recited his outline. "These are the arguments that we will present:[3]

"The revered prophet, Moses, was commanded to provide for the distribution of the Land of Canaan by lottery equally among the children of Israel.

"The prophet was also commanded to give the property of Zelaphchad to his daughters.

"The daughters of Zelaphchad are currently free to be married to any men of their choosing among the tribes of Israel.

"If the daughters of Zelaphchad do in fact marry outside of the tribe, the property which they inherited will revert to their husbands' tribes and the tribe of Menashe will suffer a substantial loss.

"The laws of the Jubilee, which are intended to maintain the original distribution of land in Canaan, will not protect the tribe of Menashe in such cases and the tribe would lose valuable property.

"We therefore request that all women inheriting land under the Zelaphchad law be required to marry men native to their tribes.

"Our first witness will be His Honor, Yehoram ben Shabtai, Chief Judge of Issachar."

The judge made his way to the witness area and Carmiel took over from Meir.

"Your Honor," Carmiel asked, "as far as the Torah is concerned, is the claim of the petitioners correct?"

"It is essentially correct, whether the out-of-tribe marriage is blessed with children or not. If there are children, they will inherit the mother's property. If there are no children, the husband will inherit it. In either case, tribal property ownership is determined by the husband's tribe and not the wife's."

"Can you explain why the Jubilee laws will not help?"

"Yes, I can. If individuals in a tribe have to sell property, it is not a permanent transaction but a sale only until the Jubilee year. At the time of the Jubilee, the property returns to the seller and his tribe. Thus, in effect, the original distribution of the land is repeated every fiftieth year. The Jubilee laws, however, apply only to real property that is sold. They do not apply to property which was lost through inheritance and marriage."

"Thank you, Your Honor."

Elchanan was hoping that the judge might know some way around the problem. He asked the judge, "Is there any way this problem can be avoided?"

"Of course. Since the out-of-tribe husband will have property, the woman can, before marriage, assign or give up her own property to the tribe. I was present at the trial of the daughters of Zelaphchad two weeks ago, however, and I heard how they struggled for twenty-five years to win their property. I very much doubt that they would be willing to give it up for any man in this world."

Elchanan had no further questions so the witness stepped away from the stand.

"My next witness," Meir said, "is His Excellency, Samuel the son of Amihud, President of tribe of Simon." The President walked quickly to the witness area and Carmiel began his examination.

"Your Excellency, can you tell us why you are especially concerned about the effects of the Zelaphchad law?"

"We stand to lose far more than other tribes because of this new law."

"Why is that?"

"Well, if all the tribes were equal in population, the law would not cause us any great concern. We would lose some land when our women married outside of the tribe, but gain some when women from other tribes married our men. The tribes are not equal, though. Simon is the smallest and poorest tribe. Our women are often forced to marry outside of the tribe because there isn't a sufficient choice of men within the tribe. On the other hand, women from the big and rich tribes are not inclined to take men from Simon."

Carmiel immediately realized that he had erred in allowing the witness to testify. Maybe another attorney wouldn't catch the mistake, but there was no chance that Elchanan would let it pass.

Elchanan struck immediately. "Your Excellency, what is your evaluation of the tribe of Menashe?

"I think it is an excellent tribe. They have vast resources of sheep and cattle, an excellent health service, an efficient tribal administration and they are now one of the larger tribes."

"Does Your Excellency think that Menashe is an attractive tribe for women to enter?

"The very best."

"In the long run, then, Menashe stands to gain more property than it would lose under the new laws. Can you then see any reason for Menashe to be the one to bring this action rather than some other tribe?"

"I cannot be expected to explain the stupidity of Menashe."

Carmiel jumped to his feet in rage. "I object to the question and the answer, and move that the judges be instructed to disregard them."

The chief judge replied. "We will certainly strike the answer, but what objection is there to the question?"

"The attorney for the opposition has no right to ask the president of another tribe to speculate about the motives of Menashe."

"The objection is sustained. The question is withdrawn."

Elchanan didn't mind because he had scored his points. He released the witness without further questions.

Carmiel hadn't planned on calling Meir as a witness, but he had to undo the damage.

"Meir, it has been suggested that Menashe will lose some territory but will be able to offset the loss by gaining more land from other tribes. If so, why did your tribe initiate this action?"

"We believe that it is important to strengthen tribal identity and that goal will not be helped by having territory circulate between the tribes. Picture for yourself the following situation. The tribe of Menashe wants to provide vital services for members of the tribe or impose some obligation upon them. All of a sudden it runs into land that really belongs to a Judean as a result of his marriage to a woman of Menashe who subsequently passed away. The landholder won't cooperate, because his allegiance is to Judah, and his status in Menashe is unclear. The reverse is also true. Will Judah provide health and school services for families of their tribe who live outside the tribal territory and within the jurisdiction of Menashe?"

When Elchanan got the witness he asked, "While the point you make may have some merit, you neglected to raise the subject in your outline. You only spoke of Menashe's potential losses, not of its possible gains. Since Menashe stands only to benefit from the new law, doesn't your case lose all validity?"

"It was an oversight. We certainly are very much concerned by the disruptive impact of the law on all tribes, large or small. We wish to have that issue included in our presentation."

It was a weak statement but Carmiel had escaped from a total disaster. Menashe just gained a passable reason for bringing the case even though no one in Menashe had thought in those terms when the case was originally formulated.

Meir then called Machla to the witness area. She still wasn't at full strength, so a chair was provided for her.

Carmiel preceded the testimony with a statement. "We are calling this witness to show that our case is not merely theoretical and that there is at least one daughter of Zelaphchad who intends to marry outside her tribe." He then addressed the witness.

"Machla, as an expert in Torah Law, is it the practice of single women to perform ritual immersion in a Mikva on a regular basis?"

"No, it is not a regular practice among the daughters of non-priestly families who are not required to be in a state of ritual purity to eat the sacred priestly foods. When single girls wish to participate in Mishkan services, they are also required to be in state of purity. Very few single women, however, choose to attend such services routinely."

"When do they start performing this practice on a regular basis?"

"Shortly before they are to be married and thereafter."

"How much before?"

"Just a few days before the wedding."

"Is there any difference in the immersion practice for brides as opposed to married women?"

"Brides are permitted to immerse before sundown."

"Did you recently perform such an immersion?"

"On grounds of modesty, it is not the practice of women to answer such questions to anyone other than their husbands."

"We have a witness."

"You are free to call her."

Carmiel asked the chief judge to have Machla stand aside while he had Bracha testify. Elchanan objected vigorously. "The attorney is putting too great a strain on the primary witness."

Carmiel argued. "The witness is evading her duty to testify, and I cannot proceed with my case until this point is proven."

The chief judge ruled in Carmiel's favor and Bracha was summoned to the platform. Bracha had not expected to be called to testify and she was quite apprehensive. She had never lost her awe of Machla and was afraid of what might happen as a result of her testimony. She had never appeared in court before and the strain of the event showed clearly on her face.

"Bracha, were you at the Mikva on Tuesday after the Zelaphchad trial?"

"I was, Your Honor."

"Can you tell us whom you saw there?"

"I saw Machla, her mother and her sister, Noah."

"You are positive?"

"Yes. I've lived with them all my life."

"What where they doing there?"

"Achla and Noah were helping Machla with her immersion."

"You actually saw Machla immerse?"

"I did, Your Honor."

"What time of day was this?"

"It was shortly before sundown."

"Were other women waiting to use the Mikva who would know Machla?"

"There were other women and volunteer attendants. Everyone in Menashe knows Machla."

Carmiel dismissed Bracha and recalled Machla.

"We have heard testimony, Machla, that you performed a ritual consistent with that performed by women who are about to get married. Are you now married or betrothed?"

"No, I am not."

"May I ask why?"

Machla did not try to mask her anger as she replied sharply. "No, you may not. The court cannot compel a woman to explain why she did not choose to marry someone."

"May I at least ask if the likely groom was from the tribe of Menashe?"

"He may have been."

"What sort of nonsense is that? You certainly must have known where your prospective husband was from."

"As was brought out at my trial, I preferred not to get married until the Zelaphchad case was resolved. It was resolved two weeks ago and from then on I was free to wed. I had two valid proposals for marriage outstanding, one of which was from a very fine gentleman from Menashe. So, I went to the Mikva and then came home to consider my options."

The judges burst out in laughter when they saw what Machla was up to. Eliav wouldn't dare testify and no witnesses could claim that Elchanan had been the scheduled groom. Noah howled with glee and said to Milka. "That's more daring than Machla has ever been. She has learned a lot from me."

"Then at least you admit you were considering a groom from another tribe.

It certainly does not seem reasonable that an intelligent woman like yourself would not know whom she would marry when she left the Mikva."

"Your Honor, I am not an idiot. Of course I know whom I would have preferred as a marriage partner, but there were external forces limiting my choices. I would like the court to know that the attorney for the petitioners had requested a court order which would have forbidden me to marry outside the tribe even before the case was heard in court. Also, the current case, which may prevent me from marrying outside the tribe, was being prepared for court. Any reasonable person would have doubts about entering a relationship that in two weeks might be ruled illegal by the Torah."

There was a loud buzz of discussion between the judges when the startling testimony emerged.

"The injunction was never granted. Why bring it up now?"

"I bring it up to show that this case has little to do with tribal property and everything to do with depriving a woman in Israel of her basic human rights."

Carmiel objected to her answer and asked to have it stricken. The chief judge wasn't at all sympathetic. "Carmiel," he said, "when one asks an unwise question he well deserves whatever answer he gets. Objection overruled."

Carmiel had no further questions. It was bad enough that Elchanan had gotten the better of him. To be outfoxed by a woman was more than he could bear.

Elchanan only asked Machla a few questions. "As an acknowledged student of the Torah, are you aware of any marital restrictions on women based on tribal origin?"

"I know of none."

"Are you aware of any inter-tribal marriages described in the Torah?"

"Yes. Aaron the High Priest from the tribe of Levi married Elisheva, the sister of Nachshon, first President of the tribe of Judah. Furthermore, while it is not written in the Torah, Caleb of Judah was married to Miriam, from the tribe of Levi."[4]

"Do you have any objections if this petition is granted for future generations but allows an exemption for the current generation?"

"I am opposed to the petition in principle. I admit, however, that if a girl knows from her childhood that she must marry within the tribe, she can adjust to it. It is grossly unfair to tell women after they have strong emotional commitments to men of other tribes, that they must give up the men they love."

"Thank you, Machla." Machla was exhausted by her exertions and Noah assisted her to the family area.

Meir summed up for the petitioners, but his heart was heavy. He had reason to feel that, based on court performance, the judges would not vote against Machla.

Before debating the case, the judges paused to find out whether there was any Divine revelation on the issue. No Divine intervention was anticipated, so the judges were not paying close attention to where the heads of the court were seated. They were totally surprised when Moses arose and walked slowly to the center of the area. In a firm voice he announced, "The Lord has made His will known to me in this matter and has said: 'The sons of Joseph speak well. Their petition is granted.' With regard to the daughters of Zelaphchad, the Lord has commanded: 'Let them marry whom they think best, but it is preferable that they, too, marry within the tribe of their father.'"

When these words came forth from the mouth of Moses, Machla let out a loud piercing shriek, "Oh, God. No." She turned white and keeled over in a deep faint. Moses halted for a moment as the four sisters scrambled from their positions and ran to Machla's assistance. Elchanan also ran over to help.

When Moses saw that the situation was under control, he continued with the Divine revelation.

"This law is given so that the inheritance of the children of Israel shall not move from tribe to tribe. Everyone of the children of Israel shall cleave to the inheritance of the tribe of his fathers. And every daughter, who possesses an inheritance in any tribe of the children of Israel, shall be wife to one of the family of the tribe of her father, so that the children of Israel may enjoy every man the inheritance of his fathers. Neither shall the inheritance remove from one tribe to another tribe; but everyone of the tribes of the children of Israel shall keep himself to the tribe of his fathers."

The sisters had no great problem with Machla. They put her legs up in an elevated position and let her smell some aromatic salts. She regained consciousness after a minute or two and she was given some water. While she was coming to herself, Joshua came over to inquire about her condition. He told

Elchanan that when Machla was fully recovered, Moses wanted to talk to her and explain the exact meaning of the Divine revelation.

"Am I right in assuming," he asked Joshua, "that it is only a recommendation that the daughters of Zelaphchad marry within the tribe? I understood from the words of the prophet that for them it is not an absolute command as it is in the case of future generations?"[5]

"You are right, Elchanan. But I must warn you that Divine preferences carry a lot of weight. Incidentally, you and Machla put up a tremendous battle. I commend you most heartily."

When Machla regained control, Elchanan told her about the rest of the revelation.

"The only thing that Meir got right today was the argument that it was not good for property to circulate among the tribes. If it were not for Divine intervention, we would have easily won the case."

"What exactly does the passage concerning us mean?"

"As I interpret it, it means that it is up to you whether you marry within the tribe or out of it. The Lord, however, recommends that you stay within the tribe." Machla had difficulty in grasping the concept. All her life she had understood the Divine will to be unequivocal. Something was either permitted or prohibited.

In her confusion she asked, "Does it mean that I will be punished if I marry you?"

"As I understand it, you will not be punished but you may fall out of Divine favor. But why trust my grasp of the situation when Moses has granted you a private audience?"

"I cannot believe it. When is it for?" What little color had returned to Machla's face quickly disappeared. She was again as white as a sheet and Elchanan was quite concerned.

"As soon as you are strong enough. I am not sure you can handle it yet."

"Elchanan, if I were on my death bed and Moses asked to see me, I would surely manage to be there."

A half an hour later she stood at the door of the Tent of Meeting and was ushered inside. The tent was not unduly large and contained only two tables. One was used for meetings with the leaders of Israel and the other for writing in the Torah. Machla's four sisters took up their vigil outside in case their services would be needed. In the tent, Moses sat at his table and Joshua, who never left the Tent of Meeting, hovered in the background. Machla trembled as Moses addressed her.

"Before we come to your individual case, I would like to say that you were magnificent at this trial and the previous one. The nation of Israel is proud of you, and I pray that in future years we will be blessed by many other women like you."

"Thank you, my Lord."

"I called you in to explain, in full, the revelation I received. I want you to understand that you are free to marry anyone you wish from any tribe of Israel. The Lord, however, has suggested that you marry someone from Menashe. Let me illustrate the matter in terms that may be easily understood. A father says to his son, 'Son, there are two schools that you may attend. The choice is up to you, but I would be much happier if you were to pick this one instead of the other.'

"Now a son may reason that his father doesn't know the schools very well or that he doesn't know his son's nature that well. So, being allowed to choose from the two, he may pick the one not preferred by his father. In the case of the Lord, He is all knowing. His judgments are perfect, so his recommendations carry great weight."

"Is the heavenly judgment based on what is best for me, or what is best for the nation of Israel?"

"I will not hide the truth from you, Machla, for you are too saintly a person for that. You are being asked to sacrifice your personal happiness for the good of the nation."

"My case won't make much of a difference if all women in the future marry within their tribes."[6]

"You are missing the point, Machla. Better than all women in Israel, you know the importance of the commandment to sanctify the Divine name. When a person sacrifices his life or happiness to do God's will, even when not required to do so, he is sanctifying God's name. That person becomes a national hero and his martyrdom inspires all future generations. Think how often we recall that Abraham was willing to sacrifice his son at God's request. Think of how Nachshon plunged into the waters of the sea? Then think of what the women of the future will say when they hear of this section of Torah. They will point out that although the law of Torah did not require Machla to marry within her tribe, she did voluntarily what others in her generation would be required to do. To abide by the Lord's will, she gave up the love of her life. The will of God in this case reflects the fact that the Almighty feels that the tribal structure is in the best interest of the Hebrew nation.

"You know, of course, that the Torah has made provision for a king and a central government should the children of Israel prefer that form of leadership. But it is clear from the Torah that God regards that option as an unnecessary imitation of the gentile nations. The Lord would much prefer the tribes of Israel to accept God as their sole king and ruler."[7]

Machla understood that a powerful king might weaken the faith of the Hebrews in their God in heaven, but she didn't fathom the need for her to be a martyr to further the cause of strengthening the tribal structure. "I can understand why God tested Abraham," she said, "but my Lord remembers that an angel intervened at the last moment to save Isaac on the altar and grant Abraham a great reward. Can I expect when Eliav is about to take me to wife, an angel will come down and say, 'Stop! Machla, the daughter of Zelaphchad, because you heeded My will and were ready to sacrifice your one and only beloved Elchanan, I will bless you and make you as great as the stars in heaven and the sands of the sea.' No, I am afraid that my sacrifice will be a real one, not just a test."

Moses waited for a moment to let Machla regain her composure after her emotional plea. In a voice full of compassion he answered, "That an angel will intervene at the last minute, I cannot tell you. I am at liberty to tell you, however, that your reward will be very great if you choose the proper course."

"I am asking about it only out of curiosity. I will not be a martyr for material rewards."

"I can tell you that your marriage to Eliav will be blessed with great happiness and, although advanced in years, you and all of your sisters will be blessed with no less than two children each. Your first child will be a son who will find special favor in the eyes of the Lord and become one of the great Torah scholars of his time. God will bless all the works of his hands."

"The blessings of the Lord are very generous. What happens if I marry Elchanan?"

"It has not been revealed to me, but I know that you will not be punished nor specially blessed. Nature will be allowed to take its course. You will take the same chances that any woman takes when she gets married. With Eliav you will have Divine guarantees and assurances."

"Let me not be ungrateful for Divine favors, but what will I do to mend the gaping hole in my heart where Elchanan is supposed to be? As a married woman, I will be required to sever all contact with him."

Moses waxed philosophical and allowed a tone of sadness to enter his response. "It is in the nature of creation that all people at some time lose the proximity of those they love. It is the duty of a person to thank God for the years of love with which he was blessed, rather than complain about the years when the loved one is absent. Machla, for the next few minutes I am going to speak to you not as a prophet but as a keeper of the books. I want you to tell me of all the events in your life where you feel that the hand of God went out against you."

"Must I?"

"Yes. It will open your eyes."

"I do so at my Lord's request. Of my own free will I would never utter any complaints against the Lord."

Machla in a low voice, almost a whisper, said, "The lord took away my father when I was five years old and left me with a mother who could not teach me Torah.

"He let my mother suffer in widowhood for forty years.

"He caused me to learn Torah in a very humiliating and debasing fashion.

"He wishes to take away the man I love without ever giving me a chance to know him physically.

"He struck me down like a stuck pig on my wedding day.

"He wants me to spend the rest of my years with a man I do not really love."

When Machla concluded her list, Moses replied. "The points you have raised are all valid. Of course, speaking of the man you love, do you recall a certain night on the border of Menashe?"

Machla blushed furiously. "I was in a state of purity that night and his intentions were honorable. He wanted me to enter a legal and proper marriage even though his methods did not exactly conform to the latest Torah laws."

"The objection is not to him putting his robe around you. All marriages contracted according to earlier practices necessarily begin with some physical contact. His sin was that he chose not to abide by the new marriage laws of the Torah. The Lord is pleased that you resisted the temptation."

Machla persisted in defending Elchanan. "He was not himself that night. He loves me as much as I love him, and he was desperately afraid that he would be forbidden by court order to marry me."

Moses reverted to the original subject. "You have made your entries on one side of the ledger, Machla. Let me make my entries on the other side.

"You were endowed at birth with a mind and memory second to none.

"You were allowed to learn more Torah than any woman in Hebrew history, save for the prophetess.

"You were privileged to teach your sisters Torah and save their lives from sin.

"You were privileged to heal the sick and save many of them from death.

"You were allowed to go unpunished for a childish conspiracy that could have endangered the sacred institution of marriage.

"You were privileged to have a fine man love you and wait for you more than twenty years. How comforting it must have been to know that if your campaign failed, you would always have a man waiting for you.

"For ten years you were privileged to love and enjoy the love of one of the greatest men of Israel, at the expense of two innocent people, Eliav and Batya.

"You were privileged to teach Torah in Judah to hundreds of teachers and thousands of students.

"You were privileged to have your name in the Torah not once but twice — an honor accorded only to the daughters of Zelaphchad among members of the younger generation.

"You were privileged to argue for your cause in front of the High Priest, the High Court and 25,000 members of the nation.

"You were privileged to win your struggle to inherit land in Canaan and have your case described in a section of the Torah named for you and your sisters.

"You are privileged to still be allowed to marry Elchanan if you so choose.

"You see, Machla, for every instance where the Lord did not treat you as favorably as you may have wanted, you received two blessings in return. The balance is in the Lord's favor. To tell the truth Machla, with all your liabilities, every last woman among the children of Israel would willingly trade places with you. There isn't a girl in Israel who doesn't pray to grow up to be a second Machla."

Machla could not deny the truth of the Divine favors she had received. Still her heart ached with her love for Elchanan. "I do not deny that my blessings are numerous and I thank the Lord for them every day. But the Lord has endowed me with a heart and with passions. He must realize that I would desire to fulfill them."

"There comes a time when compassion is more worthy than passion. There comes a time when a woman with many lambs should not deprive those who have but one lamb as their sole possession."[8]

"I understand what my Lord is saying, but I cannot give my answer now. I need to consult with those who are dear to me and seek their advice and counsel. How much time may I have before deciding which path to follow?"

"You may have one week. It is now late in our fortieth year and that part of the Torah relating to your case must be completed as soon as possible. If you abide by the suggestion of the Lord, the final verses on this subject will read:

> 'Even as the Lord commanded Moses, so did the daughters of Zelaphchad; for Machla, Tirza, and Hogla and Milka and Noah, the daughters of Zelaphchad were married to their uncles' sons: and they were married to the families of the sons of Menashe, the son of Joseph, and their inheritance remained in the tribe of the family of their father.'"[9]

"Does that mean that if we abide by the Lord's desire, we are at least free to marry anyone in the tribe of Menashe?"

"Yes it does."

"Will the verses be written before the actual marriages take place? It may take two years to marry us all off."

"Your word is as good as gold."

"Does it mean that Tirza will be restored to her rightful place in the order as you have read it just now?"

"This reference to the daughters of Zelaphchad will be in the correct chronological order. Tirza's name will follow yours."

"Thank you, my Lord. This hour in your presence was the most glorious event in my life."

Elchanan and her sisters were waiting for her as she left the Tent of Meeting. The sisters kept their distance while she spoke to Elchanan.

"Elchanan, I have a free choice to marry within the tribe or out of it, but the Lord would be more pleased if I were to stay within the tribe."

"Did Moses offer you any incentives?"

"Among other things he said that if I follow God's will, the daughters of Zelaphchad will be listed in the Torah a third time and Tirza will be listed in her right place."

"Twice is not enough? That is still two more times than most private people in our generation."

"The Torah is an eternal book, Elchanan. One doesn't treat an additional listing lightly."

"How much time did Moses give you to make a decision?"

"One week. I must advise him of my decision by next Monday afternoon."

"I won't pressure you while you are making up your mind but I will offer some inducements."

"I am listening."

"If you choose me, I will grant you the privilege of naming our first born son 'Zelaphchad' in memory of your late father. I will treat you like the queen you are, and I will love you even more than I do now."

"I certainly couldn't ask for anything more."

Elchanan left Machla and she returned with her sisters to Menashe. On the way, she explained the judgment and summarized her discussion with Moses.

"What are you going to do now?" asked Tirza.

"Well," Machla said, "if I don't want Eliav, and God does not want me to have Elchanan, maybe I will ask Chemlon to marry me."

"Oh no you won't," Tirza reacted instinctively without thinking. "He's mine. He asked me to marry him two weeks ago."

"What did you tell him?"

"Oh, nothing," she said with a smile, "I told him I was too busy to think about such things as marriage."

When Elchanan returned home, Batya greeted him warmly. "You were masterful today, I was thrilled with your performance."

"I would rather perform poorly and win a case than perform well and lose it."

"You haven't yet lost. I asked Chemlon, and he said that under the ruling Machla may still marry you."

"It's the old story," Elchanan countered. "The fox walks by the field and sees the most beautiful morsels that a fox can desire. The only problem is that next to the food is a big man with an even bigger stick waiting to smite the fox as soon as he reaches out for the food."

"I understand. I want you to know, though, that I almost prayed for you to be victorious in the case."

"Why didn't you, my dear?"

"Don't you remember?" she said with a merry twinkle in her eyes. "I traded off my rights to pray in return for Friday nights."

When Machla reached Menashe, Noah said to her, "You have had another rough day and you need rest. Have a good night of sleep. Tomorrow morning I will tell you what choice to make."

"Sleep is about the best idea you have come up with in quite a while."

The next morning, Machla awoke to plan her strategy. She would seek counsel from four people; Noah and her mother within the family, Chemlon and Malka, her former student, outside the family. Her aim was to get a balanced selection, two people who would favor Eliav and two who would favor Elchanan. She would listen to their advice and evaluate their arguments.

She knew that Noah would say to pick Elchanan. Noah was an incurable romantic, a creature of the flesh. By her own admission, Elchanan was the manliest person she had ever seen. There was no way that Noah would suggest Eliav. Her mother, she anticipated, would choose Eliav. To Achla, he was a known commodity. She didn't really know Elchanan well. Given her conservative nature, she was probably afraid of him. She also would hesitate to let her daughter be a second wife when she could be another man's first one.

Chemlon, she anticipated was in Elchanan's favor. In the last few months,

Chemlon had almost become a disciple of Elchanan. He admired his knowledge and skill and imitated his ways. A deep friendship had developed between the two and it was Chemlon who had advised Elchanan of Meir's plans.

With Malka, she also had no doubt. The girl was brilliant but extremely pious. The mere suggestion that there was a Divine preference for Eliav would cause her to cast her vote for him.

Noah was beginning to stir so Machla woke her. "You said you were going to tell me this morning whom to choose."

"Are you sure it's not too early? You know I hate getting up at dawn."

"It's almost nine. Tirza came back with the manna and everyone has left for work."

"Well, then, I advise you to marry Elchanan."

"Why?"

"Because you never listen to me. If I say Elchanan, you will marry Eliav, and that is the correct choice."

"Stop fooling around Noah, this is serious. Whom do you really prefer?"

"You will be happier with Eliav. I really mean it. Perhaps the passion will be greater with Elchanan for a year or two but he will cool off as he did with Batya. No one has ever figured out how to put two wives with one man and avoid conflict between the women. Eliav will love you forever. It will be a wonderful feeling to get up in the morning and not have to ask yourself what shall I do today to earn my husband's love or what is Batya doing today to take him back from me."

"But Elchanan is so much more learned that Eliav."

"Learned men are nice to talk to and you have enjoyed ten years of intellectual conversations. Learned men, however, don't make better husbands than good men, and Eliav is a prince. Cleave unto him."

Machla next walked to the Tribal Center to see her mother.

"I let you sleep late because you needed the rest," her mother said. "How do you feel now?

"Much better. Do you have some time to talk to me?"

"You haven't asked my advice since you were fourteen. Are you sure you need my help?"

"I told Moses that I would seek counsel from those who were close to me."

"You may not like my advice."

"It is your right to express yourself."

"Well, then, I will. Machla, I am tired of martyrdom. First my husband, then my daughters. Moses couldn't draw a list of blessings for me because my sufferings would far outweigh them. I say that enough is enough. You have delayed marriage for twenty-three years. At least that was for a good cause, one that I could understand. Now you are being asked to enter a marriage with a man you don't really love for the convenience of some tribal bookkeeping. Menashe won't lose any land. It just may have to exert itself to keep track of its holdings in other tribes.

"Machla, you are entitled to marry the man who will make you happy. Elchanan is a far greater man than Eliav can hope to be. Even as a second wife, you will be happier with him. I have nothing against Eliav, but love is an important aspect of life. If God is letting you marry Elchanan, don't hesitate." Machla was almost in shock at her mother's surprising point of view.

"Thanks, mother. It is not what I expected to hear, but it is good advice. Maybe I should have sought your guidance more often."

"If you did, I would be a grandmother today like some of my friends. By the way, the class has started sewing the wedding dresses, so hurry up and make up your mind."

Machla went back to the tent for rest and reflection. She had guessed wrong on her first two advisors and she felt she was losing her touch. She should get to know people better, she thought to herself as she fell asleep in the early afternoon.

That evening Eliav came by and took her for a walk. "You were magnificent in court yesterday. Carmiel wanted me to testify that you were not planning to marry me but I would have no part of anything like that."

"Why not?"

"Things have been running my way lately. From no chances at all, I have become a strong contender. I figured that after the trial, you would still be free to marry Elchanan. It would have been very stupid of me to antagonize or embarrass you publicly."

"You showed a good deal of wisdom there. Your chances have increased dramatically since you fashioned such a formidable alliance. Meir, Bracha and

Batya were always on your side. Now you have added the Almighty Himself. Would you still be willing to marry me after I kept you waiting all these years?"

"My offer is good until the children of Israel cross the Jordan river. What I have come for tonight is to offer some more dowry."

"It won't be necessary, but I am listening."

"If you marry me, I will give you the right to name our first son, 'Zelaphchad', in honor of your father. I will treat you as the princess that you are, and love you throughout our married life as I do now."

"Anything else?"

"I will learn Torah with Meir on a regular basis."

"That won't be necessary. Most of what you know you learned from me. Nothing would give me more pleasure than studying Torah with you."

After Eliav left, Machla decided to see Chemlon on Wednesday and Malka on Thursday.

Chemlon was direct and to the point. "Elchanan towers over Eliav. If all other things were equal, I would advise you to choose him. But all other things are not equal. There really is no free choice when it comes to Moses, the prophet. Those who went against his will, paid for it with their lives. The reason for that is that the will of Moses is the will of the Lord and the power of the Lord is awesome. He rewards those who abide by His will and punishes those who stray from it."

"I thought we were granted free will?"

"Only in a theoretical or intellectual sense. Of course, you have free will in your thoughts and can speculate about any course of action. Behavior, however, is intimately linked to consequence. If you use your freedom to choose a given path in life, you cannot escape the pitfalls that lie in wait for you on the road. Let me explain this situation in simple terms. You tell a child that he has the freedom to study or not to study. Then you add that if he studies he will get the candy and, if he doesn't, he will have to go to sleep. You really are not offering him freedom of choice. Sure, you are free to marry Elchanan, but you may have to pay a price for your choice. You have monumental achievements to your credit, Machla, because you have enjoyed Divine grace. For you to fall out of Divine favor at this point in your life, makes no sense at all. Choose Eliav, and live with the memory of the ten beautiful years that you enjoyed with Elchanan."

On Thursday, Machla went to Judah to speak with Malka. Elchanan was in court as some regular judges were busy preparing for the Sabbath. Malka was glad to see her and give her the time she needed. Having sat on the visitor's side of Machla's desk on so many occasions, Malka felt slightly uneasy with her former teacher coming to see her. Machla appeared very strained and tense.

"I never dreamt," said Malka, "that I would live to see the day when Teacher Machla comes to seek my advice."

"I learned a lot from my pupils and you are the brightest of them." Malka had matured rapidly with her new responsibilities. She was still short but her body had filled out and she was pleasant to look at. Machla related the problem she was facing and asked, "What would you do if you were in my place?"

After some deliberation, Malka replied, "Machla, you taught me that all Torah laws are wise and must be considered equal when it comes to observing them. That I do not deny. As I have grown older, I have learned to differentiate between the enduring and eternal laws and those of a more temporal nature. The new marriage law is not a great law. It is the last vestige of a tribalism that will not survive in Canaan. The Torah clearly senses that the future of our people in Canaan is in central government. There is already provision for a king and a central holy city. A parcel of land in Judah or Menashe is totally insignificant. The new law restricting inter-tribal marriages will not long be observed and, what is more, the legislation degrades women and treats them like so much cattle.[10]

"If you have a choice in the matter, even if it is not an equally balanced one, I would show my displeasure with the new law. Let the future generations of the daughters of Israel know that at least Machla, the daughter of Zelaphchad, had the good sense to say 'no.' Let the world know that you gave your life to advance the status of Hebrew women and were not ready to give back the gains you achieved."

Machla was shocked at Malka's vehemence. She was no longer the little orphan girl who had once clung to her. The woman confronting her was proud and defiant.

"The gain I made is basic and will not be lost. I admit that this marriage limitation is a setback, but progress in life is not always one-directional. We move ahead and fall back. Ultimately, we reach our goal."

"Those who are not given a choice in the matter can rationalize their acceptance of the law. I don't see how you can."

"What about Elchanan? Do you approve of him?"

"I don't know Eliav, but I can tell you that Elchanan is the most magnificent person I know. If you have the chance to marry him, don't waste it. I often dream of finding a man like him."

"Don't tell that to Batya, I gave her enough trouble already."

"Don't worry. I know I can't have Elchanan, so I am doing the next best thing."

"What is that?"

"I reasoned that if I can't have Elchanan as a husband, I can at least have him as a father-in-law. I asked Elchanan to consider me as a potential bride for his oldest son, Achituv."

"What was his reaction?"

"He said that he has to take care of Dina first and then he would talk to me."

"What are your chances?"

"Elchanan would like his children to marry aristocracy. You know how poor I am and you know that I don't look like Noah. But, you taught me how to pray and I do so every day."

"I'll put in a good word for you," Machla said as she left for home. Having spoken to all the living advisors and getting mixed and unexpected results, Machla realized she would have to turn to her ancestors who were no longer among the living. Sunday morning found her at the tomb of Joseph seeking to resolve her dilemma. This was her second visit to the holy site within a month. Unlike the first visit, when she was with her family, this time she was alone and free to pour her heart out to the founder of her tribe.

CHAPTER

FIFTEEN

"CIRCLING THE WALLS OF JERICHO"

Kneeling at the tomb of Joseph, Machla prayed:

> "O, Joseph, father of our tribe, your daughter, Machla, prays for your help. I must make a decision and I am incapable of doing so without your guidance. Shall I marry Elchanan and follow the dictates of my heart, or shall I marry Eliav and satisfy the will of those above me? Am I obligated to make more sacrifices or have I done enough? Is a recommendation merely a suggestion, or is it an order? I am so confused that I can no longer think clearly."
>
> "You cannot communicate with me directly but ask the Lord to send me a sign so that I may know the right course to follow."

Sunday night, the sign which Machla was seeking came in the form of a dream. In it, she saw herself transported to the Land of Egypt in the days of Joseph. There, from her vantage point, she was able to look directly into the home of Potiphar, the officer of Pharaoh and the employer of Joseph. A scantily clad Zoleika, the wife of Potiphar, was doing her best to seduce Joseph into coming to bed with her. She had taken hold of his garment and was pleading with him. Machla could hardly believe how beautiful and desirable she was. Joseph was about to yield to her persuasions and take her in his arms when, behind Zoleika, he beheld a large vision of Jacob, his father, frowning at him. No words were spoken, but the message was clear: A son of Jacob does not yield to the passions of the flesh and make love to a married woman. Joseph pulled out of his garment and ran away.[1]

The dream continued with Machla replacing Zoleika and Elchanan playing the role of Joseph. He was embracing her and asking her to come to bed with him. Machla was about to accede when she saw a vision of Moses behind Elchanan with an even angrier frown than Jacob had in the first part of the dream.

Machla awoke with a start. She had gotten her sign and the message was clear: a daughter of Israel does not succumb to the passions of the flesh when such action is contrary to the will of heaven. She knew that every time Elchanan made love to her, she would see the frowning vision of Moses poised beyond him.

Machla had enough. She was no match for the infinite power of the Lord. Chemlon, of all her advisors, was the one who had told her the truth. One could not escape from a God who was everywhere. One could not hide anything from a God that was all knowing or defy a God who was all powerful.

At two in the afternoon, she appeared at the Tent of Meeting ready to make her surrender official. Waiting outside the tent were the two men in her life, Elchanan and Eliav, standing about fifty paces apart. They were aware of each other's presence but were not looking at one another.

The curtain was drawn, and Machla was ushered into the presence of the prophet. Compared to the Mishkan, the tent of Moses was not ornate. The curtains were made of plain tent cloth, and did not have any special designs. Moses preferred the simple abode, in keeping with his humility. Even though this was Machla's second visit to the tent, she was still overawed by the prophet's presence. In a trembling voice she inquired, "Does my Lord know of the decision I have made?"

"The Lord has not chosen to reveal it to me thus far."

"Good. Then I take it that there is still time for some last minute negotiation."

"One may always seek favors from the Lord."

"The first request is that when I choose Eliav, someone will tell Elchanan about it other than me. I am woefully ashamed because I promised to marry him, and I am defaulting on my word. I have never knowingly told a lie in my life."

Moses understood her plight. "I shall tell Elchanan for you. All vows, if indeed you made a vow according to the Torah, are made conditionally upon the terms of the vow being acceptable to the Lord. In this case, the Lord, Himself, is annulling the vow and you are absolved from sin."

"While my Lord is talking to Elchanan, may he please ask him to forgive me and not harbor resentment against me in his heart?"

"I will seek to persuade him."

"Can my Lord bestow some Divine favor upon this noble man to compensate him for his pain?"

"The Lord is a healer of all wounds whether of the flesh or the heart."

"Can my Lord help Malka make a match with Elchanan's son?"

"I will pray to the Lord in her behalf."

"One more request?"

"The last one, please."

"May I watch you write the promised verse in the Torah?"

"You will definitely choose Eliav?"

"Yes, my Lord."

"Are you afraid that Tirza will be listed out of order again?"

"Yes, my Lord."

"Come with me then."

Moses walked over to the parchment on the table and, in Machla's presence, wrote in Torah script:[2]

> "AS GOD COMMANDED MOSES SO DID THE DAUGHTERS OF
> ZELAPHCHAD, AND MACHLA, TIRZA AND HOGLA AND MILKA
> AND NOAH BECAME THE WIVES OF THEIR UNCLES' SONS."

Machla was overcome with joy as she saw the words become part of the sacred teachings of the children of Israel.

"Here, my daughter, keep this quill as a memento of your third entry into the Torah. The nation of Israel is proud of you. May the Lord bless you for all that you have done."

Machla was ushered out of the back of the tent and Elchanan was summoned to enter. She ran to Eliav, who was very concerned when he saw Elchanan go in before Machla came out.

"Eliav, I am all yours. It has been so written in the Torah and can never be changed. I am inviting you to join us for this coming Sabbath morning meal, so that my mother can meet her prospective son-in-law and grant me her approval."

"Thank God," Eliav said, fighting to control his emotions. "What if your mother doesn't approve?"

"You can easily wait another twenty years for her to change her mind."

Eliav laughed. "May I walk you home?"

"Not yet. I have to bid farewell to Elchanan. Go home and we will talk on the Sabbath."

Inside the tent, Moses was speaking with Elchanan. "Elchanan, you have been blessed with everything that a man could desire. Wealth, good appearance, great wisdom, success in your work, fame and popularity, a devoted wife and four wonderful children. The Lord, in His wisdom, is withholding only one thing from you, the body of Machla, the daughter of Zelaphchad. The mind and the wisdom and the love of this woman you have enjoyed for ten years. Is there a man in Israel who would not be happy to trade places with you?"

Elchanan was barely listening to the final words of Moses. When he sensed that Machla was being denied to him, a wave of sadness engulfed him and tears began to well up in his eyes. He was crestfallen and defeated.

In sadness, he said to Moses, "It is difficult, my Lord, to apply rational thought in affairs of the heart. I cannot begin to describe my pain at the loss of Machla. As Jacob grieved over his son, Joseph, and could not be comforted, so do I feel at this moment. What sin have I committed that I should be thus afflicted?"[3]

"You have not sinned in this regard, my son. There was another man who wanted Machla and a woman who wanted all of you for herself. They, too, were without sin. If two men compete for a position where only one can be chosen, does it mean that the losing candidate has sinned? It simply means that the judge in the case preferred one over the other.

"I want you to know that Machla asked me to inform you of her decision because she was ashamed to face you after breaking her vows. She wants you know that her love for you never wavered and that her actions are in response to the will of our Lord in heaven. It would mean very much to her to secure your full forgiveness. She also requested me to arrange that you be endowed with some blessings to ease your pain."

"I will in time forgive her because I believe that of her own free will she would never have deserted me. As my Lord has stated, I already have received more blessings than most men. I do not seek any additional favors."

"Nevertheless, if you see it in your heart to forgive Machla, the Lord will bestow upon you some added ones. Thus shall you be rewarded:

"You will soon be appointed as chief judge of Judah.

"The Lord will open the womb of Batya, after thirteen years of being barren, and bless you with a daughter. This will not be an ordinary child, but one that will be surrounded by angels of the Lord guarding her in all her ways."

"Thank you, my Lord."

"Oh yes, something else that may turn out to be the best blessing of all. Young Malka prays every day to become your daughter-in-law. She is one of the brightest women in all of Israel, and Machla has made a special request on her behalf."

Machla waited for Elchanan as he left the tent, her eyes red and swollen.

"I cannot kiss you farewell, Elchanan, as I am not in purity. The Lord was not overly happy about our last contact either, even though I had emerged from the Mikva only a few hours earlier. I did have every intention of marrying you, but the Lord prevented me. In fact, I worked on this wedding gift for many months. She handed him a beautiful cloth of purple wool embroidered with the words:

> TO MY BELOVED ELCHANAN:
> MAY THE LORD BLESS YOU AND KEEP YOU.
> MAY THE LORD MAKE HIS FACE SHINE UPON
> YOU AND BE GRACIOUS TO YOU.
> MAY THE LORD LIFT UP HIS COUNTENANCE
> UPON YOU AND GRANT YOU PEACE.
> ETERNALLY YOURS, MACHLA

"I know that the pain is too great for you to forgive me now, but please try to do it soon for all the love that we have shared."

"The cloth is superb and I appreciate the sentiments. I am sure a time will come when I can forgive you as well." He strode off in the direction of Judah so that she shouldn't see the tears in his eyes.

Machla walked home slowly, trying to reorganize her life. When she reached the tent, her mother gave her a bowl of soup and hovered over her. Her sisters stood nearby waiting to hear the news.

"We will have company for the Sabbath. I have invited a prospective groom for your approval, mother."

"That means it's Eliav, because Elchanan wouldn't leave his wife and children for the Sabbath," Noah said.

"I thought I told you to marry Elchanan," Achla said, dourly.

"When your mother says one thing and the Lord says another, you have to listen to the Lord. Let me rest for a while. Tonight, we will have a family meeting."

At dinner, Machla showed the quill that Moses gave her and cited the verse that he wrote in the Torah in her presence.

Tirza was beside herself with joy. She kissed and hugged Machla and thanked her profusely but then she suddenly stopped. "Wait a minute. You didn't agree to marry Eliav just to get my name in the right order in the Torah, did you?"

"Of course I did. Why else would I marry him."

Tirza didn't know whether Machla was serious or not because Machla was not the type to jest.

"You didn't have to do that for me, Machla."

"Sit down," Noah said to Tirza. "You can't be such an idiot. If Machla chose Eliav, it is because that is what I specifically advised her to do. Isn't that so, Machla?

"You did advise me to do so, but the real reason that I chose Eliav is because I never was really free to do otherwise. Thank God I am at least being allowed to marry a decent man who loves me. God could just as well have forbidden me to marry anyone. Now that I am spoken for, it is my desire to account for all of my sisters. What's doing with you, Tirza?"

"I told Chemlon that I will give him an answer as soon as you have decided on your course of action. He will be coming around later to hear it. The date that we set will be at least two months after your wedding."

"That's wonderful. What's happening with you, Hogla?"

"The trial did a world of good for us and gave us needed exposure. In the last three weeks, Milka and I have received a total of ten inquiries as to whether we are available for marriage. We will study them all."

"That leaves only you Noah. Where do you stand?"

"I enjoy the single life. For the first time in my life I will have a tent all to myself."

"Speaking of tents, Noah, you had better clean it up before the Sabbath. I don't want Eliav to think that I am responsible for that mess. As to the original question, though, you can't remain single. I gave my word to Moses that all of us would marry, and that is how he wrote it in the Torah."

"I don't recall you asking me."

"You have my permission to tell that to Moses. He will gladly change the verse to read that four daughters of Zelaphchad married within the tribe. The fifth was unfortunately struck by lightning as she left the Tent of Meeting."

"Alright then, I will get married, but I am not at liberty to say to whom."

"Why not?"

"Because I will immediately be trampled to death by a horde of enraged sisters."

"We won't hurt you." They all assured her.

Noah walked about fifteen paces towards the path where she would have a head start if necessary.

"I am going to marry Meir," she shouted.

Her sisters were too stunned to chase her. Milka was the first one to react. "After what he did to Machla? How can you think of doing such a thing?"

"That's alright," said Machla. "I can't think of any more apt punishment for his misdeeds than being married to Noah. Does Meir know of the bitter fate that awaits him?"

"Not yet. But I am inviting him to our Sabbath feast and maybe he will catch on. And, don't worry, Machla, I will clean up my half of the tent."

"Noah, come back here and be serious for a moment."

Noah walked back warily.

"Listen, Noah," Machla said, "Meir is a very sober man. He spends most of his time studying Torah and teaching a few students. You saw him in his public appearances. He was thorough and well prepared in a very scholarly fashion but there was no spirit in him. You are full of life and sparkle. You and Meir just don't make a pair."

"Now that all of you are getting married, I think it is time that someone told you the real facts of life. The Torah permits married women very little freedom. No more flirting, no being alone with other men, no leading a gay life. You settle down and raise kids, feed your husband, and worry all day that he will bring home a younger woman as a second wife after you have given him your best years.

"In public life, it's a man's world. No important work is open to a married woman. Husbands are jealous and worried about their egos and they stifle their wives. If I get married, I am going to have to reform. I will be going to bed early and getting up early. I am going to have to start cooking and cleaning.

"For me, Meir is ideal. He is patient and not demanding. He will be busy with his studies, so he won't interfere with any interesting activities I may find. Do you know how many judges and commanders have proposed to me in the last three weeks? The wives are slaves to their husband's careers and have to cope with all the entertaining and all of the emergencies in the middle of the night. Then, the minute a Noah is free to get married, these men forget all about their loyal slaves and seek a good time. That is not for me. If I am going to lead a quiet life, I want a quiet man to do it with."

"How are you going to convince Meir that you have repented, that you won't put rocks in his socks?"

"I have a simple strategy if none of you interfere."

"Let's hear."

"Meir loves to teach. I am going to ask Meir to teach me, since Machla is getting married and won't be able to do so anymore. After a year, he may realize that I am a woman and might want to do something about it."

"Don't you know more Torah than Meir now?" Milka asked.

"It's hard to say. Meir may not be as sharp, but he studies an awful lot. I will not be the first woman to play the fool in order to build a man's ego."

In Judah, the situation was far more somber. Elchanan dragged himself home and went to bed. He did not eat or drink. Batya took one look at him and didn't have to be told that it was all over between Machla and her husband. Her feelings were mixed. In a way, she rejoiced that her rival was gone, but she was very concerned that Elchanan's spirit would go as well. As long as Machla was around, Elchanan was a highly motivated man. He got up early, dressed carefully and took pride in his appearance. To compensate for his feelings for Machla he was especially courteous and considerate to her. He devoted much time to the children and often had Machla talk to them about Torah. Now she was afraid that he would lose interest in life and, concurrently, in her.

She went over to Elchanan and saw that he was not asleep. Slowly she removed his shoes.

"Why are you doing that?" he asked. "I may yet have to go out tonight."

"People in mourning may not wear shoes," she said.

"Don't torment me, Batya, you have no idea how badly I feel right now."

"I most certainly do. I have felt that way every night for the last ten years. I know very well what it means to have your loved one desert you for another person. In your case, you have the consolation of knowing that she chose Eliav because she had to and not because she loved him more than she loved you. In my case, I had no such comfort."

"The wound is still open, Batya."

"You are free to mourn for two days if you wish, but then you will have to get up and help prepare for the Sabbath. We have Dina's prospective husband, Talman, as a guest, and I also invited Malka."

"Why did you do that?"

"I felt that maybe if you will have someone learned to talk to, your spirits will pick up."

"Please leave me alone," Elchanan groaned and ended the conversation.

The Sabbath at the Zelaphchad tents was a happy occasion. Machla was concerned about Elchanan, but she, herself, had made peace with her fate. It would have been nice to be the wife of a famous person but, she rationalized, most of the reflected glory would have gone to Batya anyway. There was nothing to do but accept the will of heaven.

Freed of his fear of losing Machla, Eliav reverted to his basic nature. Cheerful and outgoing, he livened up the dinner table. Even Achla began to enjoy his presence. After dinner, he and Machla went for a walk, their first chance to talk since Machla's decision. The three middle sisters went walking by themselves so that Noah could implement her strategy for Meir.

"Eliav," Machla said while walking, "if you take me as a wife you are entitled to rule over me in certain matters."

"No one can rule over Machla, daughter of Zelaphchad."

"That's where you are making a mistake. Just because I have a long list of accomplishments, it doesn't mean that I am different than other women. I plan to serve my husband and will expect him to complain if dinner isn't ready or the house is not clean. He can make love whenever he wishes and I will act as the Torah requires."

"Machla, I am not sure you believe a word you are saying, but I certainly don't. You may be biologically female but you were born with the spirit of a man, and you have always lived that way. You cannot change your nature and I am willing to accept you as you are. By the way, when are we getting married?"

"In all probability, it will be on the first day of the tenth month. I should be in a state of purity at that time."

"Are you ever going to tell me why you didn't go through with your marriage to Elchanan?"

"Who is Elchanan? I don't recognize the name."

"Elchanan ben Uriah."

"Oh that Elchanan, the fellow I once worked for in Judah. Why should I marry him when I have such a lovely man in Menashe?"

"You are not in court now, Machla, you may tell the truth."

"The truth is that Elchanan is part of my past. I will do my best to forget him and will certainly not mention his name in your presence with one exception."

"What is that?"

"If his daughter Dina gets married or, if my student Malka marries his son, I would like to attend the weddings with you."

"Is that the little girl who studied with Noah?"

"Yes. Did you ever hear her recite the Torah?"

"Quite often I passed the teaching area on the way to my tent. She reminded me of you at that age."

Malka at that moment was at Elchanan's table and she was taking part in a heated discussion. Talman was amazed at her knowledge and power of analysis while Achituv was utterly overwhelmed. When Talman took Dina for a walk, Batya suggested privately to Achituv that he offer to escort Malka back to her tent.

"I can't, mother, I am afraid she will embarrass me with her knowledge."

"Don't worry, I'll take care of that. You just ask her."

As Malka was thanking her for the hospitality, Batya whispered to her, "Tone down the intellectual level a bit, you are frightening my son out of his wits."

"Thank you," she whispered back, "I understand."

On the day after the Sabbath, Machla had a steady stream of visitors. Most of them came to wish her Mazel Tov on her forthcoming marriage. A few came to seek her forgiveness, after having offended her in the past.

Bracha came first, far more subdued than usual. "Machla, I want you to forgive me for testifying against you in court and telling the whole world that you were at the Mikva. I sinned, not out of hatred, but out of my intense desire to help my brother. If I ever hated you, it was because of his suffering. Now that you will be my sister-in-law, I want you to feel welcome in the family. I admit that I was a rotten child when I was young and I hated it when my father said, 'Why can't you be like Machla?' I feel that I have since learned to behave a little better."

"I forgive you, Bracha. I am sure that you will respect my modesty requirements in the future."

"Thank you, Machla, I will. God bless you."

Meir was next to seek Machla's pardon. They had a long talk about tribal rights and Meir admitted that, although it was a valid cause and stood up in court, the primary reason he had dragged Machla to court was to help his cousin.

"I am also your cousin."

"Yes, but you are a woman of strong faith. You will be able to survive losing your beloved Elchanan. Eliav could not have survived losing you. I feel that I saved his life. But I do seek your forgiveness for the public embarrassment and pain that I caused you."

"I will forgive you if you undertake some form of penance."

"Gladly, Machla. What would you like me to do?"

"Meir, if I get married and pregnant, I won't be able to teach Noah and counsel her. I want you to undertake to teach Noah Torah on a daily basis for the next year."

"I love to teach, and Noah, despite an obvious lack of order and discipline, is a very apt pupil. Tell me the truth, Machla, has Noah cast her eyes on me?"

"In the last three weeks, Noah has had numerous proposals from the most important judges and commanders. Who knows how many more from common people. Why should she be interested in a quiet, unassuming scholar? She would drive you crazy in less than a week."

"That is what I thought, too. But she has been very friendly lately and has spoken respectfully to me for a change."

"If, theoretically, she were interested in you, would you want to marry her?" The usually somber face of Meir underwent a dramatic transformation. A broad smile spread across his lips and a bright gleam was in his eyes. "There isn't a man alive who wouldn't be thrilled to have her. She can light up an area like no woman in the tribe. I have thought of her on many occasions, but I was afraid that she wouldn't settle down after marriage. You can't keep your wife on a chain."

"I think that Noah has reformed and will settle down. Look, Meir, Noah can't get married for over a year because it will take that long for her four sisters to precede her in marriage. She is the youngest and won't get married ahead of an older sister. If Noah behaves for a whole year under your tutelage and counsel, would you consider that a sufficient sign of repentance?"

"If Noah acted respectfully for two weeks, I would consider that a miracle. After a year, I would be happy to have her as a wife."

"I will give you a suggestion, Meir. Tell Noah that you will teach her but only at half past seven in the morning because you have to study with your learning partner later. If she presents herself at that time, it means she really loves you. But don't tell her that I gave you the suggestion. I will merely tell her that you will be happy to teach her, and that she should make arrangements with you. Since you are a man of your word, I forgive you in advance for any offenses that you may have committed against me."

Later in the afternoon, Dina came to see her. The visit didn't arouse any special notice because many of her former students visited with her at regular intervals. "I want your blessing on my forthcoming marriage, Teacher Machla, because you are saintly. If you bless my marriage, it will succeed. I will be marrying Talman in the spring and he is a scholar and a fine person. My parents think very highly of him and his parents seem pleased with me."

"I am very happy for you and your parents, and you have my sincere blessings. Is anything doing with Achituv?"

"It is strange that you asked me about that. Malka was with us for the Sabbath, and I sensed some spark of interest. The problem is that Achituv is young and Malka is so mature that she intimidates him. That girl could hold her own with the judges of the High Court of Israel."

"You can tell Achituv that I said he should not be afraid. Tell me, how is your mother?"

"I know you mean my father and I will tell you what I can. My mother asked me to thank you for deciding not to marry my father. She feels that in time she will win back his love. I feel that she will regain her confidence after you are married to Eliav and that she has a good chance of restoring her marriage.

"My father has still not overcome his grief and he feels betrayed. It will take a lot of time for him to recover. That is part of the reason why I came. Malka asked me if you could come to Judah on Wednesday morning, as she desperately wants to talk to you. If on that occasion you can greet my father and wish him well it will help him a lot. I know you won't be able to do that after you are married."

"Can you tell your father for me that, although I didn't listen to their advice, both my mother and Malka strongly urged me to marry him? Also, please tell Malka I will come to see her."

On Wednesday, Machla walked to Judah and Malka was waiting for her in Machla's old tent.

"I was sad to hear of your decision but I understand the pressure you were under. I pray that you will be happy."

"We bless God for the good as well as the evil. The evil is our test, and the good is our reward."

"I have always envied your unshakable faith."

"With my own eyes I saw the sea split and with my own ears I heard the word of God at Sinai. Why should I not believe?"

"What shall I do about Achituv, Machla? He is frightened of me. I find it hard to play dumb."

"You should never do that. If a man loves you, he will be proud of your knowledge. Achituv has many years of study ahead of him, but someday he will be on the same level as you. Bide your time and have faith. By the way, where is Elchanan today?"

"You haven't heard the news?"

"What news?"

"Elchanan was appointed chief judge of the tribe of Judah and he is now presiding at the tribal court for the very first time."

"That really is wonderful news." In her heart she realized that Moses had listened to her and helped Elchanan offset his pain.

"By the way, the tribal council is meeting now. Come with me and you will be pleasantly surprised. They walked over to the large council tent and, as Machla entered, Caleb and all seventy-five of the Judean commanders rose to honor her. Machla realized at once that she had been lured to Judah for a special ceremony.

Caleb remained standing and the commanders took their seats. "I have before me a council resolution honoring Machla, the daughter of Zelaphchad, for her learning and faith and service to the Tribe of Judah for nine full years. All in favor say 'yes.'"

There was a loud roar of approval.

"We can never repay Machla for the Torah she taught our daughters and the teachers she trained to spread the word of the Lord. The Torah mentions her name three separate times and all future generations will herald her from afar. We in Judah can offer praise to her directly. Although God will surely bless her for her efforts, we wish to show her our own appreciation in a small way. Machla, will you please come forward."

Machla walked to the front area of the tent where Caleb handed her an embroidered purse. The purse seemed only a small gift and she had no qualms about accepting it. When she lifted it casually, it was so heavy that it fell from her hand.

"What's in it?" she cried in alarm.

"A few pieces of silver, I'm sure," said Caleb.

"I can't accept money for teaching Torah."

"You are not being paid for the Torah instruction. You are being rewarded to a very small degree for administrative work and non-instructional activity. You have my permission to accept it."

Machla took the purse and made a short statement. "From the bottom of my heart, I thank the council for this tribute. The council owes me very little for my toil because I worked for the glory of heaven. The debt I owe the members of the council is far greater. They gave me the opportunity to teach the word of God. They advanced the status of Hebrew women more than any other tribe. The spirit of Torah will live in the homes of Judah. Both the mothers and the fathers in the tribe will be able to transmit the Torah to future generations.

"I want to thank the council for its support and express my gratitude to the president and legal advisor who supervised my efforts. Above all, I wish to thank my students, among whom is the new Drector of Women's Education in Judah. The trust they put in me was crucial to my success. They have made us all proud. May God bless the tribe of Judah and all the tribes of Israel with Torah and good deeds. May we all live to see our nation in the Land of Canaan, Amen."

There was a loud burst of applause as she walked back to her place holding the purse in her hand. She returned to her tent with Malka and waited for Elchanan. He came out during a court recess and greeted her warmly. "I am sorry I missed the presentation and your response, but I am glad that you received your well-deserved recognition."

"I thank you, Elchanan, for I know that you had a hand in it. When I present you with gifts they are of plain cloth. Yours are of pure silver. Elchanan, I seek your forgiveness once more for breaking my vow to you and causing you great pain." Machla was nervous in his presence, but Elchanan was now more reconciled to his fate. "I hope that you will find some measure of comfort in your new position as chief judge of the Judean court."

"I did not know that I would see you today. I was summoned to Moses yesterday to talk about the position of chief judge. The first thing he asked me was whether I had forgiven you, and I answered that I had with all my heart. He told me that in Egypt the people enjoyed only seven good years while I had ten. He advised me to store the memories of the good years to offset the lean ones. I shall follow his advice."

"God bless you, Elchanan, you have lifted a heavy weight from my heart."

Tearfully, Machla bade Elchanan farewell. After carefully tieing her purse within her robe, she walked back home.

Elchanan worked until late in the evening on the court calendar and other aspects of his new position. The children were asleep, but Batya stood at the tent entrance waiting. She had fixed her hair and donned her best robe. There was a look of contentment and happy anticipation on her face. She bowed to him and said, "My deepest respects to his exalted honor, the chief judge of the Tribe of Judah."

"I thank my loyal subject. If I don't get something to eat I will hold you in contempt of court."

"Fear not, your dinner is waiting. I hope that your new position will give you a better outlook on life. By the way, what did you have to promise Moses to get the appointment?"

"I had to agree to fully forgive Machla for deserting me."

"If you got the position, I assume that you forgave her. Was it the offer of a position that prompted you to make such a noble gesture?"

"It was not the offer of a position that prompted me nor even the second part of the blessing. I did it because Machla meant me no harm and was forced into her decision by powers she couldn't resist."

"What was the second part of the blessing?"

"Nothing much. I think Moses wanted to do something for you to make up for your pain."

Batya looked at him in disbelief. "What could make up for ten years of pain?"

"Thirty years of happiness. Moses promised us a daughter who would be specially blessed and guarded by angels while she grew up."

"Thank God. There could be nothing more valuable. By the way, did Moses say how this child would be conceived? Will it happen in the natural way or will some angel come while I am sleeping and insert the seed in my womb?"

"In all cases where the Torah mentions a Divine promise to a woman that she will have a child, the conception proceeds in the natural way."

"I hope you still remember how to go about it, Elchanan. It has been such a long time."

"I am sure you will refresh my memory, my dear."

"Who gets to name the child?"

"I do. This one I earned through great sacrifice."

"You can give her any name but Machla. I don't want you picking her up and saying 'I love you, Machla.' You might be thinking of the wrong one."

"In view of your fears, she won't be named Machla," Elchanan said with a smile on his face.

"Achla is out as well. It is too close."

"I have chosen the name, Yedida."

"That is truly a beautiful name. Now that we have settled that matter, there is only one other problem. What are you going to do with Machla's cloth? Hang it over our bed?"

"No, my dear, although I would enjoy looking at it on rare occasions."

"I will not destroy your mementos, but they can not go on permanent display either. We will work something out. Now it's time for your refresher course."

On the last day of the ninth month, Machla went to the Mikva again, in anticipation of her marriage. At noon the next day, she stood in the Tribal Center of Menashe wearing her beautiful wedding dress. Achla and her students had done magnificent work in preparing the gown. In the presence of half of the tribe of Menashe, Eliav slowly intoned: "Behold, thy art betrothed to me with this ring according to the laws of Moses and Israel." This new method of betrothal was now considered an acceptable alternative to a written document in sanctifying a woman as a wife.

The witnesses were Joshua Ben Nun and Elazar, the High Priest. The dancing featured more than 1,000 young girls from the Torah schools of Judah. It was by far the most spectacular wedding in the annals of the tribe of Menashe. After the wedding, Machla lost no time in bequeathing her half of her tent to Noah and moving in with Eliav.

"Free at last," Noah said. "I am free at last."

Three months later, in a very quiet ceremony, Tirza married Chemlon.

Meir and Noah spent a lot of time together talking and studying. Noah was really trying to reform, but she found it very hard. "If I have to be up and dressed by half past seven each morning for much longer, I will have to abandon the arrangement," she pleaded with Machla. "It is inhuman to get up that early and I don't look my best in the morning."

"I'll see what I can do," Machla said.

She spoke to Meir that afternoon and said, "Meir, you know that the Torah prohibits cruelty to living things?"

"Of course, I do."

"Noah is a living thing, isn't she?"

"I would say so. The Torah was specifically referring to animals, but cruelty to humans is forbidden under the commandment of love thy neighbor."

"Can you love Noah a little bit and let her start studying an hour later?"

"The starting time was originally your idea, but I did agree that one should get up early to serve his Father in heaven as our ancestor Abraham did."

"You don't want to lose her?"

"No, Machla, not after all that I have invested. I love her very much. She can start one hour later. No more."

Noah thanked Machla, profusely. "You have saved my life."

On the first day of the eleventh month, Machla and Eliav attended Dina's wedding in the tribe of Judah. Elchanan looked well and Batya was radiant. "Mazel Tov on your daughter's wedding," Machla said to her. "You are looking extremely well."

"I have good reason to. Aside from having Elchanan to myself, I am with child. Elchanan is happy in his new position and he is looking forward to the new arrival with great anticipation."

"That is wonderful news. I cannot be absolutely certain about my condition, but I have reason to feel that I, too, am pregnant."

"As usual, you never waste much time. How is Dodi?"

"She sends her best regards."

Machla was also able to exchange greetings with Elchanan but only briefly.

The long odyssey of the children of Israel was rapidly drawing to a close. On the seventh day of the twelfth month, Moses convened the entire nation to bid farewell to his flock. In his final messages he appointed Joshua to succeed him. He also recited a song that was so beautiful that many listeners could not hold back their tears.[4]

Machla told her sisters that the refusal by the Almighty to allow Moses to enter the Promised Land was due in large part to the stubbornness of the children of Israel. "He was denied that which he most desired because of our sins."

Achla quietly added, "Your late father also paid for the sins of others. But from his vantage in heaven, he knows that there will be a Zelaphchad on his land in Canaan. That will delight his soul."

That very day, Moses, the servant of God, ascended Mount Nebo, overlooking the Land of Canaan. From afar, he viewed the land that was destined to be the home of the children of Israel. He had led his people to the very brink of the Promised Land, but he would not be privileged to bring them onto its soil. His earlier appeals on this matter had been rejected, and he accepted the heavenly verdict with grace. On Mount Nebo, Moses was called to his eternal rest and the children of Israel mourned him for thirty days.[5]

On the tenth day of the first month of the forty-first year, the waters of the Jordan River parted and the children of Israel crossed the border of the Land of Canaan on the dry river bed. As soon as she was on the other side, Machla knelt and kissed the soil of the Holy Land, setting an example for her sisters to follow.

Achla gathered her daughters and said to them, "I was privileged to dance with Miriam at the Sea of Reeds and now I want to dance at the Jordan." Her daughters danced with her and sang hymns of praise to the Lord. Others joined with them in a mood of intense joy. The participants sensed that the Almighty had redeemed His promise to the children of Israel that He would deliver them to the Land of Canaan.[6]

A few days later, the manna stopped falling. Noah was elated that she wouldn't have to listen to her sisters telling her how hard they worked gathering the manna for her.

"Growing wheat and baking bread is much harder," Machla warned her.

"That may be true," she answered, "but it can be done much later in the day."

After the first Passover in Canaan, the Israelites began the conquest of the country in earnest. For seven days, a contingent of Hebrews circled the city of Jericho and sounded their horns. On the seventh day, they circled the walls seven times. The entire nation then shouted in a mighty voice and the walls of the city came tumbling down.[7]

The last time that Machla saw Elchanan was at the national convocation between the mountains of Gerizim and Eival near the city of Shechem. The tribe of Menashe stood near the tribe of Judah and Machla greeted Elchanan and Batya. Batya was in her eighth month and Machla was a month or so behind.[8]

"Farewell," she whispered to him, "I will never forget you."

"You were the best part of my life," he responded. "You will live in my heart forever."

It would be almost twenty years before they would see each other again.

Malka was successful in her romantic pursuit and married Achituv at a lavish wedding. She continued her educational work while Achituv studied at a higher Yeshiva. Machla was hoping to attend the wedding but, just as the wedding was taking place, she delivered a beautiful baby boy. At the circumcision ceremony, Achla conveyed the baby to Haniel, who held the boy while Meir performed the circumcision. Meir then bestowed the Hebrew name on the child. "Let his name in Israel be called Zelaphchad, the son of Machla, the daughter of Zelaphchad, and her husband, Eliav, the son of Shafat."

Not long thereafter, Hogla and Milka got married. From among the proposals Hogla received, she chose a widowed judge by the name of Shimron. Milka got married next in the Land of Canaan to a single commander who was only thirty years old. When Noah chided her for robbing the cradle, Milka responded that her husband, Yaman, felt that a daughter of Zelaphchad at any age was worth more than five women of eighteen. Noah suggested that she check her husband's mental health.

On the eve of her fortieth birthday, Noah and Meir got married. On the morning after the wedding, she slept till ten. Turning over in bed she asked Meir, who was up and around, "Are we officially married?"

"Yes, dear. You don't have to get up early anymore."

"I'm glad I married a man who understands women," she said, and went back to sleep.

Part 4

IN CANAAN

CHAPTER

SIXTEEN

"THE JOURNEY TO BETHLEHEM"

In the waning moments of daylight, the large wagon slowly approached the home of Machla and Eliav. Its wide wheels cut sharp tracks in the gravel as the driver reined his team of horses to a halt, directly in front of the main entrance. Machla had spotted the wagon from afar and marveled at its appearance. By her appraisal, it was the property of a man of great wealth. She couldn't recall ever seeing anything like it in central Canaan. The members of her tribe eked out a living tending sheep, supplemented by grain farming and a few cows here and there. Expensive wagons, of course, were well beyond their means. Transportation, when required, took the form of open-air carts drawn by donkeys.

It was still warm in the Dothan Valley, although the heat of day had broken and the sun was sinking in the west. Passover had come and gone and, with it, the last of the winter rains. The skies would remain clear until the fall, while the weather would get intensely hot. Summer in the valleys of Canaan was not a pleasant time, so Machla was determined to enjoy the beautiful springtime as long as it lasted.

The driver of the wagon was surely not its owner. He was a tall, lanky man, dressed in simple work clothes. Rough hands and a weather-beaten face identified him as a man who had spent his years in manual labor. Machla peered around his tall frame looking for passengers in the wagon but there were none. There were only empty benches, richly upholstered, and a few supply baskets.

"Shalom," Machla called, as she caught his attention. "Welcome to Dothan. Is there anyone you came to see, or are you just passing through?"

The driver descended from his perch and greeted her. "I truly hope that I have arrived at my destination. My name is Elgar and I work for Elchanan ben Uriah of Bethlehem. He sent me to deliver a letter to Machla, daughter of Zelaphchad, and await her reply."

Upon hearing the name Elchanan ben Uriah, Machla turned pale. Vivid images, suppressed for many years, flashed through her mind and painful memories surfaced. Twenty eventful years had passed since the national convocation near Shechem when he had bidden her farewell with great sadness in his voice. There had been no communication between them over the next two decades, although now and then she heard his name mentioned by travelers coming from the south. Quite famous in judicial circles, he served with distinction as the chief judge of the tribal court of Judah. He was certainly aware that she had a child because she was visibly pregnant when they parted ways. Whether he had any further knowledge of the son she bore, or of the daughter who arrived two years later, she had no way of knowing.

"I am the Machla you seek," she said, when she regained her composure. "I knew your master well many years ago. How is he? Does he still preside at court?"

Elgar hesitated and sighed. "He withdrew from the court a few months ago due to his poor health and he is very much in need of Divine mercy. I am sure that the letter I have for you will shed more light on the matter."

Elgar was pleased that Machla was looking well and appeared physically fit. He did not tell her himself that what was in store for her was a long and tedious journey, but he sensed that she would be capable of making it. He carefully opened the pouch he was carrying and handed her a rolled parchment. Her hands trembled as she undid the seal and glanced at words in Torah script obviously written by a scholar. She knew instinctively that bad news was forthcoming, because no one wasted parchment on happy events. Written notices were reserved for unpaid loans and bills and records of dire events. Her spirits, which had been high throughout the late spring day, sagged rapidly. Her heart sank as she grasped the full import of the message and tears of grief flowing from her eyes fell on her linen robe.

With the Help of God
The first day of the second month

Dear Machla,

The Lord who has been my shepherd from my youth unto
this day, is now writing the final chapter in my life. He has
stricken me with a severe illness and I am confined to bed
much of the time. Even my doctors can no longer hide the
fact from me that my days on earth are numbered.

I have no complaints to the Almighty, for He has
granted me, more than most others, spiritual blessings
and material wealth. Nevertheless, I feel that I must
resolve certain urgent matters before my end comes. I
also wish to atone for any sins that I may have committed
against my fellow men and seek their forgiveness so that I
may meet my Creator with a clear conscience.

Machla, I beg you to come see me as soon as possible
and bring with you, your beloved son, Zelaphchad. My
trusted employee, Elgar, has been instructed to assist you
in every way possible and drive you to my estate in the
wagon that I have sent. When you wish to return, he will
take you home.

With undying respect,
Elchanan

After rereading the letter, Machla wiped the tears from her eyes and fell into
deep thought. She was intrigued by the possibility of seeing Elchanan once
again. Such a visit would be an act of kindness, she rationalized, although Eliav
might view it in a somewhat different light. She turned to Elgar, who was
anxiously awaiting her reply. "This is a matter of great moment, Elgar. I can not
give you an immediate answer. My husband is in the field with my son penning
the sheep. He may object to my going on grounds of propriety or for some other
reasons. Also, my son, who studies Torah with his teacher each night, may not
wish to interrupt his sessions. My heart tells me to go but I must secure
consent."

Elgar understood her cautious approach and was pleased that the invitation was not rejected out of hand.

"Listen, Elgar," she continued. "You have been on the road for a number of days and must be very tired. Let my daughter, Tovah, help you with the horses while I finish preparing the evening meal. After dinner, I will discuss the matter privately with my husband. In one way or another, you will have your answer by tomorrow morning. We have an extra room in our house where you can stay until the question is resolved."

Elgar was relieved by her words. Her desire to go was now quite clear to him and, from all that he had heard about Machla, it was a very promising sign. She was known to be strong-willed and extremely persuasive.

"I thank you for your kind words and your gracious offer of hospitality. I urge you with all my heart to do this act of kindness for my master who is a righteous man, and who deserves to meet his Maker with peace of mind. He told me not to pressure you for a quick reply, but simply to remind you that his condition is serious and there is not much time to spare."

"I understand that quite well," Machla replied. "There will be no unnecessary delay." She called her daughter outside to meet their guest. When introductions were completed, she told Tovah that Elgar would be staying overnight. Tovah did not question her mother's invitation to a stranger as hospitality was frequently extended at her home, in keeping with the importance that the Torah attached to the practice. She guided Elgar to the barn and showed him the stalls where the horses could rest. Elgar parked the wagon and unyoked the horses. Tovah, in turn, drew the water and prepared the feed. Elgar thanked her profusely for her help. He noticed that while she was a very attractive girl of seventeen, she was not in the least pampered. She was used to heavy work on the farm, and her appearance reflected outdoor toil. As Elgar tended to his animals, Tovah took his parcels to the house and placed them in the room he would occupy.

Machla prepared the dinner with great dispatch. Although she was already well into her sixties and her hair had turned gray, she was quite spry and energetic. She now left the heavy farm work to her husband and children but she still managed the household. Her figure was trim and her face had the bronzed look of the farm women of Canaan.

"Mother," Tovah said, when she saw the table set as if for a festive Sabbath meal, "Aren't you overdoing the welcome a little? Our guest is only a wagon driver, not one of the angels who were served a lavish meal when they visited our father, Abraham."

Machla answered with characteristic patience. "Tovah, you know that all men are created in the image of God and must be treated as equals. Nevertheless, we are instructed to extend preferential treatment to the wise and elderly. Elgar is the representative of his master, a great and learned judge, about whom you will someday hear at length. In showing extra respect for the servant, I am, in effect, honoring the master."[1]

Somewhat chastened, Tovah helped her mother prepare the food. When Elgar returned from the barn, she showed him to his room and gave him a basin of water and towels for his personal needs. Elgar thanked her and said that he would return shortly. The room where the dinner was to be served was an all-purpose room to the right of the main entrance to the home. Behind it was a kitchen, with a side door leading to a storage area for logs and water. The main bedroom chamber was to the left of the entrance. There being no central hall, members of the family had to walk through the main room and kitchen to get to the two small bedrooms and spare room in the back. The children had a rear entrance which they could use when they wanted to avoid walking through the kitchen.

While Elgar was washing and changing for dinner, Eliav and Zelaphchad, returned from the fields. Eliav always felt a sense of pride when he entered his home because he had built it with his own hands. The walls of the home were made of stone. To span the area between the walls, he had used timber which was abundant in the vicinity. Some families used brick arches for the ceilings but Eliav had neither the patience nor the resources for such construction. To make the roof watertight, he filled in the spaces around the timbers with clay and mortar. Water for the needs of the family and the livestock was drawn from a well. Winter rainwater was saved to the fullest extent possible but, when the rains were insufficient, the grain crops did not flourish. Although Eliav had worked hard that day, he made a special effort to be alert and attentive at dinner time. He had taught his children that family meals were an important part of the human experience and a time for bonding. He had excellent rapport with his children, and they confided freely in him. Zelaphchad spent many hours working together with him and appreciated his father's guidance.

Once inside the house, Eliav noticed the well-set table and the special foods. "We're having company?" he asked Machla in surprise. "I don't remember you telling me anything about visitors."

"There is only a single guest and he arrived unexpectedly. While he himself is only a messenger, he comes with urgent tidings from someone you know very well. Our visitor, Elgar, is the foreman of Elchanan ben Uriah of Bethlehem. He was sent to deliver me a letter personally written by his master."

"Elchanan ben Uriah? A handwritten letter?" Eliav wondered aloud. "It has been ages since I last saw him. Is there something wrong? Has some evil befallen him?"

Machla fought to hold back her tears. "The letter contains grievous tidings. Please read it yourself." She handed him the unrolled parchment. Eliav read it slowly, silently. He read Hebrew fairly well, albeit not with the same facility as Machla.

"Sad news indeed," he said after a long interval of silence. "Elchanan cannot be much more than sixty-five and he has so much to live for. I recently heard that he declined another invitation to sit on the High Court. He apparently prefers to be the chief judge of a tribal court instead of being a junior judge among seventy." After another pause he asked Machla, "What are your intentions with regard to his invitation? Do you plan to see him?"

"It's a very delicate subject and I have not thought the matter through as yet," she replied. "If it be acceptable to you, Eliav, I would like to discuss the matter privately in our chamber after dinner. I indicated to Elgar that I would have an answer for him early in the morning."

Eliav did not mind putting off the matter until after dinner because he was one who enjoyed total relaxation at meal times. He worked very hard maintaining his property and livestock. Although he was younger than Machla, age was beginning to creep up on him. Despite his burdens, he was a cheerful man who greeted everyone with a smile. Even though farm work kept him trim, a slight stoop and a small paunch reflected the passing years.

Elgar joined the family in the main room and Tovah helped Machla serve dinner. During the meal, he had a chance to study Zelaphchad closely. The boy was tall and well built. He resembled his mother, but lacked her poise and polish. Not sure of what Machla's children knew about his master, Elgar did not go into great detail about him. He did report that Batya was in good health, albeit totally devastated by her husband's illness. She was constantly at his bedside and personally tended to his needs. She was fully aware of the letter he was carrying and subscribed wholeheartedly to the invitation. When Machla asked him about Elchanan's children — four of whom she knew by name — Elgar related that all of those children were married and doing quite well. Among them they had already produced sixteen grandchildren. He then added that Elchanan had another child, a daughter, who was born in Canaan before Elchanan had established his residence in Bethlehem. She was the only one of his children not yet married.

"What is her name?" Machla asked.

"Her name is Yedida. She just turned nineteen and is a very beautiful young woman."

After dinner, Zelaphchad left to study with his teacher in the nearby village. He wondered about the well known judge who was the subject of much conversation at the table. He did not know how the judge was connected to his family, but he suspected that it was somehow related to the famous law cases in the Torah that involved the daughters of Zelaphchad. His maternal grandfather was the Zelaphchad cited in the Torah and he knew that his parents had named him after his grandfather. In the village elementary school, the teacher devoted much time to the Torah passages which told of the Hebrew inheritance laws. These laws were modified following an appeal by his mother and her sisters but their scope was restricted after a counter appeal initiated by his uncle and teacher.

Zelaphchad knew that if he were to leave home and study in a large city, he would enjoy special attention as the son of biblical figures. Here, in the village, it meant little that several sections of the Torah were devoted to his family, because the students in the school were all related. The cousins on his mother's side shared in the distinction that their mothers' names were written three separate times in the Torah. His paternal cousins did not enjoy quite the same honor, but even they were proud of the fact that their relatives were mentioned several times as a group, in a section of the Torah devoted entirely to their case.

After reaching the age of thirteen, Zelaphchad completed the elementary school and continued studying with a private teacher engaged by his mother. His tutor, Meir, was Machla's brother-in-law and cousin. Since Meir was not disposed to work full-time at farming, he augmented his income by teaching privately and performing religious functions. The services which he rendered included circumcision of male children and ritual slaughter of animals and fowl. For more than six years he had been teaching Zelaphchad.

Many of Zelaphchad's friends worked full-time and no longer received formal religious instruction. Zelaphchad worked only part of the day, even during harvest seasons and other busy periods. The rest of the time he studied Torah. His mother taught him occasionally and he enjoyed those periods immensely. It was only recently that he had came to realize how well-versed she was in Torah. Far more than his father or teacher, his mother knew how the elders of Israel understood the intent of the Written Law. She instilled in him a love for the Oral Law without which, she claimed, the Written Law could not be properly observed.

The time his mother could devote to him was limited by her need to teach his sister, Tovah. Girls in the tribe of Menashe were not admitted to the lower schools and men would not deign to teach them privately. In the entire tribe, only a handful of women were educated. Machla and her sisters were the exceptions. Since her sisters all had daughters of their own to educate, Machla had no alternative but to dedicate virtually all of her spare time to Tovah's religious training.

Zelaphchad did not know how long he would continue his studies. Occasionally, there was talk of his leaving home to study in a Yeshiva in the south where most of the academies were to be found. He did not think that his parents had the resources to support such a venture. There was also the problem of his being an only son. His parents had married at an advanced age and it would not be long before they would need him to manage the extensive family property. A stay in the Yeshiva, however, would lead to qualification as a judge or teacher. If he pursued such a vocation afterwards, he would find it hard to be able to devote sufficient time to farming.

Tovah cleaned up after the meal and went outside for a brief stroll before returning to her room for study and prayers. Elgar retired to his room where he quickly fell asleep. It had been an arduous trip from Bethlehem and he faced a long journey back. He did not detect any hostility in Eliav and was encouraged by his warm and friendly attitude. He had had grave doubts about the mission when he embarked upon it, but now he was more hopeful. It seemed that his master, Elchanan, had correctly gauged the depth of feeling that Machla had for him and, in retrospect, the mission appeared quite reasonable.

Machla, carrying a lit candle, entered the bedroom and sat down on the bed. Eliav followed behind her and sat down on a nearby chair. They were a couple who communicated frankly and openly, especially when the matters concerned their children.

"Eliav," she began, "I need your advice and understanding. Elchanan ben Uriah is the man who helped me and my sisters achieve success. To him I owe my place in history and the property that I inherited. My sisters likewise owe their status to him. He sought only one reward for his efforts on my behalf and that I denied him. I do not regret my decision to marry you instead of him, but I am saddened that I caused him such pain and anguish. In all these years that we have been together, I have been faithful to you. I have given you my love and affection and have been a loyal wife. Never did I mention the name Elchanan in your presence or in the presence of the children. They are totally unaware of the role that he played in my life.

"I feel in my heart that it is my duty to see him before he dies. I don't know why he speaks of sins and forgiveness, for it was I who sinned against him and broke my troth. Perhaps he may have information for me that he withheld all these years. It may be that he just wants to reexamine the moments in his life that changed the course of Hebrew history. I will never know unless I make the visit."

"You are a compassionate woman, Machla, and that is why you judge Elchanan with undue kindness. I don't for a moment deny that Elchanan helped you in your case, but you underestimate your own role. It was your actions that won it for you and any competent lawyer could have done what Elchanan did. I know that he didn't charge for his efforts, but I always felt that he worked more for the love of you than for his belief in the cause. I assure you that he hasn't put you out of his mind for a single moment in all these years. His heart aches for you and he dreams of seeing you. He cannot bear leaving this world without one final look, without once again hearing your voice. What is more important, is that he does not want you to forget him after he is gone. I really feel that it would not be proper for you, a married woman, to acquiesce in such desires."

"Jealousy is warping your judgement," Machla quickly retorted with a trace of anger in her voice, "No doubt Elchanan still cares for me but time heals the pain of unrequited love for men of faith and intelligence. He has his work, his family, his scholarship and, believe me, lust will not emerge in the shadow of death. If my presence will ease the pain of his final moments, I would never forgive myself if I ignored his plea.

"Eliav, in all other matters you respect my judgment without hesitation and, in my acts of charity and service, you have given me a free hand. I will not go without your blessing but I plead with you to bestow it upon me. I knew Elchanan as a man of integrity and honor. You have absolutely no cause to be concerned."

Eliav mulled over his wife's words. Very quickly the realization set in that Machla felt a moral obligation to go. Whenever she reached such a decision there was no stopping her. That was the story of her life and success. Offering any further resistance would be futile. Nor was there any question of Machla's loyalty to him. She had never let him feel that she married him under duress or that he was her second choice. She treated him reverently and made him feel loved and wanted.

Eliav tried to ease the tension. "I can understand why he summoned you, Machla, but what makes him want to see Zelaphchad?"

To that Machla replied, "I have no doubts about that. Elchanan is a wealthy man and I venture to say that he will bestow some gift upon our son. He knows that I would accept nothing from him so he will try to bestow his favors indirectly. Surely you would not want to deprive our son of a substantial benefit?"

The conversation lasted for another half an hour, but it was all after the fact, the issue having already been decided. The discussion focused on details of the trip and the preparations that had to be made for Machla's extended absence. Before leaving the bedroom, Machla kissed her husband in gratitude. The long, passionate embrace, signaled that more of the same would be forthcoming when the pair retired for the night.[2]

"We are going," Machla announced to Elgar when she saw him in the morning.

"God be blessed," he responded instinctively. "You are doing the right thing and my master will be pleased. I already have taken care of the horses this morning and we are prepared to leave as soon as you are ready."

"Wait a minute. Not so fast, please. It's Tuesday morning and I know that we must be there before the Sabbath. Still, it will take us a few hours to make arrangements here and we will have to make several stops along the way. Let me get you some breakfast. While we eat, we can plan the journey. I also have to let my children in on the news." Machla turned and went to the back rooms used by her son and daughter.

Zelaphchad was already awake when she entered. It was a small room but it meant a lot to him. With only two children, Machla had the luxury of giving each child an individual room, not the usual practice in an area of large families and small homes. Her son was a hard-working boy, and his parents had no complaints about him. His combined program of study and work was very taxing, but he never voiced any objection to it. Although Machla would have liked to converse with him, there was no time for casual conversation that morning.

"I have good news, son, something you've been waiting to do all your life. You and I are going for a trip to the south and you will be able to see all the places that you learned about: the mountains of Ephraim, the Tomb of Rachel, the Judean hills and, above all, much of the beautiful land that God has given the children of Israel."

It took a moment for Zelaphchad to grasp the news, for he had no reason to expect a trip in the spring. The only traveling he ever did, were his holiday pilgrimages. These observances were now taking place in the holy city of Shilo after the Tent of Meeting had been moved there from the area of "Gilgal." Annually, or every other year, the family visited the religious centers located in the neighboring tribe of Ephraim. The route taken by the pilgrims avoided Shechem, so Zelaphchad never saw the towering mountains of Gerizim and Eival. As for the south, he had never been there. The historic cities of Bethlehem and Hebron were known to him only from his studies.

"When are we going and how are we traveling?"

"We are leaving before noon in Elgar's wagon. Get up now, say your prayers and pack your best clothes." So saying, Machla left the room and walked across the hall to tell her daughter the news. Tovah was quite perceptive in such matters and showed less surprise than her brother when she heard about the trip.

"I would love to come along, mother. Do I stand a chance?"

"Not really, dear. Firstly, you weren't invited. Secondly, someone has to stay here and look after your father. But don't worry, we should be back late next week."

At breakfast, Machla discussed her planned itinerary with Elgar. "We have to stop in the village of Dothan and let my sister and her husband know about the trip. Meir is Zelaphchad's teacher and he has to be advised that his pupil will be away for some time. With my sister, Noah, I have to discuss a personal problem. When we leave Dothan, we can head straight for Shechem and spend the night at an inn. In the morning, we must stop at the Tomb of Joseph and offer prayers. From there we will proceed to Shilo and stay over. Thursday, after services at the Tabernacle, we will head directly for Bethlehem. How does that sound to you?"[3]

"We can manage to do all that if you so wish. It would be easier, of course, to enter the hilly country well below Shechem, but the difference is not overly significant. I cannot guarantee that we will make Bethlehem on Thursday, however. We're talking about a long distance and the hills are steep. It may also be necessary to spend Thursday night at an inn."

"I do not wish to forego Shilo even if it means an additional night on the road. My son and I will be ready to start the trip before noon." With everyone helping, the family packed and loaded all the bags on the wagon. Eliav kissed Machla farewell and bid her Godspeed. Machla then fondly hugged Tovah in a loving embrace. Before entering the wagon, she gave her daughter some last minute instructions, mostly about the meals that she would have to prepare for her father and other chores that she would have to perform. After she was seated in her place, Zelaphchad climbed in and sat down opposite his mother. When the passengers signaled their readiness, Elgar started the horses and the journey was underway.

Elgar knew the way to Dothan but needed Zelaphchad's help to find Meir's house. Noah was out in front of the house feeding the chickens when the wagon pulled up. She was still the liveliest of Machla's sisters. In her serious moments, which were few and far between, she displayed intelligence and Torah knowledge second only to Machla. Her marriage to Meir had even helped her narrow the gap somewhat between her and her oldest sister.

All in all, Noah was a remarkably beautiful woman even at the age of fifty-eight. She made sure never to allow work to compromise her good looks. Although there was just a six year age difference between her and Machla, she looked considerably younger. The work she did with the fowl was about the only serious effort she made to labor on her farm. The original birds were bought from a camel driver coming from the east and she managed to breed them successfully. She gave each chicken a name and conversed with them as she fed them.

Elgar stopped and helped Machla down from the side ladder. Seeing her alight, Noah's mouth opened wide in surprise. "Machla, you must have discovered gold on the farm. Did you dig it up or did you find a Canaanite treasure chest? What a wagon! What a handsome driver!"

"Quiet Noah. Calm yourself. Neither the wagon nor the driver are mine. Gold? On my farm there are only rocks. Finish your work with the chickens and come inside. Better yet, let Zelaphchad feed them for you while we talk. I hope Meir is in because I have to speak to both of you."

"Meir is in the village but I can send David to get him. You must be going for an important trip. Tell me about it."

When they were sitting alone in Noah's main room, Machla brought her sister up to date. "I can not believe that Eliav agreed to the trip." Noah said. "You must have promised him the moon. But why go in the first place? What do you have to gain?"

"I am going because a dying man that I deeply respect has asked me to do him a kindness. Perhaps I will tell him again that I appreciate what he did for me and ask him once more to forgive me for what I did to him."

"I should have let you marry him if you still feel that way about him after twenty years. Listen to me, Machla, this trip is an exercise in stupidity. I know that you won't change your mind but I have to tell you anyway. You are going to walk into Elchanan's estate and your eyes will pop out of your head. Hand woven carpets on the floor, panels of wood and gold, maids and servants everywhere. I happen to know that Elchanan is very prosperous. Here you stand in your best clothes and you still look like a pauper. And what about your face? You no longer are the royal beauty of the desert. Twenty years of toil have left their mark on you and all you have to show for it are rough hands and wrinkles. Meanwhile, Elchanan has treated Batya like a queen. She has been pampered and waited upon hand and foot. She will be delighted to see you in your shape."

"I am not going with the intent of showing myself off," Machla protested. "You know that material gifts have never been important to me and, even in that regard, I have no reason to complain. I have my land, my home, my family. I want for nothing important. Batya is a noble woman who will not gloat about her wealth. In any event, it is Elchanan who sent for me and he, as the letter states, is on his death bed."

"Don't you want him to remember you as you were?"

"At this point it hardly matters. What's important is that I remember him as he was. Nothing will ever make me forget that." By now Meir had returned from the village and Noah quickly briefed him on the latest developments.

"Well, if you are going anyway, what advice are you seeking from us?"

"I stopped by to tell you and Meir that Zelaphchad will be missing his lessons for at least the next ten days. But, of far more importance, is the fact that I need your advice on a very sensitive matter."

"You hardly ever ask anyone anything, Machla, so it must be a real problem."

"It truly is. As you know, Zelaphchad will be meeting Elchanan for the first time. In all of his nineteen years, I never once mentioned the man's name to him and never told him anything about the details of our case. He doesn't even know that an Elchanan exists. I am not sure that it was right for me to withhold the information, but I did it to protect Eliav. Somehow I felt that Zelaphchad would not respect his father as much if he knew that I loved another man."

"I doubt whether that would have happened. Zelaphchad loves his father very much, and I don't think that his feelings would have been any different if he knew about your past. Of course, it might have changed his regard for you."

"What do you mean by that?"

"What I mean is that he would have seen you in a much better light. Right now you probably impress him as a straight-laced saint without any emotional depth. Perhaps, if he knew the story of your life, you would seem more human in his eyes, more fallible, a little more fragile. Eliav is an earthy man. He loves to drink and tell stories and liven things up. Maybe your image could stand some tarnishing. What do you think, Meir?

Meir spoke thoughtfully. He was still a very restrained man whose personality was in sharp contrast to Noah's vivacity. He spent an increasing amount of time studying and teaching Torah. "Zelaphchad is a mature young man already. His character and personality will not change on the basis of these disclosures. I feel that you should tell him everything, Machla, so that he will get the story firsthand and not from anyone else. He has already started asking me questions about the case, but I have not revealed more than was written in the Torah."

"I thank you both for your counsel and this time, for a change, it is close to my own conclusions. One thing still troubles me, though. How did Elchanan know that I had a son? When our ways parted, I had not yet given birth."

A touch of color began to enter Meir's otherwise pallid cheeks. "Tell her, Meir," Noah said, "because she will find out anyway." Meir spent a moment organizing his thoughts.

"I didn't say anything to you because I was afraid of upsetting you. As you know, I go for the holiday pilgrimage every Passover. About ten years ago, I met Elchanan at the Tabernacle and got into a conversation with him. He asked me about your health and that of your husband and children. I saw no reason to hide any information. Almost every year since then I met him and kept him posted. He showed particular interest in Zelaphchad. When I advised him that I was teaching the boy privately, he was even more pleased. He inquired thoroughly as to what he was learning and about the progress that he was making. He wanted to know how avid he was in his studies and the degree of his understanding. Of course, you know yourself that Zelaphchad is a superior student. I did not have to exaggerate at all."

"It makes me feel good to learn that Elchanan is still interested in me and my family. Perhaps I should have kept abreast of Elchanan, too, but that would have been contrary to the spirit of my pledge to Eliav."

"I can tell you that Elchanan is doing very well in his work. He came to the Tabernacle with his family and I spoke with his wife and daughter. Batya seems very happy and radiates contentment. The daughter is like a star in heaven. She takes after Elchanan and is the apple of his eye."

When Meir stopped speaking there was a long silence. Noah was expecting Meir to continue. When he didn't, she spoke up. "Tell her the rest of it, Meir. She has every right to know."

"I cannot do that," he answered. "Elchanan did not want Machla to know of it and I promised not to tell her."

"You may not be able to tell her, but I certainly can. The truth is that Elchanan presented Meir with a substantial purse each year that he was teaching your son. You know full well, Machla, that you pay Meir very little for the time that he puts in. What is more, you pay him now the same amount as you gave him six years ago, although the level of instruction is much higher and the time he devotes is much longer. Were it not for Elchanan's help, Meir would not be able to give Zelaphchad as much time as he does without asking you for a substantially higher fee."

Machla was stunned by the revelation. "I'm sorry, Meir," she finally said, "I didn't realize. What I pay you may not be much, but even that sum is hard for me to scrape together. Nevertheless, I would have managed to find the money somewhere. It is a sacred family duty to teach sons Torah and I am not happy that Elchanan paid for my obligation. Why didn't you tell me?"

"Time is short, Machla, and I will not waste it on polemics. Briefly, I feel that all higher religious education should be subsidized because most parents cannot afford to finance it by themselves. Too many children, both in the north and in the south, are growing up without Torah knowledge because of this problem.

"Elchanan is a wealthy man and, like others who have the means, he has been supporting Torah education for older students. He is within his rights to subsidize Zelaphchad and I saw no reason for me to reject his offering."

"Your ideas are essentially correct, Meir, but I am not sure of Elchanan's motivations in bestowing his largesse upon my son. I pray that he is not mocking me when doing so. We will continue this conversation further when I get back, but right now I must be on my way."

Machla returned to the wagon, called to Zelaphchad who was talking with his cousins and asked Elgar to get underway. She was going to use part of trip to tell her son the entire story of the daughters of Zelaphchad, but she would wait until the next morning before starting. She first wanted to pray at the Tomb of Joseph for guidance when unburdening herself to her son. The tomb was located in Shechem, where the remains of Joseph were laid to rest after traveling with the children of Israel in the desert for forty years.

Elgar's driving skills became apparent on the main roads. The horses pulled the wagon firmly and needed little control. The roads were quite dry, and the wagon was well enough upholstered to make the trip bearable. Machla was also familiar with the road, at least as far as Shechem, and she was able to point out highlights to Zelaphchad. There was a large concentration of families from Menashe who had settled on either side of the road. As she passed properties belonging to families she knew, she mentioned them to him, but she did not stop to greet anyone. She was determined to reach Shechem by sundown and avoid traveling after dark.

The road out of Dothan led almost due south. It veered slightly westward to avoid the higher elevations of the central mountains of Canaan. It was a good road and well traveled. Already in the days of Jacob, it served as the main caravan route to Egypt. Ishmaelites would travel from Gilead through Dothan, their camels laden with spices such as balsam and laudanum. In fact, it was one such caravan on its way south, whose drivers purchased Joseph from his brothers and resold him on the Egyptian slave market. Although Machla knew every detail of the history of Joseph, she relived the full story in her mind.[4]

When the road passed Shomron, it turned sharply eastward towards Shechem. The road was cut to pass between the two majestic mountains of Gerizim and Eival. Eival was due north of the city while Gerizim was to the south. Both mountains rose some 2,000 cubits in height.[5]

Machla remembered the time, some twenty years earlier, when she had stood with her tribe on Mount Gerizim and participated in a dramatic ritual ordained by Moses and carried out by Joshua, his successor. Her tribe had been among the six chosen to face Gerizim, while the six other tribes faced Eival. Levites, standing between the tribes, read a series of blessings and curses alternately to each group of tribes and the listeners answered, "Amen."[6]

It was Machla's first summer in the Promised Land. Although her pregnancy was well advanced, she stood motionless under a blistering sun until she heard the final passage, "Blessed are those who uphold the words of this Torah and abide by them." She was touched by this blessing most of all because it took the form of a broad clause that rewarded those who regarded the Torah as an indivisible unity and were not selective in their observance. Following the blessings, Machla went down to inspect the twelve stones which had the words of the Torah engraved upon them. Unlike many others, she was able to read the text fluently and identify each passage.[7]

"You were there, too, Zelaphchad. You may not have been born but you were in my womb and I consider that as being present." She described the national assembly to Zelaphchad in perfect detail, since the experience had left an indelible impression on her. Zelaphchad had learned of the event in his studies, but it was far more exciting to hear about it from his mother, who had participated in it. The hours passed quickly as she spoke to her son and by the time they drove through the outskirts of Shechem, the sun had already set. Elgar headed for an inn where he was able to secure two adjacent rooms. Machla had a room for herself and he shared one with Zelaphchad. All slept soundly because they were tired from their lengthy journey.

After breakfast, they returned to the wagon and began to travel in a more easterly direction. They went for only a parsang before reaching the base of Mount Gerizim, where there were two sacred sites. One was Jacob's Well. The other, in a grove of mulberry trees slightly north of the well, was the Tomb of Joseph. Joseph's remains were buried in the Land of Canaan in keeping with his instructions before his death. The site chosen for the internment was the plot of land purchased from the children of Shechem by Jacob, when he returned from his sojourn with Laban.[8]

Machla entered the tomb, kissed the bier and knelt in prayer. Her words were whispered but they were from the heart.

> "O', Joseph, our father, progenitor of the tribe of Ephraim and of my own tribe of Menashe, accept these words of prayer:
>
> "I, Machla, the daughter of Zelaphchad, from the village of Dothan where you were sold into slavery by your

brothers, have come to your holy resting place to beseech your blessing in these critical moments in my life.

"I pray you, as you sit before the heavenly throne in the presence of our sainted patriarchs, Abraham, Isaac and Jacob, implore the Creator of all mankind to answer these requests that I, a humble descendant of your tribe, address to Him.

"Be it Thy will, O' Lord, to provide a full measure of life, good health and happiness to me, my beloved husband, Eliav, my son, Zelaphchad, and my daughter, Tovah. Give them strength and courage to walk in Thy ways and heed the commandments of Thy Torah.

"Bestow the blessings of heaven on all the members of my tribe and all the children of Israel. May their fields drink of the dew of heaven and may the earth yield its fruits in abundance. Mayest Thou protect us from our enemies and cause us to live out our days in peace.

"I now pray to thee, O' Lord, on behalf of Elchanan ben Uriah who is at the door of death. Thou knowest that he is a pious man who has served Thee all his years with unbounded faith and total dedication. He taught many children the word of God. He brought peace and good will to men by judging them in fairness and honesty, as they stood before him in the courts of law.

"Heal him, O' Lord, from his dire illness and cause him once again to walk among his people and teach the word of God. Yet, if it be Thy will to bring his days on earth to an end, gather his soul to Thee without inflicting pain and suffering upon him. Let him experience the Divine kiss of death as did Thy servant, Moses, of blessed memory. If thou freest his body from agony, be it Thy will to do the same for his soul. Let him not feel pangs of conscience or guilt about any acts that he committed. Rather, let him die content in the knowledge that he was one who was able to propagate Thy word and fulfill Thy commandments proudly and heroically.

"I further pray that I may be of comfort to him in his final moments. Cause me not, however, to regret that I obeyed Thy will when I denied to him that which he so passionately desired. May my self-denial ever be considered by future generations as an act of sanctification of the Divine name.

"And now, if the gates of mercy are still open and I have not exceeded the limits of Divine favor, grant me these final requests.

"My son, Zelaphchad, stands at the threshold of manhood. A man is not complete without a woman to love and cherish, a wife with whom he can fulfill the Divine imperative to be fruitful and multiply. Help me find for Zelaphchad a bride who will share with him a life of Torah and good deeds. May she be the daughter of a scholarly man and possess a heart of wisdom and a soul of kindness. If she herself be versed in the Torah, so much the better. If not, let her love and respect my son for his knowledge of the law and his commitment to it. May she be as Rachel, the mother of Joseph, who, together with her sister, Leah, built the house of Israel.[9]

"Lastly, bestow upon me the gift of eloquence so that I may relate to my son the true and complete story of the daughters of Zelaphchad, for the day has arrived when I must reveal the innermost feelings of my heart to him."

Machla rose from the ground, kissed the bier again and emerged from the tomb. On the long ride to Shilo, she told her son the story of her life and times.

CHAPTER

SEVENTEEN

"FOR HE SHALL GIVE HIS ANGELS
COMMAND OVER THEE TO GUARD
THEE IN ALL THY WAYS"

 more than a full day to tell Zelaphchad the whole story, as he frequently asked questions and interjected comments. She didn't finish relating the saga until late Thursday afternoon, after they had left Shilo en route to Bethlehem. The Temple visit had been relatively brief but inspirational. Unlike major festival attendance, the crowd was sparse and it was possible to watch the sacrifices even from the women's section. Elgar and Zelaphchad observed from the main courtyard.

What pleased Machla most about Zelaphchad's first reaction was his praise for her feelings towards his father. "I never sensed anything but the utmost love and respect between you," he said. "I never had any reason to imagine that there was anyone else in your life."

"Do you think my decision was well taken?" she asked.

"I cannot say for sure, mother. It seems correct because it was the will of God, if not an actual law. But I would have argued the case somewhat differently if I were you. In a choice between personal gratification and the Divine will, the latter always triumphs. You should have suggested that as the wife of Elchanan you could have accomplished more for the glory of Torah than as the wife of a farmer. Certainly teaching Torah ranks above the property of tribes."

Machla was proud of the analytical powers of her son. "There are now many people who are willing and able to teach Torah," she said, "but not that many who will give their lives to build our land. The Land of Canaan, the Torah of

Moses and the God of Israel are all equally important and necessary for our survival as a nation."

Elgar had correctly estimated that the stops along the route would create the need for an extra night on the road. By the time the travelers reached Bethlehem, it was past nine Friday morning. Elchanan had a magnificent home and, as Noah had foreseen, there were servants at work. The home was situated on a large parcel of land close to the highway that ran from Bethlehem to Hebron. It was richly furnished and decorated. Of the immediate family, only Batya and Elchanan were home. They greeted the visitors warmly. Machla was shocked by Elchanan's appearance for he looked very gaunt and was clearly suffering from the ravages of illness.

Elchanan asked Batya to prepare a light meal while the servants helped the guests settle in. After breakfast, he asked one of the men to take Zelaphchad to visit the Tomb of Rachel so that he could speak to Machla privately. Batya helped him out to the back porch and, after a few minutes, left Elchanan with his guest. Elchanan was very pleased to see Machla and her presence kindled pleasant memories from their joint educational efforts in the desert.

"Machla, you have no idea how much your coming means to me. I would not have considered my life complete without seeing you again." Machla saw the tears welling in his eyes and she was deeply moved. Elchanan regained his composure and continued, "I hope that you have had a pleasant trip. How are your sisters and their families?"

"One of the good consequences of the second trial is that all of my sisters live close by. They are well and are all happily married. You probably heard that my mother passed away about five years ago, but she lived to hold each of the fifteen grandchildren in her arms."

There followed a long review of the families on both sides covering the number of children born to them and the activities of each couple. After a while, Machla decided to get to more urgent matters. "I am sure you didn't invite me to Bethlehem just to hear a report on my family. But, before you get to the business at hand, I wish to take care of something that is bothering me."

"What is that, Machla?"

Machla withdrew a purse from under her robe, the one that was awarded to her by the tribal council of Judah. It was lighter than it had been at the time of presentation, but it still contained a substantial amount of silver. She placed the purse down on Elchanan's table and said, "This is a reimbursement for the subventions that Meir received from you for teaching my son. It was a very nice gesture but you are not the boy's father and it was not your duty to finance his Torah education."

"I am sorry that the matter has come out in the open and even sorrier that you feel this way. If you will give me the opportunity, I will tell you why I will not accept your money and I have good reasons for my position. I know that Moses, of blessed memory, used to draw up balance sheets with people who had complaints. Let me compose one with you.

"I never told you this and it may come as a complete surprise, but my wife Batya has three sisters and no brothers. When her father died, his brothers assumed his property rights in Canaan. One day, she asked me if she were as good as Machla. As usual, I answered that in certain respects she was even better. Then she asked me if a woman would lose her rights under the Zelaphchad law if she was married before the law was enacted. I told her it made no difference. She then asked me to put in a claim for her father's property rights and she and her sisters got the land. Her uncles were very unhappy, but the law is clear.

"Now, when I took your case, I did not expect any reward. Nevertheless, I received compensation far in excess of anything in that purse and you don't see me returning the property to you.

"More directly, my appointment as a chief judge resulted from my involvement with you and I have been handsomely rewarded with great benefits for being in that position. Finally, I was blessed with one gift as a result of your intervention that is so valuable that it has no price at all. I refer to my daughter, Yedida, who is the light of my life.

"What did you get from me? A Torah subsidy for your son, some of which was not even mine. Since I am chief judge, many wealthy merchants donate funds to support students in their higher Torah studies. Such an arrangement exists as well in tribes other than Judah. I want you to know that without such support, there would be very few students studying at the academy of learning that I have established.

"All this means is that not only will I not accept any money from you but I may be directing more funds in your direction."

"How can you do that? My son is just about finished with Meir's tutoring."

"The tribe of Menashe does not have advanced academies of Torah. Judah has several where even married students can continue their studies for many years. My son, Achituv, studied at the Yeshiva in Hebron for five years and now he has been appointed as an associate judge and secretary of the tribal court of Judah. I would be willing to accept Zelaphchad into my academy and he would be sustained until he completes his education."

"You know that I cannot allow you to accept my son on your own. Your judgment may be clouded by our past relationship. I would permit him to enter, only if he were tested and accepted by another judge who does not know who he is, or where he is from."

"From what I hear from Meir, you are not taking too much of a risk. I will arrange for a colleague to conduct the examination for his admission to the academy. Nevertheless, I request your permission to interview him for another opportunity for which you will have to admit that I am the only one entitled to do so."

The real intent of Elchanan's summons was beginning to dawn on Machla. "You are not involved in a little matchmaking, are you, Elchanan?"

"It might lead to that."

"Elchanan, you are crazy. I am afraid that your illness has affected your better judgment."

"Why do you say that?"

"I have nothing but admiration for my son, Zelaphchad. In Torah knowledge he will hold his own whether you or another judge tests him. Remember, though, he is a son of a middle-class agricultural family and has grown up in a simple manner without any social graces. Your daughter, to use the Torah expression, has not even exerted herself to put her foot down on the ground. Let us look at things realistically. You are aristocracy and for twenty years have held the second highest position in the largest tribe in Israel. Your fame is nationwide and I am sure that you can select a husband for your daughter from amongst the most highly placed families in Judah."[1]

"Let me be honest with you, Machla. I have four children other than Yedida.

Three of them found their mates in the highest tribal social classes. One of them married a penniless orphan girl. My wealthy son-in-law and my two rich daughters-in-law are fine and I have no complaints against them, but I would gladly trade all three of them for another Malka. I cannot begin to tell you what she did for Achituv and how she pushed him to Torah. I cannot begin to tell you what it means to have her sit at our Sabbath table. When she speaks, everyone stops what they are doing just to listen to her. I am determined that my next son-in-law will have to pass only one test, the test of scholarship. If he doesn't have the resources to support my daughter in style, I will bestow a sufficient dowry upon him to do so."

"Do you think your daughter would be happy on a farm with the sheep and the cows? Won't she miss the city culture and social life?"

"That I cannot say. In the end, the young people have to love each other. I am now only interested in getting parental approvals out of the way because my daughter will not marry without my consent and I suspect that Zelaphchad won't marry without yours. Do I have your permission to interview Zelaphchad this afternoon?"

"I have no objections as long as I can meet your Yedida at the same time."

"It is fine with me but don't be too rigorous with her. She herself has been asking me to find her a husband for a year now. I told her that she would have to face searching inquiries and she said she would be willing to do so."

"Does she know anything about us?"

"More or less. She discovered your cloth a few years ago and we told her the story, omitting only a few details."

"On the way down, I told Zelaphchad the story as well."

Yedida arrived at noon and was introduced to Machla. The girl was clearly nervous but absolutely radiant. Machla could see how closely she resembled Elchanan. Her beauty was in a class with Noah when Noah was forty years younger. She was dressed luxuriously and conveyed a sense of aristocracy.

"Why don't you show Machla around the estate and sit a while by the pond," Elchanan suggested to her.

Yedida guided Machla around the property and Machla was impressed at the condition it was in. The grass and shrubs were neatly trimmed and rows of trees were growing along the perimeters. A flower garden was in full bloom near the entrance and a pond covered much of the back half of the property.

"Do you do any of the farming?"

Yedida seemed surprised by the question. Finally, she held out her hands for Machla's inspection. It was obvious that she had never held anything in them heavier than a spoon.

"You must have spent most of your time studying Torah I would imagine."

"I am ready to answer your questions. But please keep them fairly simple."

Machla recalled some of the examinations that she faced in her life. To her, they were a challenge that she loved and she never worried about being embarrassed. It was obvious that her awesome reputation had preceded her.

"I am sure that you know much more than I did at your age. You come from a wealthy family. Suppose someone asked your father for a loan. What may your father not do?"

"He may not charge interest on the loan."[2]

"Is there anything unusual about the way the commandment is written in the Torah?"

"It is one of a group of commandments that includes the words 'You shall fear the Lord' in the text of the commandment."

"Why was that done?"

"There are certain commandments that are very easy to evade. Unless a person is warned to fear his God who knows all, he may not observe such commandments scrupulously."

"Can you tell me how it is possible to evade the prohibition on interest?"

Yedida listed a few examples and, by the cases chosen, Machla knew at once who was responsible for Yedida's education.

"How long has Malka been teaching you?"

"How did you know it was Malka?"

"It could only be Malka or Dina because you are repeating the words that I taught them. It isn't Dina because she would not have remembered the examples in such perfect order."

"Malka taught me from the time I finished elementary school until I was eighteen."

"There is no need for any further questions, Yedida. You were privileged to have the most knowledgeable teacher available. Do you know why your father invited us to Bethlehem?"

"I have a premonition that he is trying to arrange a match between me and Zelaphchad."

"Are you ready to get married?"

"Yes. Many girls my age are already married."

"Why didn't your father take care of this before?"

"He could not bear the thought of me leaving him. Now that he is very sick, he feels that he has to get me settled as quickly as possible."

"Do you know anything about my son?"

"Yes. I have heard wonderful things about him."

"Such as?"

"I heard that in addition to being a Torah scholar, he milks the cows very well, cuts the barley quickly, and tends to the sheep perfectly."

Machla realized that Yedida had been coached very well.

"Would you be happy with a man who tills the soil? We have no other sons and that may be his required work."

"A farmer in the Holy Land serves God when he works."

"Listen, Yedida, forget all the answers that Malka taught you and answer me from the heart. Can you live on a very much lower standard of life than you now enjoy?"

"Malka told me to answer that by saying that marriage is a spiritual union, which should not be affected by wealth. I honestly don't know whether I could live poorly or enjoy working on the farm."

"I am sure that you will feel better for being truthful with me. Let me go see how Zelaphchad is faring with your father."

Yedida thanked Machla for talking with her. "I would enjoy meeting Zelaphchad."

Machla presented Zelaphchad to Yedida and Elchanan sent the two young people out to the pond.

"Machla, your son is a true scholar. He is quite sharp and his knowledge transcends rote learning. Apparently, Meir and you share the same teaching philosophy."

"The philosophy came from Azriel, Meir's father. We both learned our first lessons in Torah from him, Meir in the tent and me outside of it. I passed it down to those who learned from me. By the way, how did you ever get Malka to teach your daughter?"

"That was the dowry for Achituv. She couldn't even clothe herself when she became his bride. We gave her everything and required only that she teach Yedida when Yedida finished her first school."

"You struck a very good bargain. Your daughter exceeded my highest hopes for Torah knowledge in a woman. It goes without saying that she is also a graceful and beautiful girl. Even Noah will have to concede that point. I still have doubts, however, as to whether she would adjust to life on a farm in Dothan."

"How can we determine such things in advance?"

"I have a suggestion to solve the problem and I won't ask for any favors in return."

"You now help people for nothing?"

"There comes a time even for that."

"Let me hear your idea."

"I would like to invite Yedida to spend her summer in my home where she can share a room with my daughter, Tovah. There, she can work on the farm and learn to milk the cows and tend the sheep. In a few months, she can determine whether she is prepared to embark on such a life."

"That is an excellent idea. If she likes it and she likes Zelaphchad, then we can proceed further. If not, she will look elsewhere. Your son, however, is welcome at the academy in the fall whether or not any relationship develops between him and Yedida."

"We will be glad to take Yedida back with us."

"I will ask her. Remember when they asked Rivka whether she would go with Eliezer she didn't hesitate for a minute."[3]

Yedida didn't hesitate either. "I will go, father. Please ask the servants to donate all their old clothes so that I will not look out of place."

The Sabbath meals at Elchanan's home were very enjoyable. Malka was there with her family and so was Dina. As usual, Malka was the center of attention as people listened to her views and commentaries on various matters. During the long spring day, Machla had a chance to talk to Batya alone in the morning and to Malka in the afternoon. Batya let her know how serious Elchanan's illness was. "His heart is failing and he finds it hard to walk. We cannot tell how long it will be before it gives out entirely."

"Have these years been good for you?"

"They have been very good, Machla, very good. Even better than the ten years before he met you. He really began to appreciate me and express his love with more passion and feeling. Our wonderful daughter brought us even closer. How have they been for you?"

"Well, Eliav always loved me and I have come to love him. We, too, have wonderful children. I feel fulfilled on the land and I do not regret the long struggle to win it. As Moses said, one cannot have everything she wants in life and I already had more than a sufficient share of blessings."

"I pray you don't hate me for what I did to you. I still don't know what happened to cancel your wedding to Elchanan but he says my prayer caused it to occur."

"One never knows what causes the Lord to act, but I have never doubted that it was a Divine intervention that caused me to lose out and Moses did not deny it when I complained. You were within your rights to pray, Batya, and I cannot fault you for that."

"That is what Elchanan said as well. Each year now, on the eve of the twelfth day of the ninth month, I walk to the Tomb of Rachel and offer a prayer of thanksgiving for the kindness that the Lord granted in returning my husband to me."

"And what does Elchanan do while you are offering your words of gratitude?"

"He takes your cloth from its hiding place and walks to the pond. There he sits for a long time mourning his lost love. He laments for a couple of hours and then he puts it out of his mind until the following year."

"We have a somewhat different routine in Menashe. On the tenth day of the ninth month, all of the daughters of Zelaphchad gather at a feast to celebrate the anniversary of our great victory in the High Court. Each sister recites a section of the Torah to mark the occasion."

"What do you do on the twelfth day?"

"I thank the Lord that he didn't strike me dead on that day and I promise never to defy His will again."

"Whatever happened must have been very painful."

"Incredibly so."

"I am sorry it came to that. You must believe me that I didn't want to hurt you."

"I do, Batya, I do."

Machla spoke to Malka in the late afternoon. "You seem very happy within the family."

"I am indeed."

"I know that you spent a lot of time teaching Yedida. Tell me, wasn't it demeaning to accept such a condition in your marriage agreement, a form of bondage?"

"I must admit that my actions did not equal my own preachments. I was immature when I advised you to be a martyr for the rights of women and marry Elchanan against God's will. I am sorry for doing so and I hope you will forgive me. I confess that I, myself, deviated from my egalitarian philosophy in my desire to be part of Elchanan's family. I rationalized my actions by saying that it was worth paying such a price to be able to serve my God and my people from the highest possible vantage. In reality, I was hiding self-interest under a mask of altruism."

"It was I who solicited your guidance, even though you were young. Wrong though your advice was, I do not regret seeking it. I admired the sincerity and conviction with which it was given. So much for the past. Let's get back to the present. You know Yedida better than anyone. Do you think she can adjust to the farm life?"

"I am not sure but, if she does, it will do her a lot of good. Right now, she has little drive or ambition. Everything she desires is always at hand. If there is any hope that she will ever accomplish anything in life, she must experience what it means to struggle and fight for goals.

Sunday morning, Zelaphchad easily demonstrated his readiness for the academy and a place was reserved for him in the fall. Elchanan told Machla that if anything developed between Yedida and Zelaphchad, the pair could live in the vacant home on Batya's property during the years of Zelaphchad's studies. He then bid his daughter farewell and told her to have a good time on the farm. Anxiously, he watched Yedida enter the wagon and take the seat next to Machla. Zelaphchad sat on the facing bench.

They covered distances quickly and the wagon reached Dothan by Wednesday morning. Machla wanted to stop at Noah's house on the way home to tell her that she was back and to show off her new acquisition. Noah was out with the birds when she saw the wagon and she ran to greet Machla. Machla dismounted and then came Yedida. When Noah saw Yedida she yelled, "Meir, come quick and take a look at the gorgeous specimen that Machla picked up on the way."

Machla was no longer agile enough to kick Noah in the shins although she would have loved to. "Watch your tongue, Noah, this is the daughter of His Honor, the Chief Judge of Judah."

Noah was no longer afraid of Machla, for age had taken its toll on her one time master. "Well," she said, "Elchanan did something right for a change. Come on in for a minute for some refreshments."

When Meir came out, Noah introduced Yedida as the Queen of Judah, a name that she would never lose. "How come Elchanan let her out of his sight?" she asked Machla.

"I invited her for a vacation on the farm for a few months. City girls like to visit farms for a change of pace."

"Tell Meir what happened in Judah. I want to talk to Zelaphchad for a minute."

Machla told Meir that Zelaphchad would be continuing his studies in Judah and Elchanan would cover all of the expenses. "Thanks to your teaching, he passed the examinations with ease."

Noah was having a talk with Zelaphchad near the sheep pen. "For some reason, your mother has an unerring knack of finding beautiful people. In case you are unaware of such things, the girl you brought back with you is in a class of her own. But if you don't care for her, please pass her on to my son, David. I want to keep the tradition of beauty alive in my family."

Zelaphchad was not beyond teasing his aunt. "Looks don't mean that much, aunt Noah."

"What does count, you idiot?"

"The important thing is how well a girl milks the cows."

Fortunately, Noah didn't have anything handy to throw at Zelaphchad. "If you were my son, you would certainly know what is important!"

When the wagon arrived at Machla's home, Eliav and Tovah greeted the travelers and helped them alight.

"We have a guest," Machla said. "This is Elchanan's daughter and I invited her to stay for the summer."

Eliav grasped the purpose of the visit and raised no objections. While Tovah and Zelaphchad showed Yedida around the farm, Machla told Eliav the details of the visit. She also told him that Zelaphchad was accepted at the academy whether or not things worked out with Yedida. Eliav was more than pleased because he had no idea how he would have been able to finance an extended stay in Judah for his son.

"She is a very attractive girl and quite refined," Eliav noted. "Do you think she would enjoy the rural life?"

"Time alone will tell."

Tovah arranged a bed in her room for Yedida and the next morning Yedida, although half asleep, went out to milk the cows with her. Between Tovah and Zelaphchad, Yedida learned all about farming. There were any number of aches and pains and some tears at night but she persevered. Within a month, she was doing fairly presentable work.

"I never worked this hard in my whole life," she complained to Zelaphchad.

"It's very healthy outdoor work and we are helping to build the Land of Canaan."

"What am I going to do with all the knowledge that I gained during the last ten years?"

"Torah doesn't make you a better farmer, but it makes you a better person. It is the language of communication between Hebrew people and it makes for a moral society."

One morning, as Zelaphchad was watching her milk the cows, Yedida filled a pail of milk but failed to get the bucket out of reach of the cow. Petti, the senior cow on the farm, was otherwise a reasonable creature but she couldn't resist a full pail of milk. She lashed out at the pail and tipped it over. Strangely, the pail righted itself immediately and no more than a few drops were lost.

Zelaphchad stared at Yedidah, his mouth wide open. "How did you do that?" He asked.

"I'm sorry. I was hoping you wouldn't see what happened."

"I don't mean leaving the pail within reach of the cow. All beginners lose a few pails until they learn. I mean how did you get the pail to correct itself."

"I am afraid I cannot tell you that."

A few days later Machla asked Zelaphchad how things were coming along between him and Yedida and he said. "I like her very much and she has magical qualities."

"That is a wonderful compliment to pay to a girl. 'You find her enchanting' is the way you are supposed to say it."

"That's not what I meant. I was talking about real magic." He related the incident with the pail and Machla went into deep thought.

"You have just helped me solve a problem that has been bothering me for twenty years."

"What is that, mother?"

"When Moses told me that you would be born he said that you would be blessed by the Lord. When he told Elchanan about his daughter, he said that she would be guarded by the angels."

"I remember you telling me that, but I didn't attach any importance to it. I thought the words were merely general statements that meant that the children would be healthy and attractive."

"No, my son. Moses never spoke in generalities and every word was measured. Yedida's blessing was different than yours. Moses meant that the Lord would assign her a pair of angels at birth to protect her from all evil. In your case, you got the blessing of our tribal father, Joseph, that everything you undertook would be blessed with success and that you would find favor in the eyes of all men."

"You mean people would be well advised to never ever try to hurt Yedida?"

"Yes, indeed. You learned about Bilaam when an angel with a drawn sword stood in his way. They can be pretty frightening."[4]

"How long will these angels watch over her?"

"Moses used the term growing up. I imagine that when she gets married, the angels will leave and her husband will have to protect her."

"I am ready to do so, mother."

Machla studied Zelaphchad closely. He was fully developed and looked quite strong. She imagined that he was mature enough to build a family, but Eliav had his doubts. "Your father is not sure you are ready for marriage. Remember, we were both in our forties when we got married."

"My grandfather married my grandmother when he was twenty and it worked out very well."

"If you call producing a family of five daughters working out very well."

Zelaphchad couldn't resist the temptation. "One of them was aunt Noah."

Machla was stung. "You take that back or I won't give you my consent."

"All right. One of them was my beloved mother?"

"That is much better. Did you tell Yedida that you love her and that you want to marry her?"

"I am somewhat afraid."

"Those are things that no one else can do for you. With your blessing you are bound to succeed."

That night, Zelaphchad was walking with Yedida when he said, "I found out who straightened up the pail. It's nice to have a pair of angels protecting you from harm."

"They are somewhat over-protective. I cannot learn from my mistakes because they never let me make any. Sometimes, I get annoyed and tell them to go back to the Lord because I don't need them anymore."

"Do they listen to you?"

"No. Would you believe I went through an active childhood without a single scratch to show for it?"

"Do you want to be free of them?"

"One doesn't give up protection of that quality voluntarily."

"Yedida, I stand ready to replace the angels and take you under my wings. The angels are with you only until marriage and someday you will have to get a husband to replace them." Here he paused and, his heart racing, he whispered. "How about me?"

"I understand that you, too, received some sort of blessing when you were born."

"Yes. I have the blessing of Joseph. My work succeeds and I find favor in the eyes of men."[5]

"Will I share in your blessing if I give up my angels?"

"My success will be your success."

"What if a Zoleika comes along? Would you be tempted?"

"It would have to be an extremely good looking woman. I am told that you are very attractive yourself."

"Who told you?"

"My aunt, Noah."

"She is not bad herself, even at fifty-eight."

"You haven't yet answered my first question."

"I forgot what you asked me."

"That's strange, I seem to have forgotten it, too."

"Oh no you didn't. You asked me to marry you."

"Only indirectly."

"Make it direct."

"Yedida, will you marry me?"

"Yes. When can I stop the farm work?"

Yedida left for Judah at the beginning of the following week to prepare for her wedding. Zelaphchad left at the start of the sixth month to enroll in the academy. Eliav gave him his blessing and said, "Try to produce at least one son."

That year, all the daughters of Zelaphchad and their children went to Shilo for the holidays and continued from there to Judah for the wedding. Elchanan was very weak but was able to preside. The status of Elchanan in his tribe became even clearer to Machla when she saw none other than Joshua, the son of Nun, being led to the wedding canopy. The successor of Moses and the conqueror of Canaan was quite advanced in years but, when he heard of the impending wedding, he was determined to be present. When he was requested to bless the bride and groom under the canopy, he did not hesitate to make a moving speech.

> "My dear Zelaphchad and Yedida, this sacred moment in
> your lives brings to my mind a scene that will always live
> in my memory. In the heat of the desert sun, I once heard

the voice of a beautiful woman addressing a massive gathering of the children of Israel. In ringing tones, fired by emotions of love, she extolled the great Land of Canaan and pleaded passionately for her share of the sacred soil of our homeland. She was your mother, Zelaphchad. Together with her sisters, she wrote a glorious page in the eternal book of an eternal people. Standing by her side, Yedida, was your father, who served as the advisor and counselor of the daughters of Zelaphchad in their epic struggle.

"I was in the Tent of Meeting in the aftermath of the case. It was there that I heard my master Moses, blessed be his memory, confer upon Machla the daughter of Zelaphchad, the blessing that she would bear a son. In the spirit of Joseph, the father of the tribe of Menashe and my own tribe of Ephraim, that son would be blessed with success in all his undertakings. My dear Zelaphchad, I can think of no greater success than winning the hand of this beautiful daughter of Israel, Yedida. I was also present in the Tent when the revered prophet blessed Yedida's father with words of a psalm that he himself had composed. When he spoke of the daughter that would be born to Elchanan and Batya he said: 'For He shall give his angels charge over her to protect her in all her ways.'[6]

"The blessing that Moses bestowed on Yedida was intended to span her childhood years. Using the very words of my sainted teacher, I shall now extend her blessing to future years and expand it to include her partner in life:

'There shall no evil befall thee, neither shall any plague come nigh thy tent. Thou shalt not be afraid of the terror by night nor of the arrow that flieth by day; He will cover thee with his pinions and under His wings shalt thy find refuge.'

"Zelaphchad, as you enter the ranks of those who will study and teach our holy Torah, I want you to promise me that you will never forget that you were born amongst common people who till the soil and tend the sheep in our homeland. If you have the knowledge to teach Torah and are endowed with the ability to do so, bring the word of God to those who grew up with you and thirst for instruction. Follow in the footsteps of your mother who was a brilliant teacher and who imbued a generation of women with the teachings of Torah.

"I may very well be the last national leader of the Hebrew people for the foreseeable future. But even if we are not to be a united nation in a political sense, we must remain one people in a spiritual sense. Young couples who live according to the Torah and who teach the word of God will safeguard our future in the Promised Land.

"May God bless the bride and groom with health and happiness and may He bestow the blessing of long life on Eliav and Machla, Elchanan and Batya and their families. Amen."

The wedding feast was a gala event attended by many of Machla's former students. Everywhere she went, people still recognized her and wished her well. The reception was held out of doors on a part of Elchanan's estate from which the Tomb of Rachel was clearly visible. The festivities following the wedding lasted a full week. At one of the gatherings, those present were able to hear the words of a very distinguished guest, Othniel, the son of Kenaz, the brother of Caleb and his successor as leader of the tribe of Judah. In his greetings to the family, Othniel stressed the uniqueness of the inter-tribal marriage. "Like other young women of Judah, Yedida followed the custom of praying at the Tomb of Rachel to be blessed with a suitable husband. In Yedida's case, our mother Rachel responded by blessing her with one of her very own sons. Rachel was the mother of Joseph, the father of the tribes of Menashe and Ephraim. From the families of Menashe, Rachel chose the son of the most scholarly and pious woman in the tribe and brought him to Yedida.

"The gesture was in recognition of the purity of the soul of our beloved Yedida and in tribute to the deeds of her father, our well known scholar, judge and teacher. Judge Elchanan, who maintains the Yeshiva in Bethlehem, has won a student whom we will be proud to have in the Yeshiva.

"May this union, and the progeny that emerge from it, ever teach us that we have the duty to transcend tribal borders and build a great nation, unified by the spirit of Torah and faith in one God."

When all the feasting was finally over, Machla bid Elchanan a tearful farewell and returned home to await the sad news which was not long in coming. With it came a letter that Elchanan wanted delivered to her privately after his death.

"My love for you has remained with me until my last days on earth and I thank you again for every minute we spent together. You were God's gift to me, my wellspring of joy and inspiration.

"I return to my Creator in peace, thankful for the knowledge that in the blood of my descendants will course the blood of Machla, the daughter of Zelaphchad. You and I fought for the idea that the children of Israel are more than a collection of tribes. We saw a vision of one great people selected by the Almighty to transmit the teachings of Torah to all nations. We could not in our own lives cross the tribal borders, but our children have succeeded in doing so. They will be the symbol of our dreams and the fulfillment of our love.

"In the closing moments of my life, I see an even greater vision. From my city of Bethlehem and my tribe of Judah, will emerge great kings who will guide our descendants to previously unscaled heights and bring them to love God with all their might, all their hearts, and all their souls. Amen."

Machla rolled up the parchment, which was wet with her tears, and put it away in a private place. "Pray for me in heaven, Elchanan," she whispered, "and may God grant you the peace and happiness that eluded you on earth."

APPENDIX

GENERAL NOTES

THE CHARACTER OF THE DAUGHTERS OF ZELAPHCHAD

In recreating the story of the daughters of Zelaphchad, the author hewed very strictly to the characteristics given for them in the Talmud. In the Tractate of Baba Bathra, the Rabbis describe the daughters of Zelaphchad as being wise, righteous, and possessing exegetic skills. Some commentaries define the term "righteous" as being fully observant of the Torah. Others consider the quality of righteousness as reflecting the performance of charitable acts. Wisdom, of course, is based on knowledge of the Torah, while exegetic skills refer to ability to apply the teachings of the Torah in given situations.

In the book, the daughters are portrayed as being extremely knowledgeable in Torah. They are also shown to have skills of reason and logic, in applying the teachings of the Torah to their needs. As far as righteousness is concerned, the author follows both interpretations of the term. Their charitable deeds consisted of helping sick people, on a large scale. Their strict observance of the commandments is emphasized throughout the book.

THE PERSONALITY OF NOAH

Special emphasis is given to the unique personality of Noah, the daughter of Zelaphchad. This attention derives from the fact that the Torah itself was aware of her extraordinary qualities. Chronologically, Noah was the youngest of the five daughters. Nevertheless, on two of the three occasions that the names of the daughters are listed in the Torah (Numbers XXVI:33 and Numbers XXVII:1), the name of Noah is listed second, immediately after the name of Machla, the eldest. On those occasions, the name of Tirza, second in order of birth, is moved to the end of the list. Rashi (Numbers XXXVI:11) cites the Talmud, which explains that the listing at the end of Numbers is in chronological order, while the others are in the order of wisdom. Noah's wisdom is amply illustrated in the book. The author believes that she would not have been advanced over her sisters unless there was a special reason for doing so.

In all cases where the Torah elevated younger siblings ahead of older ones, there were special circumstances. This was true in the elevation of Abel over Cain, Ephraim over Menashe and Zebulun over Issachar. According to traditional sources, Zebulun was advanced because he was a sponsor of Torah studies. Ephraim was advanced because greater leaders emerged from his tribe. Abel was held in higher regard than Cain because of the quality of his offerings to the Almighty. To explain the elevation of Noah ahead of her older sisters, the author bestows upon her not only great wisdom but an outstanding personality.

The author further believes that the promotion of Noah was a source of friction between her and Tirza. He devotes considerable attention to this rivalry.

DELAY OF MARRIAGE

According to the Talmud, Tractate Baba Bathra 119b, the daughters of Zelaphchad delayed their marriages for many years. The Talmud tells us that the youngest of the daughters was forty years old before she was married. Instead of criticizing the Zelaphchad women for delaying a traditional religious obligation, the sages consider their delay of marriages as an act of piety, on the grounds that the women waited for men who were worthy of them.

As to why the daughters of Zelaphchad deferred their marriages, the author has little doubt. This entire novel rests on the premise that the delay was engendered by the desire of the daughters of Zelaphchad to further their case for inheriting property in the Land of Canaan. The assumption is made that the daughters knew that marriages to men who would inherit their own land in Canaan, would weaken their claim of inheritance. There was no reason to feel that judges would bestow additional land upon women who were already in possession of land as a result of their husbands' inheritances. The author feels that this was the primary motivation for deferring marriage.

Since the daughters got married to the same cousins who wanted to marry them when they were younger, it is hard to say that these men were worthy when the daughters were older, and not when they were younger. Yet the Talmud considers them to be worthy of the daughters (Talmud, Tractate Baba Bathra 119b, Rashi). It is apparent that the daughters' test of worthiness of prospective mates was whether the latter believed in inheritance of land for women. Since the cousins were opposed to this idea, the daughters of Zelaphchad considered them not worthy, until after the Torah guaranteed them their land.

If the daughters of Zelaphchad were as righteous as the Talmud considers them, there is no way that they would have deferred the sacred obligation of marriage unless they had an outstanding reason to do so. The Hebrew people have always believed in marriage and family, and traditionally Hebrew women undertake this duty at the earliest age possible. Nor is it possible to believe that the daughters remained single for lack of suitors. (Given a non-monogamous, religious society, the marriage rate ((ratio of married women to single woman between the ages of 15-45)) could easily exceed 95% or 19:1. The odds that any five single women chosen at random would remain in that state are in the nature of two and a half million to one or 19^5. If the daughters were as pious and learned as described in the Talmud, they would have been sought out by the most desirable men in the tribe. The odds on their remaining unmarried for lack of choice would then become astronomical).

It is hard to imagine any religious authority throughout the ages who would condone the behavior of women who choose to defer marriage. Nevertheless, both the Torah and the Talmud make it clear that the daughters of Zelaphchad had children by virtue of a Divine miracle, such as that which was bestowed upon Yocheved, mother of Moses (Talmud, Tractate Baba Bathra 119b). There could be no greater endorsement of their behavior than the bestowal of a miracle upon them.

In a separate paper, submitted to the Council of Young Israel Rabbis in Israel, the author justifies the behavior of the daughters of Zelaphchad on the grounds that the objective of acquiring land in Canaan is worthy of the greatest human sacrifices. He describes how Jewish men, throughout the ages, fought and died to defend their land in Israel. Deferring marriage, although quite painful, does not rank with the supreme sacrifices that Jews have made to possess their homeland.

THE SIN OF ZELAPHCHAD

In their presentation to the court, the daughters of Zelaphchad admit that their father was guilty of a major sin (Numbers XXVII:3). In several locations, the Talmud offers three options as to the nature of the sin (Talmud, Tractate Sabbath 96b ff). Zelaphchad was guilty of either a Sabbath violation, participation in an unauthorized battle with the Canaanites or joining with those who complained about desert conditions. The author is firmly convinced that the sin involved was that of taking part in the battle with the Canaanites, in defiance of a direct prohibition by Moses. While most people who receive religious education get the impression that Zelaphchad was guilty of gathering wood on the Sabbath, there are many reasons to feel that this is not the case.

Ordinarily, when the sages of the Talmud disagree on a subject, they state their opinions and leave it at that. They do not go out of their way to criticize each other's opinions. In this case, those Rabbis who felt that Zelaphchad was not guilty of Sabbath violation, claim that those Rabbis who say that he was, will have to pay the price for besmirching the reputation of a Tzaddik. In fact, the Sifri Zuta, (Numbers XV:32), claims openly that it is impossible to say that Zelaphchad violated the Sabbath.

There is general agreement that Zelaphchad was a righteous man and that violating the Sabbath was not in keeping with his character. If so, why do some feel that he did it? Tosafot (Talmud, Tractate Baba Bathra 119b ad loc.) answers that Zelaphchad wished to illustrate that the death penalty for Sabbath violations was still in effect, despite the fact that the entire generation had already been sentenced to death in the desert. This interpretation is extremely hard to accept. There is no reason to feel that anyone in his right mind would think that all of the Torah laws were suspended because the men of the generation were doomed to die over forty years in the wilderness. Even if there is merit to this concept, it is hardly likely that someone would choose to demonstrate the existence of a death penalty by bringing it upon himself. Similar explanations for Zelaphchad's Sabbath violation are equally unconvincing.

It seems unlikely that the daughters of Zelaphchad would emphasize their father's sin (Numbers XXVII:3) if it were a routine sin of this nature. They use the term "Cheto," (*his* sin), which implies a unique type of sin relative to Zelaphchad himself, and not to everyone else. Sabbath observance is a general commandment, persisting through time. The attack against the Canaanites was sinful on a specific occasion, and not thereafter. In fact, after this incident, war against the Canaanites was part of the Hebrew philosophy and expressed in a fixed command.

Furthermore, the daughters stressed that Korach sought out the support of Zelaphchad in his rebellion against Moses. Since Korach himself was a Tzaddik, it is unlikely that he would have enlisted someone to his cause who was not totally observant.

During the course of the book, the author elucidates what motivated Zelaphchad, and the others who went on the mission, to defy the instructions of Moses. Zelaphchad was a descendant of Joseph, who loved the Land of Israel. He was not ready to die passively in the desert, without a chance of setting foot upon the soil of the Promised Land.

Finally, to satisfy those who are concerned with the ultimate judgment of the virtue of

Zelaphchad, we can refer them to the passage in the Zohar, (3:157a) which states that the Almighty forgave the sin of Zelaphchad.

TORAH EDUCATION FOR WOMEN

The commentaries insist that all the daughters of Zelaphchad were well-versed in Torah (Talmud, Tractate Baba Bathra 119b). Nowhere is it revealed how these women acquired their religious education. They certainly did not receive the education at home, because they were orphans and the death of their father occurred before the oldest daughter was six years old. There is no indication that the mother of the Zelaphchad women had more than a smattering of Torah knowledge. One possibility that was open to the author was that the daughters of Zelaphchad received their education from Miriam, the sister of Moses. We know that Miriam was actively involved in teaching women (Micah VI:4, all commentaries). Another possibility was the existence of schools for women. While the existence of schools for men in Egypt was well known (Genesis XLVI:28, Rashi), there is no known reference to similar schools for women.

From Micah VI:4, Targum Jonathan ben Uziel, there may be an indication that Miriam actually established a school. The author did not feel that he could attribute the education of the daughters of Zelaphchad to existing schools without further data. He therefore chose to believe that the Zelaphchad girls achieved Torah knowledge by virtue of their own efforts. He assumed that Machla overheard Torah instruction given to her male cousins and, thereafter, transmitted the knowledge to her sisters.

THE TRIBAL COUNCIL HEARING

The hearing and censure of the daughters of Zelaphchad by the elders of the tribe of Menashe is a fictional construct. The author assumes that the tribal elders would not have permitted the daughters to defer marriage until they reached the age of forty. Menashe was a rapidly growing tribe, and emphasis on procreation was much in evidence. Wilfully postponing marriage was contrary to tribal ideals and religious traditions. The chapters dealing with the censure explore this issue, and form an important part of the novel.

The existence of a council is not fictional. The Torah refers to such bodies as "Rashei Ha-avot" (Numbers XXXVI:1) or "Rashei Ha-matot" (Numbers XXX:20). The author made use of commanders in the composition of the body in keeping with the verse in Deuteronomy I:15, which relates the words of Moses, "I selected wise and well known men from among your tribal leaders, and appointed them as your leaders — captains of thousands, captains of hundreds, captains of fifties, captains of tens, and police for your tribes."

ROMANCE OF MACHLA AND ELCHANAN

The character of Elchanan is a fictional one. The author developed this character consistent with what would be an appropriate match for Machla, the daughter of Zelaphchad. That at least one of the daughters of Zelaphchad was planning an inter-tribal marriage is obvious from the Torah. If all the daughters were intending to marry within the tribe, there would have been no need whatsoever for the Zelaphchad cousins to petition Moses to bar the daughters from marrying outside the tribe. Since one such case would create the need for the plea to Moses, the author limited the inter-tribal activity to a single instance.

INTERVENTION BY ELCHANAN IN THE ZELAPHCHAD CASE

The author is firmly convinced that the Zelaphchad family received assistance from some outside source in bringing their case to the High Court. Like any supreme court, access to the Sanhedrin is very limited. Members of the general public rarely have the knowledge and legal skills to bring a case to the High Court. In the book, the author uses Elchanan's relationship with Caleb, brother-in-law of Moses, to help the case along. Since a referral from a lower judicial entity is required before a case can be considered by the High Court (Exodus XVIII:22, commentaries), the author made provision for this circumstance as well.

In general, the court procedures described in the book closely follow the codified procedures in the Talmud, Tractate Sanhedrin. While such codification was not written until 1,300 years after the Torah was revealed, it is assumed that the laws of the Sanhedrin generally followed the oral traditions and customs passed down from Moses.

SPECIAL ENDOWMENTS OF MACHLA'S SON, ZELAPHCHAD

In all cases where normally barren women have become fruitful as a result of Divine miracle, the offspring are uniquely endowed. We need but refer to the following: Yocheved (mother of Moses), Chana (mother of Samuel), wife of Manoach (mother of Samson), and the matriarchs, Sarah, Rebecca, Leah and Rachel. The special endowments of Elchanan's daughter, Yedida, are as fictional as the father himself is.

DETAILED NOTES

Having stated the key concepts upon which the novel is based, there will now follow a chapter by chapter rendition of explanatory notes on specific items raised in the book. Such notes will be limited to matters dealing with Jewish laws and customs which regulate the behavior of the protagonists in the novel.

DETAILED NOTES

CHAPTER 1

1. RIGOROUS SLAVERY
   Exodus I:14 ff.

2. SLAVE ATTIRE
   Description based on ancient Egyptian art. See "Egypt: Descriptive, Historical, and Picturesque: G. Ebers; Cassell Publishing Company, 1878; pp. 160-ff.

3. ZELAPHCHAD FAMILY
   As a help in following the text, readers may consult the Zelaphchad family tree printed at the start of the novel on the inside cover.

4. MOSES
   The author is using the English name "Moses" instead of the more traditional Hebrew form "Moshe." He does so because he anticipates that many readers of the book will not be familiar with Biblical names in the original Hebrew. The same is true for the various books of the Bible cited in the notes. Readers who may not be familiar with the English or Latin names may consult the glossary which appears in the appendices.

5. MOSES' ACT OF REBELLION
   Exodus II:11 ff.

6. RELIGIOUS EDUCATION
   Genesis XLVI:28, commentaries. See also General Notes under the heading Torah Education.

7. ACHIEVEMENTS OF JOSEPH
   Genesis XLI:1 ff.

8. BEND THE KNEE
   Genesis XL:43.

9. HEBREW SETTLEMENT IN THE LAND OF GOSHEN
   Genesis XLVI:34, XLVII:4, 6.

10. LEVITES EXEMPT FROM SLAVERY
    Exodus V:4, Rashi.

11. ENSLAVEMENT OF THE HEBREWS
    Exodus I:8 ff.

12. INTERVENTION OF MIRIAM
    Exodus II:1, Rashi ad loc.

13. BIRTH OF MOSES
    Exodus II:1 ff.

14. BUILDING OF THE CITIES OF PITHOM AND RAMESES
    Exodus I:11.

15. PERSECUTION OF THE HEBREWS
    Exodus I:16, 22.

16. PRE-TORAH MARRIAGE CUSTOMS
    Maimonides, Laws of "Ishut," (Marriage and Family), Chapter 1. The text reads: "Prior to the giving of the Torah, a man would meet a woman in the marketplace. If it were agreeable to both parties, he would bring her to his house and have relations with her privately. She would then be his legal wife."

17. NAMING OF CHILDREN
    Various customs prevail among Jewish families as to the naming of children. There is no halachic requirement on the matter. In the Book of Genesis, most of the naming was done by men. It is to be noted that Leah, wife of Jacob, gave her children names of her choice, as did Rachel. The names she bestowed were for both male and female children. In one case, Jacob and his wife, Rachel, bestowed different names upon the same child.

18. THEY DIDN'T CHANGE THEIR LANGUAGE
    Midrash Shemot Rabbah, Chap. 1, Par. 33. "Rabbi Huna stated in the name of Bar Kapara: 'Israel was redeemed from Egypt for four reasons. They did not change their Hebrew names, they kept their language, they did not reveal their secrets, and they protected the morality of their women.'" (The above text is written differently in various editions of the Midrash.)

19. THE RETURN OF MOSES
    Exodus III:7 ff.

20. REVELATION OF THE BURNING BUSH
    Exodus III:1 ff.

21. THE SPEECH IMPEDIMENTS OF MOSES
    Exodus IV:10. There are many colorful explanations in the Midrashim as to how Moses acquired his speech defect. It is not clear whether his difficulty was in pronunciation, eloquence, or both.

22. MIRACLES PERFORMED BY MOSES
    Exodus IV:1 ff.

23. SUMMONS TO AARON TO MEET MOSES
    Exodus IV:27.

24. DEFECTION OF THE ELDERS
    Exodus V:1, Rashi ad loc.

25. DIALOGUE OF PHAROAH AND MOSES
    Exodus V:1-5.

26. DENIAL OF STRAW FOR BRICKS
    Exodus V:7 ff.

27. SIZE OF THE BRICKS
    The size is derived from an ancient illustration. See note 2 for the source of the drawing.

28. PROCESSING OF THE BRICKS
    Exodus V:7, Rashi. The Babylonian brick-making process is fully described in Genesis
    XI:3. See also the Encyclopedia Britannica under the heading, "Bricks."

29. PUNISHMENT OF ZELAPHCHAD
    Exodus V:14.

30. PLEA OF OFFICERS TO PHARAOH
    Exodus V:15 ff.

31. THE ELDERS BERATE MOSES
    Exodus V:20 ff. The identification of the elders as Dothan and Abiram is cited in Rashi,
    ad loc.

32. PLEA OF MOSES TO THE LORD
    Exodus V:22, 23. The translation of this and other Biblical verses are taken from the
    Jewish Publication Society Bible.

33. RESPONSE OF THE LORD TO MOSES
    Exodus VI:2 ff.

34. THE CHILDREN OF ISRAEL IGNORE MOSES
    Exodus VI:9.

CHAPTER 2

1. IDENTITY OF MESSENGER
   The author intended this description to apply to Joshua ben Nun. It is his feeling that
   Joshua was already identified with Moses prior to the Exodus. His appointment to lead
   the battle against Amalek (Exodus XVII:10), ahead of other distinguished leaders,
   would indicate a long standing relationship between him and Moses. A number of
   Midrashim explain his appointment and his other qualifications.

2. PHARAOH'S ADVICE TO MOSES AND AARON
   This passage is based on Exodus V:4, 5.

3. THE WATERS OF THE NILE TURN TO BLOOD
   Exodus VII:20 ff.

4. THE REMAINING PLAGUES
   Exodus VII:26 ff.

5. FIRST REFERENCE TO LIBERATING THE HEBREWS
   Exodus VIII:4, 11.

6. CONCESSIONS BY PHARAOH AFTER FOURTH PLAGUE
   Exodus VIII:21 ff.

7. DIALOGUE AFTER EIGHTH PLAGUE
    Exodus X:8 ff.

8. DIALOGUE AFTER NINTH PLAGUE
    Exodus X:24 ff. From the Torah, it appears that Moses rejected Pharaoh's offer entirely
    on his own. The reward for this display of faith was immediately forthcoming. We are
    told at the beginning of Chapter XI, that God appeared to Moses in the very presence of
    Pharaoh, and advised him that the tenth plague would soon be visited upon Egypt.

9. PASSOVER RITUALS
    Exodus XII:1 ff.

10. PROMISE TO ABRAHAM ABOUT EGYPTIAN SPOILS
    Genesis XV:14.

11. THE TENTH PLAGUE
    Exodus XII:1 ff.

12. RIOT AT PHARAOH'S CASTLE
    Exodus XII:29-33. Pharaoh's personal efforts to locate Moses are described in Exodus
    XII:31, Rashi. In the view of most of the commentaries, Moses was not truly in hiding. In
    fact, the commentaries agree that Moses spent the night of the tenth plague in Egypt
    (rather than with the Hebrew community in Rameses, which was eight parsang away).
    He did so in order to receive the command to leave Egypt without unnecessary delay.

13. THE RIGHT TO EGYPTIAN SPOILS
    Exodus XI:2.

14. THE EXODUS AND THE MATZO
    Exodus XII:34-37.

15. NON-HEBREWS AND CONVERTS JOIN THE EXODUS
    Exodus XII:38.

16. PHARAOH'S DECISION TO PURSUE THE HEBREWS
    Exodus XIV:5 ff.

17. COMPLAINTS AGAINST MOSES
    Exodus XIV:11 ff.

18. BY THE SHORE OF THE SEA OF REEDS
    Exodus XIV:1 ff.

19. BRAVERY OF NACHSHON AND THE TRIBE OF BENJAMIN
    The stories of the bravery of Nachshon and the tribe of Benjamin do not appear in the
    Torah text. They appear in the Midrash (Rabbah, Bamidbar XIII:7) and the Talmud
    (Tractate Sotah 36b).

20. SONG OF MOSES AND MIRIAM
    Song of Moses, Exodus XV:1 ff. Song of Miriam, Exodus XV:20 ff.

21. PROMISE OF CANAAN
    Genesis XII:7

22. REVELATION AND THE TEN COMMANDMENTS
    Exodus XVIII:1 ff.

23. THE ORAL LAW

The Written Law (Torah Shebiktav) includes only information revealed to Moses, the father of all prophets, and written by him. All further revelations by the Almighty are part of the Oral Law (Maimonides, Thirteen Principles of Faith, and elsewhere).

24. SIN OF THE GOLDEN CALF

Exodus XXXII:1 ff.

CHAPTER 3

1. COLLECTION OF THE MANNA

Exodus XVI:4 ff.

2. TASTE OF THE MANNA

Exodus XVI:31.

3. ELEVATION OF THE TRIBE OF LEVI

Numbers VIII:5 ff.

4. APPOINTMENT OF BEZALEL

Exodus XXXI:1 ff.

5. VOLUNTEER HELP IN BUILDING THE TABERNACLE

Exodus XXXV:21 ff.

6. THE NEW HEBREW CALENDAR

Exodus XII:1 ff., Rashi and various commentaries.

7. STRUCTURE OF THE HOLY ARK

Exodus XXV:10 ff.

8. TRIBAL PRESENTATIONS TO THE TABERNACLE

Numbers VII:54 ff.

9. SPYING MISSION TO CANAAN

Numbers XIII:1 through Numbers XIV:39.

10. THE SPIES SHOULD HAVE BEEN WOMEN

The suggestion that the spies should have been women, who loved the Land of Canaan instead of men who despised the Promised Land, appears in the commentary of the Kli Yakar (Numbers XIII:1) and is based on Talmudic sources.

11. THE RAID ON THE CANAANITE STRONGHOLD

That Zelaphchad was a participant in the attack on the Canaanite stronghold is explained at length in the General Notes in the Appendices. For the specific details of the battle, see Numbers XIV:40-45.

12. DEATH OF RAM

The Talmud in Tractate Baba Bathra relates that one of Zelaphchad's brothers died ahead of him. The author identifies this brother with Ram (Talmud, Tractate Baba Bathra 116 ff., Mishnah and commentaries).

13. DEATH OF THE TWO SONS OF AARON

Leviticus X:1 ff.

CHAPTER 4

1. MOURNING LIMITATION
   Barak was correct in saying that even Moses would not be mourned for more than thirty days. See Deuteronomy XXXIV:8.

2. CATTLE IN THE TRIBE OF REUBEN
   Numbers XXXII:1.

3. PRAYER IN VAIN
   Talmud, Tractate Brachot 54a.

4. REBELLION OF KORACH
   Numbers XVI:1 ff.

5. COURT OF SEVENTY ELDERS WITH PROPHETIC SPIRIT
   Numbers XI:25

6. GOD'S COMMAND TO ABRAHAM
   Genesis XII:1, Jewish Publication Society translation.

7. LEVIRATE MARRIAGES
   The basic laws of Levirate marriages are clearly outlined in Deuteronomy XXV:5 ff. and in the Talmud (Tractate Yebamoth in its entirety). A woman who has children, either male or female, is ineligible for Levirate marriage. This is established in the Code of Law, Eben Ha-Ezer, Chapter 156. For additional information on this matter, see Chapter 11, Note 1.

8. STORY OF JUDAH AND TAMAR
   Genesis XXXVIII:1 ff.

9. CUBITS
   Hebrew measurement. Generally accepted to be eighteen inches to half a meter. Certain sacred cubits were said to be twenty-four inches or sixty centimeters.

10. HONORING TEACHERS SIMILAR TO HONORING PARENTS
    Talmud, Tractate Pesachim 108a.

11. POPULATION OF FAMILIES OF THE TRIBE OF LEVI
    Numbers III:25 for the family of Gershom; III:44 for the family of Merari.

12. COMMAND TO COUNT THE TRIBE OF LEVI
    Numbers III:15.

CHAPTER 5

1. EVERY PERSON IS A BOOK
   The verse on which this premise is based appears in Genesis V:1.

2. LAWS OF THE SABBATICAL AND JUBILEE YEARS
   Leviticus XXV:1 ff.

3. PROPERTY INHERITED ONLY BY MEN
   Barak based his understanding of the law on all cases of inheritance described in the Torah up to the time of the discussion.

4. TORAH PROTECTION FOR WIDOWS
   Exodus XXII:21 ff. and elsewhere.

5. NUMBER OF JUDGES AND COMMANDERS
   The number of judges in a tribal court was set at twenty-three (Talmud, Tractate Sanhedrin); The number of elders was set at seventy (Numbers XI:16); The author assumes that commanders are officers of 1,000. Given that the Hebrew population of men between the ages of twenty and sixty was about 600,000, this would mean approximately 600 commanders.

CHAPTER 6

1. INDIVIDUAL RESPONSIBILITY FOR SINS
   The Talmud teaches that there is no messenger for sinful acts (Talmud, Tractate Kedushin 42b). If someone was requested by another party to perform an evil act, he must refuse to do so. If he does commit the act, then he is fully responsible and not the one who sent him. As expressed in the Talmud, the analogy is made to a master and a servant. The Talmud asks rhetorically, "If the master requests an action and the servant requests a contrary action, whom do we obey?" The master (God) instructs us to perform righteous acts while the servant (man) is requesting us to perform sinful acts. We are duty bound to listen to the master (Talmud, Tractate Kedushin 42b).

2. ADAM AND THE FORBIDDEN FRUIT
   Genesis III:17 ff.

3. MAN SHOULD NOT LIVE ALONE
   Genesis II:18.

4. FRUITFULNESS OF THE TRIBE OF MENASHE
   The fruitfulness of the tribe of Menashe is based on the blessing that Jacob bestowed upon his son, Joseph, the father of Ephraim and Menashe. Genesis XLVIII:16 and Genesis XLIX:25.

5. PROHIBITION OF PROSTITUTION
   Deuteronomy XXIII:18.

6. INTENT TO VIOLATE THE LAW IS NOT PUNISHABLE
   While people who plan to do good deeds are rewarded for their thoughts, people who plan to sin are not punished for their thoughts (Talmud, Tractate Kedushin 40a).

7. THREE COMMANDMENTS REQUIRING MARTYRDOM
   There are three commandments which may not be violated even if it means yielding one's life (Maimonides, 'Laws of the Foundations of the Torah,' Chapter 5, Paragraph 2).

8. COMMAND TO BE FRUITFUL AND MULTIPLY
   Genesis I:28.

9. VIOLATION OF POSITIVE COMMANDMENTS
   Circumcision, Genesis XVII:14. Passover, Exodus XII: 15.

10. THE COMMAND OF PROCREATION DOES NOT APPLY TO WOMEN
    Code of Law, Eben Ha-Ezer, Laws of Procreation, chapter 1.

CHAPTER 7

1. BRIBERY BLINDS THE EYES
   Deuteronomy XVI:19.

2. HOLY ARK PLATED WITH GOLD
   Exodus XXV:10-17.

3. CIRCUMCISION DEFERRED IN THE DESERT
   Joshua V:3-9.

4. DEATH OF JEWS IN THE DESERT ACCELERATED
   Deuteronomy II:15.

5. VOLUNTARY OFFERINGS
   Where time allowed, voluntary offerings were presented during the day. Otherwise they were offered at night. See Talmud, Tractate Yoma 33a.

6. THE DAUGHTERS IN A STATE OF RITUAL PURITY
   The reader may wonder why the daughters of Zelaphchad were in a state of ritual purity. If they were menstrual at anytime and did not purify themselves in a Mikva, they could not enter the grounds of the Tabernacle. This is based on the verse in Leviticus XII:4. The ban on single women going to the Mikva is less than 1,000 years old. With the destruction of the Temple and the absence of sacred food, there is no need for single women to be in a state of purity. In the early history of the Jewish people, when the Temple was in existence and unmarried daughters of priestly families ate sacred foods, they were required to be in ritual purity. The daughters of Zelaphchad were not from a priestly family, but they did visit the women's area in the Temple on a frequent basis. It is therefore assumed that they did undergo ritual purification.

7. TORAH SCRIPT
   The author is following the Talmudic teaching that the Torah was written in a simple form of "Ktav Ashurit." (This script was further refined by Ezra the scribe. His refinements brought this script to its current form). This means that the Torah was written in Hebrew. Furthermore, the author accepts the traditional dating of revelation (more than 3,200 years ago.) While some modern archaeologists believe that no Hebrew writing existed before the eighth century BCE, such opinions are based on the mistaken belief that the Hebrew alphabet was Phoenician in origin and that the Torah was not revealed by the Almighty. While this footnote is not the place to elaborate on the defense of Orthodox traditions, suffice it to say that belief in the Written Law is one of the principles of faith of the Jewish religion (Maimonides, Thirteen Principles Of Faith, Commentary to the Mishnah, Sanhedrin:10).

8. THE NAME MACHLON
   Machlon, the Hebrew equivalent of Machla, was the name given to the son of the judge, Elimelech (Ruth I:2).

9. SONG OF MOSES
   Exodus XV:1 ff. Jewish Publication Society translation is used for the quotations in this chapter.

10. BLESSING TO THE TRIBE OF JUDAH
    Genesis XLVIII:8 ff.

11. GENERATIONS OF ESAU
    Genesis XXXVI:5.

12. THE VERB "VAYASHKEM" IN THE TORAH
    Three times for Abraham (Genesis XIX:27, Genesis XXI:14, Genesis XXII:3);
    Once for Avimelech (Genesis XX:8);
    Once for Jacob (Genesis XXVIII:18);
    Once for Laban (Genesis XXXII:1);
    Twice for Moses (Exodus XXIV:4, Exodus XXXIV:4);
    In the past plural form, "Vayashkimu":
    Treaty of Isaac and Avimelech (Genesis XXVI:31);
    Worship of the golden calf (Exodus XXXII:7);
    Battle with the Canaanites (Numbers XIV:40);
    Future imperative plural form "Vahishkamtem":
    Request of Lot to the angels (Genesis IX:2).

13. EXCHANGE OF ANIMALS THAT WERE TITHED
    Leviticus XXVII:32 ff.

14. TORAH GIVEN TO WOMEN
    Exodus XIX:3, Rashi.

15. NOT TO STRAY AFTER THE SIGHT OF ONE'S EYES
    Numbers XV:39.

16. CALEB MARRIED TO MIRIAM
    Exodus XXIV:14, Rashi, ad loc.

CHAPTER 8

1. CREATION OF THE WORLD IN SIX DAYS
   The question and answer on the length of creation are based on the text in 'Ethics of the
   Fathers,' Chapter 5, Mishnah 1.

2. INSECTS CREATED PRIOR TO THE CREATION OF MAN
   The insects and crawling animals were created on the fifth day of the creation, Genesis
   I:20 ff. Man was created on the sixth day, Genesis I:26 ff. Concerning the moral lesson of
   humility in this order of creation, see Talmud, Tractate Sanhedrin 38a.

3. CONSULTING WITH ANGELS BEFORE CREATION
   Based on Rashi, Genesis I:26. This verse also illustrates the humility of God.

4. CALEB'S SURVIVAL TO AN ADVANCED AGE
   Numbers XIV:38 and elsewhere.

5. ABRAHAM'S TRAVERSAL OF CANAAN
   Genesis XIII:17.

6. CALEB'S TRAVERSAL OF CANAAN
   Numbers XIII:21 ff. Caleb made the crossing of Canaan as a member of the spying
   mission sent by Moses to investigate the Holy Land.

7. TESTING OF ABRAHAM
The ten tests of Abraham are described in 'Ethics of the Fathers,' Chapter 5, Mishnah 4, and elsewhere.

8. ABRAHAM'S REWARD AFTER THE AKEIDA
Malka was quoting from the Book of Genesis XXII:16-18. The 'Akeida' refers to the binding of Isaac. Jewish Publication Society translation.

9. MACHLA PERMITTED TO MARRY ELCHANAN
The prohibition on plural marriages was not in effect during the years prior to the common era and for 1,000 years thereafter. The ban on plural marriages was established for western Jews by Rabbi Gershom about 1,000 years ago.

10. AVI'S ILLNESS
The illness described is a form of roseola.

11. USING A SANCTUARY AS A SHORTCUT
The prohibition against using a sanctuary as a shortcut was codified in the Talmud, Tractate Berachot 62a.

12. HONORING PARENTS AND TEACHERS
Exodus XX:12, plus various commentaries.

CHAPTER 9

1. NUMBER OF GIRLS BETWEEN THE AGES OF ELEVEN AND THIRTEEN
The commander estimated that there were 7,500 girls in Judah between the ages of eleven and thirteen, based on data provided in the first census of the Hebrew tribes (Numbers I:27). There the tribe is listed as having a population of 47,600 men between the ages of twenty and sixty. In the second census, the tribe of Judah is described as having 67,500 men of the same age (Numbers XXVI:15). Since the conversation took place about thirty years after the first census, we can interpolate that the number of men at the time of the council meeting was about 62,000. Because the men of this generation died off rapidly in the desert and none survived beyond sixty, we can estimate that there were about 80,000 women in Judah above the age of twenty (women above sixty were not sentenced to die in the desert). Assuming that the medium age of the population was twenty, it is safe to estimate that there were also 80,000 women below the age of twenty. Dividing twenty age groups equally among the 80,000 younger women, yields about 4,000 girls in each age bracket or 8,000 for the combined eleven and twelve year old age groups.

2. IMMERSION IN THE MIKVA FOR SINGLE WOMEN
This matter is explained in Chapter 7, Note 6.

3. MACHLA'S VIEW OF LIFE AS A COMPULSION
Machla's view that birth and life were compulsory was later reflected in the teaching of 'Ethics of the Fathers,' Chapter 4, Mishnah 29.

4. USING THE LEVITICAL AREA AS A SHORTCUT
This subject was covered previously in Chapter 8, Note 11.

5. WOMEN AND THE STUDY OF TORAH

This subject was discussed in part in the General Notes. Women are not commanded to study Torah because they were specifically exempted by the verse "thou shall teach them to thy sons" (Deuteronomy XI:19). This aspect of the subject is discussed in the Talmud, Tractate Kedushin 29b. That persons who are exempt from a commandment may perform these mitzvot voluntarily, is well established in the Talmud. Maimonides, ('Laws of Torah Study,' Chapter 1, Paragraph 13), rules that women who study Torah are rewarded for it, but not on the level of the male counterparts because they were not commanded to do so. In the case of teaching daughters Torah, however, there were some Rabbis who prohibited it (Talmud, Tractate Sotah 20a). The halacha does not rule in accordance with these views in so far as the Written Law is concerned (Maimonides, ibid.) In seeking court rulings and interpretations, Machla may have gone beyond the halachic rulings of later generations. In her time, it was not prohibited and the daughters of Zelaphchad were praised for their exegetic skills. See General Notes.

6. ASSAULT AND BATTERY OF HUMAN BEINGS

That assault and battery of one human being by another is forbidden, emerges from the laws recorded in Exodus XXI:12 ff. Elchanan was not referring to physical contact between a man and a menstrual woman. Such contact is forbidden when affection is involved. A kick in the shins is not an affectionate gesture.

7. RENDING GARMENTS IN MOURNING

Talmud, Tractate Moed Katan 26a.

CHAPTER 10

1. TWO SISTERS FORBIDDEN TO BE MARRIED TO ONE MAN

Leviticus XVIII:18. While it is forbidden for a man to be married to two sisters at the same time, a man may marry his wife's sister after his wife passes away. The penalty for such an infraction is very severe. While the patriarch, Jacob, was married to two sisters, Leah and Rachel, simultaneously, that was before the Torah was given.

2. LOCATION OF THE TENT OF MEETING

Although there are many opinions on this matter, the basic source is to be found in Exodus XXXIII:7 ff.

3. FACE OF MOSES COVERED BY VEIL

Exodus XXXIV:29.

4. ITAMAR'S RESPONSIBILITIES IN THE TABERNACLE

Itamar was responsible for the Gershon family of Levites (Numbers IV:28) as well as for the Merari family (Numbers IV:33).

5. COMPLEX MATTERS REFERRED HIGHER

Exodus XVIII:26 indicates that matters which could not be resolved by lower officials were brought to the attention of Moses.

6. ELCHANAN'S RULING ON JUDICIAL AUTHORITY

The wide ranging authority given to the courts of Israel to make rules and laws for the benefit of society are fully described in Deuteronomy XVII:9-13. Although the enactments of the Judicial authorities are Rabbinic in nature, disregarding Rabbinic promulgations is considered a violation of Torah law. It is assumed that these laws were put in place in the fortieth year of the sojourn in the desert in preparation for entry into the Land of Canaan.

7. REVELATION OF THE DIVINE WILL

In the case of the second Passover, Moses requested a ruling from the Almighty and received it (Numbers IX:8 ff.).

8. INVALIDATION OF TEMPORAL LAWS

Temporal laws can be invalidated by courts that are greater in number and wisdom than the court which first enacted the law (Talmud, Tractate Megilla 2a).

9. UNANIMOUS VOTE TO CONVICT THE MURDERER

If all judges of a court vote to condemn a murderer, the verdict is set aside and other procedures are adopted. These rules are discussed in the fourth chapter of the Talmud, Tractate Sanhedrin 32a ff.

10. ABRAHAM'S DEPARTURE TO CANAAN.

Genesis XII:1.

CHAPTER 11

1. LAWS OF THE LEVIRATE

Deuteronomy XXV:5 ff. The fact that the birth of a daughter, as well as that of a son, disqualifies a woman from Levirate marriage is described in the Talmud, Tractate, Baba Bathra 109a. In the Artscroll English edition of the Tractate Yevamot 22b, Note 17, there is a lengthy summary of the reasons for equating sons and daughters in this respect. Three major reasons are given as proposed by various groups of early scholars. Depending on the opinions, some are derived from interpretations of the Torah text. Others stem from logical inferences.

2. LAWS OF SON PREDECEASING FATHER

If a child predeceases his father, and the father has no living children at the time of his death, his wife is eligible for Levirate Marriage (Talmud, Tractate Yevamot 92a).

3. DEATH OF AARON

Details of the death of Aaron, including the closing of the eyes, appear in Numbers XX:29, and in Rashi XX:26. The actual date of death is given in Numbers XXXIII:38.

4. QUALITIES OF AARON

The remarkable character of Aaron is best described in the words of Hillel ('Ethics of the Fathers,' Chapter 1, Mishnah 12).

5. ATTACK OF THE CANAANITE KING, ARAD

Numbers XXI:1 ff.

6. EVENTS IN THE FORTIETH YEAR

The schedule of events listed with regard to the wars against the Amorites and the Bashanites are listed in the Seder Olam, ad loc.

7. ROLE OF ELAZAR AT THE HIGH COURT

Elazar presided at the High Court following the death of his father, Aaron. He was the presiding judge at the first Zelaphchad trial (Numbers XXVII:2).

8.   SINS WITH THE DAUGHTERS OF MOAB
Numbers XXV:1 ff.

9.   WAR AGAINST THE MIDIANITES
Numbers XXV:16 ff.

10. SECOND CENSUS IN THE DESERT
Numbers XXVI:1 ff.

11. MENASHE'S CENSUS RESULTS
Population totals for Menashe in the second census are given in Numbers XXVI:28 ff. There, the daughters of Zelaphchad are listed individually for the first time.

12. LISTING OF THE DAUGHTERS OF ZELAPHCHAD
The first two times that the daughters of Zelaphchad are listed in the Torah, the order places Noah second immediately after Machla. In the final listing Noah is placed last. The Talmud and most of the commentaries claim that the first two listings reflect the intellectual status of the sisters while the final listing reflects their order of birth. Eben Ezra takes exception with this distinction and claims that the final listing reflects the order in which the daughters of Zelaphchad got married. (Numbers XXXVI:11).

13. ESAU'S REACTION AFTER LOSING HIS BLESSING
Genesis XXVII:41.

14. LISTING OF EPHRAIM AND MENASHE
Jacob advanced Ephraim ahead of Menashe (Genesis XLVIII:13 ff).

15. LISTING OF ZEBULUN AHEAD OF ISSACHAR
Genesis XLVIII:13,14.

16. LISTING OF TRIBAL PRESIDENTS OUT OF ORDER
Numbers VII:11 ff.

17. STORY OF CAIN AND ABEL
Genesis IV:1 ff.

18. ABRAHAM'S DEDICATION TO DIVINE SERVICE
Genesis XXI:3 and elsewhere.

19. NOT TO HATE ONE'S BROTHER
Leviticus XIX:17.

20. MARK OF CAIN
Genesis IV:16.

21. STORY OF REUBEN AND GAD
Numbers XXXII:1 ff.

22. MOSES CALLS FOR TRIBE TO JOIN REUBEN AND GAD
The request by Moses for another tribe to join Gad and Reuben is found in the Ramban, (Numbers XXXII:33). Some have sought to associate this request allegorically with the verse in the Book of Deuteronomy XXXIII:20.

23. IF THERE'S NO BREAD THERE'S NO TORAH
See 'Ethics of the Fathers,' Chapter 3, Mishnah 21.

24. HISTORIC REFERENCES BY TIRZA
Abraham propagating the faith (Genesis XII:5, Rashi);
Isaac digging wells (Genesis XXVI:18 ff.);
Jacob's Ladder (Genesis XXVIII:12);
Joseph's coat of many colors (Genesis XXVII:3).

CHAPTER 12

1. RETURN OF THE SPIES
Numbers XIII:26.

2. THE SISTERS TESTIFY SERIATUM
That each sister testified a single part of the Zelaphchad plea sequentially, is stated in the Yalkut Shimoni, Numbers XXVII.

3. MIRIAM'S ROLE IN EDUCATION FOR WOMEN
Miriam played an important part in the religious education of women in the desert. See commentaries Micah VI:4 and the longer explanation in the General Notes.

4. JOSEPH'S LOVE FOR CANAAN
See Rashi, Numbers XXVII:1.

5. LEVIRATE MARRIAGE FOR WOMEN WITH CHILDREN
See Chapter 4, Note 7.

6. TRIBE OF DAN
This event is entirely fictional. While there is no doubt that some prostitution prevailed among the tribes of Israel in the desert (see the incident with the daughters of Moab at Baal Peor in Chapter 11, Note 8), no reflection is being cast on the Tribe of Dan. Dan was selected because it is considered the least noble of the tribes having descended from Jacob's servant wife. In the selection of architects for the building of the Tabernacle, the commentaries contrast the appointment of Bezalel, of the most noble Tribe of Judah, and of Ahaliav, of the most lowly Tribe of Dan. They point out that architects from the highest and lowest tribes were involved in the project.
In addition to all of the above, the single mention in scriptures of a Hebrew woman of ill repute referred to a member of the Tribe of Dan (See Leviticus XXIV:11, and Rashi ad loc. Also refer to Rashi, Exodus II:11).

7. INHERITANCE OF ZELAPHCHAD
The full extent of the Zelaphchad inheritance in the Land of Israel is described in the Talmud, Tractate Baba Bathra 116a, ff.

8. COMMAND TO ABRAHAM TO GO TO CANAAN
Genesis XII:1 ff.

9. LAWS HELPING WEAKER ELEMENTS OF SOCIETY
Most of these laws appear in the twenty-second Chapter of Exodus and in the nineteenth Chapter of Leviticus.

10. PASSAGES CITED BY MACHLA
Machla's closing remarks are taken from Deuteronomy VIII:7-10. Jewish Publication Society translation.

11. VOTING ORDER OF JUDGES

This procedure is described in the Talmud, Tractate Sanhedrin 32a, in the Mishnah.

12. PRAYERS OF RACHEL AND LEAH

The Almighty enjoys hearing the prayers of the pious (Midrash Rabba, Genesis, Chapter 45, Section 5).

CHAPTER 13

1. NEW LAWS FROM THE ZELAPHCHAD CASE

Numbers XXVII:7-11.

2. WOMEN AFFECTED BY THE ZELAPCHAD CASE

Chemlon's estimate of women affected by the Zelaphchad case was very low. Statistically speaking, the number of women in families with only daughters will vary according to the birthrate. A table is given below for the Tribe of Menashe and for the Nation of Israel as a whole. The number of tribal families is derived from the Torah.

TRIBE OF MENASHE

FAMILIES	BIRTHRATE	FAMILIES AFFECTED	WOMEN AFFECTED
52,000	4	3,250	13,000
52,000	5	1,625	8,125
52,000	6	812	4,872

THE NATION OF ISRAEL

FAMILIES	BIRTHRATE	FAMILIES AFFECTED	WOMEN AFFECTED
600,000	4	37,500	150,000
600,000	5	18,750	93,750
600,000	6	9,375	56,250

The tribe of Menashe was extremely fruitful, so Chemlon may have been justified in assuming a birthrate of six children per family. While we cannot be certain of the birthrate amongst the children of Israel in the desert, an average of six children per family seems high (When the birthrate increases, the occurrence of families with all female children is far less likely).

3. MARRIAGE RITUALS PRIOR TO THE TORAH

See Chapter 1, Note 16.

4. CURRENT MARRIAGE RITUALS

Current rituals of Jewish marriage are based on Rabbinic understandings of the passages in the Torah starting in Deuteronomy XXIV:1 ff. While not stated in detail in the Torah, they are fully clarified in the Talmud, Tractate Kedushin. The author cannot determine exactly when the new marriage regulations were put into effect. He is simply following the chronological order of the Torah where such laws were revealed in Deuteronomy. The latter book was written in the fortieth year of the Jewish experience in the desert.

5. CONDITIONS OF BETROTHAL
The Talmud states that anyone who wishes to marry a woman always does so on condition that the match would meet with Rabbinic approval (Talmud, Tractate Ketubot 3a).

6. LAWS OF THE ZAVAH
The laws of the Zavah appear in Leviticus XV:25 ff. The difference between Zavah procedures and regular menstrual purification are not significant today because observant Jewish women now observe seven clean days following the menstrual period. In Biblical times, the seven clean day requirement applied only to a Zavah condition and not regular menstrual bleeding. Consecutive bleeding for three days at a time, other than the regular menstrual cycle, caused a woman to be Zavah under Torah regulations.
In the Halacha, there is a dispute whether a marriage is valid if it is conducted when the bride is a Nidah or Zavah. The validity is in question because the marriage is not subject to consummation at the time it is performed. Given the piety of the daughters of Zelaphchad, it is clear that they would not enter into a marriage under questionable circumstances.

7. TORAH TEXT OF THE ZELAPHCHAD CASE
Numbers XXVII: 1. Jewish Publication Society translation.

CHAPTER 14

1. ELAZAR'S ABSENCE AT THE ZELAPHCHAD SECOND TRIAL
Elazar presided with Moses at the first Zelaphchad hearing (Numbers XXVII:2). He is not listed as being present at the time of the second hearing (Numbers XXXVI:1). It is the author's feeling that the absence was deliberate. The reason for this feeling is that the Torah was very specific in listing the fact that the Tribal presidents and the heads of families were on hand. Thus, the omission of Elazar was not a casual matter.

2. INTERVALS BETWEEN MARRIAGES IN A FAMILY
The tradition that a younger child cannot get married until seven days have passed since the marriage of a sibling, dates back to the days of Laban (Genesis XXIX:26).

3. ARGUMENTS OF THE FAMILIES OF MENASHE
The outline of the case presented by the families of Menashe was taken from the Book of Numbers XXXVI:1 ff.

4. INTER-TRIBAL MARRIAGES
Marriage of Aaron and Elisheva (Exodus VI:23).
Marriage of Caleb and Miriam (Exodus XXIV:14, Rashi).

5. TRIBAL MARRIAGE OPTIONAL FOR THE SISTERS
The commandment given to the daughters of Zelaphchad that they should marry within the tribe (Numbers XXXVI:6) was optional rather than mandatory. This is the view taken by the Talmud, in Tractate Baba Bathra, and all other Torah commentaries. It is based on the way the verse is written which states that while they are free to marry whomsoever they please, they should marry within their father's family.

6. MARRIAGE LAW APPLIES TO ONE GENERATION
    In actual fact, only members of the generation that entered the Land of Israel were bound by the law prohibiting inter-tribal marriages (Talmud, Tractate Baba Bathra 120a and b).

7. OPTION OF A KING AND CENTRAL GOVERNMENT
    The Torah allowed for the possibility that the Jewish people in the Land of Israel would someday prefer a monarchy and a central government in preference to tribal rule (Deuteronomy XVII:14 ff.).

8. ANALOGY OF THE LAMBS
    This analogy compares to the words of the prophet Nathan to King David (II Samuel XII:1-7).

9. MARRIAGES OF THE DAUGHTERS OF ZELAPHCHAD
    That the Daughters of Zelaphchad married within their tribe is confirmed by the Torah (Numbers XXXVI:11, 12). Jewish Publication Society translation.

10. QUALITY OF THE LAW RESTRICTING MARRIAGE
    The words of Malka on the quality of the law restricting inter-tribal marriages for women who have inherited property are quite correct. The Talmud, Tractate Baba Bathra 121a, states that the law lasted only for one generation. Even more telling is the passage in the Talmud explaining the fact that the national festival of the 15th of Ab was in part due to the fact that this was the day that the ban on inter-tribal marriages for women inheriting property was fully rescinded (Talmud, Taanith 30b).

CHAPTER 15

1. JOSEPH'S VISION OF HIS FATHER
    When Joseph was tempted to sin with the wife of Potiphar, he beheld a vision of his father which prevented him from doing so. This teaching is quoted in Rashi, Genesis XXXIX:11 and is derived from the Talmud, Tractate Sotah 37a.

2. MOSES WRITES OF THE ZELAPHCHAD MARRIAGES
    Ibid. Chapter 14, Note 9.

3. JACOB MOURNING OVER JOSEPH
    Jacob could not be comforted following the disappearance of Joseph (Genesis XXXVII:35).

4. JOSHUA APPOINTED TO SUCCEED MOSES
    Deuteronomy XXXI:7. The farewell song of Moses, Dueteronomy XXXIII: 1ff.

5. MOSES VIEWING THE PROMISED LAND
    Deuteronomy XXXIV:1 ff.

6. CROSSING THE JORDAN INTO JERICHO
    Joshua III:14 ff.

7. BATTLE OF JERICHO
    Joshua VI:12 ff.

8. CONVOCATION AT MOUNT GERIZIM AND EIVAL
    Joshua VIII:31 ff.

CHAPTER 16

1. MACHLA'S REMARKS TO TOVAH
   All men created in the image of God (Genesis I:26). Preferential treatment for the elderly and wise (Leviticus XIX:32).

2. MARITAL RELATIONS PRIOR TO SEPARATION
   It is the custom of married couples to engage in relations prior to periods of separation (Code of Jewish Law, Orech Haim, Section 240, Paragraph 1).

3. TOMB OF JOSEPH IN SHECHEM
   Joshua XXIV:32.

4. HISTORIC IMPORTANCE OF DOTHAN
   The area of Dothan was on the caravan route leading to Egypt (Genesis XXXVII:25).

5. LOCATION OF MOUNT GERIZIM AND EIVAL
   Current maps of Israel list Mount Gerizim and Eival as being on either side of the city of Shechem. This is confirmed in Rashi, Deuteronomy XI:30 where the term "Elonei Moreh" appears. Rashi states that this term refers to Shechem and he cites a verse in Genesis XII as proof.

6. MENASHE ON MOUNT GERIZIM
   The Tribes of the sons of Joseph, Ephraim and Menashe, were assigned for the blessings on Mount Gerizim (Deuteronomy VII:11). There are later references in the commentaries to the effect that only half of the tribe of Menashe, the half that would settle on the west side of the Jordan, was facing the direction of Mount Gerizim.

7. VERSE ABOUT THOSE WHO UPHOLD THE TORAH
   Although the Torah states the verse in negative form, i.e. "Cursed is he that does not fulfill the words of this Torah," tradition has it that all verses in this section were read in both positive and negative forms. The positive form is used in this novel. This appears in Rashi, Deuteronomy XXVII:12 and is based on the Talmud, Tractate Sotah 36a.

8. TOMB OF JOSEPH
   Ibid. Chapter 16, Note 3.

9. RACHEL AND LEAH AS MATRIARCHS OF ISRAEL
   Machla's view of Rachel and Leah as the matriarchs of Israel is reflected in the Book of Ruth IV:11.

CHAPTER 17

1. CHARACTERIZATION OF INDOLENCE
   Machla's description of a woman who has had a very easy life is reflected in the Torah passage, Deuteronomy XXVIII:56.

2. INTEREST ON LOANS
   The prohibition on charging interest for loans appears several times in the Torah. The one referred to here containing the words, "You shall fear your God," is taken from Leviticus XXV:35.

3. REBECCA'S WILLINGNESS TO FOLLOW ELIEZER
   Genesis XXIV:58.

4.   THE ANGEL CONFRONTING BILAAM
     Numbers XXII:22 ff.

5.   JOSEPH BLESSED WITH SUCCESS
     Joseph was blessed with success in all his undertakings (Genesis XXXIX:2).

6.   THE ANGELS PROTECTING YEDIDA
     Psalm 91, which contains the words, "He shall give His angels charge over thee," is
     attributed to Moses in many of the Midrashim. It immediately follows Psalm 90, which
     contains the superscripture, "The prayer of Moses, man of God." The Midrashim assume
     that the heading means that Moses was the author of Psalm 90. Since the Talmud,
     Tractate Baba Bathra 15a, considers Moses to be one of the authors of the Book of
     Psalms, it is reasonable to assume that the Psalm which bears his name is the one that he
     wrote. The Midrashim add that he is also the author of the eleven Psalms which
     immediately follow Psalm 90.
     The view of the Midrashim is supported by Liturgical practice. In the Sabbath morning
     prayers, we recite Psalm 90 and 91 together. In the Sabbath evening prayers we link the
     last verse of Psalm 90 to Psalm 91.
     There is, however, a dissenting opinion of Rabbi Saadiah Gaon, who feels that Moses
     wrote neither Psalm 90 or 91. He claims that the reference to Moses simply means that
     these Psalms were sung by the sons of Moses but were not written by him. The Tosafot in
     the Talmud, Tractate Yebamot 64a, supports the opinion of Saadiah.
     For a full discussion of this subject, one may consult Daat Mikrah, published by Mosad
     HaRav Kook (Book of Tehillim, Psalm 90, Note 37).

BIBLIOGRAPHY

WORKS CITED

TORAH

GENESIS   בראשית

General Notes: A-6;

Detailed Notes: Chapter 1, Notes 6, 7, 8, 9; Chapter 2, Notes 10, 21; Chapter 4, Notes 6, 8;
Chapter 5, Note 1; Chapter 6, Notes 2, 3, 4, 8, 9; Chapter 7, Notes 10, 11, 12; Chapter 8,
Notes 2, 5, 8; Chapter 10, Note 10; Chapter 11, Notes 13, 14, 15, 17, 18, 20, 24; Chapter
12, Note 8; Chapter 14, Note 2; Chapter 15, Note 3; Chapter 16, Notes 1, 4, 5; Chapter 17,
Notes 3, 5.

EXODUS   שמות

General Notes: A-7;

Detailed Notes: Chapter 1, Notes 1, 5, 10, 11, 12, 13, 14, 15, 19, 20, 21, 22, 23, 24, 25, 26, 28,
29, 30, 31, 32, 33, 34; Chapter 2, Notes 1, 2, 3, 4, 5, 6, 7, 8, 9, 11, 12, 13, 14, 15, 16, 17, 18,
20, 24; Chapter 3, Notes 1, 2, 4, 5, 6, 7; Chapter 5, Note 4; Chapter 6, Note 9; Chapter 7,
Notes 9, 12, 14, 16; Chapter 8, Note 12; Chapter 9, Note 6; Chapter 10, Notes 2, 3, 5;
Chapter 14, Note 4.

LEVITICUS   ויקרא

Detailed Notes: Chapter 3, Note 13; Chapter 5, Note 2; Chapter 7, Notes 6, 13; Chapter 10,
Note 1; Chapter 11, Note 19; Chapter 12, Notes 16, 9; Chapter 16, Note 1; Chapter 17,
Note 2.

NUMBERS   במדבר

General Notes: A-1, A-4, A-5, A-6;

Detailed Notes: Chapter 3, Notes 3, 8, 9, 11; Chapter 4, Notes 4, 5, 11, 12; Chapter 7, Notes
12, 15; Chapter 8, Notes 4, 6; Chapter 9, Note 1; Chapter 10, Notes 4, 7; Chapter 11, Notes
5, 7, 8, 9, 10, 11, 12, 16, 21, 22; Chapter 12, Note 1; Chapter 13, Note 1; Chapter 14, Notes
1, 3, 5, 9; Chapter 17, Note 4.

DEUTERONOMY דברים

Detailed Notes: Chapter 4, Notes 1, 7; Chapter 6, Note 5; Chapter 7, Notes 1, 4; Chapter 9, Note 5; Chapter 10, Note 6; Chapter 11, Note 22; Chapter 12, Note 10; Chapter 13, Note 4; Chapter 14, Note 7; Chapter 15, Notes 4, 5; Chapter 16, Note 6; Chapter 17, Note 1.

TORAH COMMENTARIES

KLI YAKAR כלי יקר

Detailed Notes: Chapter 3, Note 10.

RAMBAN רמבן

Detailed Notes: Chapter 11, Note 22.

RASHI רשי

General Notes: A-1, A-6, A-7.

Detailed Notes: Chapter 1, Notes 6, 10, 12, 24, 28; Chapter 3, Note 6; Chapter 7, Note 8; Chapter 8, Notes 3, 12; Chapter 11, Notes 3, 24; Chapter 12, Notes 4, 6; Chapter 14, Note 4; Chapter 15, Note 1; Chapter 16, Note 5.

ZOHAR זוהר

General Notes: A-5.

EBEN EZRA אבן עזרא

Detailed Notes: Chapter 11, Note 12.

SAADIAH GAON סעדיה גאון

Detailed Notes: Chapter 17, Note 6.

DAAT MIKRAH דעת מקרא

Detailed Notes: Chapter 17, Note 6.

TANACH

JOSHUA יהושע

Detailed Notes: Chapter 7, Note 3; Chapter 15, Notes 6, 7, 8; Chapter 16, Note 3.

II SAMUEL שמואל ב'

Detailed Notes: Chapter 14, Note 9.

MICAH מיכה

General Notes: A-6.

Detailed Notes: Chapter 12, Note 3.

RUTH רות
Detailed Notes: Chapter 7, Note 8.

TEHILLIM תהלים
Detailed Notes: Chapter 17, Note 6.

MIDRASHIM

MIDRASHIM מדרשים
General Notes: A-4.

Detailed Notes: Chapter 1, Note 18; Chapter 2, Notes 1, 19; Chapter 12, Notes 2, 12; Chapter 17, Note 6.

TALMUD

BABA BATHRA בבא בתרא
General Notes: A-2, A-3, A-4, A-5.

Detailed Notes: Chapter 3, Note 12; Chapter 11, Note 1; Chapter 12, Note 7; Chapter 14, Notes 5, 6, 10; Chapter 17, Note 6.

BRACHOT ברכות
Detailed Notes: Chapter 4, Note 3; Chapter 8, Note 11.

ETHICS OF THE FATHERS פרקי אבות
Detailed Notes: Chapter 8, Notes 1, 7; Chapter 9, Note 3; Chapter 11, Notes 4, 23.

KEDUSHIN קדושין
Detailed Notes: Chapter 6, Notes 1, 6; Chapter 9, Note 5; Chapter 13, Note 4.

KETUBOT כתובות
Detailed Notes: Chapter 13, Note 5.

MEGILLA מגילה
Detailed Notes: Chapter 10, Note 8.

MOED KATAN מועד קטן
Detailed Notes: Chapter 9, Note 7.

PESACHIM פסחים
Detailed Notes: Chapter 4, Note 10.

SABBATH שבת
General Notes: A-4.

SANHEDRIN   סנהדרין
Detailed Notes: Chapter 5, Note 5; Chapter 8, Note 2; Chapter 10, Note 9; Chapter 12, Note 11.

SOTAH   סוטה
Detailed Notes: Chapter 9, Note 5; Chapter 15, Note 1; Chapter 16, Note 7.

TAANIT   תענית
Detailed Notes: Chapter 14, Note 10.

YEBAMOT   יבמות
Detailed Notes: Chapter 11, Notes 1, 2.

YOMA   יומא
Detailed Notes: Chapter 7, Note 5.

CODES OF LAW

MAIMONIDES   רמב"ם
Detailed Notes: Chapter 1, Note 16; Chapter 2, Note 23; Chapter 7, Note 7; Chapter 9, Note 5.

SHULCHAN ARUCH EBEN HAEZER   ש"ע אבן העזר
Detailed Notes: Chapter 4, Note 7; Chapter 6, Note 10.

SHULCHAN ARUCH ORECH CHAIM   ש"ע אורך חיים
Detailed Notes: Chapter 16, Note 2.

HISTORY

SEDER OLAM   סדר עולם
Detailed Notes: Chapter 11, Note 6.

SECULAR

"EGYPT: DESCRIPTIVE, HISTORICAL, AND PICTURESQUE"
Detailed Notes: Chapter 1, Notes 2, 27.

ENCYCLOPEDIA BRITANNICA
Detailed Notes: Chapter 1, Note 28.

GLOSSARY

CHAPTER ONE

Taskmaster, taskmasters — נוגש, נוגשים

Zelaphchad — צלפחד — Son of Chefer (See inside front cover)

Egypt — מצרים

Pharaoh — פרעה — Name carried by successive Kings of Egypt

Azriel, Shaphat, and Ram — עזריאל, שפט ורם — Names assigned to the brothers of Zelaphchad

Jacob — יעקב — Grandson of Abraham (See inside front cover)

Judah — יהודה — Fourth son of Jacob; also name of largest tribe in Israel

Joseph — יוסף — Son of Jacob (See inside front cover)

Goshen, Land of — גשן — Province of Egypt occupied by the Hebrews

Ephraim — אפרים — Son of Jacob, name of tribe in Israel

Levi — לוי — Son of Jacob, name of tribe in Israel engaged in religious service

Nile — יאר — Principal river in Egypt

Amram — עמרם — Judge of the Hebrews, father of Miriam, Aaron and Moses

Pithom and Ramses — פתם ורעמסס — Egyptian cities built by Hebrew slave labor

Chefer — חפר — Descendant of Menashe, father of Zelaphchad

Achla, Achlama — אחלה, אחלמה — Name assigned to wife of Zelaphchad

Machla — מחלה — Eldest daughter of Zelaphchad

Tirza and Hogla — תרצה וחגלה — Second and third daughters of Zelaphchad

Adina — עדינה — Name assigned to wife of Shaphat

Eliav — אליאב — Name assigned to first-born son of Shaphat

Meir — מאיר — Name assigned to first-born son of Azriel

Tziporah — צפורה — Wife of Moses

Jethro — יתרו — Midianite Priest, father-in-law of Moses

Sinai — סיני — Name of mountain where the Torah was received, located in the desert of the same name.

Aaron — אהרן — Brother of Moses, Judge of Israel following the passing of Amram. Later served as High Priest for the children of Israel.

Horeb — חורב — Alternate name for Mount Sinai

Gamliel — גמליאל — Elder and later first president of the tribe of Menashe

Noph — נף — A major city of Ancient Egypt

Asher — אשר — Son of Jacob, name of tribe in Israel

Pagiel — פגעיאל — Elder and first president of the tribe of Asher

Reuben — ראובן — Eldest son of Jacob, name of tribe in Israel

Dothan and Abiram — דתן ואבירם — Chronic complainers among the children of Israel

CHAPTER TWO

Yocheved — יוכבד — Wife of Amram, mother of Miriam, Aaron, and Moses

Pi Hahirot — פי החירות — Egyptian City where the Hebrews encamped. Alternate name for Pithom.

Cubits — אמות — Measurement derived from average length of hand from elbow to tip of the fingers. Authorities differ on the actual length. (See Note Nine in Detailed Notes for Chapter Four)

Sea of Reeds — ים סוף — Body of water miraculously crossed by the Hebrews on their way out of Egypt. Sometimes erroneously translated as the Red Sea.

Benjamin — בנימן — Youngest son of Jacob, important tribe in Israel

Nachshon — נחשון — Brother-in-law of Aaron, first president of the tribe of Judah

Written Law — תורה שבכתב — First five books of the Torah revealed to Moses

Oral Law — תורה שבעל פה — Oral laws and traditions revealed to Moses and others. These laws were later incorporated into the Mishnah and Talmud.

Chur — חור — Son of Miriam and Caleb

CHAPTER THREE

Manna — מן — Heavenly food that sustained the Hebrew people in the desert.

Omer — עמר — Biblical measure, equivalent to half a liter or a pint.

Exodus — יציאת מצרים — Departure of the Hebrew people from bondage in the Land of Egypt

Cohanim — כהנים — Descendants of Aaron who served as priests in the Tabernacle and Temples.

Bezalel — בצלאל — Grandson of Chur, who was the major architect of the Tabernacle

Menorah — מנורה — Seven branched candelabrum in the Tabernacle.

Cherubs — כרבים — Sculptures of young angels emplaced upon the Holy Ark.

Issachar — יששכר — Son of Jacob, name of tribe of Israel

Zebulun — זבלון — Son of Jacob, name of tribe of Israel

Simon — שמעון — Son of Jacob, name of tribe of Israel

Gad — גד — Son of Jacob, name of tribe of Israel

Dan — דן — Son of Jacob, name of tribe of Israel

Naphtali — נפתלי — Son of Jacob, name of tribe of Israel

Cloud of Glory — עמוד הענן — Cloud that guided the Hebrew people daily in the desert.

Joshua — יהושע — Disciple of Moses and, ultimately, successor to him.

Caleb — כלב — Husband of Miriam, member of the spying mission to Canaan, and second president of the tribe of Judah.

Amalek — עמלק — Evil desert nation that attacked Israel on the way out of Egypt.

Gadi ben Susi — גדי בן סוסי — Leader of the tribe of Menashe, who served on the spying mission to Israel.

Hebron — חברון — Ancient city in the Land of Canaan, burial place of the patriarchs.

Shamua — שמוע — Leader of the tribe of Reuben, who served on the spying mission to Canaan

Hittites, Jebusites, Amorites, and Canaanites — חתים, יבוסים, אמרים וכנענים — Early Canaanite nations, living in the Land of Canaan.

Pillar of Light — עמוד האש — Pillar of Light that guided the Hebrew people nightly when traveling in the desert.

Sodom — סדם — Evil city in Canaan during the days of Abraham.

Korach — קרח — Cousin of Moses, who rebelled against his leadership.

Arad — ערד — Name assigned to commander in the tribe of Ephraim, who led the attack against the Canaanite stronghold on Mount Paran.

Mount Paran — הר פארן — Mountain in the southern part of the Negev in the Land of Canaan.

Tent of Meeting — אהל מועד — Tent which served as the office of Moses (See Note Two in the Detailed Notes of Chapter Ten).

Hormah — חרמה — City in Canaan to which the Amalekites and Canaanites pursued the Hebrews who attacked Mount Paran.

Nadab and Avihu — נדב ואביהוא — Sons of Aaron who perished in the Tabernacle.

CHAPTER FOUR

Yiscah — יסכה — Name assigned to wife of Azriel.

Paran — פארן — Desert in which the Hebrew people traveled. Exact location is uncertain.

Shur — שור — Desert in which the Hebrew people traveled. Exact location is uncertain.

Abiram — אבירם — Name assigned to commander in tribe of Menashe.

Arnon — ארנון — Name assigned to commander in tribe of Menashe.

Yakira, Amnon, Joseph, and Ahuva — יקירה, אמנון, יוסף ואהובה — Names assigned to children of Azriel.

Boruch, Bracha, and Tehila — ברוך, ברכה ותהלה — Names assigned to children of Shafat.

Milka — מלכה — Fourth daughter of Zelaphchad.

Noah — נעה — Fifth daughter of Zelapchad.

Levirate — יבום — The laws under which the brother of a man who dies without children takes the widow in marriage. (See Note Seven in the Detailed Notes of Chapter Four)

Barak — ברק — Name assigned to commander of 1,000 in the tribe of Menashe. Zelaphchad and his family reported to this commander.

Er, Onan — ער, אונן — Children of Judah in the Land of Canaan.

Tamar — תמר — First married to Er, and then by Levirate marriage to Onan.

Gershon and Merari — גרשון ומררי — Families of the tribe of Levi.

CHAPTER FIVE

Jubilee — יובל — (See Note Two in the Detailed Notes of Chapter Five)

Sabbatical — שמטה — (See note Two in the Detailed Notes of Chapter Five)

Nechama — נחמה — Name assigned to wife of Meir, who passed away in childbirth.

Ekron — עקרון — Name assigned to the brother-in-law of Meir.

CHAPTER SIX

Nimshi — נמשי — Name assigned to commander in Menashe who was recused from voting on the Zelaphchad case.

David ben Nimshi — דוד בן נמשי — Name assigned to son of Nimshi.

Chanan — חנן — Name assigned to commander in Menashe who was recused from voting on the Zelaphchad case.

Zeldan — זלדן — Name assigned to commander in Menashe who was recused from voting on the Zelaphchad case.

Oran — אורן — Name assigned to the son of Zeldan.

Abba — אבא — Name assigned to commander who was appointed prosecutor for the Zelaphchad case.

Zila — צילה — Name assigned to the daughter of Patar, who testified against the daughters of Zelaphchad.

Simon — שמעון — Name assigned to the son of Hosea, who served as carrier of judicial report of Elchanan ben Uriah in Zelaphchad case.

Benjamin — בנימן — Name assigned to the son of Michael, who served as carrier of judicial report of Elchanan ben Uriah in Zelaphchad case.

Elchanan ben Uriah — אלחנן בן אוריה — Name assigned to judge in the tribe of Judah. He served as Director of Higher Religious Education and as advisor to the tribal council. Later, he developed a close relationship to Machla, the daughter of Zelaphchad.

Rodeph — רודף — Literally, "pursuer;" One who pursues another person with intent to kill or to rape.

CHAPTER SEVEN

Machlon — מחלון — Son-in-law of Naomi, first husband of Ruth.

Song of Moses — אז ישיר — Sung by Moses after the crossing of the Sea of Reeds.

Esau — עשו — Twin brother of Jacob.

Ahalivama — אהליבמה — Daughter of Ana, who was the daughter of Zivon. She married Esau, and bore him Yeush, Yalam and Korach.

Yeush, Yalam, and Korach — יעוש, יעלם וקרח — The children of Esau and Ahalivama.

Vayashkem — וישכם — Hebrew word meaning, "to rise early."

Hagar — הגר — Concubine of Abraham, mother of Ishmael.

Isaac — יצחק — Son of Abraham, one of the Hebrew patriarchs.

Abimelech — אבימלך — King of the Philistine people.

Laban — לבן — Brother of Rebecca, father-in-law of Jacob.

Lot — לוט — Nephew of Abraham.

Tithing — מעשר — Ten percent of crops and animals donated for religious purposes.

Batya — בתיה — Name assigned to wife of Elchanan ben Uriah.

Dina — דינה — Name assigned to eldest daughter of Elchanan ben Uriah, and pupil of Machla.

Malka — מלכה — Name assigned to pupil of Machla.

CHAPTER EIGHT

Aviva — אביבה — Name assigned to daughter of Yafa, pupil of Machla.

Avi — אבי — Name assigned to son of Elchanan and Batya.

Achituv — אחיטוב — Name assigned to son of Elchanan and Batya.

Michael — מיכאל — Name assigned to son of Elchanan and Batya.

CHAPTER NINE

Mikva — מקוה — Ritual pool of rainwater or well-water used in purification.

CHAPTER TEN

Dodi — דודי — Literally, "My beloved;" Nickname assigned to Noah, the daughter of Zelaphchad.

Aryeh — אריה — Name assigned to Judean commander, who worked with Elchanan and Machla.

Elazar — אלעזר — Son of Aaron, presiding judge at Zelaphchad trial, successor to Aaron as High Priest.

Itamar — איתמר — Son of Aaron, presided over priests at the Tabernacle.

CHAPTER ELEVEN

King of Arad — מלך ערד — Canaanite King who attacked the children of Israel after the death of Aaron.

Sihon — סיחן — Desert king of Amorites defeated by Israel.

Og — עוג — Desert king of Bashan defeated by Israel.

Moab — מואב — Desert nation related to Israel.

Midian — מדין — Desert nation led by Jethro at the time of the Exodus.

Chemlon — חמלון — Name assigned to legal advisor and alternate judge of the tribe of Menashe.

Gilead — גלעד — Son of Machir, son of Menashe (See inside front cover). Name also given to territory occupied in Trans-Jordan by tribe of Menashe.

Cain — קין — Son of Adam. Slayer of Abel.

Abel — הבל — Son of Adam. Slain by Cain.

Trans-Jordan — עבר הירדן — Territory on the eastern side of the Jordan River.

Haniel — חניאל — Second president of the tribe of Menashe.

Machir — מכיר — Son of Menashe (See inside front cover).

CHAPTER TWELVE

Yerachmiel — ירחמיאל — Name assigned to son of Ophir, witness at the Zelaphchad trial.

Ariel ben Abba — אריאל בן אבא — Name assigned to chief judge of Asher, witness at the Zelaphchad trial.

Armon ben Karni — ארמון בן קרני — Name assigned to senior commander of the tribe of Dan, witness at the Zelaphchad trial.

Abraham ben Kalman — אברהם בן קלמן — Name assigned to witness at the Zelaphchad trial.

Zavah — זבה — Woman bleeding beyond the regular menstrual period (See Note Six in the Detailed Notes on Chapter Thirteen).

CHAPTER THIRTEEN

Carmiel — כרמיאל — Name assigned to sage of the tribe of Naphtali, prosecutor for the second Zelaphchad trial.

Asenath — אסנת — Wife of Joseph.

CHAPTER FOURTEEN

Yehoram ben Shabtai — יהורם בן שבתאי — Name assigned to chief judge of tribe of Issachar, who testified at the Zelaphchad trial.

Samuel ben Amihud — שמואל בן עמיהוד — President of the tribe of Simon.

Elisheva — אלישבע — Wife of Aaron, sister of Nachshon.

CHAPTER FIFTEEN

Zoleika — זליכה — Wife of Potiphar, attempted to seduce Joseph.

Potiphar — פוטיפר — Egyptian officer, master of Joseph.

Talman — תלמן — Name assigned to husband of Dina, daughter of Elchanan and Batya.

Yedida — ידידה — Name assigned to daughter of Elchanan and Batya.

Mount Nebo — הר נבו — Final resting place of Moses.

Jericho — יריחו — Ancient city in Canaan that was captured by Joshua.

Gerizim — גרזים — Mountain near Shechem, where tribes who offered blessings stood.

Eival — עיבל — Mountain near Shechem, where tribes who pronounced imprecations stood.

Shechem — שכם — Ancient city in Canaan, burial place of Joseph.

Zelaphchad ben Eliav and Machla — צלפחד — Grandson of Zelaphchad ben Chefer.

Yaman — ימן — Name assigned to husband of Milka

Shimron — שמרון — Name assigned to husband of Hogla

CHAPTER SIXTEEN

Dothan — דותן — Ancient city of Canaan where Joseph was abducted by his brothers.

Bethlehem — בית לחם — Ancient city of Canaan where Rachel was buried and King David was born.

Elgar — אלגר — Name assigned to servant of Elchanan.

Tovah — טובה — Name assigned to daughter of Eliav and Machla.

Gilgal — גלגל — Ancient city of Canaan which served as headquarters of Joshua during conquest of Canaan.

Tomb of Joseph — קבר יוסף — Final resting place of Joseph in the City of Shechem.

Shilo — שילה — Ancient city in Canaan, religious center of the tribes before Jerusalem.

David ben Meir and Noah — דוד — Name assigned to son of Meir and Noah.

Shomron — שמרון — Ancient city of Canaan in the Galilee, later became capitol of the Northern tribes. Now known as Samaria.

Tomb of Rachel — קבר רחל — Final resting place of Rachel, wife of Jacob.

CHAPTER SEVENTEEN

Bilaam — בלעם — Pagan prophet employed to curse Israel in the desert.

Othniel ben Kenaz — עתניאל בן קנז — Younger brother of Caleb, judge of the tribes of Israel after Joshua.